THE BROKENHEARTED

THE BROKENHEARTED

AMELIA KAHANEY

An Imprint of HarperCollins*Publishers*

HarperTeen is an imprint of HarperCollins Publishers.

alloy**entertainment**

Produced by Alloy Entertainment
1700 Broadway, New York, NY 10019
www.alloyentertainment.com

Library of Congress Cataloging-in-Publication Data
Kahaney, Amelia.
  The brokenhearted / Amelia Kahaney. — First edition.
    pages cm
  Summary: "When seventeen-year-old Anthem Fleet is suddenly transformed into an
all-powerful superhero, she must balance her old life with the dark secret of who she
has become"— Provided by publisher.
  ISBN 978-0-06-223092-8 (hardback)
  [1. Superheroes—Fiction. 2. Adventure and adventurers—Fiction. 3. Secrets—Fiction.
4. Love—Fiction. 5. Family problems—Fiction. 6. Ballet—Fiction. 7. Social classes—
Fiction.] I. Title.
PZ7.K12243Bro 2013   2013014336
[Fic]—dc23   CIP
                                                                 AC

Design by Liz Dresner

13 14 15 16 17 LP/RRDH 10 9 8 7 6 5 4 3 2 1

First Edition

For my parents, who gave me wings, and for Gabriel, who gave me someplace warm to land.

Let us dream of blood and pulse and ebb and flow. Let us consider tide and beat and throb and hum. Let us unweave the web of artery and vein, the fluttering jetties of the valves, the coursing of ions from cell to cell, the sodium that is your soul, the potassium that is your personality, the calcium that is your character.

—Brian Doyle

AFTER

A girl, alone.

Legs tucked up inside a baggy black hoodie, she perches on a metal grate atop one of the tallest skyscrapers in Bedlam City. She is watchful, still and silent as a gargoyle. The city heaves beneath her, but all she can hear this high up is the whistling of an icy wind.

This building, Fleet Tower, shares her name. When her parents die, she will inherit all eighty-seven stories of it. *Lucky girl*, the papers say. But Anthem Fleet's luck ran out a long time ago.

Beneath her, in the penthouse, is her bedroom. Inside it, objects she once loved. The varnished mahogany ballet barre bolted to the wall, where she practiced till her feet bled. The king-size bed she looked forward to crawling into each night, back when sleep came easily. Underneath the bed, a metal lockbox. The place she kept everything he gave her, until what he gave her turned into something no box could contain, something no girl would want to keep.

Above her, an indifferent sky shot through with searchlights, long fingers of light groping at the purply dusk. Gray thunderheads forming over a bruise-colored lake. Scattered fires raging, always raging, downtown.

And inside her, a cold steel ball. A ticking bomb that beats just like a heart. Pain and rage in equal measure. *Tick tock.*

While she sits and watches, waiting for nightfall, she makes a list of lies.

Time heals all wounds. Not all of them, it turns out. Some wounds cut too deep, and some kinds of heartbreak aren't temporary.

There's something good inside everyone. Some people are born into this world to do harm. She knows this now but wishes she didn't. Nothing matters to her more than keeping those people away from the ones who can't fight back. Away from the kind of person she used to be, before.

You only live once. What she's been through these past months should have killed her, but it didn't. She has a second life now, one she would never have chosen, but it's all she's got. Her life, her little square of rooftop, and a heart that beats too furiously.

She narrows her green eyes to slits and stands up, swinging her arms a little, bracing herself for the jump. She turns her gaze to the darkening streets downtown, to the sprawling, seething mass of inhumanity beyond the Midland River, better known these days as the Crime Line. The jagged scar of the river is what separates the gleaming north side from the lawless south.

Past the Crime Line, somewhere in the maze of the South Side, is where Anthem went from whole to brokenhearted. Where she stopped being the girl with all the promise in the world and turned into a shattered, damaged thing.

4

And every day since then, Bedlam City and the people in it have managed to break her heart all over again. She's learned this world is a beast, a bully that keeps on kicking you long after you're down.

In Bedlam, you either learn to take a beating, or you find a way to fight back.

BEFORE

CHAPTER 1

Here's the choreography: school, ballet, homework, sleep. Repeat the steps until you turn eighteen, keep perfect time, twirl like the ballerina in a jewelry box, and someday it will all pay off. Keep the routine, and the routine will keep you safe. This is what I've been brought up to believe.

But today, just this once, I can't.

As I walk through the front door of 87P, I compose my face. I shrug my ballet bag off my sore shoulders and drop it next to the statue looming next to the coat closet—a black marble griffin with its sharp teeth bared, oversize hundred-dollar bills clutched in its claws.

"Stop staring," I whisper to the marble beast, reaching up a hand to cover its beady eyes.

I pass our sunken sitting room, the plush white of it blazing orange as the sun falls below the horizon, and spot my father through the sliding glass doors. He speaks in low tones to Serge, his right hand, driver, and bodyguard, while pacing on the balcony. Serge's back is to the window, but I see his head nodding yes, his huge shoulders straining against his usual black suit. When my father turns around and sees me through the glass doors, he flashes me one of his showstopper smiles, his handsome, unlined face radiating an easy confidence that sells buildings all over Bedlam. Tonight he wears his black tailcoat and a white bow tie. *The full penguin*, he calls it.

I pad down the long hallway toward the master bedroom, rolling my neck from side to side and listening to each vertebra pop and crack.

"Mom?" I call as I take a few tentative steps inside my parents' empty bedroom suite. I brace myself for whatever version of my mother awaits me. Will it be Vivirax-mellowed Helene? Liftivia-energized Helene? Giggly, flushed Helene, deep into a bottle of Amnesia Vineyards chardonnay? Heading toward my mother's massive dressing room, I slide my eyes along the enormous oil portrait of twelve-year-old Regina sitting cross-legged in a field of wildflowers, a perfect miniature version of my mother. Regina with her big blue eyes, imperious lips above a pointed chin, white-blond hair hanging halfway down her back. The sister I never had. The daughter my mother wishes she still had.

But when I enter the dressing room, Helene isn't there. Instead, I'm met with my dress, light as air and fluttering a little on its hanger. I stare at the princess-cut gown, the iridescent material glowing white, blue, pink, and purple all at once, like the sky at dawn reflected off an ocean. This is more than a dress, I realize. It's a promise. Of a certain kind of night. Of the right kind of future.

And I can't put it on.

The evening was supposed to go like this: I would wash up

after ballet practice, put on this dress my mother picked out, and head to the mayor's house for the South Side Orphans' Association Ball. I would nod, smile, make polite, demure conversation, and dance with my boyfriend of six months, Will Hansen, under a twinkling chandelier. Then Will and I would slip off to a suite at the Bedlam Grande. He would lay me down on the bed, my long red hair fanning out in all directions, and deflower me. It would hurt a little, according to my best friend, Zahra, or maybe it wouldn't. We would lie there together until the wee hours, my parents assuming we were out at the heavily secured Young Philanthropists after-party in the hotel lobby. As the sun rose over the Bedlam skyline, Will would drive me home in his silver Huntley. I would kiss him good-bye and watch his car crawl quietly away, rejoicing in my bright future with the district attorney's son.

The vision pops like a soap bubble when my mother joins me in the closet, luminous in her seaglass-colored ball gown. Her golden hair is wound into a low, loose bun, and her angular face glows in the pinkish light.

"Hello, darling," she murmurs when she sees me. Our eyes meet in the gilded, pink-lit mirror of her ivory vanity, where she keeps her gold-handled makeup brushes, her lipsticks and shadows, lined up with military precision. In one corner are five crystal jars that hold all her prescriptions. Her heavy-lidded gray eyes are full of Viviraxed calm as she gestures toward the dress. "I had it steamed."

"It's beautiful," I start, a hot blush crawling up my chest. "But . . . I can't go tonight. I'm sick. I threw up in the middle of ballet."

I wrap my arms around my midsection and hunch over, willing my face to drain of all color. Staring back at me in the mirror is a damp-looking redhead, mascara dripping beneath her eyes, her pale skin covered in a constellation of ginger freckles. Next to the perfect human specimen that is Helene Fleet, I really do look ill.

Her eyes narrow as she studies me in the mirror, but I can't quite tell if she's concerned or just annoyed. She walks toward me and places a cool, smooth hand on my forehead. "You feel fine," she murmurs. "Maybe you just need to lay down for a little while. Have you had some water?"

Just then, my father stalks into the dressing room, his skyscraper-shaped cuff links jingling in his palm. "Five minutes, my loves."

"She's sick." My mother frowns, her lower lip sticking out like a pouting child's, her disappointment evident. "A stomach bug. She says she's not going."

"Not going?" My dad's smile droops. He turns and looks at me sideways, waiting for the punch line. "Of course you're going. Chin up, kitten. The Fleets never get sick."

"I know, Dad," I say, staring at the floor. I've been watching the parade of frail South Side children at the start of the Orphans' Ball since I was ten. I can almost smell the prime rib, can almost taste the puréed peas dotted with flecks of gold the mayor serves us once the orphans are whisked away. "But I just don't—"

"Think of poor Will," my mother chides, turning away to press a button beneath the vanity table. Instantly, her mirror slides up the wall, revealing dozens of steel jewelry drawers behind it, each one holding an individual necklace or bracelet or a couple of pairs of earrings. "He'll be bored stiff without you."

Poor Will. My nose wrinkles. *If only you knew what I was supposed to do with poor Will tonight.* "Will is a big boy. I'm sure he'll be fine," I say quietly.

When Will first asked me out, it felt like winning a prize. At Cathedral Day School, Will is practically royalty: class president, debate champion, and the leading man in all the school plays. I'm the ballet nerd, the perfect student whose shyness gets interpreted as snobbery. When Will began to pay attention to me, I became visible. Not just a brain but a flesh-and-blood girl. So of course I swooned over the flowers he sent, the feeling of walking down the halls with his arm around my shoulder— any girl with a pulse would have done the same.

But everything I felt at first has faded. The more Will insists it's time we take things further, the less I want to. This morning during mass, wedged in the center of the fifth pew from the altar, I whispered to him that I might not be ready for the suite at the Grande. That maybe dancing under the mayor's crystal chandelier was as far as things should go tonight. His expression froze, then twisted into a smirk. "I can think of a few girls who would be happy to take your place," he said, and for an instant I saw in his faded blue eyes that he wasn't joking. Then he put his school-president-perfect mask back on and smiled. "Kidding. We'll wait as long as it takes."

Helene presses a series of numbers into a glowing panel next to the jewelry safe. After a low beep, she pulls out the bottom drawer and selects a platinum-and-diamond necklace set with seven rubies the size of peppermints. She holds it up to her neck, the jewels dripping down her collarbone.

"Gorgeous, Leenie," my father murmurs approvingly, moving to fasten the clasp at the nape of her neck.

"It's perfect," I breathe. I think back to last Valentine's Day when he gave it to her, whispering to me that night that it was a *steal* at $50,000. "You look beautiful."

My mother smiles wanly at me before closing the drawer

and lowering the mirror again. "Thank you. But tonight is all about the orphans."

Tonight is definitely *not* all about the orphans. My parents rely on these events to get the ear of the mayor and other local politicians. The real estate market in North Bedlam is cutthroat. As developers, Helene and Harris have to constantly grease the political wheels—including schmoozing with District Attorney Hansen and Mayor Marks—for the best building sites. "I'll just rest here awhile. If I feel better, I'll take a cab to the ball later," I suggest.

"I hope it isn't the flu," Helene says. "You can't afford a flu right now, with rehearsals for *Giselle* and your studies and—"

"Let's leave Anthem be, darling. She's already a workaholic just like her parents," my dad interrupts, winking at me so I know he's on my side. "We'll keep an eye on Will for you, kitten. Just take it easy tonight."

My mother sighs. "Lily's here until nine."

I nod. Lily is our cook, and I can probably convince her to leave a little early. My parents check the mirror for one final appraisal. In this light, they look twenty-five. It's as if they never age. I form my hands into the shape of a camera and squint through the imaginary lens.

"Picture perfect?" Harris asks, his arm around Helene's waist.

"The perfect couple," I reply. And in this instant, I almost believe it.

If not for the drowned blond beauty found floating in Lake Morass eighteen years ago, anyone would think we had it all. But Regina is the fly in our amber, the error in our opal, the crack in our façade. Harris has his buildings to console him. Helene does, too, along with her charities, her pills, her chardonnay.

Which just leaves me.

A year after Regina's life ended, mine began. I'm the replacement daughter, the girl who was supposed to make everything better. A living, breathing antidepressant. Two dry kisses and one cold compress later, the perfect couple is off to the ball, leaving their far-from-perfect daughter in the dressing room to rest. When they're gone, I stay in the closet awhile, to stare at my all-too-ordinary face in the mirror.

CHAPTER 2

By ten, Zahra and I are far away from the tinkling champagne flutes at the Orphans' Ball, racing through the black streets of the riverfront district—a once-industrial section of the North Side that abuts the Midland River—toward a warehouse party just east of the Bridge of Forgetting. We're both wrapped in long wool coats, freezing in the drizzly late-February air.

"This place is giving me Bedhead," I mutter through chattering teeth. I shove a gloved hand into my pocket, my index finger searching out the round red button on my pepper spray key chain. Even fearless Zahra looks a little unnerved by the dimly lit neighborhood, chewing her cuticles and scanning everything around us for clues.

"I think it's this way." Z aims her wide-set violet eyes in the direction of a street sign twirling on its pole like a weathervane. We're at the corner of Arsenic Avenue and Thorn, both of which are unfamiliar streets. I almost never leave Upper Bedlam—the district made up of the neighborhoods of Lakeside, Church Hill,

Museum Mile, and Bankers Alley—where things are safe and orderly. But staying home and brooding about Will was even less appealing than one of Zahra's "underground" parties in a rough part of town.

"Aha," Z says triumphantly when we reach the corner. She grabs me by the crook of my elbow and pulls me toward a row of industrial warehouses scrawled with graffiti, hunched against the wind.

The sidewalk is deserted but for a couple of drunk girls teetering past us on five-inch heels, their laughter whiskey-scented and high-pitched. The first four buildings on the block are semidemolished, their windows either shattered or covered over with rotting boards, but the last one in the row blazes with multicolored light.

"Looks great, right?" Z says, her hips already swaying to the thumping bass of "Kiss Me on the Apocalips" by Suicidal Stepchild. It's been this way since the first time I met her, when she snuck into my kitchen during a charity luncheon my mother was hosting. Six-year-old Zahra scandalized me by stealing a whole tray of petit fours before lunch was even served, demanding that I lead her to my room where we could devour the treats. Zahra's always been daring, up for anything, anytime. Me, I need a lot of convincing to choose new and risky over safe and predictable. Always have.

I shrug, wishing I'd stayed home with an Epsom salt bubble bath and my tried-and-true DVD of Olga Inkarova's all-time best ballet performances. If I'd stayed home, I would be asleep by now, ready to get up early and head to the studio, with an hour of ballet to myself before our Saturday morning practice. This is the year I get to try out for the Bedlam Ballet Corps, when I find out if my twelve years of dedication to ballet have been enough to make a career out of it.

As we walk closer to the massive warehouse, a rainbow of colored lights passes over us, and doubt starts bubbling up inside me like acid indigestion. Is this party really worth a sluggish day at ballet tomorrow? "Are you sure we should be here, Z? Because I don't think—"

But then the double doors at the top of the building's stairs swing open as if sensing our arrival, and my words evaporate on my lips. A thin blond man in a worn velvet top hat slithers out of them and extends a hand to Zahra, who's standing a few feet closer to him than I am. He has a long, skinny black star tattooed beneath each of his eyes.

"Come inside, sparkly girls." His smile reveals a missing tooth and several gray ones. "Be corrupted."

A South Sider. I take a reflexive step backward and freeze, the dumb smile of a foreigner in a strange land glued to my face, hoping my initial revulsion at his teeth doesn't show. But Zahra grabs his hand and follows him in without a second thought.

"Let's go, Anthem." Z turns around for a moment and thrusts her pointy chin toward the party, a wicked little grin lighting up her face. "This is exactly where we should be."

And then she's inside, leaving me no choice but to follow. I let the man in the top hat pull me up the steps, his grip so firm it hurts a little. Then I walk with Zahra through two sets of shabby velvet curtains until we find ourselves on an enormous checkerboard dance floor.

A tickling heat travels along my spine as I ogle the revelers: guys in bespoke suits and leather pants, women in high heels and shiny vintage dresses, feathers and jewels dripping from their shimmery shoulders. On the edges of the massive room are stations for drinks, each staffed by bartenders in top hats like the doorman's. Swooping from the ceiling are women on trapezes, wearing nothing more than a sticky-looking wax, each with a set of tattered black wings sprouting from her shoulder blades.

"Told you. Party of the year!" Zahra shouts over the music, stepping out of her boiled wool trench. Gold hot pants cling to her tiny butt, and a white cotton tank with a red-and-black silk bra beneath it is tasked with harnessing her ample chest. Five long strings of black pearls dangle from her neck. "Give me your coat."

I fiddle with the last button still fastened at my collar, take a deep breath full of sweat and smoke and alcohol fumes, and finally unbutton it.

"How did I let you talk me into wearing this?" I scream, but my words are lost in the noise. Zahra insisted I wear my costume from last year's ballet recital, so I'm dressed as Juliet. As in, Romeo and.

She looks at me and smiles tenderly. "You look beautiful," she says, leaning into my ear so I hear her.

"The *costume* is beautiful," I correct her. Juliet wears a purple-and-black corset with real whalebone in it, paired with a black lace tutu edged in zippers. It makes my waist even tinier than it already is and gives me the illusion of cleavage. It screams *Look at me*, and I'm not someone who likes to be looked at. Not unless there's an orchestra playing and I'm onstage, having rehearsed my every move for months. In real life, I never quite know where to stand or what to do with my hands.

"I'll stash these and find us some drinks," Z shouts, taking my coat.

I nod and sway self-consciously to the music, my eyes glued to the angels swinging on their trapezes. Seconds later, I feel two women dancing too close on either side of me, feathers from a peacock boa scratching my right forearm, then fingernails digging into my left hip. I try to dance out of the way, but a third woman, this one short and stocky in a leather catsuit, steps in front of me, blocking my way, keeping me planted.

"Ballerina," the one with the boa whispers in my ear, her breath hot. I step backward, but I'm surrounded. She's got SYNDI tattooed on her bare shoulder, and the word ripples as she reaches for my tulle skirt as if appraising its value. "So young," the one on my right hisses. She's skinny but sinewy and strong, clad in a tuxedo jacket, frilly bloomers, and heels, her bobbed hair neon yellow on one side of her part, black on the other.

"She's just the right size," Catsuit says, twirling around to face me. Her pink hair is shellacked into a towering pompadour, and one of her eyes lists slightly to the left. She grins, and her teeth are sharp and small, feral.

I turn to look for Zahra, my heart racing, but her back is to me and she's headed toward a row of speakers along the far wall. I start to back up, my lips frozen in a panicked smile.

"Don't go," Boa pouts. She's the prettiest of the three, tall with flawless bone structure, but her head is shaved down to the scalp and her eyes are ringed in two-inch orange false eyelashes. Her hands are around my waist, pulling me toward her. "We like nice girls like you, don't we, ladies?"

"My friend is there—" I say, too softly. I stick my elbows out and get ready to thrash, gulping in air. But just then the one in the catsuit takes a step away from me, motioning for her friends to do the same. "Forget it, bitches," I hear her mutter.

Their eyes are glued to a tall, shaggy-haired guy in a crisp white shirt and a velvet jacket. His rangy body and sharp cheekbones are freshly torn from the pages of a magazine. He's walking toward them. Toward *me*.

"There you are," he says, smiling as he opens his arms. An expectant smile plays on his lips. "I've been looking for you everywhere. Let's dance."

I cautiously take his hand in mine, too shocked to do anything else. A heartbeat later, we're twirling around the room in a loopy, confident waltz. My body goes into ballroom mode even as my eyes stay glued to the bald woman, who winks at me before she turns away. In seconds, they've all faded into the crowd.

"I think you have me confused with someone else," I stammer.

"Nah." He smiles, his eyes crinkling at the corners. "I thought you might need an escape route from those Syndicate girls. The dance was a bonus."

Syndicate girls. My skin prickles at the mention of Bedlam's crime ring. Everything bad that ever happens here—murders, muggings, gambling, prostitution—is said to be the Syndicate's doing. "We can stop now," I say. "They're gone."

"How about one more dance?"

I look up at his face. It's broody and square-jawed, with thick, straight eyebrows above beautiful eyes. He has a half-wilted white flower stuck in his lapel. For a moment I think there is something harsh, even mean in his expression, but then his mouth softens into another disarming grin.

I crane my neck over his shoulder to check on Zahra and spot her up on a platform, waiting in line for drinks. She flashes me the thumbs-up and mouths *yummy*, which is Zahra-speak for *handsome*. I swallow a smile, then pull my head back so he can see my face when I nod yes.

He pulls me closer, and we begin to move again. He leads effortlessly, his hand warm on the center of my back. As we spin under the chandelier, I notice a splotch of blue in the brown iris of his left eye, as if it's been erased.

"Where'd you learn to dance like this?" I ask as he pulls me smoothly out of the way of a group of performers on stilts.

"Here and there. You?"

"Cotillion, starting at age seven. And ballet every day since age four." Immediately, I wish I could take it back, unlabel myself as a snooty rich girl.

"Then you can probably do *this*," he says, dipping me so low my hair sweeps the floor.

When he suggests we go to the windows and look at the view, I stammer out something about needing to find my friend. But like magic, Zahra's behind me, putting a drink in my hand and pushing me toward him.

She winks at him, then waves like she's sending us off on our honeymoon. "See you on the dance floor."

The boy slides his jacketed arm through my bare elbow. "I'll bring her right back to you." He smiles at Zahra and leads me away.

We climb through an open window onto a kind of make-shift terrace covered in tar, where a few people are gathered in couples or small groups, speaking in low voices. A soft steam rises from our warm skin.

"Gavin Sharp," the boy says, pushing a tumble of sandy-brown hair out of his eyes. He pulls a leather pouch from his back pocket and starts shaking tobacco into two rolling papers.

"Anthem Fl—Flood," I say, changing my name at the last second. I don't feel like being a Fleet tonight—not here, not with him.

He nods. His eyes flick across mine for an instant, and then back down as he licks the paper closed on the two expertly crafted rollies. "Want one?"

"No thanks," I say. I never smoke. Dancing as much as I do takes lungs of steel.

Gavin runs a silver lighter along his jeans and cups his hand around it to protect the flame from the wind. His fingers are long and elegant. My mother would call his hands "artistic." He smokes quietly, and I bring the plastic cup Zahra brought me to my lips and finish off the bitter green drink in two swallows. We stand side by side and stare at the brooding city, the night lit up under an almost-full moon.

Feeling slightly calmer from the alcohol, I study the view. Gleaming skyscrapers and stately mansions glitter on the north shore of the Midland River. On the other side of the water, the night is many watts darker. In the tangle of poorly lit streets, low-slung buildings yawn on their foundations. The South Side looks not just like a different city but like it exists in a different century.

I sneak a look at Gavin's profile and then move my gaze eastward, drawn to the arctic smoothness of Lake Morass. Still covered in a layer of pale blue ice, the lake is the only pure, blank space in the otherwise teeming city. The one place where nothing moves and nobody gets hurt. Not since Regina's accident, anyway. My parents have made sure of it by funding the lake patrol themselves.

"Right there . . ." Gavin squints and points into the warren-like streets of South Bedlam. All I see is a ragged collection of burnt-looking structures. "That's my building. The one with the water tower on it."

My eyes travel over dozens of water towers, perched like giant, frozen tarantulas on top of buildings. A tickling curiosity springs open inside my chest. "What's it like . . . over there?"

"We're not all thugs and criminals, you know." Gavin takes a last squinting drag from his rollie and pinches it out between his fingers, stuffing the butt back into his leather pouch to reuse later.

"Of course not." I rush to agree, to assure him I don't believe everything they print in the *Daily Dilemma*. "It's just, I've never . . . I don't get there too often. I guess because—"

"It's not safe. That's what they want everyone to think, right?" His eyes flash with something, a challenge maybe, but his mouth is still curled into a smile. Then he shrugs. "Seems all right to me, but I have nothing to compare it to, really. It's the only place I've ever lived."

"I'm sure it's like anywhere else," I suggest, "and has its bad days and its good days," though I don't really think that can possibly be true. South Bedlam is the murder capital of the country. There are more arrests per capita in South Bedlam than anywhere else in our hemisphere. It seems like every day is a bad day there.

I stare at the puff of white my breath forms in front of me, thinking guiltily of my nightly rides home from ballet practice in our cream-colored Seraph, an imported car so rare and expensive it elicits stares from people in the streets. The glass in the windows is bulletproof, and we live in the *safe* part of town.

Gavin nods. "I guess."

During the beat of uncomfortable silence that follows, I look toward Fleet Tower. If I squint, I can see my room on the top floor, the faint glow of the desk lamp I'm always forgetting to turn off.

As if reading my mind, he asks if I live nearby.

"Not far, yes. You can't see my place from here, though," I tell him, wishing it were true.

"So how do I find you again if I don't know where you live?" Gavin turns and studies my face, his eyebrows raised above those beautiful, playful eyes.

Find me again? I stare down into the melting ice in my cup, holding it with both hands because I worry if I don't, they might start to shake.

"Um . . ." I grope for words, blushing so violently that I'm sure he can see it in the moonlight. Before I can decide what to say, his eyes leave my face and focus on something over my shoulder. His expression turns hard. He leans in, his mouth against my ear, and my body tingles a little from the closeness of his lips, the tickle of his shaggy hair on my skin. "Party's over. Put this over your nose and mouth, and *run*." He presses a soft gray bandanna into my hand.

"What?" I whirl around to look behind me through the tall windows, but all I see is the party raging inside. "What do you—"

"I'll catch up with you," he says sternly, pushing me forward. "Just go. *Now*."

And then the first feargas canister skitters across the floor.

It all happens so fast. Gavin practically shoves me inside through the open window. I spot Zahra's black pixie cut in the crowd—she's still dancing, still breathing, oblivious to what's coming—and run toward her, holding my breath. Then people begin to scream and the lights go out in the building, leaving only candlelight from the chandelier diffused with purple gas from the canisters. Riot police fan out across the room, helmets down, black glass covering their faces.

I press the bandanna over my mouth and nose and pull Z toward the doors. She's coughing on the thick purple fumes, already hallucinating, screaming about snakes and spiders and roaches. I drag her out into the black night, repeating *Everything's okay, nothing to be afraid of,* as she cries hysterically. Police raids and gas-and-dash are so common in Bedlam that we've been trained at school on what to do if we inhale feargas, giggle gas, cyanide spray, arsenic oil. This is the first time I've ever seen the effects of feargas up close.

I usher her through the crush of people spilling out onto the sidewalk and manage to lead her down the block, toward an empty lot between two derelict warehouses.

"Sit down, Zahra," I tell her in my calmest voice. She falls to the ground, her hands swiping at her short hair as if it's infested with fire ants. I pull her up until we're sitting across from each other, all alone on a weed-choked patch of earth. I take a breath and try to block out the terrified sounds of other screaming feargas victims. The electronic twang of the riot police on their bullhorns is deafening even here. They're ordering everyone out. "PHOTOGRAPHERS WILL BE ARRESTED," they keep saying through the megaphones. "DISPERSE IMMEDIATELY."

I concentrate on Zahra's panicked eyes. "Let's say the meditation," I say, putting both hands on her shoulders. "Just like in school, okay?"

We huddle together and begin, repeating the meditation over and over again: *This too shall pass. This too shall pass.* Is it seven times, is it ten? We say it ten times just to be sure, and Zahra's movements slow down. She stops yanking on her hair and scratching at her arms, her sobbing reduced to a low series of moans. When we begin to count backward from a hundred, I feel her shoulders soften. Finally, we practice focusing on the objects around us, waiting for the feargas to work its way through Zahra's frontal cortex.

"The moon, I see the moon," I whisper, holding Zahra's head in my lap, stroking her hair.

"But it's bleeding, Anthem. Why is it bleeding?"

"Shhhh," I whisper, a shiver running down my spine as I look down at Zahra's eyes, normally so fearless, now wide with terror. "It's not, sweetie, I promise."

"A broken window," she says hoarsely a few minutes later.

"Good. A clump of grass."

I feel her nodding, snuffling a few last tears. "I found a dandelion. That's a good thing, this time of year."

Much later, when Zahra is able to walk again, we head out into the night. Zahra twirls the dandelion between her fingers and leans on my shoulder as we hobble toward the corner to wait for the cab I've called. The screaming and chaos from the raid has stopped long ago. My thoughts keep circling around the boy with the erasure in his eye, the waltzer, Gavin Sharp. *He's fine*, I tell myself. *He knew just what to do.*

And yet I can't stop hoping he's okay, wondering how he knew what he knew, and what he meant when he said he'd catch up with me.

CHAPTER 3

"And that's all the time we have for propaganda and the rule of law today," says Dr. Tammany, our sprightly, old politics teacher, as she perches on the edge of her desk. "Please come in tomorrow with an example of propaganda from a newspaper or the street."

Dr. T points a tiny remote control at the ceiling, clicking off the last picture in her slideshow from the time of the South Side riots—a picture of a mob of people holding signs, their mouths open in fear as they run away from police on horseback. The headline doesn't match the picture: BRUTAL RIOTS KILL TWO POLICE OFFICERS. The last real riot happened when I was three. One of my earliest memories is of an angry mob amassing in the pocket park across the street from Fleet Tower.

"How do we know that this class isn't just another form of propaganda?" a boy's voice pipes up from the back of the room. Everyone laughs, but a chill goes through me as I think of the billboards on all the highways that say A SAFER BEDLAM IS IN YOUR HANDS with a picture of a scared-looking woman on the phone and the police hotline, 999-TIPS, in red beneath her. Did someone phone in the party on Friday? I can still hear the police on their bullhorns on Friday night. *Photographers will be arrested.*

"You don't," Dr. T says evenly, her ears reddening as she tucks her peach-colored bob behind them. Just then, the church bells begin to ring, signaling the end of class. "Let's explore that question tomorrow."

Dr. T pushes her glasses up her long nose and winks at me. "Interesting drawing, Miss Fleet," she says when the clamor of the bells dies down. "Very lesson-appropriate."

I smile politely from my desk in the front row by the stained-glass windows—the seat I've taken in nearly every classroom since kindergarten—and look down at the row of faceless police I've drawn across the top of my notepaper, each with an oversize arm raising a baton high into the air. For a second, I consider telling her I've drawn the image from memory. But I keep quiet. I can't risk being sent to the school counselor for an anxiety assessment. Or worse still, a concerned phone call to my parents.

As the class erupts in the chaos of pre-lunch socializing, a shadow falls across my desk. When I look up, Olive Ann Bang and her two henchgirls, Clementine Fitz and Ronda Hatch, are lined up in a row in front of my desk. I'm at eye level with their plaid skirts, six inches shorter than Cathedral's regulation dress code. Their shiny legs are dappled with colored light from the stained-glass windows, and a blurry imprint of the Virgin Mary's face reflects off Olive Ann's bare knees.

"Hey," I say at last, flashing a noncommittal smile.

"Long time no talk," purrs Olive Ann, pursing her lips in a glossy pout. Olive Ann is the youngest daughter of Cathedral's principal, the grim and steely Winnifred Bang. Neither Bang likes me very much, probably because Olive's been one spot behind me in the class rankings since freshman year. Now that it looks like I'll be valedictorian in a few months, Olive's usual disdain for me has gone from a slow simmer to a full-on boil.

"We heard you didn't make it to the Orphans' Ball," Clementine says, her voice faux-sympathetic. "Will said he had to go without you."

"I was sick." I shrug.

"He told us to give you this," Olive Ann says, glaring at Clementine for piping up without permission. "It's sealed, don't worry."

"I wasn't worried," I mumble as Olive Ann produces a small, cream-colored envelope with a stylized *WH* embossed on the back flap. "Don't be a stranger, Anthem." Olive's nose wrinkles as she flashes me a tight smile.

"Okay." I nod, my face a mask of neutrality. Then the three of them whirl around, sling their book bags over their shoulders, and walk, with near-perfect symmetry, out of the room.

After such an elaborate delivery, Will's note is anticlimactic.

Missing you, Red. Meet me in the chapel. I'll be waiting.
—Will

I've never liked being called Red. As I've explained to Will a dozen times, nobody's ever called *Brown*. I stand up and press my books against my chest like a bulletproof vest. I haven't returned Will's calls or texts all weekend because I'm afraid something will slip about what I really did on Friday. Zahra doesn't remember much—one of the few good things about feargas is the amnesia—but I can't get the sound of her screaming out of my mind.

I also can't stop thinking about Gavin Sharp.

• • •

I'm heading toward the intersection of Hemlock Street and Catechism Way, trying not to feel like a terrible person for blowing off Will. At lunch period, I took the coward's way out and stuck a note in his locker saying I'd meet him tomorrow. When I round the corner onto Hemlock, my eyes are drawn to a flash of reflected sunlight across the street.

A boy in a black leather jacket is leaning up against a motorbike. He's reading a book. I freeze on the sidewalk and stare, making sure I'm not mistaken. My eyes travel over his lanky, broad-shouldered frame, the sandy-brown swatch of hair falling jaggedly over his eyes. The sharp jawline ending in a cleft chin.

He folds down a corner of the page he's reading and shuts his paperback, an ancient-looking copy of *The Great Gatsby*. A slow smile lights up his face as he looks up. "You're here."

I cross the street in three long strides. Standing just a few feet away from him now, I set my ballet bag down on the sidewalk and clear my throat, a mix of anticipation and nervousness tingling in my chest. "Doing some reading?" I ask lamely.

"Gatsby kills me every time." He shoves the book into the back pocket of his jeans. There's a charged beat of silence between us. "Guess I'm a sucker for an unhappy ending."

Two bunheads wrapped in coats rush by us, and I break eye contact with Gavin to watch them disappear through the studio doors. It's Constance Clamm and Clarissa Bender, both in level six, too worried about being late to look up and notice me. When the doors slide shut behind them, I finally ask the obvious. "How did you find me?"

"I asked a few friends where the best dancers in North Bedlam practiced. All roads led to Swans." Gavin's cheeks turn the faintest hint of pink. "I hope you don't mind."

"No, I don't mind." I look up into the glass-walled third floor of Seven Swans, where nine bunned heads tilt in unison above nine pairs of shoulders. Nine bare, sinewy arms reaching gracefully up, bending toward the windows, then up again. Like the legs of a giant, graceful caterpillar.

"They're starting practice without me," I murmur, transfixed for a moment by the scene. In twelve years, I've never watched this ritual from the outside.

"Take a ride with me," Gavin says. "I want to show you something."

My mind whirls with a million reasons I should say no, the main one being that I never, ever miss ballet. Two more: My parents would kill me if they found out I was on a motorcycle with a South Sider, and Serge picks me up from ballet every night at seven. A sharp gust of wind hits my back, as if urging me toward Gavin.

His voice is gentle. "Don't think too hard."

I squint up at the studio one last time, at the girls at the barre, a lifetime of routine beckoning me back into its safe embrace. I think of my parents, of my homework, of ballet, of Serge, of Will. And then I stop thinking entirely.

"Let's go."

CHAPTER 4

I ignore the alarm bells going off in my head and tell myself to focus on the little details: the thrum of the bike underneath me, the wind in my face, the way my stomach flutters when Gavin's warm back is pressed against my chest.

We hurtle through Bankers Alley and the Bank of Bedlam rears up before us, its mirrored façade slicing our reflection into dozens of tiny triangles. The downtown office of Fleet Industries is only two blocks away—my parents could be anywhere among the suited businesspeople bustling down the street.

We pass a cluster of twenty tents and my gaze fixes on a sign that says EAT THE RICH, a huge pair of garish lips around the words. Another sign reads THE REAL BEDLAM WILL RISE UP AGAIN. The protest encampment has been a fixture here since before I was born, its scruffy members chanting about justice and equality. Every couple of weeks, the police come and break it up, but the protesters always reappear the next day, stoic and bruised, with new signs that say things like COPS ARE NOT ABOVE THE LAW. When I look up again, we're about to ride across the Bridge of Forgetting and enter the South Side.

"You okay?" Gavin yells over his shoulder as the bike idles.

"Yeah, I just haven't been over the bridges in a long time," I yell back, the wind sucking the words out of my mouth. *Or ever.*

"It's safe, I promise," he yells. "At least when you're with me." He guns the bike, and we take off across the bridge.

Hundreds of locks hang from the balustrade's filigreed stonework, left by couples who have walked this bridge, locked padlocks to it, and tossed the keys into the river to symbolize their unbreakable bond. I wonder how many keys are at the bottom. Hundreds? Thousands? How many romantic declarations have been made here over the years?

Once we're off the bridge, Gavin pulls the bike over to the curb and cuts the engine. "Let's walk from here."

The slate-gray sky is beginning to fill with faint streaks of pink and orange. Unlike in the north, with its industrial wall along the river to prevent flooding, the South Side is lined by a grassy embankment that slopes easily down toward the rocky shore. Circus birds, Bedlam's neon-red-and-yellow finches, hop about on the ground, chirping and joyful.

As we travel along the sidewalk bordering the river, I take a closer look at the dilapidated townhouses and brick apartment buildings that line Feverfew Street to the south. There's graffiti everywhere, scrawled over the bricks and fences, JUSTICE and THE SOUTH IS NOT AFRAID. And over and over again, a million different tags: SYNDIC8. LIVING IN SYN. SYNLIFE.

Gavin guides me down a narrow dirt path toward a thin footbridge jutting into the river, marked by a rusted metal archway that reads BRIDGE NINE in gothic script. At first, I wonder why I've never seen it before. But then I take a closer look and see that after a hundred feet or so, the bridge just . . . stops. It ends in the center of the river, as if someone sliced half of it off. Boards have been nailed haphazardly across the bridge's abrupt endpoint. "What happened?"

"We call this the Bridge to Nowhere. When I was six or seven, they blew up the north half of it. This is what's left."

"They?" I ask.

Gavin shrugs, the light in his eyes flicking off the way it did just before the party ended the other night. "People who didn't want South Siders walking to the museum district and scaring the tourists. Same people who killed the Hope, maybe."

I shoot him a dubious look. The last time I heard anyone mention the Hope, I was in the seventh grade. He was a crusader for justice who supposedly almost ended the crime wave just before the South Side Riots started. Most people believe he was just an urban legend. At least that's what I've always learned in school. He was killed before I was born, if he ever existed at all.

"But couldn't it have been an accident?" I ask. I don't want to suggest the other scenario that floats through my mind: that South Siders blew it up themselves during the riots.

Gavin stares out over the river. "Maybe. But then why didn't they ever rebuild the thing?"

The path spirals past the bridge and slopes downhill, opening up a moment later into a circular courtyard with an ornate stone fountain at its center. It must have been beautiful once, with three mermaids at the center, their tails flung gorgeously into air. But their faces have crumbled, the stone chipped away. One mermaid has only a chin. Gavin puts a hand on each of my shoulders. "Turn around."

In front of us is a curved wall, about ten feet tall and thirty feet wide, encircling the courtyard. A mural covers every square inch of it. Layers and layers of spray paint, but also oil paint, judging by the level of detail. The bottom half is all blues and grays, a mob of angry police, hundreds of them receding into the background, an infinity of cops. So much like my doodle in class today, it's uncanny. But here, they're looking up into the sky, at . . .

My hands cover my mouth as I take it in. A ballet dancer stands on one arched foot atop a raised police baton. She's mid-turn, with one slender leg bent and her arms clasped above her. Her hair is red. She wears my Juliet costume.

And her face, slightly tilted and fierce with concentration, is mine.

Unconsciously, I've walked up to the mural to study it up close. I reach up and touch the hem of the ballerina's tutu—*my* tutu. The paint is dry. There are at least four shades of gray layered together to form the folds of glittery tulle.

At last, I turn to Gavin, my face hot. "You painted this?"

He shrugs. "I was looking for a way to finish the mural. Once I met you, I knew how to do it."

"Nobody's ever done anything like this for me," I say.

"Oh, I'm sure you've inspired a lot of admirers on the North Side."

"Not exactly." I turn away from him, hiding my blush as I gaze at the painting. Will once gave me a pair of earrings with a silly little card: *You're my Anthem, and you make me want to sing.* But Gavin's painting took hours of painstaking work. I turn around to face him.

"I need to tell you something. My last name isn't Flood. It's Fleet."

He raises one thick eyebrow, pulling a hand through his hair. Then he shrugs. "Okay."

I move to stand beside him and aim my index finger at the top of our building. "We live in that tall building with the spire. Fleet Tower. On the top floor."

"Huh." He nods, seeming indifferent, like it's all the same to him. Like me and my address aren't inextricably linked. "Must be nice to live somewhere like that."

I sigh, relieved that he's not mad at me for lying to him. "I guess."

"You *guess*?" He grins. "I'm hoping it's at least sort of nice."

He flips his hair out of his eyes and stares at me playfully. I open my mouth to explain, but it takes me some time to find the words.

"It isn't always . . . as nice as it seems," I finish lamely, sucking all the flirtation out of the conversation.

"No?" he asks, turning to me, his face growing serious.

A cold blast of metallic air hits my face, and I flip my coat collar up. "My sister drowned when she was seventeen, and my parents never really got over it. My mom, especially."

Gavin winces, then grabs my hand. "I wasn't born yet." I go on, conscious of his fingers resting lightly around my wrist. "The only reason they had me was to replace her. I think my dad hoped I would give my mom a reason to live again. But I'm starting to realize that no matter how perfect I try to be, I can't ever make up for what they lost."

A car alarm bleats in the distance. Gavin pushes his hair out of his eyes again. When he stops to face me, the smile he wears is sad. "It must be tough to not only live your own life but to try to finish someone else's."

"Sometimes, yeah," I whisper, thinking of my mother's episodes of immobilizing sadness, her monthlong bouts of depression that come out of nowhere, dragging us all down with her. I'd give anything not to turn out like her. Scared of everything. Too sad to really live.

"You're enough, you know."

"Enough?" I blink hard, the image of my mother vanishing, replaced with Gavin's face earnestly studying mine.

He shrugs. "You're amazing."

Gavin carefully tucks a lock of my hair behind my ear and bends his face toward mine. We both go quiet. I rise onto tiptoes and my hands find the nape of his neck, his hair blowing against my fingers. Our lips come together, gently at first. Desire surges through my body, so powerful it weakens my knees as the kiss becomes more urgent and we move closer together.

I've kissed Will more times than I can count, but it's never made me feel like this.

Gavin pulls back eventually. His arms stay wrapped around my shoulders. "Sorry," he says. But the dazed grin on his face tells me he's not.

"Don't be," I breathe, a dazed grin stretching across my face. I link a few of my fingers with his and steal one last look at the ballet dancer on the wall as we begin to walk back up the hill.

The sky has turned a purple gray in the twilight. Across the river, the old-fashioned streetlamps are beginning to flicker on. Here on the South Side, with no streetlights to speak of, the dark begins to wrap around us like a cocoon.

When we get to the top of the embankment, Gavin points toward the sky past the bridge. His hand finds mine again, the heat of it and the closeness of his body warming me. We watch hundreds of circus birds fly from west to east, a neon cacophony in the darkening sky.

CHAPTER 5

"Will?" My voice echoes softly in the cavernous stone chapel the next day. The flying buttresses and soaring ceiling designed a century and a half ago are supposed to make God-fearing Bedlamites feel small and awestruck, and even though I know it's a trick of architecture, it works.

The chapel, I realize as I walk slowly up the aisle, is the last place I saw Will. I pause at the pew I was sitting in on Friday, the place where I realized I didn't want to go to any party with Will Hansen ever again. The unpleasant memory dissolves as I notice a rustle of the burgundy curtain in front of the confession booth. I slip off my shoes and tiptoe across the marble floor. Two black shoes peek out under the confessional curtain. I slip soundlessly into the booth on the other side of the wooden partition and close my half of the curtain. Pulling back the screen in the wall between us, I wait for my eyes to adjust to the darkness.

I clear my throat and adopt a stage whisper. "Father, forgive me, for I have sinned."

Will leans his forehead against the screen, so close I can smell the expensive cedar hanger his shirt hung on this morning. "And I thought the problem was you haven't sinned *enough*."

"Will," I whisper nervously.

"I know. You were *sick*." Though I can't see Will's face, I can almost hear him sneering. "It was a joke, what I said about other girls taking your place," he says from the other side of the booth. "I sent you about thirty texts apologizing."

I nod, dreading what I know I need to do, guilt sticking in my throat. Will may be kind of obnoxious, but he deserves better than this.

"You could have called me the next day to see how it went."

"Sorry," I mumble. There are no good excuses for ignoring him the way I have been. "I should have called."

"You're not exactly in the running for girlfriend of the year," Will continues.

"Then break up with me," I hear myself say.

Silence. I press my spine against the mahogany wall, letting out an involuntary puff of air through my nostrils.

The curtain rings scrape against their rod as Will leaves the confessional. He pulls back my curtain and stands in front of me, a wounded look clouding his broad face. "Seriously?"

"I—I don't know. It just doesn't seem—" I fumble, letting the sentence hang.

He turns away and looks at the huge fresco painted beneath the east-facing windows of the cathedral. I follow his gaze until I see it, the image of Judas betraying Jesus, his evil kiss on Jesus's cheek. I turn away, but the kiss of the betrayer is imprinted on my vision.

"I had other options, you know," he says, shrugging. "But I chose *you*. That should count for something."

"I should be grateful, you mean, because a popular guy like you is interested in a loser like me," I whisper, blood suddenly roaring in my ears. I force myself out of the booth.

"All I'm saying is you should think about what you want in life," Will says calmly, his eyes dead and bored-looking. He sighs loudly. "I'm a patient guy. I'll wait for you to realize what's in your best interests. Until then, you might want to be more careful about where you go dancing."

My mouth falls open, but no words come out. "What do you mean?" I finally manage.

"Just don't do anything you'll regret. This is Bedlam, remember? People are watching you."

"What people?" I say, my voice strangled. I search Will's face for clues. Is he threatening me?

"Don't worry about it, Anthem." Will pauses, his eyes glittering with malice. "But I'd love to know—who's the guy?"

"What *guy*?" Does he somehow know about Gavin?

"Forget it. You don't have to tell me," Will says, checking his watch. "I'll be here when you change your mind."

"I'm not changing my mind," I say sharply. I push past him, but he grabs my wrist before I can clear the pew. I whirl around and yank my hand away, opening my mouth to speak but not finding any words.

"Lie to me all you want, Anthem, but don't lie to yourself." He pulls his leather satchel over his shoulder and straightens up to his full six feet. Before I can think what to say, he turns and stalks heavily out of the chapel.

My hands are trembling as I adjust the burgundy tie at my collar and slowly, mechanically smooth out my pleated plaid skirt. I bend to slip my oxfords on and wait a few minutes before I leave. My eyes wander back to Judas and his false kiss. Under someone's ordinary face can lurk the most sinister thoughts. The church bells start to clang again, but all I can hear is Will's voice.

People are watching you.

CHAPTER 6

When the final bells of the school day begin to clang at 2:55 P.M., I bolt up from my seat in Honors English and hurry out the forty-foot arch of Cathedral's front doors. Checking over my shoulder to make sure Will is nowhere in sight, I pass the security booth at the school gates. Blake and Meechum, the armed guards on duty in the afternoons, stand at the ready, watching for criminals or vagrants.

Meechum nods hello. His hand rests casually around the barrel of the BulletBlower 27 he wears strapped around one arm. "Afternoon, Miss Fleet."

"Hi, Meech." I smile. I've known him since kindergarten. He's getting on in years, but just last week he chased down a couple of punks who'd threaded their way among all the high schoolers boarding school buses, catching them with half a dozen wallets and two Pharm-inhalers stuffed in their pockets.

I move past him onto the sidewalk and start to weave through the crowd of burgundy, navy, and white–uniformed kids milling around. Then I feel my phone vibrate in my skirt pocket.

Gavin: Can you get away? I miss you.

I look up the block toward Seven Swans. The answer should be *I've got ballet today,* but yesterday was too good.

I walk quickly around the block where it's quieter, then call Madame Petrovsky. It turns out to be disconcertingly easy, lying to her.

When she answers, I tell her I overdid it on Sunday and twisted my ankle, and that I missed rehearsal yesterday because I was seeing the doctor. "He said to elevate it and rest for a while longer, until the swelling goes down," I lie.

"Oh dear," she says, pausing to emit a long sigh. "Please rest. No walking. Lots of ice. We are choosing parts for *Giselle* very soon," she reminds me, a trace of panic creeping into her voice. "I suppose I can put it off a little longer. . . ."

I can almost hear her frowning, can almost see the crease between her eyebrows deepening. I do my best to shake off my guilt. I'm not bragging when I say I'm among the best dancers she's got in level six. I can practice at home, at night, I tell myself. I can still land the prima role. A few days can't erase twelve years of training.

"Sorry. I know it's terrible timing." I rise onto my toes and hold on to a light post, then move through a sloppy pas de bourrée, my guilt about lying now almost completely overtaken by my excitement about a whole afternoon with Gavin.

We sit side by side on the deserted beach of Lake Morass watching the cotton-candy fog roll in off the water, so thick we can almost hold it in our hands. He tells me about his mother dying when he was just nine years old after being sick with a wasting disease for years; about how his father, who moved away when Gavin was a baby, never came to claim him from the orphanage he was sent to live in when his mother died. When I ask him about what the orphanage was like, he shrugs, and says simply: "The kind of place you do everything you can to get away from. I left when I was thirteen. Been supporting myself ever since."

I ask him how he supports himself now, and he tells me he paints houses on the North Side. The work is seasonal, so he's busy in the summer and free in the winter to work on his art.

"Drawing was all I had for a long time," he says. "I used to steal coal from the kitchen and sketch on old newspapers. It was the only thing I could do that felt like an escape from being me. So I kept doing it."

I nod, knowing exactly what he means. When everything else is terrible, a day of dancing is all it takes to remind myself of what's good. I think guiltily of the studio and wonder for a second what sequence the level sixers are doing now.

Later that afternoon, we buy cups of tea from a nearby café and sit next to each other, staring out over the river with our pinkies linked on the table. The silence between us is comfortable, somehow familiar.

He drives me back with ten minutes to spare. I wait for Serge in the lobby of Seven Swans, doing my best to shake the sand from my hair.

Each day this week, I've called to check in with Madame and report on my ankle, then walked to a meeting place Gavin and I have chosen, just a few blocks from Seven Swans. I've never missed this many days of practice in my life.

It happens fast. My feelings for Gavin grow exponentially more intense each day, and I'm becoming one of those girls I normally cannot stand. Those dreamy, dopey gigglers who see the bright side of everything, who seem almost stupid with love. It was never like this with Will.

"It's almost better," I say to Madame on the phone on Friday, the fifth day in a row that I'm missing ballet. I check furtively around me for anyone I might know as I wait at the designated corner for Gavin to pull up on his bike. "I have a physical therapy appointment today, and if I get the all-clear, I'll be at Saturday practice."

"Very good, Anthem. You've been very responsible about this injury. We look forward to your return."

Ugh. *I've been the opposite of responsible,* I think as Gavin's bike pulls up. This has to stop, or I'll have no hope of catching up. . . .

When he pulls his helmet off, Gavin's face is half-hidden by his shaggy hair, but his expression is so eager that I lose my train of thought. "Me too," I say to Madame, and click the phone off.

"Where to?" I grin.

He takes me to his studio, in the old rail yards deep in Southeast Bedlam. When we pull up between two rows of rusted trains surrounded by tall thickets of grass and scrub, the first thing I notice is how quiet it is. Then I hear the cooing of circus birds and look up to see a nest on the closest train car, all but eaten up by deep red rust. A large albino crow announces itself on the roof of another rail car a few feet away, its sharp beak open to the gray sky.

"That's Money," Gavin says, whistling at the crow, who regards us with one red eye.

"Money?"

"He's here today, gone tomorrow." Gavin grins. "I named him when I first started painting out here."

He leads me toward an ancient-looking train car wrapped in desiccated vines that will probably become bright green in the summer. He unlocks a heavy padlock and slides open the door. My breath catches when I get inside.

It's a riot of color. The walls are coated in layer upon layer of paint, and there are several half-finished canvases—some stunning, haunted landscapes that look inspired by this rail yard, where plants overtake the buildings and the cars. There's a triptych of townspeople standing in front of a country church, all of them staring at the sky, horror etched into their faces, their mouths open in silent screams. Another of a couple, their bodies elongated as they run from a fire.

"This is your studio?" I breathe, moving in a slow circle to take in all the art. In one corner of the room are a few dozen large cans of house paint, some rollers, a pile of tarps.

"Yep. Also my storage space for the day job."

"How do you stay so clean?" I ask.

"What do you mean?"

"If I hung out here, I'd be covered in paint every day," I say.

"Coveralls," he says. "Also, um, I'm trying to impress you with my best duds. Is it working?"

I look him over. Worn black pants with a small hole in the knee. Combat boots. A button-down shirt with a frayed collar. All topped with a motorcycle jacket. "Totally."

I walk toward him and lean upward for a kiss. When we break away, I want to tell him he could show up in ripped rags and I'd still like him. A lot. I clear my throat. "You should stop worrying about impressing me."

"It's just hard to believe a girl like you would bother with someone like me," he says softly, his eyes trained on the paint-splattered wood planks of the train car's floor.

"A girl like me would definitely bother." I laugh. "Though *bother* isn't the word for it."

The unspoken part of this conversation is that up until now, we've been keeping our time together a secret. He hasn't asked me why I haven't shown him my neighborhood haunts, my apartment, my favorite place to get coffee, but I know he senses that my parents wouldn't approve of what we're doing, and not just because I've been skipping ballet.

"It's been a good week," he says, then moves to a far wall and turns an easel around. There's a palette set up, oil paints glistening on it, still wet from use. Above it, a small canvas, half of it filled with my face. He's even done my freckles, the few darker ones under my eye and the lighter gingery ones across the bridge of my nose. "I started working on this early this morning."

"How can you do this from memory?" I breathe.

He shrugs, studying the painting, then glances at me to check how accurate he was. The answer is *very*. He must have a photographic memory. "I just think about you, and this is how I picture your face."

"I'm here now," I suggest. "If you want to do the other half . . ."

"Nah," he says, quickly flipping the easel back around to face the wall. "Not enough light. Maybe next week." I bite my lip at the mention of next week. I have to get back to ballet. The only way to spend time with Gavin is in the evenings, and that means telling my parents. But I'm pretty sure telling my parents I've been seeing a South Sider will mean being instantly grounded, or at least forced to go everywhere with Serge. It will be the end of my time with Gavin Sharp.

And if there's one thing I'm absolutely sure of, it's that I don't want this to end.

CHAPTER 7

On Monday I stuff my books into my locker and turn my blood-shot eyes to the crowded stone hallway. I walk slowly through the sea of crisp white button-down shirts and plaid skirts. My throat is raw from lack of sleep; I stayed up talking on the phone with Gavin till 1:00 A.M. But being exhausted has never felt so good.

The halls have been humming with an extra intensity today—everyone's talking about the girl from Midland Prep who was stabbed last night outside her house on Juniper Street. Snatches of conversation reach my ears—the stabbing, prom tickets on sale next week, Principal Bang's appearance on *Channel Four News Roundup* early this morning to speak about protecting the children. *A droopie deal gone wrong*, I hear some-one say. *No way*, says another. Only lowlifes do droopies. It's all smokestacks and gigglepills for Midland Prep girls.

"How do you say, 'We're cutting Latin' in Latin?" a familiar voice chirps in my ear.

"Zahra!" I exclaim, turning to link arms with her. It's been a while since we've really talked, I realize guiltily. I haven't exactly been avoiding her, but I've been pretty evasive when we've hung out at lunch, guarding my afternoons with Gavin as if telling anyone would somehow pop the bubble we've been living in each day. "Where have you been?"

"*Veni, vidi, vici*. I came, I saw, I yawned. We need an emergency debriefing session," Zahra says, her eyes covered by a pair of vintage cat-eyed sunglasses. "*Now.*"

"The usual spot?"

Z nods. "Act nonchalant. Blandsen and Bang are watching you."

I laugh nervously as I swivel my head around and look for Will and Olive Ann, but Zahra squeezes my elbow and frowns. Suddenly I have the distinct suspicion I'm on display, a glass slide under the Cathedral Day microscope.

Five minutes later, we're racing through the stacks of the school library, inhaling the smell of old leather and wood polish. We reach the spiral staircase at the back of the main study area and quickly clatter up it until we're well into the Thesis Tower. It's lined with dark wood shelves containing the bound thesis projects of every student who has ever attended Cathedral. All this insulation makes it the perfect place for a private conversation—especially compared to the rest of Cathedral, where the gray stone halls are known for their echo-chamber effect, the architecture of the school encouraging the spreading of secrets and lies.

Zahra and I have been coming here to decompress, together and sometimes alone, ever since we discovered it freshman year. We've vowed never to take anyone else up here.

At last, Zahra lifts her sunglasses. Her violet eyes are flat and clinical as she looks me up and down, appraising me. As if she doesn't quite trust me.

"If you keep looking at me like that, I'm going to need an

anxiety assessment," I say.

Zahra raises her eyebrows, her mouth sealed shut. She plucks a thesis—*Machiavelli in Bedlam: Today's Power Brokers and Their Quest to Rule*—from the curved shelf that snakes up the tower and starts to flip through it. "I can wait here all day until you start talking. Some great reading material here. And unlike you, I'm not averse to ditching classes."

I blink hard and try to hold her gaze, but her expression is so steely I have to look away. It's clear she's waiting for me to spill. "Okay, there's some stuff I haven't been telling you. But I guess you know that."

"Um, yeah." She smiles tightly, shutting the thesis and gesticulating with it still in her hand. "What in Bedlam's balls is going on? You've been off in the clouds all week, and now I hear that you broke up with Will?"

"You were right about him," I say, thinking of the countless times Zahra's suggested Will wasn't with me for the right reasons. I lean my forehead against the wall of books and close my eyes, the red splotches behind my eyelids dancing like poisonous blooms. Maybe I'm just paranoid, but I could swear Will's been shooting me nasty looks every chance he gets this week. "I should have ended it a long time ago."

She nods, nibbling her bottom lip. "What finally broke the camel's back?"

"Well." I grin and clear my throat, savoring the chance to shock my unshockable best friend. "For one, there's someone else."

"Bandanna boy?" Z squeals, slapping me hard on the hip with the Machiavelli thesis.

"Uh-huh." I beam back at her, the thrill of finally sharing my feelings for Gavin sending a pleasant shiver down my spine.

Z grabs my hands in hers. "Why didn't you say anything before? I tell you everything!"

"Sorry. I meant to tell you. I just . . ." I trail off. *I just wanted to make sure it was real.*

"It's okay. Forget it. You've told me now, at least."

"Anyway." I sigh, my stomach twisting with the knowledge that whatever Gavin and I have will collapse like Bridge Nine the moment we're discovered. "It's not like it can last."

"Why not exactly?" Zahra asks.

"Zahra, think about it." I lower my voice to a whisper. "Gavin's from the South Side. And we're—"

"Yeah, your family owns half of Bedlam. So what? Opposites attract."

"But I could never even introduce him to my parents."

"You don't know that," Z says brightly, waving her hand through the air as if erasing all my doubts. "Maybe your dad will look at him as a project."

"Maybe," I say, but I seriously doubt it.

"And if not, know what?" Zahra throws her arm around my shoulders.

"What?"

"You're eighteen in a few more months. Your parents aren't in charge of you forever."

Just then, the bells begin their frantic noontime ringing.

As we head back down the spiral staircase, I let my thoughts drift back to Gavin. The spaces in between seeing him feel like the blurred background of a photograph, whereas our afternoons together are crisp and clear in a way I've never felt before. Just three more hours, I tell myself, until everything comes into focus again.

"Here," Gavin says, holding his leather jacket over my head and shoulders. We're huddled under a narrow fire escape in the alley behind Seven Swans. An electrical storm opened up on us as we were driving back on the bike, and we're both drenched.

"You're soaked," I protest. "Keep it on!" His thin white T-shirt sticks to his chest and stomach, but he just shakes his head and holds his jacket over me.

There's a deafening crack of thunder, and he pulls me to him. Rain drips off our noses as we kiss. I shudder in his arms, happier in this moment than I've ever thought I had a right to be. The knowledge that our afternoons together are ending suddenly feels catastrophic and horribly unfair.

I managed to buy one more day from Madame by telling her the physical therapist insisted, but tomorrow I have to go back. If I don't, I risk not just my role as the lead in *Giselle* but also the entire winter performance.

"Anthem," Gavin says, grabbing my hand and looking me in the eyes. His lashes are wet and bunched together.

"Gavin," I whisper, just as a car pulls up around the side of the alley. I glance down at my watch. Seven. Time to meet Serge. "I'll call you later." I pull my hand away and grab my ballet bag from the back of Gavin's bike, slinging it over my shoulder.

"Stay two more minutes. I want to tell you something—"

"Sorry." I flash him a pained smile. "I have to go."

"Tonight?" his eyes are pleading. "Can you sneak out? Come see me?"

I hold his gaze for a beat. I've never tried sneaking out before, at least not while my parents were at home. But it can't be that hard. I've lived in Fleet Tower my whole life, and by now, I'm sort of an expert at being invisible. Finally I nod, my heart somersaulting in my chest.

I dart out of the alley and head for our cream-colored Seraph, idling at the curb. "Hi, Serge. Some storm, huh?" I say as I slide into the backseat.

"Indeed. Perhaps you should have stayed indoors after

practice," Serge says evenly.

I catch sight of Serge's coal-black eyes in the rearview, the whites bright against his skin. I flick my eyes away, guilt and paranoia washing over me. Serge has been with our family since before I was born. On her good days, my mother jokingly calls him her backup husband. He has never done anything but protect me and take care of me, and I've been lying to him for the past week and a half.

"I thought I dropped something, so after practice I went to go look for it . . ." I trail off, unable to finish the lame excuse.

"I cannot help but notice your attire, Anthem," Serge says, as he pulls the Seraph away from the curb and begins to pick up speed. He grew up a child soldier in an African republic, and he's worked as security for dictators, government officials, and CEOs all over the world. He's seen it all, and he's always prepared for the worst—I'm pretty sure the gun he keeps in the glove compartment of the Seraph is loaded and that it's not his only one. He is not someone who is easily fooled, and he doesn't deserve to be lied to.

I look down at my soaked jeans and belted trench, my rain boots. "I changed upstairs," I say quickly.

Serge nods, but I can tell by the silence hanging in the car that he doesn't believe me.

As we roll through the streets toward home, I open my mouth to try to make conversation, but I don't quite know what to say. Instead, I reach into my ballet bag, where I've kept Gavin's gray bandanna in a small zippered pocket for the past week. I touch the soft material with my fingertips, my gaze locked out the window, excitement overtaking my guilt as I think about what I'm going to do tonight.

CHAPTER 8

South Bedlam after midnight is different than the run-down but charming place I've gotten to know over the past week. Though the reflected moon bounces off the rain-slicked streets, the main thing I notice once we cross the Bridge of Unity is the darkness. Only one out of every twenty streetlights seems to work over here. We pass by a bar with a wide, cracked bay window displaying two girls no older than I am, dancing listlessly in tassels and top hats and not much else. Mournful accordion music wafts out into the street, and a small crowd of people gather on the sidewalk to watch them through the window.

The motorcycle roars down one side street, then another, until we turn right on a street marked Oleander Way. "This is my block," Gavin shouts back at me over the revving engine.

He slows the bike, and I notice a group of droopie dealers in the doorway of a burnt-out brick building. Several shiny black cars idle at the curb, snaking slowly toward the corner. Two pale boys, dressed too lightly for the chilly night, scurry to the first car's window. One boy drops something the size of a matchbook through the two inches at the top where the window is cracked, then the other takes what must be the payment and stuffs it in his pocket.

I pull my arms tighter around Gavin's midsection, my hands finding the pockets of his leather jacket. I can feel his stomach muscles tighten through the silky lining, and my fear melts into desire.

We pull up to a building in the exact center of the long, treeless block. Gavin parks the bike in front of a squat concrete loft that must have once been a fish processing plant, the words MACKEREL TUNA ANCHOVIES stenciled in faded yellow lettering on the front wall above a large metal grate.

"Here we are," he mumbles as I dismount the bike. He flashes me a pained half-smile, his eyes darting up and down the block, deserted on all but the one busy corner.

"Don't look so worried," I say, not quite sure if I'm reassuring him or myself.

He pulls me toward him, wrapping his arms around my shoulders. He leans down until his forehead rests against mine, until our eyelashes brush up against each other. I lift up onto my toes and press my lips against his cheek, his jaw, his mouth, until I don't care what neighborhood we're in—this is the only place I want to be.

Gavin unfastens the metal grate and pulls it up with two hands, then unlocks a series of bolts on a sliding metal door. When at last he pushes open the heavy industrial door, I follow him inside. His apartment is a cavernous room with cement floors and a corrugated tin ceiling crisscrossed with metal beams. Canvases are stacked against each wall, six deep; but other than the vibrant swirls of color in his paintings, the place is colorless, sparse. There is almost no furniture, nothing to keep our footsteps from echoing.

A threadbare dark-purple couch takes up the center of the room, a coffee table covered in partially melted candles just in front of it. Off to one side, sheer white fabric hangs down from the ceiling, forming a sort of partition, the vague outlines of a low-slung bed visible behind it.

I follow Gavin to the couch in the center of the room, my forearms tingling with goose bumps, and pull the sleeves of my hoodie down over my wrists. It's colder in here than outside.

Gavin pulls a tartan camp blanket off the back of the couch, revealing a long rip in the upholstery. He shakes the blanket loose from its folded rectangle and wraps it carefully around my shoulders.

"It's not much, but it's home," he says, fussing with the blanket until it's around me like a cloak.

"I love it." I gather up the edges of the blanket so they don't drag on the cement floor and walk over to the kitchen, just a hot plate with two burners and a dented pale-green refrigerator that looks a hundred years old. On the fridge is a lone magnet—flat, blue, car-shaped—that reads HARRY'S AUTO PARTS—FOR THE CAR AND MOTORCYCLE CONNOISSEUR. Underneath is a photograph of a three-year-old boy with sandy-blond hair sitting on his mother's lap, snapped during what looks like a camping trip. She's leaning back and laughing, her face strikingly beautiful.

"Is this you?" I turn around to find Gavin running his metal lighter against his jeans. When it sparks to life, he bends down and begins lighting the candles.

"Me and my mom." He looks up. "Before she got sick. It's the only picture I still have. I should probably get a frame for it."

I nod and swallow hard, a mist of tears springing into my eyes when I think about everything he's had to go through.

"I'll get you a frame," I murmur as I walk toward the flickering candlelight. I think back to all the complaining I've done about my own mother, and a hot wave of disgust washes over me. "It must have been so hard, growing up without . . ." I trail off, not knowing how to finish.

"A lot of people have it worse." Gavin shrugs as he lights the last candle and looks up at me, his eyes twinkling. "I got you something. Hang on."

He jogs over to the curtained-off bedroom, and I hear the scrape of a drawer opening. The naked bulb on the floor throws his shadow onto the opposite wall of the room, elongated, a scarecrow on stilts. I sit down on the couch and lean my head against the worn purple velvet as Gavin moves back toward me.

I shut my eyes, willing myself to remember every detail of tonight. A moment later, I feel Gavin's weight as he sits next to me on the couch.

"For you," he says, placing a small square box just above my knee. It's an ancient candy tin, imprinted with a woman in silhouette, her hair curled around a flowered hat. Above her, written in deco script, is the word PASTILLES, the last two letters blotted out by a patch of rust blooming on the greenish metal.

"You didn't have to get me anything," I say, my chest hot.

"Open it." Gavin scoots closer to me until our legs are touching. I can feel the heat of him through my jeans. I wiggle the lid back and forth until it slides off the box. Inside a twist of yellowed tissue paper, I find a heart-shaped gold pendant on a delicate gold chain.

"It's beautiful," I breathe, holding the chain up in front of me and letting the heart dangle and flip from side to side. The pendant is thinner than a dime and made of hammered gold, the heart shape artfully lopsided, long and thin, with a perfectly round hole the size of a grain of rice punched into its right side. When it stops twisting on its chain, a faint ray of light bleeds through the hole.

"Fourteen karat. One of a kind, the guy said." He looks up at me through his lashes, his expression serious.

I shake my head, realizing how expensive this must have been. There's no way I can keep it.

"I love it, but it's too extrava—"

"Don't worry about it," he interrupts sharply. "Painting pays pretty well in the summertime. I'm not as poor as you might think."

"Sorry, I didn't mean . . ." I trail off, fearful I've offended him.

He waves his hand as if to say *Forget it*, then turns on the couch so he's facing me squarely. His gruffness has softened now, gone as quickly as it came. The candlelight flickers in his eyes as he stares intensely into mine. "I can't stop thinking about you, Anthem."

Gavin takes the necklace from me. He unclasps it, lays it gently on my throat, and moves to fasten it behind me. It fits perfectly between the ridged bones of my clavicles. I close my eyes and let myself feel his breath on my hair, his hands fastening the chain at the nape of my neck. "Me too," I murmur.

I slowly pull away from him and stand up. The candles flicker on the table behind me, and the naked bulb in the corner of the room forms a sort of spotlight. It feels like the most natural thing in the world when I pull my hoodie off over my head, my gaze locked with his.

"Are you sure you want to do this?" He searches my face for fears or doubts. "We don't have to—"

"I'm sure," I say firmly. I can almost see myself from above, as if I'm dreaming this. But it's real.

My stomach full of butterflies, my skin tingling, my head reeling with the force of the moment, I take Gavin's hand and pull him up from the couch. We walk slowly toward the gauzy curtains. Toward whatever comes next.

CHAPTER 9

My eyelids fly open when I hear the crash. The glowing red numbers on Gavin's clock read 4:08. I can't see anything else in the pitch-black corner of the loft, but what I hear makes my heart start to race: metal scraping against metal, a brief silence, and then voices. Some male, but at least one gravelly, high-pitched female, joined together in a teasing sing-song like a church hymn gone terribly wrong.

La-la-la-LOVERS. It's oh-oh-oh-OVER. Da dum da dum dum.

I pull my arm out from under the heavy wool blankets and grope beside me, feeling Gavin's arm curled around his pillow. I shake his shoulder until he turns over, reaching to pull me against him again, to cradle my body in his. This was how we drifted to sleep together, just two hours ago. I shake him harder.

"Whas wrong?" he mutters, his voice still cottony with sleep.

"Wake up," I whisper, my body tensed with fear. "Someone's here."

Just then, the metal security gate screeches open in front of the old factory doors. I kick the covers off and scramble around the sides of the bed. I search frantically until I find my jeans on the floor. I pull them on, but my stomach sinks when I remember my hoodie is in the living room by the couch.

The banging on the inner doors gets louder. Gavin switches on a bedside lamp, the dim bulb casting a low, sinister light under its tasseled red silk shade. His eyes look panicked.

He pulls his own jeans on, and the deep red light glows along his bare chest. Just three hours ago, I ran my hands along that stomach, tracing the outlines of each muscle. "Grab your shirt and hide." He shoots a nervous glance toward the door, then yanks a bunch of canvases out from under his bed. "Under here," he motions.

I run to grab my hoodie off the living room floor. My bare feet race across the ice-cold cement as the ominous metal-on-metal sounds keep coming from the door. When I reach the couch, I pull my sweatshirt on so violently I hear a seam rip along the armpit.

Pepper spray, I think as I begin searching through my pockets. But except for a lint-covered Relaxamint in the right pocket of my jeans, there's nothing. My heart sinks. I was so eager to see Gavin tonight that I forgot the one thing I never travel without. And now that I actually need it, the canister is in my coat pocket in the hall closet at home.

Gavin's rummaging in a kitchen drawer. He grabs a paring knife, then runs toward me, tucking the blade into his back pocket. "Get under the bed," he whispers, pulling me toward it. "Don't say a word."

I crawl under the low-slung bed, my heart racing. *La-la-la-LOVERS. It's oh-oh-oh-OVER.* My stomach drops when I hear the dead bolt turn in its tumbler.

I hear the crash of the metal door flying open, and suddenly the loft is filled with radiant moonlight. My body goes rigid with fear as I crane my neck to see the doorway, where they appear, five figures in silhouette. They come in slowly, casually, as if they're here for a party.

They're all wearing gas masks, and two of them are carrying guns. In these terrible masks, remnants from some old war, the intruders look like giant cockroaches. Black rubber tubes dangle where their mouths should be; their eyes are bizarrely wide-set, blue-green lenses the size of saucers, and frayed leather straps wrap around their hair. The two men aim their guns squarely at Gavin and fan out on either side of him.

My eyes are drawn to the woman, who comes into view in my six-inch window between the mattress and the floor. The leather straps of her mask wrap around a white-blond bob with blunt bangs. She wears army-green coveralls, spotless but for a finger-size smear of white paint beneath her left knee. She's around my height, but carrying an extra thirty pounds of muscle and curves. The green glass of the gas mask hides her eyes, so my gaze fixes on her blue surgical gloves. They're too big on her, bagging at the wrists and fingertips. All five of them wear them, like a team of demented, roachlike surgeons.

It dawns on me in a sickening rush. The gloves, the gas masks. Gas-and-dash. It's been happening in the Bedlam subway system for years now—entire cars in the Bedlam Tube poisoned with giggle gas, people either killed or so drugged that they can't fight off the teams of criminals who methodically search them for wallets, belts, shoes, purses, jewelry. Anything they can sell on the black market. Gas-and-dash has become so common that now only the poorest citizens venture underground to use the Bedlam Tube.

"Get out of my house," I hear Gavin say.

The cockroaches respond to this with uproarious laughter. One of them has a high-pitched giggle that could break glass. I hear the sounds of cabinets opening and closing. Then someone is in Gavin's tiny bathroom, where I hear the rustle of the vinyl shower curtain. I pray that they will find something they want to steal and leave peacefully. But the shoes emerge from the bathroom and then turn, pointing in my direction. Slowly, steadily, they approach the bed. *Please turn around. Please take what you want and leave.* The steps halt right in front of me. I feel myself trembling as the thick legs bend lower, and when his horrible roach eyes meet mine, I scream.

"Found a dust bunny under the bed." A hand closes around my ankle and drags me, thrashing and kicking, across the rough cement floor.

"Get away from her!" Gavin yells, and then someone else yells out in pain.

I begin to scream, clawing at the masked thug like a wild animal, until I feel the cold steel of a gun muzzle against my side.

"Let's sit down on the bed, sweet pea." The girl's raspy voice is muffled slightly by the hideous rubber tubing.

I freeze, the spot where the gun touches my ribs now the only part of my body I can feel.

"Well, come on." She yanks the shoulder of my hoodie up from the ground, and I quickly stumble to the bed. As soon as I'm seated on the edge of it, she sits next to me, just an inch away, her gun cocked and pointed casually at me from her lap, her finger on the trigger. I look toward Gavin and see the bald roach has a gash on his forearm. Blood streams out of it and drips all over the floor. He has wrested Gavin's paring knife away from him, and his good arm holds it against Gavin's neck. One flick of the wrist, and the knife will pierce Gavin's throat.

"No," I whisper. "Please."

"Don't hurt her." Gavin's eyes burn into mine. "Get the gun away from her, *now*."

Tears leak down my cheeks, onto my hoodie, falling fast. I don't dare move to wipe them away. I don't dare breathe.

"Please," I moan, not breaking eye contact with Gavin. "I have money. I'll give you whatever you want. Just let us go."

"Money!" the girl exclaims, her voice dripping with sarcasm. "Well, why didn't you *say* so, sweet pea? Boys, let's make it happen. He's not gonna gag himself." She snaps her fingers, and the rubber surgical glove rustles.

"Don't touch her!" Gavin screams, kicking wildly as two of the roaches move toward him. "Anthem, don't give these assholes anythi—" But then the skinny guy stuffs something in Gavin's mouth and seals it with a long strip of silver duct tape. They bind his wrists, securing them behind his back. Satisfied, they finally lower the paring knife away from his neck.

"That's better. Now I can hear myself think," the girl says, the rubber tube on her buglike mask bouncing as she talks. In my head, I name her Miss Roach. She turns to Gavin. "We're not going to touch her, Romeo. We plan to let your walking bank account run home to Daddy."

He tries to break away, but they push him to the cement floor, where he lands face-first with a sickening thud. One of the masked men wedges a black boot into Gavin's back, and another puts a gun against the back of his head, cocking the trigger. Gavin's face contorts in a pained wince.

"*NO!*" I scream, leaping up from the bed.

The girl jumps up, too, wiggling her gun, a tiny pearl-handled pistol, in my face. I sink back down to the bed, shaking uncontrollably.

"Put your hands where I can see them, on the bedspread. And no more yelling. I'm not going to hurt you or your boyfriend unless you do something stupid."

I nod, looking over at her quickly, then turn back to see Gavin's face still smashed against the cement floor.

"Nice and easy, nice and easy," the big one says, pulling the gun away from Gavin's skull. Gavin looks up at me from the floor, his eyes panicked.

"I'll give you whatever you want," I whisper.

"I know, sweet pea, I know," she says. In front of us, the muscular bald thug pulls Gavin to his feet.

"So let him go," I plead. "It's me you want, not him." Once I've said the words, it hits me that they're true, and that Miss Roach knows it. Why else would she call me a *walking bank account*? We must have been followed. Someone saw a rich girl in the South Side and decided to cash in.

They start to move him, half walking, half dragging him toward the door. The tall one keeps his gun near Gavin's head. Gavin's eyes remain trained on the floor. He's ashamed, I realize. Embarrassed that I'm seeing him so helpless. I gasp at the sight of his duct-taped hands, bound so tightly they're turning purple.

"Here's what happens now," Miss Roach says, her tone as neutral and crisp as a flight attendant's, but her stance is menacing as she leans toward me, her face just inches from mine. She pulls the bottom of her gas mask away from her mouth again so her words are crystal clear. Her matte red lips curve into a smirk, her breath a mix of cigarettes and bubblegum. "We take your boyfriend away to a special place we know. You get us $250,000 by midnight on Friday. Someone—*one* person, *un*armed—delivers the money to Dimitri's on the Water, on the south side of the Bridge of Unity. We'll be waiting there, watching carefully for any cops."

I nod, my eyes glued to Gavin's. He looks both furious and fearless, propped up by a masked thug on either side, his arms wrenched tightly behind him. A vein bulges on his forehead, and he shakes his head, communicating one thing: *Don't do it.* I stare into his eyes, refusing to back down. Hoping my gaze reassures him somehow.

"Sweet pea?" the girl says, poking the muzzle of the gun deeper into my ribs. "Pay attention, okay? Here are the rules. You go to the cops, he dies. You don't bring the money in full, he dies. Your delivery guy shows up at Dimitri's on the Water with someone else, he dies."

"Take me instead," I moan quietly, even though I know they won't. "Kidnap me and go to my parents. They'll give you anything. Just let him go."

"Too risky. You'd be splashed all over the papers. We'd rather roll the dice with loverboy."

"Gavin!" I choke out as they drag him toward the door. "I'll get the money. Just stay alive!"

And then they're gone, out the door, pulling him with them. The girl leaves last, her gas mask fixed over her face again. She backs out, her gun aimed at me the whole time, then gives me a little finger-wagging wave and slams the metal grate back down over the door. I'm left alone, sitting still as a statue on the bed where earlier tonight I lost my virginity. Where I drifted off to sleep in Gavin's arms. A hot wave of anguish presses in on me from all sides followed by a thudding fear that I'll never see Gavin again.

Gavin's blood glistens on the cement floor, a boot print's edges tracing the wet, black smear. I swallow down a mouthful of bile and concentrate on what I have to do. Thanks to years of memorizing dance sequences and teachers' lectures, I remember every word of her instructions. Any wrong move has the exact same consequence.

He dies. He dies. He dies.

CHAPTER 10

I walk and walk.

In the hushed darkness of 5:00 A.M., I begin to retrace the path we took on Gavin's motorcycle. It's much slower on foot, and terror has made me disoriented. Twice, I turn down dead-end alleys before I find the artery that takes me north again. On the sidewalk opposite me, a man with a face like a gnarled tree trunk pushes a shopping cart full of cans. His body is bent, feet swollen, bluish toes poking out of his broken shoes. "Kill 'em all!" he shouts, his voice surprisingly loud and clear. "Every last one of 'em. Explode the whole city, start again!"

I pull my hood up around my face and avert my eyes, quickening my pace when I see the Bridge of Sighs looming up ahead, ornate and shining, illuminated by spotlights from below. *Light.* In the dark grid of busted streetlights and abandoned buildings, light means safety—and help for Gavin. The bright order and logic of North Bedlam is just across the bridge. I aim myself like a missile toward it, not daring to run but walking fast.

The entrance to the bridge is only two blocks away, then one block. *Almost there.* I whisper the words to myself in time with my footfalls, until they become a mantra: *Al-most-there al-most-there al-most-there*.

The pedestrian entrance to the Bridge of Sighs is marked on either side by stone carvings, the olive-wreathed heads of goddesses with their mouths open, serene eyes tilted skyward.

"Yougotanypills?"

My stomach drops. A low voice keens in my direction. Out of the shadows lumbers a hugely fat man, his wide nose webbed with broken capillaries. Tufts of woolly greenish hair spring at funny angles from his head. He's fashioned a voluminous robe from hundreds of tattered pages of newsprint, all scrunched together, the edges of it shredded and filthy. The sleeves rustle in the wind like feathers on a great carnivorous bird. He lurches toward me, his eyes askew. A pale slice of his stomach peeks out from a rip in the robe, garish and pale in the light of the moon.

I shake my head and turn away, but he comes closer. His teeth are splayed out in all directions.

"AnypillsIaskedyouaquestion." He steps between me and the waterfront, leaning close enough to engulf me in the fetid cloud of his breath.

"No pills," I say hoarsely, my eyes scanning the bridge for signs of life. I turn to run, but my foot catches on his leg and I stagger forward against the balustrade. My forehead smashes against the stone filigree, and I crumple to the ground. A sticky warmth drips down my face. When I sit up and reach to wipe it away, my fingers are covered in blood.

He looms over me, his walleyes looking in two directions. He bends toward me, and his laugh is the high-pitched squeal of a pig.

"Pretty." He strokes my hair until his filthy hands catch in the tangles. I don't even scream when I feel the paper feathers of his sleeves tickling my neck. Not even when they're followed by ten thick fingers encircling my throat.

"Prettygirl. Iusedtoliveinahospitalbuttheysetmefree." His grip on my throat begins to tighten.

I come back to myself as his grip gets tighter, clawing at his wrists, desperate for air. "Let me help you," I whisper. "I'll find you some medicine." But my windpipe is shutting. I claw wildly at his feathery wrists, bits of paper flying into my mouth as I try to rip his hands off me, but he's far stronger than I am. The world starts to fade to black, a few white stars flaring and dying out—

"Hands off."

The birdman's grip suddenly loosens, sending me falling back against the balustrade. His leering face lunges toward me again, only to be pulled away by a set of strong arms reaching around his huge paper shoulders.

"I said to leave her alone!"

From the ground I watch as the birdman turns and fights back, flailing his paper-covered arms. After a short struggle, a punch lands squarely between his lunatic eyes. He falls backward, whimpering in that same high-pitched, piggy squeal, and lands faceup on the bridge, arms spread wide, eyes rolling into the back of his head before shutting altogether.

"You okay?" My rescuer stands over me, his teeth stark white against his olive skin in the moonlight. He wears a thin, black long-sleeved tee with a rip at the collar, his wide shoulders straining against the fabric. His forehead gleams with sweat, and a bead of it crawls down his smooth cheek. He looks like he's been out jogging.

"Yeah," I say, still slumped on the ground, shaking a little.

"They never should have closed the asylums," he adds under his breath. He crouches down to my level, taking care to be gentle as he studies the cut on my forehead, his brow creasing above his dark eyes. He offers me his hands, gently pulling me onto my feet. "You're going to need stitches."

"Thanks," I croak, bringing my hands to my throat, rubbing the places the birdman squeezed, the sensation of his fingers crushing my windpipe still lingering.

He nods, his eyes zeroing in on my neck. I reach up and feel the delicate chain of the heart necklace Gavin gave me, miraculously unbroken.

"You shouldn't be out here alone late at night," he says. "But since you're here, and we're meeting like this, I'd accept a little reward."

I shake my head, hoping I'm misreading the covetous expression clouding his face. "I don't have anything," I whisper, panic ricocheting through my torso.

"Come on," he coaxes, impatiently shifting his weight from one sneakered foot to the other. "Nothing at all?"

My heart racing, I take stock of him. He's tall and built to hurt. My eyes flick past him, toward the South Side. No way am I going back there. I've got to get across the bridge and head north.

Adrenaline flooding my veins again, I do the only thing that makes sense. I pirouette around on the narrow pedestrian walkway, and I run.

"Really?" he shouts, incredulous. "Hey! I'm not going to hurt you!"

I sprint harder than I ever have before, my lungs burning

with every step. Behind my own ragged breath and the slap of my shoes on the cement, I hear him following me.

"Wait up!" He catches up to me easily and grabs my hand. "Calm down, I'm not—"

"No!" I twist desperately away from him, lunging backward toward the bridge's worn stone railing. The stone has crumbled into nothing, leaving a gap in the railing that puts me on the edge of the bridge. "Get away from me!"

His eyes wide with alarm, he offers his hands to me again. "I'm sorry I scared you." His voice is quiet, no longer playful or irritated-sounding like before. "Come away from the edge, okay?"

"Walk far away from me, and I will." I shudder and almost lose my balance before I grab on to a section of the railing to my right. The chemical decay of the river hits my nostrils. He shakes his head again and backs away, raising his hand to show he means no harm.

Just as I'm about to move away from the edge, the corner of the stone railing I've grabbed on to breaks off in my hand. I look down at it, dumbfounded, as a strong gust of wind pushes me backward, sending my right foot out from under me. I flail, my arms reaching wildly in front of me as my body careens into thin air.

I try to grab on to the bridge again, but my fingertips barely graze it. I see the jogger's face twist in horror as he races to the edge, and then all I see is the starless sky.

He's too late. His hands clutch at the air, his mouth a black circle of shock.

I turn midair to meet the greasy gray-green of the Midland churning beneath me, its surface dotted with small chunks of ice.

My scream is one long, shrill cry of horror.

And then I'm

    falling,

        falling,

            falling

                through

                    the

                        empty

                            moonlit

                              sky.

CHAPTER 11

I wake with a gasp.

My vision floods with blinding white light. A blade of pain slices through my skull, so sharp it sends my head slamming back down against hard, unyielding metal. I'm ice-cold. I move to wrap my arms around myself, but they're tied down, my wrists and elbows secured with thick straps.

Wincing, I squeeze my eyes shut again, longing to return to the darkness of unconsciousness—to an endless, floating dream—for just a few more minutes. In the dream, I drifted through icy green water, through murk and rot, all alone but for the occasional one-eyed fish. I was neither dead nor alive. I felt no pain.

Being awake is agony. Every tiny movement brings a new kind of hurt, every part of me searing or frigid or sore. I concentrate on the sensation of my torso rising and falling with every breath. There's heaviness in my chest, an itchy, tingling sensation. Something inside me seems almost to be *whirring*. It feels simultaneously like a spinning disk and like a hundred tiny needles pricking me from the inside. As my panic mounts, the whirring seems to get faster, louder.

I open my eyes to slits, letting the bright light in a little at a time. Shapes begin to come into focus, textures emerge and start to make sense. I'm in a small, dank room. At eye level is a rolling metal table scattered with small scissors and gleaming scalpels. Rusty old machines, tubes sprouting from them like weeds, line the gray walls. The walls, the machines, and the floor are all speckled with something dark and dried. Blood. I quickly turn away.

I lift my head and peek at the long expanse of my body. I'm covered in a thin paper hospital gown and strapped to a narrow metal gurney. An IV is affixed to my hand, and the pole stands next to me, a clear bag sending drips of pinkish liquid down a long tube one at a time.

My eyes are drawn to movement in the corner of the room. A high-pitched squeak is faintly audible under the humming of the medical equipment. Four glass aquariums sit on a metal table in the corner. One contains a cluster of tiny light-brown hamsters, and in another, a swarm of black mice with pink ears scurry over one another. Nearest to me, a pair of albino lab rats with blood-red eyes run frantically on an exercise wheel in a glass cage.

How did I get here?

Everything comes rushing back to me—the kidnappers in their gas masks; the cold steel of Miss Roach's gun in my chest; the anguished look on Gavin's face before they took him away. I cringe at this last image. The bridge. The birdman's hands around my windpipe. The bridge railing. Falling into the river. An icy sweat starts to pool under my arms. I need out of here, *now*. But the straps dig into my arms when I try to move again.

I open my mouth and cry out for help. My voice is hoarse-sounding, barely louder than a whisper, though I'm trying to shout. After a few minutes when nobody comes, I resort to banging my head against the metal table in the hope that someone will hear.

A tall, slim, silver-haired woman wearing goggles and army-green scrubs races through the door, a surgical mask pushed down around her chin. She's followed by the jogger from the bridge. He stands to one side of the gurney, and the surgeon stands on the other. I thrash on the metal table, my hospital gown billowing up around me like a sail.

The woman places her hand on my head, gently patting my matted hair. Her eyebrows furrow with concern beneath her mass of silver curls, the color an odd contrast to her youthful, unlined face.

"Don't touch me," I hiss. "Get your hands off me right now!"

"She's ferocious." She grins at the jogger, seemingly impressed. Her bloodshot blue eyes shine with evident pride as she writes something down on a clipboard. "A very good sign."

"Where am I?" I demand. "And why am I tied up?"

"I'll get those. Sorry about that. You kept trying to pull out the IV." The jogger starts to unbuckle the restraints binding my wrists to the table. "We didn't know if you were going to make it." His ears turn red as he releases the last of the straps pinning me down.

"What happened last night?" I whisper, struggling to sit up. The effort makes the room spin. I instinctively reach my hands to my throat. The necklace is still there, the flat gold heart cool in my hand.

"Three nights ago, actually," the woman chirps as she presses a stethoscope to my chest.

"Three nights?" The blood drains from my face, and I will myself not to pass out. The boy rests a hand on my back to steady me, and I don't have the strength to shake him off.

"Easy now, take it slow. You don't want to lose consciousness again," the doctor murmurs. Through my dizziness I notice a large tattoo on the inside of her forearm. It's a double helix, two curved strands of DNA. Surrounding it is a complex series of interlocking hexagons and pentagons dotted with letters and numbers. I think back to last year's bio lab, where we were always drawing symbols like this. Nucleotides. The basic elements of genetic reproduction. A second tattoo near her wrist is of a small heart, encircling a name in delicate script. *Noa.*

"You remember falling into the river, right?" the jogger says, a guilty, pained expression on his face.

I nod, wishing I could forget the icy water flooding my lungs, the instant freezing of my limbs, the polluted kerosene stench of the Midland, the certainty that my life was over.

"Sorry about that. I shouldn't have asked for a reward." He pauses for a moment, and I notice his eyes are a clear brown but red-rimmed and tired-looking. "I don't know what I was thinking.

"Anyway," he goes on, "you were carried down the river, but I jumped in after you. When I finally reached you, I took you straight to Jax's lab. I'm Ford, by the way, and this is Jax. She saved your life. Jax, this is . . ."

"Anthem."

Ford's cheeks redden a little, and he nods. "We, uh, actually already know your name."

I look from one to the other, my chest suddenly skipping like a broken hard drive. "You do?"

"You've been in the papers," Ford says carefully, avoiding my eyes. "The whole city is looking for you."

"Oh my god." I picture my mother and father being

interviewed on *Channel Four News Roundup,* and goose bumps rise on my forearms at the realization that they probably think I'm dead. Then a thought occurs to me—maybe they've found out about Gavin, maybe somehow the kidnappers have changed their plan. "Did the news mention a kidnapping?"

Ford eyes me curiously, but shakes his head. "Just you."

"I . . . the reason I was on that bridge so late is because my boyfriend was kidnapped and I was going for help."

"Sorry." Ford lowers his head. "About everything. Really."

"It's an honor to meet you, Anthem," Jax jumps in, her fingers closing around mine, pumping them up and down a little too enthusiastically. "Ford used to be a boxer before he got on the wrong side of a few fights. It may have made him into the reckless idiot he is today. He didn't tell me he was responsible for your death until later. I was furious when—"

"My *death*?" I look down at my paper gown and notice something black and wormlike swimming beneath it, near the center of my chest. I start to lift the hospital gown, but Ford lifts my chin up, his eyes carrying a warning.

"Better not look just yet."

"Why not?" I manage, my voice scraping my throat. Again I notice the tight, tingly hum in my chest, the whirring sensation.

Jax interrupts. "The river was ice-cold. Your heart stopped. Ford tried mouth-to-mouth, but it was too late. You were . . . clinically dead. Until we brought you back, of course."

"Brought me back how?" I whisper, putting a hand onto the metal table to steady myself. The lab animals. The scalpels. The—oh, *God*. The *walls*. The blood spattered across them. I begin to shake so violently that my body rustles the paper on the gurney.

"Maybe you should lie back down for a minute?" Jax says,

her lips pursed with concern. She presses two fingers against her wrist, on top of the heart tattoo. "You're still extremely weak. I'll need to keep you for observation for at least a couple more days—"

"I'm fine," I lie, my throat constricting, my larynx strangled by a crushing fist of dread. "Just tell me what you did."

Jax nods. "I dabble in a lot of different sciences. Chemistry, biology, genetics, a bit of physics—" She titters nervously. "I was actually the youngest professor ever hired in the bioengineering department of Bedlam University, before a couple of experiments got away from me and they raided my lab." Her expression grows stormy.

"Total mad scientist, in other words," Ford interrupts. "She's wanted by the Feds, which is why she never leaves this lab. I do her errands, buy her equipment, that kind of thing."

Jax scowls and perches on a rolling metal stool, her face now level with mine. "Yes, Ford, I don't know what I'd do without you. But enough about me, right?" More nervous laughter spills from her mouth, and she stops abruptly, growing serious again. "After three minutes without a heartbeat, a person is pronounced clinically dead. Your heart stopped for approximately forty minutes, but because of the lake, you were also experiencing hypothermia, which is very good for a dead person. The river may have saved your life every bit as much as the surgery."

Surgery. I feel bile rise in my throat and swallow it down. "I hooked you up to the ventilator for a while." Jax waves her hand toward a huge, hulking machine with accordions encased in glass tubing above six rusty dials. "But your heart refused to restart on its own. So I intervened."

"You intervened," I repeat dumbly.

"See those sweet little guys?" Jax points to the corner of the room. I force myself to look at the table with the cages, where the rats are frantically racing on their creaky wheels. "Maybe we should go take a closer look at them, if you think you're strong enough to get there."

I nod, sliding slowly off the metal table and following Jax and Ford toward the cages, careful not to move too far from the IV pole still dripping pink fluid into my veins. We stand side by side and watch them run. They're moving so fast in their exercise wheel that their feet are just a white blur.

"About a year ago, I used recombinant technology to culture stem cells from a hummingbird and grow a powerful chimeric heart. These little speed demons each have one."

I stare at the furry blurs of motion, transfixed by their speed. Their little legs move as rapidly as hummingbird wings. "Chimeric? As in a chimera?" I think back to Greek mythology and flash on the sculpture in our foyer, his eagle head, his lion body. "Like a griffin?"

"Like a griffin, yes . . . in that their hearts are formed from a combination of more than one species."

"And . . . how does that relate to me?"

Jax turns to me, her expression delighted. "Well, now you have one, too."

I watch her mouth move as she goes on excitedly, spirals of her silver hair bouncing as she talks, her eyes dancing. But all I hear is the whirring, louder now that I know its terrifying source. So loud it's thudding inside my head. I start to feel faint, the room stretching out like a funhouse mirror.

"Just like a hummingbird's," she's saying, "your chimeric heart beats ten times per second. It's working so hard and so fast that it appears to have already reversed all the effects of hypothermia. Lucky, because I didn't want to have to amputate your legs. . . ."

My eyes move back to the rat cage. The rats appear to speed up, their bodies almost flying in their wheel. I'm not sure if it's because of their unnatural speed or my blurred vision. I put a hand to my chest, resting it lightly on top of the jagged line Ford warned me against examining. Knotted wires poke through the hospital gown. Stitches.

Picturing it, the edges of my vision turn black. My legs start to give out. I stagger back to the gurney and grab hold of it. Inside me, there's that fluttery sensation again, only now I know its source. A freakish hummingbird heart, beating ten times faster than my old one. Racing at 600 beats per minute. Pushing the blood through my veins faster than any human heart could, or should. Pumping hard and fast until the day it burns itself out.

"My clothes," I mumble, my eyes flicking across Ford's face before I squeeze them shut against the dizzy whirling of the room. "I'm cold."

He nods, springing toward the door. "I bought some stuff for you. I'll grab it."

"How long will I live?" I whisper frantically to Jax the moment Ford leaves the room.

"If you're very careful to resist torpor, you'll live to a hundred, maybe longer."

"If I resist what?"

"Think of your heart as like an engine. If a car sits in the garage for too many days, the engine will cease. Your heart is the same way. Your blood flow will slow if you're too still for too long, or if you deprive it of fuel. This slowing of the system is called torpor, and it can kill you if you aren't careful."

"What about when I sleep?"

Jax shrugs. "We'll observe you over the next few days and see how the heart responds to eight hours of REM state. After that, we'll know more."

But I don't have a few days, I want to scream. All I can think about is Gavin being dragged out the door by the kidnappers. If I've been here three days, I have less than forty-eight hours to get them their money.

Jax taps the IV pole. "This is glucose. It's been keeping your blood sugar steady. Once we disconnect you from the IV, you might find you'll need to eat more often than you're used to."

"I need to go home," I say, my voice thick. "My parents . . ." I silently add, *Gavin*. Everything depends on getting that money to the kidnappers by tomorrow night. My stomach sinks as I stare at the rats trapped in their cage. Ford comes back, holding a carefully folded sweatshirt and workout pants with a pair of tube socks sitting on top. Under his arm are two shoeboxes. The tags are still on everything.

"I had to guess your size," he says apologetically. "I hope some of this fits."

I look at him, then at Jax. "Could I have some privacy?"

"Of course," they say in unison.

Jax pauses in the doorway and turns around, her eyes tearing up. "Your recovery is truly astonishing, Anthem. If only this were legal, we would make history." Her eye twitches as she leans into the room and continues. "Every scientist in the country would give their right arm to study you in their lab. For now, it's best that we keep this between us."

A shudder ripples through me at the thought of being studied, hooked up to wires for the rest of my life. I nod and force a weak smile as she backs out of the lab.

Alone again, I grit my teeth and rip the IV out of my hand. It stings and burns at the same time, but I manage to swallow my scream. There's a little blood, so I grab a roll of gauze from the metal table and wrap it around my hand, ripping it with my teeth and tying it in a sloppy knot. I slip into the workout pants, rolling the waistband so the bottoms don't drag on the floor, and carefully untie the strings on my hospital gown. Nobody thought to find a bra, thank goodness. This is one of those times when it comes in handy not to really need one. I stop myself from looking closely at the black line of stitches and pull on the huge maroon sweatshirt, careful to avoid brushing it too roughly against my bare chest.

After I lace up the sneakers, I slowly turn the door handle, peering out into what must be the main room of Jax's lab. She's bent over a Bunsen burner in the far corner, heating water in a large beaker, humming an aimless tune.

I dry-heave a couple of times when I see the rest of the lab. Along each wall are dozens and dozens of animal cages, full of rats, rabbits, mice, and even a monkey, black and scrawny with a large tuft of white chest hair. My heart whirring, I begin to move quietly in the direction of the door. As it creaks open, I see Jax's frizzy head whirl around from the corner of my eye. But by the time she makes it to the door, I'm already halfway down an alley. She won't chase me too far, I realize as I gather speed. A fugitive can't risk being seen.

And then I'm running, running, running, a lab rat loosed from its cage.

CHAPTER 12

At first, I run slowly, nervous I'll hurt myself so soon after major surgery. I stop for a moment behind a smoldering tire fire to gauge how I'm holding up physically. I should feel like collapsing, but I don't. I feel energized. My muscles are warm and loose. I put a hand over my whirring chest. What was it Jax said about my heartbeat? Ten times per second? It's so fast I can't differentiate between the beats at all. It feels more like a vibration.

I take off again, and with each block I'm pushing harder, daring myself to go faster. The longer I run, the more the tightness in my chest fades. Soon it's nothing but an internal itch. My feet pound the trash-strewn streets of the South Side, my pace quickening until it feels as if my sneakers are barely touching the ground. The rhythm of my toes on the sidewalk, the blast of cool air in my lungs, the simple fact of being alive after everything that's happened makes me feel that even with this . . . *thing* inside me, I'm still healthy and strong.

Maybe I'm more than just healthy, I realize as I speed past a couple of ragged street kids on skateboards. They stop to watch me, their mouths hanging open.

Concentrating on my newfound speed allows me to temporarily shove all the horrors of my back-alley operation into a tiny corner of my brain, slamming a door on the whole mess of it and locking it tight. The operation, I can block out. But Gavin—held in some dark room somewhere, suffering, at their mercy—fills my thoughts.

After I run twenty more blocks in the empty dawn-saturated streets, I start focusing less about running away from the lab and more about running toward home. I have maybe forty-two hours to get the kidnappers their money. I know they won't think twice about killing him if I don't meet their demands.

I turn right, then left, then right again, marking a zigzag course. When the skyscrapers of North Bedlam loom into view, I begin to run even faster. My arms pump through the cool air, my legs lunge higher and harder with every step—until I see a flash of blue in the street just behind me, keeping pace.

I skid to a stop and instantly fold over, putting my hands on my knees and pretending to breathe harder than I really am, for the police cruiser's benefit. It pulls up alongside me, and a bitter laugh escapes my lips. Now—when I don't need them—they show up.

My laughter dies as I catch my reflection in the smoked glass window. A rectangular swatch of gauze is stuck to my forehead, a blood spot the size of a grape seeping through it at my hairline. The gash from the birdman, I realize, shivering slightly. My hair is a wild red rat's nest tumbling around my shoulders, but my cheeks are rosy and flushed.

The window lowers halfway down, and the cop smiles at me. "Running from someone?"

"Just out for a jog, officer."

"In this neighborhood. At five forty-five in the morning. Kind of risky, don't you think?"

"Well . . ." I start, not sure what I can say to make myself look like a reasonably sane person. The cop has two deep laugh lines on either side of his mouth and intelligent blue-gray eyes.

"You're right, it's probably not the best idea," I admit, my hands wandering nervously up to my bandage.

"How about letting me drive you home," the cop says. I look out at the sky over the Midland, now blazing orange and red as the sun rises behind the glass towers of Upper Bedlam. The tightness in my chest morphs into an ache.

"Okay, officer." I smile and open the door to the backseat, slipping inside the car.

The bulletproof glass separating the front and back seats has a small door in it, which he opens so we can talk. "I'm Detective Marlowe." Our eyes meet in the rearview, and he flashes me a professional, polite smile.

"Thanks for the lift," I say, craning my neck to get a glimpse of Fleet Tower in the near distance.

"You're the Fleet girl, aren't you?" he asks casually. "A lot of people have been looking for you."

I stare into the rearview and take a breath before I answer, careful to keep my words and expressions as light and straight-forward as his. "That's me, yes."

"Mind telling me what happened?" His eyes flick from the road to the rearview, maintaining their neutral, patient gaze.

I stare at the back of his neck for a minute, his light-brown hair buzzed close to the skin, neat and tidy under his blue police hat.

"I'd love to, officer," I say, pasting the bewildered, dazed expression of an amnesiac onto my face as I allow my eyes to meet his again in the rearview. "But the truth is, I can't remember a thing."

Half an hour later, I'm seated alone at the kitchen table, my stomach in knots. I've already hugged my parents tightly while Detective Marlowe looked on. They finally sent him on his way, but before he left, he instructed them to take me in for questioning once I've had some rest. *Once she's got her memory back*, he added, winking at me as if we both knew the truth about my amnesia.

As my mother and father move toward the kitchen, I pull the sleeve of my too-big sweatshirt over my bandaged hand and hide it under the table. When they sit down on either side of me, the silence in the room is thick enough to slice.

"We thought you were dead," my mother says finally. I can tell she's heavily sedated by the way she's slurring her words. A single tear travels down each of her pallid cheeks. "This was our worst nightmare come true, Anthem. We've already lost—" Her voice breaks, and a sputtering cry of grief breaks through her narcotic haze. My father moves his chair next to hers and hugs her against his chest as she buries her face in his shirt, her body shaking with muffled sobs.

"Since you've already lost one child," I finish for her, an irrational swell of anger rising in my throat. Normally when my mother brings up Regina, all I can feel is guilt. But right now, I feel indignant. Even now, after all I've been through, I have to compete with my dead sister for center stage. It's a competition I can never really win.

"I'm sorry," I say tightly. *Sorry I've disappointed you. Sorry I'm not as perfect as I've led you to believe.* I look away from her, not wanting to meet her blank sedated face. The clock on the oven says 6:21. Time is inexorably ticking by, the kidnappers' deadline getting closer. I have to get them their money by midnight tomorrow. My father is keeping it together, his eyes red but dry, his voice steely. "What happened out there? I don't believe for a second that you've got amnesia."

I swallow hard, trying to buy some time and collect my thoughts. If I open up the floodgates, I risk letting everything out. Not just the kidnapping but the attack, my deathly swim in the river, the operation. The best thing, I decide, is to tell them as little as possible and focus on the money.

My mother pulls her head away from my father's chest, her blond ponytail lumpy and askew on the side of her head. She looks so fragile and frayed, worse than I've seen her in years. Too fragile to find out her only living daughter is a medical experiment. I take a breath and cautiously try to explain what I can. "It sort of started the night of the Orphans' Ball. Will and I—"

"We've spoken with the Hansens and the Turks," she interrupts. "We know Will broke up with you. And we know from Zahra that you've been seeing a boy from the South Side."

I sit back in my chair, stunned. It didn't occur to me that they'd already know about Gavin. "*I* ended things with Will, actually, not that any of it matters now," I say, my voice thick. The kidnapper's bloody footprint on Gavin's floor flashes through my mind, and I shudder in my chair.

"We just don't understand," my mother starts. "Will was perfect for you—"

"Enough, Leenie," my father stops her. "We need to know what happened, and whatever it was has nothing to do with the Hansen boy."

"It was all my fault," I begin, shaking off my mother's comment about Will. "And I will never forgive myself for putting you both through this." I take a deep breath and tell them about meeting Gavin. About sneaking out to his place, about the kidnappers in their horrible masks, about their demands. I leave out everything that happened after the criminals left, saying instead that they knocked me out and that a neighbor found me a day later, bandaged me, and helped me get back on my feet.

My parents sit back, stunned and horrified. Their eyes meet and exchange a look of raw fury, then turn back at me.

"I don't know where to begin," my mother says, tears welling up in her eyes once more. "You come home in a stranger's clothes, half dead, having been God knows where. It's like I don't even know who you are."

"I'm sorry," I say quietly. "Everything with Gavin happened really fast. I couldn't tell you because I knew you'd never approve—"

"How could you be so stupid?" my father interrupts me, his booming voice making me jump. I've never seen him this angry.

"I don't know what you mean," I whisper, stung by his words. My father is usually the parent I can rely on to be levelheaded and calm no matter what.

"They knew who you were," he seethes, his elegant hands balled into fists. "They knew—they *know*—that you come from a family of means. . . . They *tracked* you."

I nod, afraid to say anything because the vein on my father's forehead is pulsing with rage. I shiver when I remember what Miss Roach called me. *Walking bank account.*

"You're right. I brought this on him," I say, my voice strangled and desperate. "If I don't give them the money tomorrow, they'll kill him. And it will be my fault."

My father stands up abruptly, his chair clattering behind him as it falls onto the heated stone floor. His hair, usually arranged more precisely than a Japanese rock garden, is wild. His nostrils flare with anger. "Your *circumstances* brought this on him. We've worked so hard your whole life to protect you, Anthem, and then you just threw it all away for a boy you barely know. You're lucky you're alive."

He stalks out of the room, and a moment later, I hear the clink of the crystal decanter at the bar. My father hardly ever drinks anything but wine, and never in the morning. I look at my mother through fresh tears. She puts her hand over mine and squeezes. Her touch is warm, if not comforting.

"He's right," she says. Her ashen face has a look of mourning, not for what's already happened but for what will. For the mistakes I'm sure to make in the future, the ways I will disappoint her. "Promise me you'll never do anything this foolish again. I don't want to lock you in your room, but I don't think I'll be able to bear it if you ever—"

"I promise," I say. "Never again." And in that moment, I mean it with all my heart.

Then again, my heart is in a jar somewhere in Jax's lab.

My mother wields her sadness like a weapon sometimes. It controls our family and has for as long as I can remember. I think of the time four years ago when I found her passed out in bed, a vial of MemErase scattered across the silk sheets. She checked into Weepee Valley Psychiatric for a full month that time.

My father comes back in, holding a tumbler filled with two inches of scotch. The smell of the alcohol reminds me of the sterilizer that filled the air at Jax's lab.

"Please," I whisper, looking up at my father. "I'm sorry. I really screwed up, and I let you guys down. I know I don't deserve your pity or your help, but you have to give them the money."

My mother slumps in her seat like a wilted lily and shakes her head. "No. We need to go to the police."

"Mom, you don't know what they're capable of," I start, my heart whirring so violently I'm afraid my parents will hear it. "If they see the police coming, Gavin will die."

"But, darling—" my mother protests.

"*No.*" The violence in my voice startles even me. "You might as well pull the trigger yourself."

My mother pulls back, surprised and a little scared. She looks at my father, who nods, before turning back to me. "Okay, sweetie. If that's what you want. The police can go on thinking you don't remember anything."

My father gulps down an inch of scotch and sits down heavily on one of the barstools at the kitchen counter. "Anthem, you have to understand. Even if we do give them this money, what will stop them from asking for more? They know who you are, they know who your father is. If we give in now, it will never stop."

At the words *It will never stop*, I lose my thin layer of self-control. I'm sobbing again, my head in my arms, crumpled over the table like a used napkin.

I feel my father's heavy hand on my back, then stroking my tangled hair. "Shhh. Don't cry," he whispers. It's the worn-sounding plea of someone who has spent the last seventeen years telling his wife the same thing.

"Please. They'll kill him, don't you understand?" I say through my tears as I look up at him, at his stubbly chin, his worried eyes.

He shakes his head, and my eyes focus on his Adam's apple bobbing up and down as he swallows. "I know it seems scary now, but there's a very good chance they're bluffing and that they'll release him once they realize there's nothing in it for them." The conviction in his face is hard and unbending, a brick wall my fragile hopes have smashed against, shattering into dust. "We will not negotiate with terrorists, Anthem."

"Please," I repeat over and over, my whole body shaking now, a mix of hysteria and rage hot in my chest.

"Someday you'll understand," my father says gruffly, his eyes avoiding mine. I know now that there is nothing I can say to change his mind.

"Anthem." My mother lays a hand on my head, gently smoothing my hair. Her red-rimmed gray eyes bore into mine insistently. "You've got to see we're only trying to protect you."

I slow my sobbing enough to stare back at her, my mouth trembling defiantly, while inside any lingering threads of hope have all snapped, leaving a sour, burning disgust in their wake.

"I understand," I lie.

I turn to look out the window at early-morning Bedlam. A fog has rolled in now, blanketing the city in a deceptively serene layer of white. I stare out at the city wrapped in its veil, wondering where they've taken him, my monstrous heart itching in my chest, whirring blindly in my ears.

CHAPTER 13

It takes a half hour to refuse all my mother's exhortations: to let a doctor visit the house and examine me, to start memorizing our cover story for the media, to eat something. This last request I give in to, demolishing a plate of eggs and three bowls of Lily's bread pudding without tasting any of it. After that, I convince her that all I need right now is sleep.

I finally escape to my room with a box of cookies and two Brawn Bars tucked under my sweatshirt. I yank down the shades on my glass wall to block out the brightening day and collapse into bed. Hot tears begin to flow, faster than before. I press my face into my silk pillowcase to muffle the jagged wails emerging from my throat. When the fabric is soaked through, I grab my noise-cancelling headphones from the bedside table and crank up the score of *Giselle* as loud as it can go. I pull my thick white comforter tight around me like a straightjacket and start to weep again, this time silently, my body shaking with the force of raw grief.

I'm crying so hard I'm beyond language, beyond rational thought. All I see when I close my eyes is a film reel on repeat: the barrel of a gun pressed to Gavin's temple, a hand squeezing the trigger, Gavin collapsing like a rag doll.

Finally, after two loops of *Giselle*, my throat and eyes feel like pounded meat. As the tears subside, a single coherent thought swims to the surface of my mind: *I can't let him die.*

I pull off my headphones and listen to the thudding silence of my room. I look at my alarm clock—9:23 A.M. I force myself to stand and peel off the clothes Ford gave me, replacing them with a gray cami and a crumpled pair of jeans I find draped over the ballet barre bolted to my bedroom wall.

Standing next to the barre, my bare feet at just the spot where I've practiced pliés, pirouettes, and chassés for hundreds of hours, my eye is caught by a glittery twinkle on the top of my dresser. Two hair combs adorned with cheap crystals—part of the snowflake costume for last year's *Nutcracker* recital. I reach for them, turning them over in my palm, a plan already forming.

Slowly, silently, I open my bedroom door and cock my head to listen. Lily's in the kitchen, humming the chorus of an old rock ballad. Under her humming, I hear the tapping of eggs against the corner of the counter, the sound of the yolks plopping into a ceramic bowl. From my father's office, located on the lower floor beneath the kitchen—much too far away to be able to hear anything—I hear an avalanche of keystrokes as he types. I concentrate and listen, the keystrokes growing louder the more I focus on them. Like he's typing on a keyboard attached to my ears. I lean my forehead against the door frame and close my eyes, still listening, trying to understand how. I shouldn't be able to hear any of this. It's like my ears are supercharged.

What has Jax done to me? I cover my ears up with my hands, and the sound goes away. I uncover my ears, and it's back. I shake my head in wonder. As long as I can hear my parents, I know exactly where they are.

My heart revving, I round the corner of the master bedroom and push open the door. My mother lies sprawled across my parents' enormous bed, a thin line of drool snaking from the corner of her mouth and pooling onto the brocade bedspread. She's breathing heavily, her chest rising and falling slowly. I think of the commercials for Dreamadine: *Dream it, live it, Dreamadine. Just one pill, eight full hours.* She insisted on giving me a few pills after I finished eating, and they now sit untouched on the base of my ballet-slipper lamp.

I dart through the master suite, my heart roaring in my chest. My mother doesn't stir, but my father could walk in at any moment.

I race to the vanity and reach under it to find the little button. The mirror slides up the wall, and I face the keypad in a blind panic. I don't know the code. *Think.*

My fingers travel over the glowing keys. If I get the code wrong, an alarm will go off that will wake my mother. I've spent enough time with her here to know the code is six digits. Our zip code? My parents' anniversary? No, I realize. It's simple. There's only one set of numbers Helene Fleet would choose.

I punch Regina's birthday into the keypad with shaking fingers, for once grateful for all the September twenty-sixths I've spent at the cemetery. The low beep and the faint sound of the steel unlocking tells me I'm in. Just then I hear a door open down the hall.

There are dozens of drawers to choose from, but I don't have time to browse. I think back to the Orphans' Ball, to my mother's $50,000 valentine. I have no idea if her other jewelry is worth more than that, or less. The ruby necklace will have to do.

I open the bottom drawer and pull the necklace off the black velvet it sits on, stuffing it into my back pocket. I shut the drawer and push the button, rearming the security on the jewel safe. I race past my mother again, who has turned toward the wall in her sleep.

A moment later, I'm in my room, conscious of my father speaking to Lily in the kitchen. With shaking hands I bring the largest ruby to my lips, kissing the cold, bloodred stone the way the nuns in school kiss their rosaries.

After stashing the necklace in a box under my bed, I consider the cloud-shaped blue pills my mother gave me. *"Dream it, live it,"* I whisper, putting them both on my tongue and heading to my bathroom for a swig of water to wash them down. If I'm going to try to hand the necklace over in exchange for Gavin's life tomorrow night, I'll need to get some sleep.

Before the drug hits my bloodstream, I dig my cell phone out of the bottom of my backpack and send Zahra a quick text— *i'm ok. don't worry. will call u tmrw, too tired now. xox.* Then I quickly turn it off, unable to cope with whatever communication is stored inside.

I spend the next eighteen hours obliterated on Dreamadine.

All day and most of the night, I slip in and out of an uneasy sleep. Sometimes in my dreams the Midland River is filled with boiling acid and when I fall in, my skin peels away in sheets. In other dreams, the kidnappers douse Gavin in kerosene and light a match, and I wake up sobbing.

In the last one, I'm standing at the observation window of a sleek hospital operating theater, powerless as Jax sews the head of an ostrich onto Gavin's body. Its hideous black beak opens wide as it squeals and shrieks with pain.

CHAPTER 14

I wake up scratching at my chest through my sweat-damp T-shirt at 4:06 A.M. on Friday morning. For a few blank seconds, I'm disoriented enough not to remember what's happened. But when I run my finger along the seam of my stitches, it all comes crashing back. This is almost the exact time Gavin was kidnapped three days ago. Thoughts of what has to happen tonight start to run through my mind, and soon I'm too wired and anxious to sink back into sleep again.

I flip on my bedside lamp and wait for the sun to come up, wishing there was some way I could stop myself from imagining the horrible things that are happening to Gavin, from wondering if he's even still alive. I need to stay off the internet and away from the news, since according to my parents, I'm all over it. They've already come up with a cover story at the urging of the Fleet Industries' lawyer and PR consultant, Lyndie Nye.

"You were visiting your cousin in Exurbia and went for a walk in the woods by yourself, and you got lost. Your phone was dead. You found a cabin and waited for your cousins to find you," my father muttered through my closed bedroom door last night. I opened the door and gave him a look that said I didn't like how stupid the story made me sound, but he just turned his palms up like it was out of his hands. "It's already out there. You'll have to live with it."

As the predawn sky moves from black to periwinkle, I pick up the copy of *Gatsby* Gavin loaned me on our fifth date and find the places he's highlighted, looking for solace. My breath catches at a line he's double-underlined in black ballpoint:

> *. . . and Gatsby was overwhelmingly aware of the youth and mystery that wealth imprisons and preserves, of the freshness of many clothes, and of Daisy, gleaming like silver, safe and proud above the hot struggles of the poor.*

I read it twice, wondering if Gavin thinks of me the way Gatsby thought of Daisy. I hope not. If I was ever gleaming, if I was ever safe and proud, I'm not now. I want more than anything to be able to tell him that I don't care about money. To tell him we're not doomed the way Gatsby and Daisy were, because we can remake our lives somewhere else. But that might never be possible.

Everything depends on tonight.

By the time seven rolls around, I've decided the only way to stay halfway sane today is to go to school. At least the crowded hallways of Cathedral will distract me from the twisted images swirling through my mind like chunks of black ice in the Midland. And anything will be less stressful than the silent fury I feel in the presence of my father. I've just started buttoning my school uniform shirt, a white blouse with the *CDS* crest on the pocket, when I hear my mother's delicate fingers tapping on my door.

"Just a minute," I say, but she pushes it open anyway. I turn quickly so that I'm facing away from the door and hurry to button the shirt from the top down, my hands shaking.

"Hi, Mom." I finish the final button with a numb smile on my face.

"School so soon? I thought this morning we could go to Doctor Sprogue's office—"

"I told you, I'll go to the doctor in a few days," I say, roughly pulling on the brick-red knee socks that complete the Cathedral uniform. "I'm fine, really. The pills calmed me down a little. School will help me get my mind off everything."

She nods slowly, her lips squeezed into a rosebud of resignation. She gives in more easily than I expected. "I guess the doctor can wait. Let me see the cut," she says, lifting my curtain of hair off the right side of my face.

This morning when the sun rose, I unwrapped the bandage and discovered my wound completely healed, nothing more than a thin white scar along my hairline. "All better." I shrug, hoping she'll drop the subject. "It was just a scrape."

"Thank goodness for that. Have you done something different with your makeup?" she asks, her gray eyes puzzled.

I shake my head. What makeup? Apart from glancing at my healed forehead, I haven't had the guts to face the mirror.

"Your whole face looks . . . different, somehow." She smiles. "You look beautiful."

I shrug and turn away to rummage through my backpack, not wanting her to examine me too closely.

"Never mind," she says, leaning over and grabbing me in a tight hug. "I'm just so glad you're back."

I breathe in her sugared-lemon smell, pretending for a moment that I'm still six years old, still her little doll. Our hug is cut short by an embarrassingly loud growl from my stomach. "Is Lily here yet? I'm dying for some pancakes."

When my mother pads back down the hall to find Lily, I turn to the mirror and look at my reflection. She wasn't exaggerating. My eyes are a vibrant, richer green. My lips are pink. My normally pasty skin is flushed with color. But the biggest change is my hair. The usual carrot orange has morphed into a shiny, wine-soaked red, glowing bright as fire. My heart whirs with alarm, and I lean so close to the glass that my forehead almost touches the mirror.

A half hour later, I'm in the backseat of the Seraph, being driven to school by Serge. I lay my head against the white leather seat back. Up above us, through the sunroof, the glass-and-steel skyscrapers of North Bedlam whizz by.

I put my hand in the pocket of my plaid pleated skirt and finger the ruby necklace, my fingers traveling over one jewel at a time.

"So." I clear my throat and address Serge. "Some week, huh?"

"Quite a week, yes. I'm pleased to see you are looking . . . remarkably well," Serge says evenly as he turns the Seraph onto Thorn Street and begins to pick up speed.

"Did my parents . . . brief you?" I have my fake story for the press, but I can tell by the silence hanging in the car that Serge knows about Gavin.

He nods. "I understand they have chosen not to negotiate."

"Yes," I manage to say.

"Sometimes fortune surprises us, Miss Fleet." Serge's eyes look at mine a little too carefully in the rearview mirror. I sense a question in his gaze, but he doesn't ask it.

He pulls the Seraph up to the curb in front of Cathedral,

and I gather my books, tugging at my collar as I exit the car. As I walk up the ancient stone steps of the school, the hairs on the back of my neck stand up. I suddenly have the distinct impression Serge knows more than he's letting on.

I arrive at school eight minutes after the morning bells. I keep my head down and walk as quickly as I can to take my seat in homeroom with Mr. Brick, a former soldier turned social studies teacher. The room smells soothingly of camphor, from the cream he applies to his knee between classes.

When I slide into my desk in the front row, the class erupts in loud chatter. I hear my name over and over and immediately flush bright red.

I stare helplessly at Mr. Brick.

"Quiet down, people!" he barks. The class does as it's told, but they only stare at me harder.

I shift my eyes down to the desk. My fist clenches the tangle of rubies in my pocket.

"We thought you were dead, Miss Fleet," Mr. Brick says in a stage whisper, his eyes widening ominously. "I was writing a *speech*."

I understand that *speech* is code for *eulogy*, and a shiver passes through me. Then I think of Zahra, and my stomach twists with guilt. She must have been terrified—and now she's probably livid that she can't reach me. My cell is somewhere in my backpack; I haven't turned it back on since sending Z the text last night.

"I'm fine," I squeak out. My heart does its new electronic revving, so loud I'm sure Ginger McGeorge next to me can hear it, as I recite Lyndie Nye's fabricated story word for word. I shoot a look at Ginger and see curiosity and concern in her eyes, nothing more. I try to focus on her soft brown ringlets, still damp from a shower, as I finish my little speech.

"Anyway," I continue, hoping I sound traumatized instead of coached, "it was really dumb of me, and I was lucky to make it out okay. I'd rather not talk about it too much right now, if that's all right."

"Of course, Miss Fleet. We respect your privacy and your bravery, and I speak for the entire school when I say we're glad you're back, safe and sound," Mr. Brick allows. I slump down in my seat during roll call and whisper *Here* at my name, still feeling all eyes focused on me.

After a few minutes, I can't stand the scrutiny. I grab the bathroom pass hanging on the wall and race from the room.

Zahra's homeroom is four classrooms away from mine. I skid to a stop outside the closed door and peer through its narrow glass window, hoping to get her attention. But true to form, Zahra has taken her time getting to school. Her desk is empty.

I clench my fists in frustration and take off again, hurtling down the drafty, locker-lined hallway, which is blessedly free of straggling students. I have all the space in the world to run, and I can't seem to help running *fast*. My legs stretch as I lengthen my stride, my arms pumping furiously. I'm moving so quickly that as I turn the corner, I collide with someone and fall to the floor, hard.

"Ow," I grunt, rubbing my tailbone and patting my hip to make sure the necklace is still safe in my skirt pocket.

"You're back."

Will. I hurry to gather the books that have fallen out of my bag and get to my feet.

"Looks that way," I say cautiously, focusing my eyes on his blond curls, the perfect creases in his khakis. Anywhere but his eyes.

"Have fun out there with your boyfriend?" His mouth curls into a sneer.

"Let's not do this." Not today, not when Gavin is tied up and half-dead in a dark room somewhere. Not on what could be my last day at Cathedral. It's not lost on me that what I'm doing tonight is risky enough to get me killed.

"Do you have any idea what people have been *saying* about you?" Will takes a step closer to me, so close I can feel the heat of his breath in my hair. "I heard you ran away with your drug dealer, that you're addicted to droopies—"

"I don't care what they've been saying," I whisper. "You're the one who's always cared about that kind of thing."

"Really, though, where *have* you been? I know you haven't been lost in the woods." Underneath his controlled tone, I hear the trace of something cruel. "Slutting around in dangerous places with your poverty case?"

Everything around me fades to white, until all I can see is Will's smug mouth. His sky-blue eyes that almost hide the ugliness inside him. Almost, but not quite. I see my foot curving through the air, the toe of my leather oxford smashing into his lower lip and chin, slamming his head backward, nearly knocking it off his neck. He staggers back and looks at me with his mouth hanging open, his face a cartoon portrait of shock. Teeth smeared with blood. A long, thin string of red drool dangles for a second from his lips before falling in slow motion to the floor.

Now Will's nasty smirk is gone. His eyes widen at me in horror, a gurgling, shocked howl coming out of his bloody mouth, his hands covering the mess of his face as he backs away from me.

My senses start to return to normal, though my heart keeps

pounding hard and fast. I look down in amazement at my right foot.

"You're a psycho! A *freak*," Will slurs, a slick of blood falling from his mouth and down his chin. I stand frozen in place, my eyes glued to the mess, not fully believing I'm the one who made it.

"You're going to pay for this," he snarls. Then he turns and runs, lurching down the hallway and out of sight before I can think of what to say, leaving me alone, shaking a little as I contemplate what I've just done. And what else I'm capable of doing.

I'm sitting on the front steps of school twenty minutes later, running my fingers along the octagonal cuts of the jewels in my pocket, when Zahra finally shows up, striding up the sidewalk in a pair of high-heeled boots that are a total uniform violation. In her familiar embrace, breathing in the smell of her hair pomade and her coconut-scented lip gloss, I realize I'm trembling. Zahra just strokes my hair until I've calmed down, wiping a few tears from my face.

"So . . . are you ready to tell me?" she finally whispers. "I got your text, but what the hell happened to you? I've been a wreck."

"It's Gavin," I whisper, taking her arm in mine and pulling her through the deserted courtyard toward the chapel. "We spent the night together at his place, and—"

"You spent the night on the *South Side*?" Z stops walking, her mouth hanging open until she clamps her hand over it.

"I . . . yeah." I haven't even gotten to the point of the story, and Zahra already looks pale with worry. "That's where Gavin's place is, so."

"Sorry, go on," she says. "I just. . . can't believe you did that. You must really like this guy."

I swallow and nod. "Anyway, there was a break-in." I struggle to keep my voice level, to show her I'm okay. "Gavin was kidnapped."

Z's violet eyes widen with fear as I go on. Looking at her as she absorbs the story of the kidnappers, their masks, their guns, and the knife against Gavin's throat, I know I can't tell her about my heart or what I'm going to do tonight. I end the story with the terms of the ransom.

"Oh my god," Z breathes, grabbing my hand in both of hers. "I have no words. You poor thing. Are your parents giving them the money?"

I shake my head sadly. "No."

"Oh my god," Z repeats, panic creeping into her voice. "What's going to happen to him?"

I look past her to the guard booth, where a young guard stands at attention, within hearing distance.

"I don't know," I murmur, wishing I could tell her about the necklace in my pocket. But she's always been fiercely protective of me. If I tell her, she'll feel like she has to help me, or to find someone who will. Maybe she'd even go to the cops.

She grabs me in a hug and a few tears escape my eyes.

I'll tell her everything as soon as Gavin is safe, I decide. Better not to burden her with the whole truth. Better to have her think I'm still fully human, still ordinary Anthem. The sensible friend she's always known. The friend who doesn't jump off cliffs, and certainly doesn't confront a group of armed thugs in the dead of night.

When she lets go, I pull my blouse down in the back, paranoid that my collar will somehow slip down low enough to reveal the line of black stitches snaking down my chest.

We walk across the courtyard to the empty chapel and take a seat in the last pew. I think back to the last time I was here, when I broke up with Will. Then I picture my heel colliding with his jaw, his blood splattering Cathedral's white tile floor. I shake my head and shut my eyes, scared of my own strength and of what I might do next time, if I lose control. When I open them again, I find Zahra looking at me wonderingly.

"You dyed your hair," she murmurs, twirling a lock of it around her fingers. "It's a little darker, right?"

"Henna shampoo," I lie. "My mom thought it would cheer me up. As if that's possible." My head wants desperately to tell Z the truth about tonight, about falling in the river, everything. But my heart thrums out a warning that feels strangely like the beating of wings against a cage.

CHAPTER 15

Dimitri's on the Water is a sagging, half-demolished restaurant on the South Side riverfront. Its burnt-out neon sign is shaped like an enormous lobster, with menacing antennae and suspicious, forlorn eyes. During better times in Bedlam, people must have come here for special occasions and fancy dinners. Now the windows are boarded up, and the stucco peels from the outside walls.

I'm pressed against the trunk of a diseased oak tree on the perimeter of the parking lot. It's deserted but for two cars parked close to the restaurant, a white van with SYNDK8 spray-painted on the side in fat, spiked letters and a garish yellow dune buggy with rust spots on the bumper and a swirly, snakelike *S* painted in green and black on the roof.

I check my watch. 11:42. After waiting to hear my mother's heavy, Dreamadine-induced snores and my father's even sleeping breaths, I snuck out and ran all the way here, covering the three miles in under ten minutes. I press my fingers to my temples and rub them, attempting to stay calm. *I just ran a three-minute mile.* And the weirdest part of it is that I know I could have run it a lot faster. I begin the walk across the parking lot toward the swinging wooden doors of Dimitri's and grimace as I pat my chest, checking that the ruby necklace is still stowed in the inside pocket of my jacket, just beside my stitches. As I reach the doors, my hands shaking at the thought of what I'm about to do, of just how much depends on it, I feel a hand clamp down on my shoulder. I whirl around.

Serge towers over me, his jaw set.

"You followed me." I look past him and spot the front bumper of Serge's car—not the Seraph he drives for us, but his personal vehicle, a black Motoko sedan—sticking out from the side of the building.

"You're not going in there. They're *Syndicate,*" he whispers through gritted teeth, motioning toward the van and the yellow jeep. His French-African accent is more noticeable than usual, maybe because he's angry. "You could be killed."

I shake my head, desperate to make him understand. "I have to bring them something. If I don't try, they'll kill him." I search his face, half expecting him to pick me up and drag me into his car.

Instead, he nods. "I understand. But you should have enlisted my help."

My mouth falls open. Serge is here to *help* me?

"I will deliver your offer. You will wait in the car. I cannot allow you to risk your safety."

I nod dumbly, my mind struggling to catch up with the change of plans. He escorts me to the car and opens the back door, pulling a tan leather briefcase from the backseat and opening it on the roof of the car.

"How much have you brought?"

With shaking hands, I pull the necklace out of the inner pocket of my jacket. He looks at me wordlessly, eyebrows raised. In the silence, his disappointment comes through loud and clear.

"His life is worth more than this," I mumble, feeling simultaneously pathetic and guilty. "But they wouldn't help me."

Serge nods and carefully places it into the briefcase. Then he snaps it shut and motions for me to get into the backseat. I have a feeling this isn't the first time he's negotiated with criminals. He quit working for dictatorships many years ago, but his steeliness and his ability to intimidate hasn't left him.

"Is it going to work?" I ask, grabbing the sleeve of his suit.

"I'll do everything I can," he says, his voice even. "This type of element usually prefers to get something rather than nothing."

When the car door slams shut behind me, I watch him straighten his tie and button his black suit jacket as if preparing to walk into a boardroom. Another wave of guilt knifes into my abdomen when Serge turns the corner, briefcase in hand. He's risking his life, all because of me.

The lines in my palms fill with sweat as I sit and wait, staring out the car window at the parking lot. The asphalt glitters with broken glass; discarded plastic bags blow past like tumbleweed. I stare down at my watch. 11:56. *Four minutes to go.*

Before I can think through what I'm doing, my hand is opening the car door. I need to at least see that Gavin is alive. *Or if he's not.*

I sprint from the car to the rear of the restaurant, looking for someplace to peer in. Two Dumpsters sit close to the wall, and I shimmy on top of them, easily pulling myself up, and climb a rusted drainpipe up to the roof.

I creep along the unstable red shingles until I've come to a hole about three feet wide and one foot high, large enough to give me a clear view of the vast, decrepit dining room. I crawl cautiously toward the opening, praying my movements aren't audible from inside.

The room was once painted in fishing-themed murals, but now graffiti is scrawled over the sea full of happy, frolicking crabs, lobsters, and fish. There are a few tables turned over here and there on top of the rotting anchor-patterned carpeting.

Most of the lights in the cheap chandeliers are burned out, but a few still work, casting a dim light. Serge stands in the doorway, briefcase in hand. He faces the shattered room with a calm, steely expression.

I suck in my breath when the platinum blond and her three thugs step into view, this time wearing lightweight plastic animal masks designed for children. Miss Roach is a wide-eyed deer. The biggest of them—the fat bald one who held a knife against Gavin's neck—wears a bunny mask. The tall, thin one is a smiling skunk, and the shorter, dark-haired one is a squirrel. But then I notice three more people off to one side. One is a tall, thin woman with a boyish frame and long purple hair streaming down her back behind her pig mask. The other two—both wearing sheep masks—still have the bodies of young boys, not men. They couldn't be older than fourteen. They puff up their chests and walk close to Serge, though, and if they're intimidated by him they definitely hide it well. The silver barrel of a hunting rifle flashes in the skunk's gloved hands.

"Where is the boy?" Serge's voice fills the room, his tone clipped, no-nonsense.

The woodland creatures murmur among themselves. They seem disorganized, unsure of how to proceed. The smiling skunk lifts his rifle slightly, training it on Serge, then lowers it again as Miss Roach whispers something in his ear.

My heart cartwheels in my chest. This is the moment. The moment they bring out Gavin. The moment I know he's all right.

"Where's the money?" the fat one finally grunts from behind his bunny mask.

"We are prepared to offer a piece of jewelry valued at fifty thousand dollars." Serge's silky, deep voice floats up to me.

Please, I think. *Let him go.* I lift my head from the hole in the ceiling and gaze out at the Bridge of Hope, its pointed arches illuminated above the stinking snake of the Crime Line like a constellation of stars.

"Is this a joke?" Miss Roach's scratchy voice rasps, prickling my skin. I press my face back into the hole, a cold sweat trickling down my spine.

She keeps her distance from Serge, standing fifteen feet away from him. My eyes are stuck to her, frozen with the memory of her bubblegum-and-cigarette breath, the feel of her gun in my ribs. She puts her hands on her hips.

"This is our only offer." Serge's clipped voice is louder now. "Not a penny more. Your window of opportunity will be closed after tonight."

And so will Gavin's. Silent tears slip from my eyes.

"Maybe your boss just needs some more incentive," she chirps behind her deer mask. "Smitty, care to start?" Light bounces off her white-blond hair as she nods to the gun-toting skunk. My breath in my throat, I watch helplessly as he rushes toward Serge from behind, holding the rifle like a baseball bat. Serge reacts quickly and reaches into his suit jacket, but before he can defend himself, the skunk smashes him over the head with the gun barrel. I gasp as Serge collapses to the floor.

"Do we kill him, or just cut off his hand?" Smitty asks Miss Roach.

An animal scream rises up in me as I smash a foot through the hole in the ceiling to widen it, jumping through it feetfirst and landing lightly. All I hear is the insane ricocheting of my wild heart.

For a moment, all seven of them are too shocked to shoot. They weren't prepared for this, and I'm not about to wait for them to regroup.

I gather speed as I run toward them, my foot flying through the air until it collides with Smitty and sends his hunting rifle flying. He gets up fast, but I'm still faster, kicking my leg up as hard as I can, making contact with his crotch. With Smitty doubled over in pain, I have a second to look around at the others. I move toward the fat, greasy bunny and kick the shotgun out of his hand. It slides along the moldy rug under a pile of broken chairs.

Then a popping sound comes from the direction of the pig and her two sheep, and I twist my head as something whizzes a millimeter to my right, barely missing my ear. I am all adrenaline as I run to Serge's unconscious body, and without thinking, I reach both arms around his midsection and grab him by the waist. Picking up Serge should be physically impossible, and yet I hoist him up like he's a feather pillow. I stagger forward in what seems like slow motion, another bullet, two, barely missing my feet. Serge hangs over my shoulder, still unconscious. His arm flops against my back. I hurl myself toward the door, taking care to keep Serge from tumbling out of my arms. A half second later, I'm slamming through the swinging doors and into the parking lot, my feet barely touching the floor. The necklace is all we leave behind.

CHAPTER 16

I have no idea how long it takes me to race Serge's still-unconscious body to the car, or how much time I spend searching his pockets for the keys with shaking hands. I find them just as he wakes up and clutches his bleeding head. I guide him into the backseat and hop in the front.

By the time they start shooting again, I've already started the car.

It's only when I peel out of the parking lot and a bullet flies through the back window, shattering the glass, that the rules of time and space begin to conform to something resembling normal again. I whip my head around to make sure Serge hasn't been hit, then push the accelerator to the floor. The speedometer swings to 110 as I reach the Bridge of Unity.

"Anthem," Serge says from the backseat. "You can slow down now. It is not in their interest to follow us." His eyes meet mine in the rearview mirror, his expression a mix of awe and—if I'm reading him correctly—pride. I slow the car down to eighty and take a deep, shuddering breath. My mind is utterly blank as the adrenaline in my veins begins to ebb. How can I possibly explain to him what just happened? How can I explain it to myself?

"How's your head?" I ask him, turning my eyes to the road again.

"Just a small cut," Serge says, pressing a handkerchief to his forehead. "And a headache."

"Serge," I start. "I'm so sorr—"

"You've run two red lights," he says as I speed through an intersection. "I see your powers of driving, at least, are not greatly enhanced."

I think of him teaching me to drive in this same car, the Motoko, just a year ago. I managed to knock off both his side mirrors in one week. He was so patient both times. So much more patient than I had any right to expect.

"This is the first time I'm driving *you* somewhere," I joke lamely.

"We have experienced a number of firsts tonight, you and I."

"Sorry I didn't stay in the car." I say, wanting to say more but instead falling quiet again, not sure how to talk about what's just happened. But Serge doesn't push or prod me for answers.

He leans forward in the backseat, his head near mine, speaking softly. "I'm sorry tonight didn't go the way it should have."

"Me too," I say, my stomach twisting, when I think about what the kidnappers might be planning now.

"You realize their demands will continue to escalate. They are neither intelligent nor reasonable." Serge draws out that last word, his upper lip curled in disgust at the memory of the masked gang.

I nod miserably, wiping my sweaty forehead with my sleeve. I've spent the last few hours not letting myself think the unthinkable, but now I can't help it. "Do you think he's still alive?"

My gaze meets Serge's in the mirror again. "Yes." He pauses. "For now."

I press my lips together and blink hard, concentrating on the movement of traffic ahead of me. A hole opens inside my chest as I picture Gavin being struck again and again, a gun barrel pointed to his head. A part of me wishes I had never walked into that party that night, if it could save his life. And yet I can't imagine a world in which we never met. Tears gather at the corners of my eyes, blurring the brake lights in front of me into streaks of red. "For now, but not for long," I whisper.

Serge is quiet for a beat. "I have always admired your open mind, Anthem. Especially considering how you were raised."

"You mean, considering the money?"

"The money, yes, and always with the ballet, working so hard, with such focus."

I'm not quite sure what he's getting at, so I keep quiet as I pull the car into the garage under Fleet Tower. When I park in the empty spot next to the Seraph, Serge pushes down the lock on my door. I sit back in my seat, surprised.

"But you must be more careful. A gifted person like you cannot afford to be careless with her life."

I turn around and face Serge in the backseat.

"Especially now, when it appears there are gifts you are just discovering. You cannot risk confronting them without protection." He reaches toward the dash and flips open the car's glove compartment, just long enough for me to see the glint of a pistol. Then, without a word, he shuts it.

"Thank you," I whisper. Right now, there is nothing more to say.

• • •

Half an hour later, I dart down the hall and sneak into my room. I dig through my backpack and find three Brawn Bars I packed this morning. My exhausted body perks up after my first leaden swallow, and I quickly force down two bars, saving the third for later. I crumple the plastic wrappers into a ball and begin to pace the perimeter of my room. *It's time*, I think. Time to look at what I've become.

I walk toward the ballet barre bolted on the far wall. Even now, after everything that's happened, my body automatically falls into the battement combination we've been doing for our *Giselle* rehearsals, running through a few dozen pliés and positions with one hand resting lightly on the barre. I move from fourth to fifth position and back again, scissoring my legs faster, faster, pushing my feet out and back until they seem barely to touch the wooden floor.

I try an experimental leap, a grand jeté from the barre all the way to my bed.

The rules of physics say there's not a chance in hell I'll make it.

But I do. I land lightly and soundlessly in the center of my bedspread. I look back over at the barre, estimating the distance at about fifteen feet.

Maybe it's just a fluke. Except I know it isn't. I'm certain, deep down, that I can do it again and again.

I grit my teeth in concentration and spring forward off the bed, whizzing soundlessly through the air, almost hoping I'll crash down on the carpet and discover my limits. But I land lightly, balancing on top of the barre itself, my bare feet curving around the smooth, varnished wood.

I hop off the barre and spin in a series of fouettés toward the mirrored wall in the corner of my room. At three feet away, my reflection confirms that I'm still me. Still the skinny girl with the skeptical eyes and stubborn mouth, the pale redheaded features, the faint constellation of ginger-colored freckles. But up close, when I lean in, my eyes glow a rich emerald, no longer the heather green they used to be.

I take a deep breath and yank my turtleneck sweater over my head. I cross my arms over my bare breasts, covering most of the scar in the center of my chest. Same tiny shoulders, bony neck. Same scrawny arms. Same perfect posture, the product of years of ballet. I throw back my shoulders and lower my arms. Same almost-flat chest. And in the middle of it, a line of black plastic stitches, neatly knotted at each end.

At last, I let my eyes run along the long, jagged wound. I find a wiry piece of plastic sticking out from the scar and begin to tug, methodically untying the series of tiny knots until I'm able to pull several of my stitches out, to slide the plastic wire from beneath my skin. I barely feel any pain, just a minor pinch. Gritting my teeth, I keep pulling, untying. The stitches leave behind nothing more than a faint pink welt with pink dots on either side of it. Apparently, my new heart doesn't just make me fast and strong. It also lets me heal at hyperspeed.

The scar extends from my sternum to the tops of my breasts. The cut is sealed, my mutant heart trapped firmly inside my chest. My newfound rage, and the ability to act on it by hitting until I break bones, to run until I'm nearly flying—all of this is a part of me now, forever sewn inside me. Lodged in the same place I keep my pain, my fear, my love.

I look into my bright green eyes in the mirror and smile sadly, mourning the person I once was. The old Anthem Fleet is gone now. I'm no longer the shy, small girl who spun in perfect circles in a mirrored room. Now it's up to me to find a way to break the kidnappers, to spin fast enough to save Gavin. I begin a series of pirouettes in front of the mirror, first spinning to my right, then to my left. Every second turn, I let my bare foot fly out in front of me, imagining it making contact with Miss Roach's masked face.

My heart whirs with stubborn, stupid hope.

After a dozen kicks, I put a hand to my scar. I think of Serge's warning. I'm ready to risk everything if it means Gavin will live.

CHAPTER 17

I slice through the water, focusing on the burning in my muscles and the rhythm of my breath. The sun hasn't come up yet. I'm in our resistance pool, an extra-long, skinny rectangle of teal one lap wide in an all-glass room across from my father's office on the lower level of the penthouse. Anxiety propelling me forward, I swim freestyle against the push of the synthetic current.

As I swim, my fear and exhaustion turns to angry energy, and I feel more and more certain that Gavin is still alive. With each overhead stroke, my determination to get him back grows surer, more urgent.

Soon I'm paddling and kicking hard enough and fast enough to send great sheets of water pouring out over the lip of the pool, soaking the whole room. I recalibrate, reminding myself not to push as hard as my new heart can.

I swim until my arms feel like snapped rubber bands, then pull myself out of the pool and put on a black terry robe with

FLEET INDUSTRIES embroidered on the back. I sprawl out on the chaise longue, barely winded. An unusually beautiful sunrise streams through the glass wall—such a bright shade of fuchsia that it almost makes Bedlam look good—and I take it as a sign that Gavin is still on this earth.

I shut my eyes and lean my head against the mesh of the chaise, telling myself that after breakfast I'll figure out how to find them, destroy them, do anything it takes. I get lost in fantasies of sneaking up on Miss Roach, grabbing her by the hair, making her talk . . . until I hear the *ping* of a text message.

I wipe my hands on my robe and fish the phone out of the pocket. It's probably Zahra checking in with me for news of Gavin, or maybe my mother texting from upstairs, looking for me.

But an unfamiliar number pops up, full of zeros and fours. A hot balloon of dread begins expanding in my stomach when I read the message.

> Good morning Princess. Pleasure to see you last night. U R crazier than we thought. We need the rest of the $$$ by midnight on Sunday. If you fall short, this is the last time you'll ever see Loverboy alive. No theatrics this time.

My breath catches in my throat when a second text pops up. It's a photo of Gavin, a light-brown shock of hair falling over his face. The one eye I can see squints against the flash of the camera as if he hasn't seen light in a long time. A yellow bruise covers half his face, his eye swollen, encrusted with something dark. He's flinching from the camera, holding up the front page of the *Daily Dilemma*, the bottom half of it smeared with blood. I touch the picture and zoom in with my fingers. The date printed on the masthead of the paper is today's. It is proof that Gavin is alive.

My hands begin shaking so violently that I drop the phone. "Damn it!" I shout, scooping it up from the puddle under my chaise longue and frantically drying it off with the corner of my robe.

I bite the insides of my cheeks and suck air through my nostrils. There's no way I can get the rest of the money—not even close to that amount—by Sunday. My father was right. They're just going to keep asking for more. I think longingly about my trust fund, but it's locked away until I'm eighteen, which isn't for another seven months.

I wrap the robe tighter around me and stand up on shaky legs, my mind racing. The only solution is to find him, I realize, my fingernails digging into my fisted palms. To find him and take him from them by force. But how? My thoughts spin to Serge. We have a tacit understanding now. But Serge won't let me anywhere near the kidnappers alone. And I can't let him risk his life again—next time, I might not be able to swoop in and pull him out.

I drift out of the pool room, pausing in front of my father's half-open office door. An enlarged aerial photograph of Bedlam fills a whole wall, all of North Bedlam shaded green—for renewal, for hope, for money—and the rest of the city the dull gray of pigeons, cement, and guns.

To find people in the South Side, I realize as I study the winding streets on my father's map, I have to get help from a South Sider. And if I have any hope of forcing Miss Roach to give up Gavin, I'll need help from someone who's not afraid to play dirty.

I know only one person who fits the job description.

An hour later, I'm sitting in a cab with my Seven Swans bag next to me on the seat, headed over the Bridge of Sighs. I told my father I was headed to the studio to try to get back in the groove, and he patted me absently on the head, saying *Atta girl, there's the old work ethic I know and love.* Luckily, my mother is having one of her weeks where she doesn't rise until noon.

"You sure you want to go there?" the driver says. He's missing both front teeth, and the identification card reads ISHMAEL GREEN. I nod as I scan the twisting knot of streets ahead of us. I have no idea how to find Ford, but I'm pretty sure I remember how to get to Jax's lab, and I'm hoping she will lead me to him. Not that I relish the idea of visiting the lab. The thought of setting foot in there again makes my skin feel too tight for my body.

When we're just a few blocks away, I actually *see* Ford. He's in his usual sportswear, a black vinyl Windbreaker with white piping on the sleeves and matching pants, ducking into a MegaMart.

"Stop here," I say, and hastily shove a crumpled wad of bills into the cab's Plexiglas money slot. "Keep the change." I dash from the cab toward the sliding glass doors.

Inside the MegaMart, I'm greeted by a pimpled guard no older than I am, an Uzi strapped to his chest. He looks me up and down and yawns, then passes me a flier with today's specials on it.

"Welcome to MegaMart," he says listlessly. "Keep it moving." I wipe my sweaty palms on my pants and nod, then head into the cavernous aisles to find Ford. I have no idea what I'll say to him. The aisles of the MegaMart are narrow and grimy, everything coated in a thin layer of dust, packed to the rafters with crates of goods sold in bulk. All around me, squabbling families are piling their carts with blocks of cheez product, cases of beer, cans of beans the size of oil drums. A bent old woman sorts through an enormous bin of tube socks marked THREE FOR THREE, FIVE FOR FOUR.

I've seen commercials and billboards for MegaMart—the chain has been spreading like kudzu through the South Side—but I've never been near one before. At the end of each aisle is another guard, another preposterously large Uzi at the ready.

As I round the end of the aisle past a pyramid of fifty-pound bags of Hound Healthy dog food, I spot Ford. He's near the pharmacy, studying a wall of BuffShake canisters. I move to stand next to him, careful to keep a few feet between us.

"Bulking up?" I ask.

He whirls around, his face carved into a tough-guy mask until he recognizes me. "Anthem!" he says, breaking into a wide grin. "You came back! Jax'll be so happy I found you."

"I think it's me who found you," I correct him.

"Whatever." Ford shrugs. Then his face darkens a little. "You shouldn't have run off so soon. It's dangerous. For your, you know." He looks down at my chest, waving his hand in an embarrassed circle. "For that whole . . . situation."

"Well, I'm fine. Good as new," I mutter, my face turning purple.

A guard approaches us. "Keep it moving," he says. Ford nods, eyeing the Uzi. *Keep it moving* must be MegaMart's slogan.

"This place is the worst," he says under his breath. "They think people are going to riot over shaving cream and tuna fish."

"Listen, I need to talk to you about something—" I start.

"Not here," Ford interrupts, grabbing me by the arm. "There are cameras everywhere, and these little punks are trigger happy. Let me just pay for this"—he holds up a canister of shaving cream—"and we'll talk somewhere else."

I walk with him toward the cashier, who looks even younger

than the guard, and wait while Ford counts out $23.59 in singles and change. When we're finally out the door, he exhales, jogging a few paces and doing neck rolls as if he's just finished a workout. "I hate that place, but it's so damned cheap."

"So anyway," I try again, conscious of the four security cameras bolted above the MegaMart doors, turning my face away from them. "I need some information."

"Not here. I know a place," he mutters, zipping up his Windbreaker. "It's just up the block."

"Not the lab," I say. "I'm not going back there."

He nods and takes off, walking fast. I have no choice but to follow. He crosses the street and makes two quick rights, then stops at a pockmarked green door.

"Try to look older," he mutters, then pushes the door open with his shoulder. "And uglier."

Like anyone can see me in here, I think when I cross the doorway's threshold into the barely lit space. The room is dominated by a large bar, at least a dozen stools already occupied by slouching boozehounds even though it's only 10:00 A.M. The place is so dark that I need to wait for my eyes to adjust before I keep walking. Ford pulls me by the sleeve of my coat toward a booth in back, past the bar. The smell of grain alcohol, beer, and rollies is thick.

The bartender, a buxom girl with bad skin and a blue bouffant, smiles brightly at Ford. She scowls when she catches sight of me, but I hustle past her.

"I'm so glad you're okay," he says after we slide into a wooden booth toward the back. "Lemme buy you an EnergyFizz or something."

"No thanks," I say, taking a breath and preparing to state my case. "I'm actually here for a favor."

"You name it."

"So, they still have Gavin."

Ford nods and rubs his stubbly chin with his hand, but his brown eyes are blank. "Who?"

"Gavin? My boyfriend. The reason I was running across the bridge. He's the person who gave me this, by the way," I add, grabbing the pendant and holding it away from my neck. I give Ford a pointed look.

"Hey, slow down. I remember all that. I was asking *who* still has him," Ford says, crossing his arms.

"Right. Sorry." I go on to describe the kidnappers using the few details I have. The way they spoke, their reaction to Serge. Their guns, their masks, their car.

After I finish, Ford leans back in the booth. My eyes are fully adjusted to the light now, and I can see a small scar on the right side of his chin. Probably from a bar brawl. "I don't know these people, but they sound like Syndicate professionals," he says. "Have you considered the possibility that you're in over your head?"

"Pretty much every minute of every day," I admit. "But I can't afford to believe it. I don't care who they are. I just want them to let my boyfriend go. Can you help me?"

Ford sighs and presses his lips together in thought, a crease forming between his perfectly straight, thick eyebrows. "If I had to put money on it, I'd guess they're somewhere in Hades. But that's not going to help you any."

"Why not?" I ask. "Where is Hades?"

"It's what we call the old mall, out past the stadium. The bottom floor is all black-market traders. Everyone with a stake in the Bedlam scum community has a guy there. But you can't just *show up* there, Anthem."

"Of course I can," I say, though I don't sound very

convincing, even to myself. "I found you, didn't I?"

"You have no idea what you're saying," Ford insists. "A girl like you? They'll eat you alive. You won't last ten minutes in there."

"Don't be so sure of what a girl like me can do." I lean across the booth, my voice rising in pitch and volume. "I'll be fine. Especially if you come with me."

"Not going to happen," Ford says quietly. "I stay as far away from the Syndicate as I can." He looks past me toward the bar, his mouth pressed into a line.

"Me and the Syndicate . . . there's a history. It's a bad history."

"Please," I say. "I have no choice."

He grabs at the back of his neck as if massaging a knot of tension. Then he sighs, which I take as a good sign. "You must have really liked him," he says finally.

"I did. I mean, I do." A silence opens up between us. "I can't just sit back and let him die," I add quietly. "Haven't you ever gotten in over your head for someone you loved?"

Ford takes a deep breath and holds the air in his mouth so his cheeks puff out, then lets the air out slowly, like a deflating balloon. "Yeah."

"So you understand," I say gently.

"He's a lucky guy," he says quietly, shooting me an unreadable look. "I hope he knows it."

Then he shoves his body out of the booth and stands next to me, offering his hand. I look down at the thick calluses on his knuckles, then tentatively take it.

"Thanks," I start. "I know this isn't exactly—"

"Let's just get going before I change my mind," he says, pulling me to my feet.

CHAPTER 18

Outside the bar, I keep pace next to Ford and pull my scarf over my mouth to escape the fumes from a garbage truck rumbling by. Our heads are bent against the wind as we head southeast, mist and damp coating our faces.

I start lagging a pace or two behind Ford, staring at the back of his head, his buzzed hair in a gray beanie above his wide shoulders. I'm grateful he's willing to help me. But what if he's right? What if I'm in way over my head? Then I take a surreptitious look at the picture of Gavin on my phone, wincing at his blue-black bruise. The gash in his chin. The newspaper dripping blood.

There is no choice. No decision. I can't leave Gavin to die. I'm already suffering, I tell myself as I tighten the strap of my bag over my chest and catch up with Ford. May as well do it in hell.

After we walk in silence for ten blocks or so and I catch back up with him, Ford clears his throat. "I gotta ask, what's it like?"

"What's *what* like?"

"Your new heart!" he says, too loud for comfort. I duck my head, furtively looking around to see if anyone heard us. Luckily, the block is deserted. There's nothing moving here except a feral-looking jackrabbit nibbling the tall grass growing around the perimeter of a derelict building.

"It's pretty weird," I say vaguely. "I mean, I don't recommend letting Jax near you with a scalpel anytime soon."

"I saw you running," he whispers, moving closer to me. "When you left the lab. I saw you speeding down the alley like a . . . I mean, I couldn't see your legs. That's how fast you were going."

I blush, embarrassed that he saw me without my knowing it. "It feels easy, running like that. All part of the weirdness." I touch my sternum through my shirt, feel the slight rise of the skin around my scar.

"Tell me more. I mean, you don't *have* to tell me, but ever since I saw you run, I've been thinking about . . . like . . . what if you're part hummingbird? How cool would that be?"

I smile tightly, my face still warm. "I'm pretty sure I'm not *actually* part hummingbird. The heart is mostly mechanical. I guess there's tissue around it, but I notice it whirring like a hard drive all the time. Especially if I'm nervous or moving fast. I keep thinking it's going to burn out on me."

"Jax says it won't. I grilled her about it," Ford says, suddenly looking shy.

"You did?" I'm surprised he cares so much.

"I was worried." He shrugs. "Especially after I failed epically as a surgical assistant."

"Oh, God," I squeak, realizing Ford was probably in the room when Jax cut my chest open. "I, um, we don't have to talk abou—"

"I passed out," he interrupts with an embarrassed grimace. He looks pale and queasy just thinking about it. "The second she picked up the scalpel, I was on the floor."

"So you didn't . . ."

"I missed the entire operation," he admits sheepishly.

We walk in silence along the snaking shore of the Crime Line until we pass the southernmost bridge of Bedlam, the Bridge of Peace. Brotherhood is the roughest part of the city, the place most often cited in the *Dilemma*'s crime blotter.

A few blocks south of the bridge, Ford hangs a right underneath a freeway overpass leaking green water onto the street below, though it isn't raining out, just cold and dreary like it has been for weeks.

"Running fast isn't the only thing I can do," I say, surprising myself. I start to tell him about what happened with Serge. Being able to maneuver around bullets. The insane strength I was able to find when I needed it. His walking slows to a halt when I describe the way time seems to slow down whenever my adrenaline kicks in.

"You dodged bullets? That is *sick*," he breathes, shaking his head in wonder. "I'd give anything to be able to do something like that."

"Don't say that. Trust me, there are a million things you wouldn't want to give up." *Like Gavin*, I think. For one.

He nods, his thick eyebrows knitted together. "I guess not."

"You're the only person I've told about this," I say quietly. "Thanks. For listening, I mean."

"Don't worry, I'm good at keeping stuff to myself. Comes with living with three people in a one-bedroom apartment," he says. Then he waves his hand at a giant building rearing up ahead of us. "We're here."

When I see it, I stop short and let out an inadvertent laugh, a short, miserable *ha* that disappears into nothing in the silent gray parking lot. It's an old mall, like Ford said, once named Hillside Palisades. Now most of the letters have fallen off the sign, leaving faded, ghostly letter impressions between the intact *H* and the *ades*.

The crumbling, fortresslike exterior of the mall encloses two full city blocks, with a mostly deserted parking lot surrounding it like a moat.

We slow our pace when we reach the parking lot's inner depths, and I concentrate on listening for sounds coming from the mall. All I hear is the whoosh of cars from the nearby freeway and the cooing of a few pigeons pecking listlessly at a ripped package of hot dog buns. In the gray light of 11:00 A.M., the massive parking lot is dead quiet, with fewer than fifty half-wrecked cars scattered sparsely among the rows. All this open space would almost be peaceful if we weren't about to walk into hell.

We come to a set of glass double doors with a sign above them marked HEESECAKE, and Ford pauses with his hand on the door.

"Sure you want to do this?" His dark eyes are full of misgivings. "It's not too late to change our minds."

I nod, swallowing an acid fear rising in my stomach as I bear down on the bar of the other door, expecting it to be locked. To my surprise, it opens easily.

Inside, it's as busy and loud as the outside is deserted and silent. In the dilapidated marble courtyard at the center of the mall, crowds of people—including dozens of children as young as six or seven—gather in clusters around makeshift stalls. The sound of barkers yelling, people laughing, fighting, and hag-gling, echoes in the cavernous space. There's no electricity but for a few generators powering a couple of Klieg lights, and the edges of the ground floor are bathed in shadow. I pull my coat tighter around me.

Ford sticks close to me. I'm happy to have him here. "We're being followed," he says, pointing downward and behind me, toward a kid of maybe seven or eight with frizzy curls and caramel skin. He has blue hearing aids looped around each ear, and the top of his head is level with my elbow. Ford nods hello and smiles at the kid, and in a second he falls into step next to us.

"Smokestacks, droopies, giggles," he recites, grinning, not quite able to be as serious as the adults selling car parts, food, medicine, bullets. We turn randomly down another aisle and stand on the edge of a crowd of people encircling a felt-covered table, the air thick with rollie smoke. The dealer throws a set of dice, announcing "sevens" with a flourish of his arms, and the crowd erupts in angry shouts. I keep walking, averting my eyes from a small stage where a woman in a top hat is yelling at three younger women wearing see-through negligees, black lace gar-ters, and sparkly, cheap-looking high heels. "I need six hundred today, each, or don't bother showing up here tomorrow," she says, and I shudder a little at the thought of what they'll have to do to get it.

The boy keeps looking at me like he's trying to peg me. "Let's see, you ain't here for ammo or biogenics, and you're not one of the rent girls. . . ."

I turn to look at him. "Biogenics?"

He perks up, his posture straightening. "You want BodMod,

hearts and parts? Three dollars and I'll take you there," he says, holding his hand flat in front of him.

Hearts and parts. A chill goes through me. "No, little man. We're okay for today," Ford says.

I put a hand on Ford's forearm to get him to slow down. "I want to see it." I have to see it. Could there really be others like Jax, people here who tamper with human bodies on the same scale?

"You sure?" Ford asks, looking uncomfortable.

I nod. "I'll give you a dollar," I say to the kid, "*after* we get there."

"Two's about as low as I can go," he beams, proud of his negotiating.

"Deal," I say, and I try not to look like I'm following him as we turn right, passing by a few food stalls selling boiled peanuts, blood sausages, and beer, and turn into a long, dark hallway that smells like formaldehyde and under that, the metallic rot of flesh and blood. I'm instantly on my guard, my heart tapping out a warning in my chest.

We walk by a few ancient, ratty recliners set up in front of TVs broadcasting cartoons and soap operas. An old woman, a kid, and a young guy about Gavin's age are lying in the chairs, their arms hooked up to IV poles.

"Transfusions, chemo, stuff like that," the kid whispers. "Is that what you want? 'Cuz I know the guy for that."

"No, I'm good." I don't need any more illegal organs, I feel like telling him. One is more than enough. Up ahead, a café with the windows boarded up has been repurposed into a makeshift medical clinic. A bored-looking woman with a candy-colored pink swirl of hair sits at the counter and above her, what was once a coffee menu now reads:

CHOP SHOP

Kidneys: $25,000 + labor

Prosthetic arms/legs: $9,000 + labor

Artificial Heart: $100,000 + labor

Liver: $15,000 + labor

Pancreas: $20,000 + labor

Eyes: $6,000 each + labor

Breast augmentation: $2,000 + labor

Specialty organs on demand: inquire within

"Bedlam's balls," I mutter, suddenly feeling faint. I grab Ford's elbow for support, worried I might pass out if I don't get away from here. "Is that for real? Eyes? Do people actually buy dead people's *eyes* and reuse them?"

"I tried to warn you," Ford says, moving me away from the Chop Shop and back toward the main market in the lobby. "This place is no joke. Let's just do what we came here to do and get the h—"

"Gimme my two dollars and I can show you stuff way crazier than this," the kid cuts in as we retreat, his blue-lit hearing aids illuminating his whole head in the dim light. "This floor is nothing compared to upstairs."

"We're looking for some people." Ford stops, bending down on one knee and looking at the kid with a serious, respectful expression that makes me wonder if he has younger siblings at home. "But kid, we can find them on our own. They're bad people."

"I know all the bad people in here," the kid says proudly. "I do errands for them."

I squint at the upper floors of the mall and see a few Pharm-pumped men milling around, the glint of rifles slung across some of their overmuscled chests. I dig in my jeans pocket for two crumpled bills and pass them to the kid.

"Five more dollars if you can help us find someone," I say to him. "She's got blond hair, she wears red lipstick, and she carries a tiny pearl-handled gun."

The kid puts one thin finger to his cheek and thinks for a second. "What's her biz?"

"I don't know. Thuggery, kidnapping, thievery. She has a friend she calls Smitty. Big guy, bald," I add, hoping a name might help.

He bites a piece of dead skin off his chapped lips and chews it thoughtfully. "Let's try the third floor. There are a bunch of big bald guys up there."

We follow the kid up a broken escalator with one of the railings missing. His steps are light and fast, and we almost have to run to keep pace. We round the corner on the second floor and head up another frozen escalator to floor three.

When we get to the third floor, I swallow hard. The vibe here is hushed and tense, with scowling bodyguards pumped full of BodMods standing in front of various repurposed stores. All of them seem to be watching us.

My mouth feels like it's filled with glue as we walk past an empty lingerie store with live women displayed like mannequins in feathers and lace in the window. A red curtain flutters in the doorway as a woman and a man, both dressed in business suits, walk inside. The kid walks fast in the direction of a derelict bookstore. I follow close behind.

The glass of the bookstore's windows has been completely papered over by comic book pages and *Dilemma*s so old they've turned brown and curl at the edges. There's just a four-inch-square section at the bottom where we can see in.

The kid points downward, indicating I should peek inside.

Ford hangs back, but I squat down and look, and sure enough, I spot a big bald head that could be Smitty's. He's sitting on the floor, leaning up against a broken bookshelf, and reading a comic book. A tall pile of books sits to one side of him, and I can see a metal door toward the rear of the store. My eyes are drawn to the door, my fingers tingling as I stare at it. Could Gavin be behind it?

"That him?" the kid whispers.

I nod. The shiny dome of his head is exactly as I remember, a V-shaped divot in the pate of his skull.

I watch Smitty aimlessly flip the pages of the comic book. Then the metal door opens and a curvy blond steps out. Her hair isn't the white-blond bob I'm expecting. That must be a wig. Her real hair hangs around her face in pretty golden waves, and her whole demeanor is softer and prettier than I remember. But I know from her sharply lipsticked brick-red mouth that it's her. She grabs a canvas bag from one of the bookshelves and starts to rummage through it. Even with my heart revving like a jet engine, I can hear her singing a few bars from an old folk song:

> Of all the crooks in Bedlam, you're the only one I crave,
> of all the crooks in Bedlam, it's you who makes me brave,
> but honey pie, you cheat and lie,
> And that is why I gotta put you in the grave.

Her voice is the same scratchy pitch I hear in my nightmares. I squeeze my eyes shut for a second, resisting the urge to charge in without a plan. I turn to whisper to Ford, waving him closer. "It's her." He leans in, his head just above mine, and looks through the window. When I get up close to look again, she's got the canvas bag on her shoulder and looks like she's about to head out.

"She's leaving. Let's go," Ford says roughly, already pushing me down the hall, putting his body between me and the doorway. "You too, kid. *Now*."

I stumble and almost fall, but Ford's hand wraps around my shoulder and yanks me up, and the three of us take off fast down a dark hallway reeking of urine off the main shopping thoroughfare. When we're in near-total darkness at the end of the hall, Ford hurriedly thanks the kid and presses some bills into his hand.

"Don't tell anyone we were here. You gotta promise," Ford says, his voice kind but stern.

"Promise." The boy nods, his face glowing from the blue light of his hearing aids. "You comin' back?"

"Probably," I say at the same time that Ford says "No." He shoots me a surprised look, but I just shrug. Gavin is somewhere nearby, I'm sure of it. I just have to come up with a plan to make them let him go.

"Here's my biz card," the kid says, passing me a hand-lettered card.

Rufus Mitz

Hades tour guide, marbles champion,
small hands for big jobs

"If you come back, you'll probably need my help," he says.

"Thanks," I say, and I mean it. We would never have found the bookstore without him. I reach out a hand to ruffle his tight curls for a second before he squirms away.

"I'll show you a better way out of here, free of charge," he offers, and we follow him down a set of back stairs filled with other kids his age. I wonder if all of them are orphans or if their parents are here somewhere, working the black market. I wonder if all of them sell drugs, if their bellies are always empty, if they sleep here, but I don't ask. I don't want to know the answer.

When we get outside again, Ford gives me a hard look. "Don't do it."

"Do what?"

"You know *what*," he says. "Don't go back there. Not until you've got an army to go with you. Ambush them somewhere else. Not here. People die in this building, and nobody ever knows about it, Anthem. And the setup of that bookstore," he goes on, pacing the blacktop and flipping his hood up to keep the drizzle off his head. "I don't like it. If you get inside, you have only one way out. They could lock you in. . . ."

I nod, but I'm only half-listening. Because no matter what Ford thinks or says, I *am* coming back. Alone.

By three that afternoon, I'm back at home wolfing down a bowl of pasta with sugar sprinkled on top, watching Lily prepare a pumpkin soufflé in the kitchen, thankful for her easy company that doesn't require me to pretend or really to say much at all. When I hear my parents arrive home from wherever they've been, I paste on a bright smile and take a deep breath, waiting as they hang up their coats. Lily looks up from her stirring and winks at me, and I wink back. Under her black Fleet Industries baseball cap, her soft, full face and big green eyes register the fact that there's been tension in the house—it's pretty impossible to miss it—and I think she knows that our PR story is a lie, but I haven't told her what's really going on.

My mother comes in and gives me a dramatic kiss on both

cheeks, her skin still cold from the outside. She sits down next to me at the kitchen barstool and daintily clears her throat. "We've been talking, sweetie," she says quietly. My father comes into the kitchen and leans against the threshold of the door. He nods hello to me and smiles flatly. "And since we haven't heard anything about your . . . friend . . . it's probably time to go to the police—"

No. I stiffen, my mind running through what to say. We can't go to the police. If they somehow figure out where the kidnappers are, and move too fast, Gavin could be killed. I can't let anyone interfere now—not when I'm so close to taking care of it myself.

"I was just about to tell you," I say, looking at the counter and speaking softly, trying to fake a combination of relief and sadness.

My mother rubs my back. "Tell us what?"

"They let Gavin go. This morning. He called me. You were right, when we didn't pay they just gave up." I slouch a little, trying to draw wetness to the corners of my eyes. "But don't worry—I ended it. It would never have worked out."

Lily looks up from her soufflé batter, and I take care to avoid her eyes. It's one thing to lie to my parents, but it's another to lie to Lily.

"Well." My mother pauses and looks unsure about what tone she should strike. Her eyes dart across my face, trying to read me. "Thank goodness the ordeal is over."

"This happened today?" my father says.

"This morning. He came to see me after ballet, and I broke up with him," I say robotically.

"And you're . . . okay?" my mother asks.

"I'm fine," I sigh. "Sad, but fine."

My parents nod and look seriously worried about me, but they both soon find excuses to go to their respective parts of the house—my father to his office, my mother to her bedroom to lie down.

I'm left alone with Lily, who hands me the bowl from the soufflé batter to lick, just like she used to do when I was ten. "Ant. Really?" she whispers.

I shake my head and put my finger to my lips.

"Are you okay?" she whispers. "You don't seem okay."

"Not so good," I admit, barely holding back tears. I used to tell Lily everything when I was a kid. Not anymore. "But I'm going to fix everything."

She nods cautiously. "I'm here," she says. "If you need anything at all. And not that you're asking for my advice," she adds, "but boys aren't always worth the time we spend on them."

"This one is," I say. "You'll meet him someday. You'll see."

At 8:27 P.M., when I know Serge is upstairs with my father and Lyndie Nye for an emergency public relations meeting about the controversial Fleet Industries Stadium project, I'm in the garage of Fleet Tower, holding my breath as I press my thumb to the keypad on the door handle of the Seraph. My stomach jumps when I hear the muted thump of the Seraph unlocking. I pull the tiny glove compartment key filched from my father's desk drawer out of the pocket of my jeans.

I've known about the gun Serge keeps in the glove box since I was ten years old, and as I turn the key on the lock I'm back inside the memory, waking up from a nap in the backseat and seeing Serge calmly, methodically cleaning a gun, unpopping the cartridge and disassembling each part, polishing every section of it before putting it all back together and stowing it in a compartment inside the glove box. I was scared of what I'd seen at the time and pretended to go back to sleep, but as I grew older I found it comforting that with all the crime in Bedlam, at least our car was armed and our bodyguard knew what he was doing. Until last week, I considered myself lucky to be so well-protected. Now I know that it was an illusion—nobody's immune to danger, not in this city.

I'm terrified of even touching a gun, but I'm out of options. I can't steal any more of my mother's jewelry. It's a miracle she hasn't noticed the necklace has disappeared yet. I have nothing to offer the kidnappers. And when you run out of carrots to cajole a stubborn mule, you have to move on to sticks.

I open the glove box's outer lock and feel along the side of it for the plastic seam. When my fingers find it, I snap the lid open, and then the cool matte plastic of the gun is in my hand. It feels heavier than it looks. I assume it's loaded, not that I know how to shoot it. I just have to hope that pointing it at the right person might be enough to buy me some leverage. *A life for a life*, I think, and my forearms prickle with goose bumps. *If it comes to that.*

I wedge the gun into the back of my jeans and say a little prayer that I don't accidentally shoot myself. Then I close up the glove box and shut the car door as quietly as I can. I flip the hood of my wool jacket over my head and set out on shaking legs, telling myself all kinds of lies to get my feet to keep moving: *This is a solid plan. You can do this.* Because even though I'm scared witless, my determination is all I have. Determination, and a gun I don't know how to use.

CHAPTER 19

The third floor of Hades is full of people at night. The crowd is a little less rowdy than the marketplace down below, but here and there clumps of people—mostly men but some women, too, all of them in dark clothes, their faces weathered and wary—are gathered, talking quietly, playing cards, or drinking from paper-bag-shrouded bottles, and some of the same kids I saw on the back stairs shuttle envelopes and packages from one abandoned store to another. My chest rattles with adrenaline and nerves as I make my way toward the bookstore.

I slow my steps when I get near it, every cell of me alert for signs of Miss Roach or her people. If they're all there together, I know I'll have to come back later. When I reach the open door, the main room of the store appears empty. The same teetering book towers tilt on the carpeting. Smitty's comic book lies open on the counter where the cash register once sat—now there's nothing on it but an ashtray overflowing with lipstick-rimmed rollie butts and a few empty bottles of Blackout Vodka. I linger in the door awhile to listen with my supercharged ears, trying to focus on what's behind the walls of the store and assuring myself that nothing is moving and nobody's there. I finally approach the counter. The open comic book is called *Killerella*— in it, a girl in a skintight dress and pigtails with eyes that take up half her face points a giant gun at a sea creature, a sort of half-man, half-squid. *Girls with guns,* I think, and a slick of nervous sweat blooms where Serge's gun rests against my skin. I roll my shoulders back and straighten my posture, my eyes on the metal door in the back of the room.

Just then, I hear something moving. A grunt. And then a stack of books topples to the floor behind me.

I whirl around to see a thin, strong-looking guy in his twenties with dirty-blond hair and a black leather jacket hurtling toward me, the butt end of a rifle raised above him. Instantly, my adrenaline spikes and my ears fill with the roaring of an ocean of blood. The moldering bookstore with its empty shelves fades to white all around him, and the moment stretches out into a series of micro-movements. Suddenly, I can predict where his feet will fall and see his lank yellow hair bounce up and down as he runs. And in the molasses crawl of the moment, I have all the time I need to attack.

I move toward him, my leg flexed, my foot raised high, my boot toe about to make contact with his head. But he knows how to fight. He ducks to the side and I land badly, stumbling into a sloppy roll on the carpet, momentarily stunned. Then he lunges at me again, the butt of his rifle aimed at my head.

I roll away just in time to avoid the blow, moving onto my feet again and leaping up—*way* up, higher than the laws of gravity should allow. I land on top of him, knocking him onto his back on the carpet, sending the rifle clattering against a metal bookshelf.

I straddle his chest and struggle to pin his arms under my knees. My heart is galloping so fast it hurts. There's a sharp, glass-shards feeling in my chest, and for a split second, I wonder if this is it, if Jax's creation will give out on me at the exact moment I need it to work the hardest. Then the pain passes, and I refocus on the man struggling underneath me.

His eyes meet mine, his thin lips curled into a sneer.

"Well, hello, princess. You are something else, aren't you?" he purrs, his eyes glittering. I glare down at him, my fingers tensed, and imagine clawing his eyes out. A second ticks by, enough time for him to free one arm and grab me by my bun of red hair. A scream comes out of me that is inhuman and full of rage, and a second later, before I can even think about it, I've pulled the gun from the back of my jeans. I cock the safety with my thumb—*How do I know to do that?* but somehow I do it—and press the muzzle to his head.

"Hands on the floor. I've come for Gavin." My voice is calm, but every cell in my body is thrumming with fear.

"Rosie," he shouts, grinning at me crazily. "Get out here. You have a visitor."

We stay like that—me on top of him, pressing the gun into his forehead, holding it with both hands, trying to keep my hands from shaking. His forehead is clammy with sweat, but he keeps smiling, defiant, his eyes mocking me.

A minute later, the metal door at the back of the store squeaks open. Suddenly, she's right in front of me. Close enough that I can tell the gum she's chewing is grape flavored and freshly unwrapped, even though I'm on the floor straddling her goon and she's towering above me. Miss Roach herself. *Rosie*, I sneer inwardly, disgusted by the floral sweetness of her name. Her hair falls around her face in soft waves. Her makeup is severe, deep chrome eye shadow and harsh lipstick, but she's lush and curvy in a pleather dress, and the makeup doesn't disguise the fact that she's younger than I thought—in her early twenties at the most. Her pug nose and wide blue eyes make her look innocent, babyish. Smitty follows behind her and closes the door behind him. They each have a gun in their hands.

"I will kill him," I say simply, grinding the muzzle of the gun against my captor's temple, feeling him squirm beneath my legs. "Before your bullet reaches me, I will have already shot through his brain. So put your guns on the ground in front of you."

And slowly, miraculously, they do. Smitty goes first. Then Miss Roach snorts and rolls her eyes, but she bends down, and then there is her gun, in front of me on the carpet.

"I'm here for Gavin," I repeat, my voice hoarse with what I hope they mistake for ruthlessness or insanity. "I won't leave without him. Step away from your weapons and let Gavin go, or I shoot."

"Ain't got any sense in that pretty head," Smitty mutters as he steps away from his rifle. His double chin is flecked with lettuce shreds as if I've caught him in the middle of a taco dinner. Miss Roach—*Rosie*—doesn't say a word. She calmly adjusts her thigh-high boots and takes a few small steps backward, aiming her bright blue eyes at mine. She raises one thin eyebrow, a pitying half-smile twitching on her rose-red lips.

At last she shrugs, motioning to Smitty. "Just do it," she says flatly. "Bring him out of the hole."

Smitty lumbers over to the counter and presses a few buttons on the cash register. He stares at the counter. Nothing happens.

"Whatzit again?" he says to Miss Roach.

"Christ, Smitty. Your lobotomy is showing," she snaps, then goes to type the numbers into the register herself. The countertop slides open, and Miss Roach leans over the counter to peer inside, muttering something that I strain—and fail—to decipher. It echoes inside the counter, leading me to believe that there's a lot of space under the floor that they use as some kind of a holding chamber.

"Turn over," I bark at the blond as I stand up off him, keeping one eye on the hole under the counter. "Hands on your head."

After he's turned over onto the floor, I kick Rosie's pearl-handled snub and Smitty's rifle behind me, still standing over my hostage, aiming my gun with both hands at his skull.

The seconds tick by. Nothing moves. I hear music coming from the outside of the bookstore, accordions and drums now in addition to the brass band that was already playing downstairs, the pounding of dancing feet drifting toward us. Good, I think. A crowd will help me get Gavin out of here unnoticed. Gavin—I stop myself. Can it really be that Gavin is here? Inside the counter of a "bookstore"? It could be a trick, I tell myself. Brace for the worst. They are animals.

But then a pair of hands grips the edge of the counter. And then the top of a head. Light-brown hair. Suddenly Gavin's face pops into view.

"Hi, Anthem," Gavin sighs, smiling at me weakly before hoisting himself out of the hole under the counter. He squints against the dim light cast by the store's one working bulb and struggles to stand.

"Gavin!" I cry out, tears springing to my eyes. Up until this moment, I couldn't let myself give up the fear that they had actually killed him. But now he's standing four feet away from me, plain as day. The bruise under his eye is yellowing slightly, the upper and lower lid swollen and dark, so he's in a permanent flinch. Otherwise, he looks unharmed. His hair is ratty and matted, but his clothes appear clean, and he hasn't grown noticeably thinner. Every particle of my body wants to embrace him, to grab his hand and run, but Smitty and Rosie have quickly moved to stand on either side of him. Both of them are grinning a little, and suddenly something about what I'm seeing feels wrong.

"Are you okay?" I ask stupidly. Of course he's not okay.

"I'm fine," he says. "But Anthem, you should go." He looks pleadingly at me.

"We'll leave here together," I say. Doesn't he see that I'm the one with the gun? That I've come to get him out of here? But then I notice that there's something attached to his shoe. He turns three-quarters to the left and I see he's been shackled. A thin metal band wraps around his ankle and the band is attached to a thick cable that snakes back inside the counter, attached somewhere inside the hole he crawled out of.

"I said to let him go," I shout, moving to stand over my hostage again, aiming my gun straight down at his head. "Or I shoot your friend."

"I have a better idea." Rosie smiles at me. One of her teeth has a smear of lipstick on it. I look down for a second and discover to my horror that she's got another gun in her hand, this one an old-fashioned silver revolver. "I could just kill Loverboy right now. Which one of us has the guts to shoot, I wonder? Me or you?"

"I'll do it!" I scream, shutting my eyes and getting ready to squeeze the trigger, bracing for the impact of the gun . . . but I just stand there, frozen. I picture his skull exploding, the blood spattering everywhere, the ending of his life, however sorry a life he has led, and I can't make myself do it. My arms begin to shake and falter. My only hope is that Rosie is bluffing, too.

"I thought so." Her gravelly voice floats toward me. When I open my eyes, her gun is aimed at Gavin's chest. He's not struggling. Not begging for his life. Just staring into her eyes and waiting. "I think it's time we ended this game. It's getting boring."

"No!" I scream. "I'll put down my gun." But she just smiles in a carnivorous way. I hear her take a breath.

And then time folds in on itself. There is the deafening pop of the gun going off, and through the ringing air I watch Gavin fall to the floor, a circle of blood blooming on his gray T-shirt, the stain widening and widening until his entire torso is black with it. My throat burns with an endless scream of NONONO and I'm shaking all over and in the space of that unreal instant, they are on me. Smitty's hands cover my mouth and the other one pries my gun from my fingers and dumps the bullets out. They bounce like spilled jelly beans across the carpet.

I rip myself away from them and run to Gavin, thinking I can drag him out of here, take him to the hospital, take him to the clinic downstairs even, thinking someone somewhere can fix him, but his face is gray and his eyes—thank God for this one small mercy—are closed. His chest leaks blood left of center, exactly where the heart is located in the human body. If there is one anatomical fact I am certain of, it is this.

I cradle his face in my hands, frantically smoothing his hair, all the while someone is still screaming NONONO in a shrill and painful and earsplitting way, and it's only when Rosie slaps me in the face that the screaming stops.

"Shut up!" she says, her short body above me now, standing, the pearl-handled snub again in her hands. "It's over. So go away, princess. Just get out of here, and don't come back. I'd rather not have to kill you, too. Hard enough burying one corpse without a string of cops up my ass."

The barrel of the gun weaves back and forth in front of my eyes as she talks. My mouth fills with saliva. I spit a wad of it at her, daring her to shoot.

"Get her the hell away from me, gentlemen," she says softly, wiping my spit from her forehead. "Backup, puhleeze!" she calls out.

They grab me under my armpits, one of them on each side, and drag me across the carpet. The last thing I see is Gavin sprawled out on the ground, his whole shirt soaked through all the way to the sleeves, blackened with blood, and Rosie turning away from me, kneeling down to inspect the damage she's caused.

I'm strong now. Impossibly strong. I should be able to throw them off me. I flail and kick and Smitty goes flying, but then a door in back of the bookstore opens up and there are three more of them. Two boys who might be twins—small, wiry, olive-skinned—come charging at me, along with a six-foot-tall woman with long purple hair. I remember them from Dimitri's. The second string of Rosie's team.

They pile on to me, each one of them in charge of one of my limbs. It's too much for me. Too many people holding me down. I struggle, my body straining to shake them off, but I get nowhere.

Then Smitty gets back on his feet again. The last thing I see is his fat hand encircling the neck of a Blackout Vodka bottle and bringing it toward my head.

And then everything goes as black as Gavin's blood.

I'm dead to this world and all the horrors it has delivered.

I wake up on the tiled main floor of Hades, Serge's gun stuffed under my coat and sticking me in the ribs, Rufus kneeling over me, his small hands shaking my shoulders. "Come *on*," he cries. "Before they see you." There's a jamboree of some sort in the lobby of the mall, drums and tubas and accordions and people singing a fast song in the mournful key of a funeral dirge.

For Gavin, I think senselessly. *They know Gavin is dead.* But of course they don't. Rosie would make it her business to cover it up.

Rufus is pinching my ears and cheeks. "Get *up*, dummy."

I look at him, his skin soft and brown, his baby-pink cheeks, his hearing aids glowing in the dim light.

"Okay," I say, feeling nothing, seeing nothing. I would like to rush into the crowd and wave Serge's gun around until someone sees fit to kill me. I would gladly die here and enter the next world with Gavin. But out of respect for Rufus and what little chance he has of growing up into a sane adult someday, I don't. I let him pull me away from the drum circle and toward the back staircase. For him, I walk, one foot and then the other, through the gluey swamp of my devastation, and make my way out of here.

"What you need is candy," Rufus says as he escorts me through the back stairs and out a side door, unwrapping a cinnamon disk from cellophane and placing it in my hand as if it is a priceless jewel. "Candy always helps."

There is no help for me anymore, I think. No hope. Not here, not anywhere. But I put the disk in my mouth and let it melt on my tongue.

"Thank you," I whisper. "Do me a favor, Rufus?"

"Favors aren't free," he says, and I think of Ford eyeing my necklace on the Bridge of Sighs what seems like a million years ago now. *Nothing is free,* I think sadly as my fingers travel to the heart around my neck. Everything in life costs too much.

But Rufus shouldn't know that yet. He's just a kid. A kid

with a tough beginning, but still. I wish he'd get far away from here, take a train or a bus to anywhere else, but I know he won't. Hades is all he's got.

I put twenty dollars in his hand, then run my fingers over his soft, kinky hair. "Don't go to the third floor anymore. It's not a place for kids."

Rufus nods reluctantly. "I guess."

Later, after a numb good-bye and a fit of private, gulping sobs against the stucco back wall of Hades, I shut down, drained of everything. Somehow I walk, not daring to look back at the hulking mall where Gavin's body is hardening to stone.

I walk home under a fingernail moon, a shining sliver of light in a world that doesn't deserve it.

When I get back to the Seraph to return the gun to the glove compartment, Serge is there waiting for me. I must look terrible, because he jumps out of the car and comes around, his arms open wide. I fall against him, my whole body shaking.

"Tell me," he says, one of his hands around the top of my head. "You're bleeding."

I remember the bottle smashing over my head, but all the pain I feel is in my midsection. My head feels fine.

"Gavin is dead. They killed him in front of me," I say, my voice flat and hollow, like it belongs to someone else.

He doesn't say anything, but I hear him exhale.

I pull away from him and take the gun out from the waist-band of my jeans. "Sorry for taking this. I didn't use it."

Serge takes the gun from me and puts it inside his suit jacket. "I'm the one who should say I'm sorry. I should have been with you."

"I had to go alone," I say. "I couldn't risk anyone else getting . . ." My teeth are chattering so badly that it's hard to finish my sentence.

"Anthem. You are in shock. Let's sit in the car awhile."

Serge starts the car and turns the heat on high, but even when the internal thermostat reads 83 degrees, I'm still cold. He goes to the trunk and finds an old school sweater of mine, and I put it on in the car. Time passes where we just sit together quietly, and eventually I stop shaking and my teeth stop chattering.

"I am so sorry you lost this boy, Anthem. But you are well," he says. "Your parents need not ever find out."

I press my still-icy fingers to the car vents. "I'm never going to be well," I whisper. "Never."

"One day at a time," Serge says. "One day at a time."

CHAPTER 20

When I get upstairs, the clock in the foyer tells me it's a reasonable time of night to arrive home—only ten fifteen. I can't understand how so little time has gone by and yet I feel decades older than I did this morning. I hear polite voices and the scraping of bone china cups against saucers in the living room. My parents have company. I pinch my cheeks and quickly knot my hair into a bun that hides the blood on the crown of my head, preparing to paste on a tired, just-coming-from-the-library expression on top of the half-crazy, dead-inside face I glimpse in the hall mirror.

I fell asleep in the library, I rehearse silently. *I'm beat. Heading off to bed.* But when I reach the archway of the living room, the person drinking tea with my parents is Will. I freeze, not knowing what I'm supposed to do, unable to process his presence. I open my mouth, but all I can muster is a cough.

Will jumps up from his spot between my parents and runs to me, kissing me wetly on the cheek before moving his head next to mine, his mouth beside my ear. It takes every ounce of my will not to step away from him.

"Relax and smile," he whispers. "I told them you forgot your physics book at the library and had to go back. They bought it."

I nod imperceptibly to tell him I understand he's covered for me, smiling through gritted teeth as Will leads me into the sitting room toward my parents, his sweaty fingers cuffed around my wrist. Panic kicks in my chest as I wait for someone to tell me what's going on.

"Hi," I say cautiously.

They're all smiles. I haven't seen them this pleased with me since before my disappearance.

"I was just telling your parents how happy I am that we're back together," Will says, a joyless grin plastered on his face.

I turn to him, matching his fake smile with a horrified one of my own.

"I had a feeling you two would find your way back together one of these days," my father says, winking at me. "When it's right, it's right. Am I right?"

The room fills up with our nervous laughter, and the sound is so loud and false it makes me wince.

"Best news we've heard in ages," my mother says, her s's and g's softened and fuzzy from too much wine. "I was so sad when you two had . . . your bump in the road. . . ." Her eyes glisten with emotion as she swirls the last sip of chardonnay around in her goblet.

"Well, we're so young . . ." I start, backpedaling as hard as I dare, trying to steer my parents away from the assumption that we're together again. But my words dissolve when Will's fingers tighten around my wrist.

"Would you guys excuse us?" He beams the patented

Hansen smile—top and bottom teeth exposed, photo-ready—at my parents. "I'm gonna steal Anthem for a minute." He winks at my dad.

"Of course, William." My father smiles, returning the wink. "Steal away. You kids go chat in Anthem's room. It's great to have you back, Will."

"Oh, likewise, sir," Will says, but when he turns away from my parents, his smile lingers, his eyes glittering with a creepy sort of intensity. "See you both very soon, I hope," he calls over his shoulder. "Let's go, *sweetie*," he says to me, pulling me forcefully down the hall.

"Let go of me," I whisper, twisting my wrist free when we're out of earshot of my parents. "What the hell do you think you're doing?"

"All will be revealed in your bedroom, dear," he snorts. "And I do mean all. Ha-ha."

My skin prickles with heat as I shut the door. I walk a few feet away from him and turn to face him, hands on my hips. "What is this?" I ask, my nostrils flared and my jaw clenched. "Why are you here and lying to my parents?"

"Oh, sweetie!" Will cries, flopping onto my bed and opening his arms. "Let's just cuddle a little and then I'll explain."

"Will."

"It was a joke, Anthem. As usual, you have no sense of irony. I get that you find me less than appealing these days. I'm not stupid."

"Then why are you here?"

"*Well*," Will says, stretching the word out, "did you know you broke one of my teeth with your little burst of aggression the other day? This one's a temporary. They're making me an implant. All very time-consuming. Very expensive," he says, tapping a finger on one of his canines and then plucking it clean out of his mouth, holding the tooth up in front of his eyes to examine it. "And in the dentist's chair when they were pulling the broken one out of me and scraping out the dead nerve, I started thinking, how did Anthem get strong enough to land a kick like that? I mean, she's a ninety-eight-pound little *shrimp*. No offense, but you are." He turns his glittering blue eyes to me to see how I'm reacting, pausing to gulp some air, since he's been talking so fast.

"Get off my bed," I manage.

"Soon, *sweetheart*. But no, I don't want to get off your bed. Not at all, actually. It's just so . . . cozy!" He squeals with laughter. Something is very wrong with him, and it's not just the gap where a tooth should be.

"Anyway," Will says, stretching out on his back and putting his arms behind his head in a manner of the utmost repose, "something didn't add up. So I decided to solve the mystery."

"And what did you come up with?" I ask in a whisper, though I can tell I don't want to know.

"It made you prettier, your little experiment." Will yawns. "I mean, you used to be maybe a seven, but now . . . you could compete with tens."

"Funny, the more you talk, the uglier you get," I say, my voice choked with rage.

"I just hope that *scar* heals," he goes on, giggling crazily. "A scar can be hot, but that one's a doozy."

I freeze, my heart punching through my chest so forcefully it makes me dizzy. Does he *know*?

"What are you talking about?" I grab him by the collar of his oxford shirt, pulling him up off my bed until his face is an inch from mine, close enough so that I can smell a trace of the almond cookies my parents gave him. Did my shirt slip when I kicked him? Has he been watching me somehow?

"I know *everything*, freak show. I know what you can do. And I have it all in my computer. Now, let go of me."

"What did you do?" I whisper. I throw him down onto my sheepskin rug, where we once made out for hours.

I race over to lock the door, then return and stand over him. My body hums with the urge to fight and destroy.

But I don't. I can't. Certainly not here.

"I don't think you want to mess with me too much right now." Will grimaces. He crosses his legs and straightens up, hands on his knees, looking as if he's about to do yoga. His sky-blue eyes twinkle with pride at whatever sick thing he's dangling in front of me. "Considering the footage I have on you."

"How dare you," I whisper, suddenly exhausted. I sit on the carpet a few feet away from him, my shoulders sagging, deflated. Gavin is gone. Why does anything else even matter?

"Oh, Anthem. You cannot imagine how easy it was. I came over one Saturday while you were out at ballet or wherever it is you go. I brought your mother some flowers. Told her my plan to get you back, to win your heart, blah, blah, blah. Made her promise to keep my love for you a secret. Your parents want us to be together—I'm sure you know that already. Then I zipped in here and planted an itsy-bitsy camera when she thought I was in the bathroom." He shrugs. "I guess I'm just the kind of guy who likes to know what people are up to." He dangles his keys in front of me, a small red flash drive glinting on the ring.

"Where is it?" I whisper, blood roaring in my ears. My hands are shaking with fury.

"Oh, I'm not sharing the information. It's all for me. The footage of you jumping around your room like a crazy-assed grasshopper? I'm keeping it all to myself. You just have to do one thing for me."

"Where is the camera?" I hiss, lunging at him. He rolls away from me, flinching a little as he rights himself at the foot of my bed.

"You threaten me again like that, and the footage goes straight to a website. I was thinking AnthemFleetIsaFreakofNature.com. Has a nice ring to it, doesn't it?"

"What do you want?" I whisper, sitting back on my heels with a thud. I look out the window at the thin slice of moon hovering uselessly in the black night and swallow a sob.

"People at school think you dumped me. Did you know that?" Will's mouth twists into a grimace, his face flushed with the memory of this humiliation.

"No. What does it matter?"

"It doesn't . . . now," Will says softly, plucking hairs out of the rug and balling them up between his fingers. His eyes avoid mine. "Because we got back together, just like I told your parents."

"But we didn't—"

"But babe, we *did*. See, that's how this whole blackmail thing works. You're going to be my girlfriend again. You stand quietly like a good little ballerina by my side again. You hold my hand when we're in front of people. You kiss me like you mean it before we go to class."

"But why?" I cry. "Why would you want that? You *hate* me," I remind him. But that's the point, I realize, the force of what Will is after rocking through me. *Control. Dominance.*

"Why? Because nobody breaks up with Will Hansen. And nobody kicks Will Hansen in the teeth. And mostly, Anthem? Because I *can*."

"And if I say no?" I ask. But I already know the answer.

"If you say no, I post the footage when I get home. I'm pretty sure someone would be interested in the illegal activities of whatever back-alley nutjob did this to you. I'm quite certain you'd spend the rest of your days being studied by the medical community. And there goes your life." Will smiles and sits back against the wall, grinning crazily.

"Get the camera," I squeak. "And get out."

"Tell me we have a deal first."

A long beat of silence. We lock eyes, and there's nothing but hatred between us. I look away first, all the fight suddenly gone out of me.

"We have a deal."

"Great," he says, and walks toward a framed picture I have on the wall above my bed, a black-and-white shot of two dancers midleap, their bodies flexed and straining, hands entwined in the air. He plucks a tiny piece of white plastic from the top of the white frame. "I'll miss seeing you undress," he smirks. As he brushes past me, he eyes my unmade bed. "But maybe I won't have to wait too long before getting another look."

He pauses, his hand on the door. "We have unfinished business there, don't we?" His eyes travel to the bed and back to me, traveling slowly up my body.

"Get out," I whisper.

I push him out the door and shut it hard, sliding down the back of it. As I do, my hair falls out of its bun. I move to touch the cut on my head, but aside from the dried blood in my hair, my head is healed. I can't even locate a scab.

Hugging my arms around my knees, I wait for the tears to come. But they never do. There's just a yawning emptiness, an icy cold inside me that never thaws.

CHAPTER 21

I stay in my room for days, barely sleeping, barely eating.

Sleep delivers no rest, only blood-soaked nightmares, so I lay in the dark, staring at the ceiling, a faint crack in the plaster traveling from the light fixture in the center of the room to the crown moldings, watching the glowing red numerals on my clock move from morning to midday to night and back again. I eat a few bites of the food Lily brings me three times a day and push the rest away, my stomach recoiling. It all tastes like dirt and blood to me. I eat just enough to keep my lips and fingertips from turning blue, to keep away torpor, but no more.

Every morning my mother comes in and sits at the foot of my bed, feeling my forehead, her face pinched with concern. *Still so hot*, she says wonderingly, pulling her hand away quickly, as if I've burned her. It seems my new heart has given me the ability to generate heat in my body just by concentrating hard, holding my breath a little, and balling my hands into fists.

I mumble something from deep within the three extra

blankets my mother has piled onto my bed, trying to reassure her just enough to avoid a visit from Dr. Sprogue, but not so much that they'll question my skipping school. I dutifully swallow the fever-reducing pills she brings me, gulping water from a glass already starting to sweat on my nightstand and smiling weakly, whispering *Thanks, Mommy* before shutting my eyes again to sleep the "flu" off. Mostly, my parents leave me be, relying on Lily to check in every couple of hours while they're at the office. Some evenings, both of them come home so late that they skip coming in to see me altogether.

I mark the start of each day by deleting whatever text Will has sent me in the night. Usually it'll say *Miss your face* or *Can't wait to hold your hand again*, but by the morning of the fourth day, he's grown tired of waiting. The latest text, sent at 2:00 A.M., says, *You can hide, but not forever*.

When Lily comes with a bowl of rice porridge for me, I can tell by her expression that I'm a sorry sight. "Ant," she says gently, her green eyes soft and sympathetic, "I'm going to run you a bath. I have some lavender oil—it'll be just the thing to heal you. And if you ever want to talk," she says, lowering her voice, "about anything—I'm here."

I shake my head and turn toward the wall. "No thanks," I mumble, unable to meet Lily's compassionate eyes.

She runs it anyway, and the smell of lavender oil fills my room. My hair is greasy and my scalp itches, but I just lie there, stuck like a fly trapped between a window and a screen. I can't find the energy or the will to get up and do it. The weight of Gavin's death pins me to the bed, so heavy I still can't summon the energy to cry.

On Friday, after I've stayed home from school nearly a week, Zahra tells me she is coming over. She's been texting and calling, but I don't have the energy. The phone sits in my bathroom on its charger, vibrating. Once or twice a day I write back, something along the lines of:

Still sick

Or, when she asks if something bad happened:

No, just sick as a dog

This is the kind of text that sends Zahra into a rage: the unspecific information, the lack of detail, the obviousness of the excuse. It reeks of me keeping secrets. And I'm supposed to be done with all that, after my disappearance. I'm supposed to be the same Anthem I always was, the girl who tells Zahra everything. Before, no detail was too small to share with Zahra. If I was stuck somewhere without a tampon and bled on my jeans, she'd want to know how big the spot was. That was how things used to be, anyway. But now I've got nothing to give her but lies and half-truths. I'm as incapable of being a friend as I am of showering, of eating, of bothering to raise my blinds and look out the window.

Before I can write back to her and tell her not to come, she arrives, carrying a bouquet of purple dahlias so big it obscures her head.

"That was fast," I croak. She must have texted me when she was already standing outside the building.

Z lays the massive bouquet next to me in bed, looking down on me as if I'm a corpse and she's come to pay her final respects. "When's the last time you opened a window in here?" she says, wrinkling her nose.

She heads to the sliding glass doors that lead to my balcony, yanks the cord that opens the wooden blinds, and slides both doors open. "Much better. You need air, sweetie. Don't take this the wrong way, but you look terrible."

I recoil from the light, shielding my eyes with my hands, and sit up in bed. "I guess. I've been sick." *I want to die* is what I'm thinking.

"Uh-huh. So you tell me. Funny how you've never, ever been too sick for school before, and now it's been days. Remember when you won the spelling bee in seventh grade and then passed out onstage and it turned out you'd been hiding a 103 fever?"

A sigh spills out of me. "Yeah. I'm older now," I say. "Or maybe just sicker."

"Uh-huh," Z says again, her hand smoothing and twisting chunks of her short hair as she studies me. I can tell she's not convinced. "Listen, I can't even imagine how awful you're feeling, waiting to hear about Gavin. I just wish you felt like you could talk to me about it."

A silence opens up between us, and I spend it biting the inside of my cheeks, wanting desperately to tell her what's happened. But if I begin to tell the truth, I won't be able to stop. I'll uncork everything I'm working so hard to keep buried. My visits to the South Side. The trips to Hades. My chimeric heart. Will's threats. Z would never let me go along with Will's scheme. She'd do something—threaten him, expose him—and in turn, he could expose me. *Oh, Z,* I think as I smile weakly at her. *Forgive me.*

"I'm fine, Zahra." My voice sounds more hostile than I mean it to. "I told you, I'm just sick."

Zahra looks down at the bed, and I can see her trying to decide if she'll sit on it. She doesn't. "I can't help you if you don't talk to me," she says flatly. "But maybe you just . . . don't want me in your life anymore. That's what it feels like lately."

She stares down at the carpet, then looks at me for a second before turning to look out the window, daring me to answer.

"Of course I do," I say. "I'm just . . . I'm going through a lot. And, um, I've been thinking a lot lately about what's right for me, because—" I pause.

Don't say his name, I tell myself. *If you say his name, your heart will break open and you will never be able to gather yourself up again.* But then I say it. And the lies start pouring out of me. "Because, actually, Gavin and I broke up . . ." I trail off, my throat closing like a stopped drain.

"Broke up?" Zahra comes closer to my bed. "So they let him go?"

I nod. "I'm sorry I didn't tell you. I just . . . I've been so confused. They let him go a couple of days ago. He got in touch. He's fine. But I decided it just wasn't going to work. My parents . . ." I wave my hand in the air, too exhausted and disgusted with myself to finish the lie.

Zahra bites her lip, her eyebrows knitted in sympathy as she stares down at me. "But it might still work out with him. Maybe when you're a little older and your parents aren't monitoring your every move."

I nod and squeeze my eyes shut. Nothing will ever, in any way, work out with Gavin, I want to shout. Instead, I open my mouth and keep lying.

"Maybe someday. But for now . . . I'm moving on." I feel my face flush with shame, as if I'm desecrating Gavin's memory, as my words fill the room.

"Moving on?" Z says, surprised.

I can't look at her. "I'm thinking of getting back together with Will, actually." My voice barely a whisper, my mouth fills with a sour taste just saying the words, like I've drunk a glass of spoiled milk. "I know you won't approve, so I've been kind of distant because of that, too, maybe."

What a crock. The words out, I stare miserably up at the ceiling for a beat before I dare to look her in the eyes. *Zahra will never believe me.*

But she does. She recoils visibly, as if I've punched her. "You're not thinking straight," Zahra mutters. "Like, *at all*. God, Anthem, do you realize this is classic codependence? The definition of codependence"—Zahra begins to pace the room, her hands gesticulating as she makes her point—"is when you wake up in the morning and you don't know how you feel without looking at your boyfriend."

"Maybe you're right," I manage, my voice far away and thick.

"'Will is the biggest prick among a sea of contenders at Cathedral,'" she says, blinking back tears and shaking her head. "That's a quote from Anthem Fleet, circa two weeks ago. He treated you like dirt. Have you forgotten all that?"

"I changed my mind," I say numbly, willing her to storm away so I can stop lying. I stare at her shoes, big shit-kicking combat boots laced up to her thigh. "I was wrong."

"I'm going to go now," Zahra says slowly, as if she's not sure I even understand English anymore. "Call me when the Anthem I know returns, if she ever does. Because this?" She waves her hand over me like I'm a plate of inedible food, a ruined painting, a stained dress. "I don't know who *this* person is."

You're right, I think sadly as Zahra runs out, slamming my door hard behind her. Zahra has no idea what I've become. And I don't know, either.

CHAPTER 22

That night I'm awoken by a hand pressed lightly around my shoulder, shaking me. I'm up like a shot, leaping out of bed and onto the floor, racing to get to the door. *They've come to finish what they started.*

A voice inside me whispers *no*.

I scoop a discarded leather belt from the floor and I have one hand on the door when a voice breathes my name.

"Anthem. It's me."

I lower the belt to my side as my eyes adjust to the darkness. Ford's teeth glow in a slice of moonlight coming in through a couple of twisted slats in the closed venetian blinds. My fight-or-flight adrenaline instantly morphs into anger.

"How did you get in?" I whisper, my heart still ricocheting through my chest. I move to lock my bedroom door in case my parents heard something and decide to check on me.

He shrugs, like it was so easy it's not worth talking about.

"I'm good at breaking and entering. Don't worry, I didn't come through the lobby. Nobody saw a thing."

I stand there in boyshorts and a tank top flecked with carrot soup, openmouthed, a tiny part of me impressed that he found some other way into this fortress of a building. But a bigger part of me is furious.

"What the hell, Ford?" I ask. But then the effects of low blood sugar start to hit me: I feel dizzy, my vision dims, and I'm about to fall over. I stagger to my desk and open the bottom drawer, where I keep a stash of carbs. It's the opposite of a ballet dancer's diet, all of it, but my new heart and the fear of torpor has done funny things to my eating habits. I pull out a box of SugarKrisps, digging into it for a few handfuls of flaky cereal, a bunch of it escaping my hands and falling onto the floor, like snow atop the mountains of dirty clothes.

"Whoa," Ford says, staring at me. "Your lips are blue."

I nod, shoving cereal in my mouth.

"My fingers too," I mutter, putting a hand in the air for Ford to see. My fingertips look as if I've dipped them in light blue ink.

I blink at Ford, chewing a final mouthful of SugarKrisps, the cereal scraping painfully down my throat. *Just leave*, I think. I want to fall back into bed again and lay there, numb and sleepless and alone until the morning comes.

Ford looks around my moonlit room, then back at me. "You look . . . um . . ."

"Not good," I croak, cutting him off. "I know." I rest my hip on the corner of the desk and wait a beat, but Ford stays silent. "Why did you come here? Just checking up on me?"

"I heard about what happened," Ford says, sitting down on the edge of my bed, a dark shape in the mass of white covers. "When you didn't come around again, I went to Hades. I found the kid, Rufus. He told me everything, after I paid him seven fifty, of course. I came to see if you're okay."

"Thanks. I'm not." I drop the box of SugarKrisps on the floor, the cereal spilling out onto the carpet. I leave it there, making no effort to clean up the mess. "How did Rufus seem?"

"The same. Cute."

"Too bad he'll probably die in there or get hooked on drugs by the time he's twelve," I say bitterly.

"I know how this feels, you know."

"How what feels?"

"When someone close to you dies. How dead inside you feel. How hopeless and angry and totally, shittily alone."

"I thought you said you lived with three other people," I say flatly.

"I do. My uncle and his two daughters. My parents were droopie addicts. It killed them in the end. If my uncle hadn't stepped in to raise me, I'd be dead, too, probably."

"I'm sorry, Ford. That's awful." Chastened, I look down at my fingers, the blue tinge already receding.

I walk over to the window and open the venetian blinds a little, filling the room with bright moonlight. The scythe-shaped moon is enormous, so close it looks like I could reach up and break a piece off it. I turn away from the view—I don't want to see anything beautiful.

"You shouldn't have *gone* there," he groans. "Not alone, anyway. I told you not to."

"It's too late now," I say, too tired to stand anymore. I sink to the floor, next to the spilled cereal. "He's dead, and rethinking what happened can't change that. Believe me, I've tried."

Neither of us says anything for a minute. *Now go away*, I think as I pull my knees up to my chin and rest my head on them. I want my bed and the crack in the ceiling and my tiny silent bubble where nothing moves. "So see you around, Ford. It's over now."

He shakes his head and pushes himself up off my bed, then walks toward me. He stands in front of me and offers me both hands. I don't take them. I look down at the carpet, pluck a few SugarKrisps from the shag, and drop them into the box. "Come on. Get up," he says. "It's not *over*. You're still alive, aren't you? Even if you're not acting like it right now."

"I'm not in the mood for a pep talk," I mutter. "Just leave."

"No," he says simply, his hands still outstretched, close enough to me now that I see the tiny cuts on his knuckles, a callus on his thumb. I remember what Jax told me: *He used to box, until he landed on the wrong side of a few bets*. I shake my head a little, but he doesn't move. Ford may be a fighter, but all the fight went out of me the moment the bullet left Rosie's gun.

"The last thing you need right now is to be left alone," he says firmly. He looks like he might throw me over his shoulder if I don't cooperate.

"When we found out my dad overdosed," Ford continues, "I didn't speak for a month. My mom was still alive at that point, totally high and living in the subway tunnels with my dad until he died. My uncle got her cleaned up enough to come to the funeral, and she tried to put her hands on my shoulders. I ran away, hid behind a gravestone for the rest of the funeral. I just wanted to die right along with my dad."

He grabs my arms, and I reluctantly let him pull me up from the floor and onto my feet. "And then after some time went by, I started talking again. My uncle taught me how to box. I decided to live."

"I don't want to decide to live," I croak, my voice like a

rusted hinge. "I'm in mourning."

A car backfires, the sound echoing in the empty streets below. I cover my ears, sick of my supercharged hearing.

"This is how you mourn him? By going catatonic?"

"And how would you suggest I do it?" I snap.

"By fighting back," he says, daring me to doubt him. "*Especially* if I could run a hundred miles an hour."

"I'm done fighting." My chest and ears begin to burn. I flutter my hands up to my chest, wondering if he can see my scar in the moonlight. "Sorry to disappoint you."

I hear his heavy sigh, his footsteps moving toward the door.

"You know what?" he says. When I face him again, his eyes are hard. "The world doesn't need another brokenhearted girl."

Before I can respond, he slips out of my room. I stare at the door with my mouth hanging open, a paltry comeback lodged in my throat. *I don't care what the world needs.* And then, because I let my guard down, the memory of Gavin crumpling to the floor rears up again. The bloodstain growing wider on his shirt, the lifelessness of his hands in mine. And Rosie looking down at him and *smiling*—could she really have been smiling?

I bite the insides of my cheeks and struggle to breathe, to shake off the image, to forget about Ford and relax enough so sleep might be possible tonight. But when I look down, I find my hands have curled into fists.

CHAPTER 23

"Welcome back, Anthem," Principal Bang says, sizing me up from behind her enormous desk. She scoots her short, round body closer to me, and her professional smile falters.

"Thank you," I say warily, waiting for her to tell me why I've been pulled out of homeroom on my first day back at school. I've showered and combed the knots out of my hair, but I can't wash away the hollows in my cheeks. I swallow what feels like a mouthful of gravel and zero in on the mole above her right eyelid. The mole is safe. Her small, dark eyes set deep into her pudgy face—eyes that are looking at me a little too carefully—are not.

Principal Bang purses her lips, her chubby hands tented under her chin, her elbows propped onto her desk blotter. Behind her is the Cathedral Wall of Power—a grid of hundreds of framed pictures of successful politicians, CEOs, talk show hosts, athletes, and other luminaries who have passed through the school's hallowed halls since it opened two hundred years ago. "You do not look terribly well," she sniffs. "Are you sure you're well enough to be here?"

Nothing about me is well, but after Ford's visit, I started feeling like maybe enough was enough. I announced my "recovery" to my mother yesterday, then spent all day cleaning my room, furiously scrubbing and vacuuming between long bouts of staring blankly into space. And today, despite the sadness wrapped around me like a lead overcoat, I scraped myself out of bed early and got to school an hour before the morning bell.

"I'm fine." My voice sounds hollow and far away, like I'm hearing it through water. I clear my throat and force my spine to straighten up from my slumped position in the uncomfortable chair facing Bang's desk. I curl my mouth into a smile, hoping I'm doing it correctly. It's been so long.

"I feel I should tell you there has been talk of an anxiety assessment for you."

My body recoils at these words. "It was just a bad flu. Mentally, I'm . . ." I tap the side of my head, groping for adjectives. "Clean. Calm. Collected." There is no way I'm signing up for a day in the nurse's office being interviewed and observed by a team of psychiatrists.

Bang narrows her piggish eyes and cocks her head. "With everything you've been through lately . . ." Traces of a knowing smile flash across her face as she leans closer. "Wouldn't a little MoodEase help?"

I stare at her openmouthed. I've never heard an adult speak so openly about Pharms, especially an adult who regularly goes on Channel Ten to rant about the illegal ones circulating in the city. The room starts to shrink around me, the smothering velvet curtains on the tall, narrow windows creeping closer. Can Bang force an assessment on me?

Assessments are for problem kids. I've never caused trouble at school, except for outranking Olive Ann in the senior class. The kids who are on MoodEase are easy to spot—their complacency shows on their faces and in their newly placid personalities—and there are dozens of them at Cathedral. At least a fourth of the upper school is on Pharms: MoodEase or Concentra or Stabiline. Each of them tinkering with neurons and brain chemistry to make them happier or more focused or less of a problem.

I don't want any part of it. The anxiety assessment is a full day of interviews and stress tests. I would never make it through without spilling everything that's happened out of me like water from a broken vase. But I also don't want to be numbed out on Pharms. However agonizing my pain is, it is mine. It's a part of me.

"Thank you for your concern," I say tightly, looking down at my bitten-to-the-quick fingernails and picking at a ragged cuticle. "But I'm fine. I'm going back to ballet tomorrow."

"And your classes? How will you catch up?" she asks, her brow wrinkled with false concern. I can almost hear her gleeful thoughts of Olive Ann's potential ascent to valedictorian. I wish I could tell Bang that Olive Ann can have it—I don't care about being valedictorian anymore. "A course of pharmaceuticals could help you deal with the stress of all th—"

"I'm working out plans today with each of my teachers to make up all the work I missed." My words get high-pitched and squeaky at the end of my sentence. "Really, I'm *fine*." *So drop it.*

"Very well, Anthem. Let's talk again at the end of the week. I'll hold off on scheduling anything until then."

I nod curtly, staring at a paperweight on Bang's desk, a scorpion frozen in amber. I stand up and pull my book bag onto my shoulder, my vision darkening momentarily due to low blood sugar. I have to eat more now that I'm not laying in bed all day, I tell myself. Then I remember the only thing I can use to get her off my back. "My father has always been very against the assessments," I lie. I have no idea how he feels about the yearly assessments. We've never talked much about them. "He might be kind of upset if he hears about this," I add.

Bang's already-flushed cheeks flush a darker red. Dad is Cathedral's biggest donor. Bang's job could be in jeopardy if she gets on his bad side.

"We are only looking out for the well-being of our students," she sighs, exasperated. "Let's see how you're doing at the end of the week. If we move forward, it will be a decision we undertake together, with you and your family."

While she talks, I scan the Wall of Power behind her and locate my mother's picture toward the bottom left. She's next to a young Maurice Dodge, now the jowly, gray-faced investigative reporter for Channel Ten who's always shouting *Manny Marks is soft on crime!* My mother was gorgeous in high school, with fluffy blond hair and beestung lips that smiled sweetly, back when she was carefree and seventeen, back when her name was Helene Harkness instead of Helene Fleet.

"Fine. See you at the end of the week, I guess."

"All right." Bang nods good-bye and picks up her phone, where three lines have been flashing.

What happened to that girl? I wonder as I walk out of Bang's office. She looked so full of hope in her senior portrait. Nothing like the haunted, medicated woman I know as my mother.

I pause in the reception area of the wood-paneled main office. I'm going to be my mother, I realize. If I don't drag myself out of this somehow, I'm going to be joyless and numb for the rest of my life. But the thought evaporates when I push open the heavy door to the hallway and see who's waiting for me.

"There you are, Red." Will wears his killer smile—all teeth, dead eyes. As if he's being filmed. "That took for*ever*. I was starting to think you'd passed out in there. What'd the old hag want?"

I open my mouth to mumble something about making up my coursework, but he interrupts. "Forget it. Doesn't matter. We don't have much time, so lemme get you up to speed on our relationship."

I nod miserably, letting him pull me along by the crook of my arm. I feel limp as a dishrag, completely unprepared to cope with Will and his twisted charade.

"We're taking it slow for now," Will says, lowering his voice as we walk toward the east wing, where we both have first period. He's speaking so softly that I lean toward him to hear. From the outside, this body language probably looks intimate.

"Smile, Red!" He elbows me in the ribs, furious at my lackluster performance. "There's no grace period. You need to get it right, or else you-know-what's going online," he says between clenched teeth.

"Fine," I mutter, trying not to punch him.

"Now I'll say something, and you laugh. Pretend you're a nice girl who wants her boyfriend back."

And because I can't think of any way out, I open my mouth and do it. A barking laugh erupts from me like a cough. I even manage to smile. People are watching, waving, welcoming me back, processing the fact of me and Will together with their eyes.

With every minute that ticks by, I die a little more inside.

We pass Zahra in the hall, and I stop walking, reach a hand toward her, but Will pulls me forward, his hand clamped around my elbow. "Zahra . . ." I start, but the look on her face is pure, wide-eyed disgust, and it feels like a punch in the gut. I never should have returned to school, I realize. I don't have the strength for the performance Will is demanding. I'm too lonely to be this alone.

As we near the physics lab, I hear whispers in the hall and feel a hundred pairs of eyes on us. Will feels it, too, I guess, because he stops to grab my hand and whispers in my ear: "See their faces?" he hisses. "They're relieved. The perfect couple is *back*. They need us, Anthem. Like peasants need their royalty."

"You're repulsive," I whisper, trying to pull my hand away.

Will just snorts and squeezes my hand tighter, until it starts to cut off my circulation. I start squeezing his hand back, imagining ripping his hand off his arm, twisting it off like the lid of a jar, the bones and sinew snapping wetly in two. . . .

"Ow!" Will yelps, almost falling on the floor as he pulls his hand away from me. My thoughts snap back into the hallway, where everyone has turned to stare. "What the hell was that, you freak?" he whispers, shaking out his hand and wiggling his fingers to make sure they're not broken.

"Sorry." I smile, for once enjoying the fact that everyone's watching us. "Guess I don't know my own strength."

"See you after class," he hisses. "Do that again and I take my footage public." And then he's striding down the hall, mingling with the "peasants."

I walk into the physics lab, my jaw clenched with worry. I don't know if I'm more afraid of Will or of myself for the violent thoughts I'm having. I don't look at anyone as I slide onto my usual lab stool in the front row and take out my physics notebook, flipping methodically to the notes from a week ago. My last page reads:

REVIEW OF NEWTON'S FIRST LAW

An object that is at rest will stay at rest unless an unbalanced force acts upon it.

An object that is in motion will not change its velocity unless an unbalanced force acts upon it.

As Mr. Shrum starts writing a formula on the board for a pop quiz that I'm sure to fail, I bite my pen and consider the words scribbled in my notebook.

I think of Ford pausing at my bedroom door, the disappointment in his eyes. *The world doesn't need another brokenhearted girl.*

"Okay, everyone, let's begin," Mr. Shrum says, nodding in my direction and pantomiming the shutting of my notebook.

I pull out a blank sheet of paper and put everything else back into my knapsack. I write my name at the top of the page. I write the date. Then I stare at the paper until the blue lines blur into the white space, still chewing on Newton's law.

I don't want to be the object at rest anymore, I realize. I need to figure out how to get back in motion.

CHAPTER 24

At a quarter after midnight, I slip from the passenger seat of Serge's Motoko into the unmarked bar Ford took me to a few weeks ago. An old song wails from the speakers, a chorus of string instruments and a lone slow drumbeat behind a woman singing mournfully that *everything was black and blue, everything was me and you, when you was my man.* The air in the bar is thick with rollie smoke and something else—a chemical sweetness, a faint pink haze coming out of a few pipes of a group slumped in a corner booth.

As soon as my eyes adjust to the dim light, I zero in on the bartender. My body relaxes a little when I see it's the same girl as before, with the blue pompadour and the red patches of acne on her otherwise pretty face. I move to stand in front of her as she fills three shot glasses with brown liquid. Her eyes flick toward me in acknowledgment before she walks to the other end of the bar to deliver the shots. I loosen the thick gray scarf I've wrapped around my neck and glimpse myself in the mirror behind the bar—under the black newsboy cap pulled low on my forehead, my face is painfully thin, my eyes gaze warily out from hollow sockets. I look almost as haunted as I feel.

When she comes back, I surprise myself by pointing to the unmarked bottle of brown stuff. "One more of those," I say.

She nods curtly and pours it. "Nine," she says.

I slide a ten along the bar and take the shot, tipping the liquid down my throat all at once. It tastes like battery acid, but I manage to get it down without embarrassing myself. A second later, I feel a pleasant heat in my chest. "One more thing," I say when I regain my ability to talk.

"Yeah?"

"I'm looking for Ford."

She grabs a wet pint glass from under the bar and begins to dry it with a rag. "And why's that?"

I pick up a tattered coaster from the bar, then quickly drop it when I see the words Blackout Vodka, remembering my last moments of consciousness in the bookstore after Gavin died, the bottle in Smitty's hand swinging toward my head.

"I need his help."

She studies my face for a beat, trying to decide if I'm okay. I notice a small home-inked tattoo on her wrist: *We will rise.*

"Don't mess with him," she says flatly as she scribbles something on an order pad. "Or I'll find someone to mess with you."

I nod slowly and wonder what kind of past this girl and Ford might share. "He's a friend," I say. "I promise."

"Whatever," she mutters, ripping the bar tab out of the book and folding it once before handing it over. "Here's where he goes at night sometimes. If he's not there, I can't help you."

I thank her and leave, floating a little from the alcohol. When I unfold it, the bar tab says *Jimmy's Corner—Bergamot and Vine.*

• • •

When I get back into the Motoko and tell Serge where we're going, he just nods. "Thanks for driving me," I say, trying to fill the silence of the car. I was about to head out by myself, but Serge intercepted me when I got out of the service elevator in the garage and insisted that he wanted to drive me.

"No need to thank me."

I clear my throat. "Aren't you wondering what I'm doing?"

"I trust that it's important," Serge says. He stares straight ahead, alert and seemingly not sleepy in spite of the late hour. "And necessary."

"It . . . might be," I mumble, then go back to staring out the window. As the scenery rolls by, I'm glad I'm in a car and not moving on foot through this neighborhood.

Bergamot Street is a wide avenue with old-growth trees that must have once been a shopping district. Now every storefront is boarded up and their spray-painted walls read BLACK MOLD and TOXIC—DO NOT ENTER among the usual SYNDC8 tags. Each storefront has two or three stories of apartments above it, also boarded up. Jimmy's Corner is easy to spot—it's on a shallow hill, on the second floor of the only building on Bergamot that still has electricity.

I tell Serge I might be a while and that he should go home.

"I'll wait," he says simply.

"Serge."

He holds my gaze a long time, his wide nostrils flared with determination. I'm never going to win this argument, I realize, and finally look away and nod. "Okay."

I stand outside on the deserted sidewalk for a few minutes, listening to the *thump-thump-thump* of fists hitting a bag, wondering if it's Ford.

Only one way to find out, I tell myself, and press the buzzer for number two. The thumping stops, and I hear footsteps coming down the stairs, then the sound of a face being leaned toward a peephole. Nothing. No movement.

"Ford?" I call out tentatively.

Silence.

"Yeah?" he finally says.

"Hey, um, want to open the door?"

"I don't know," he calls. "Should I? I'm still thinking about it."

"It's cold out here, and dark." Bergamot is in the neighborhood of Lowlands, famous in the papers as a bad area ever since a series of floods cut most of it off the electricity grid.

"Okay, okay. Sit tight," he says. By the sound of it, he's unlocked at least four bolts.

When the door swings open, he's grinning. And sweaty. And shirtless.

"Sorry. I wasn't really going to keep you waiting out there," he says, pulling me inside to the narrow vestibule and sticking his head out the door to look in both directions. "You are alone, right?"

"Of course," I say, squeezing into the tiny space as he shuts the door behind us, doing my best not to brush up against him. "Who would I come here with?"

"Dunno," he murmurs as he relocks the bolts. Ford wraps his arms around his chest, as if he's just realized he's half-naked. "How'd you find me?"

"Bartender at that bar you took me to. She likes you, I think."

"Oh, Michelle? We went out when we were in the seventh grade. She's just an old friend."

There's another awkward silence.

"Listen, I thought about what you said." I clear my throat,

making sure my eyes stay on his face and not on his stomach muscles. "And you're right."

"What did I say again?" The bare bulb in the vestibule flickers, then goes out, and he bats at it with his hand to turn it back on. "Sorry. Jimmy steals all his electricity."

"There's actually a Jimmy at Jimmy's Corner?"

"There are two Jimmies, actually, Jimmy Senior and Jimmy Junior. Jimmy Senior lets me train here after hours. I like to keep a low profile." He pauses. "Anyway, you were about to tell me what I was right about."

"You said you could maybe help me," I remind him. "I . . . I was thinking it might be time for me to learn how to fight."

He nods and looks me over for a minute, his expression serious. "Are you sure you're ready to say good-bye to these scrawny excuses for arms?"

Then he grabs my upper arms and squeezes my biceps.

My face goes hot again, and before I know it I'm back to staring at Ford's torso. "I guess so?"

"Then come on." He starts up the narrow stairwell, taking the steps two at a time. He turns and motions for me to follow. "Let me show you my office."

CHAPTER 25

"Again!" Ford shouts. I watch him in the mirror, standing at a safe distance behind me, doing his usual bounce from foot to sneakered foot, occasionally swiping a fist at the air as he watches me attack the six-foot punching bag bolted to the ceiling in the center of Jimmy's Corner, which turns out to be kind of charming for a decrepit old boxing gym that smells like the inside of a dirty sock. The equipment is all at least a hundred years old, but it's unlike anywhere I've ever been before, with pictures on the walls of prizefighters and at least a hundred different objects to hit and kick and pummel. "Low jab, upper cut, then a kick to the stomach. Like you mean it, Green!"

I suppress an annoyed grimace and do the sequence, my eyes focused on the red vinyl bag, my ungloved fists punching the living guts out of it, the bag finally swinging up at a slight angle, responding to my relentless kicks and hits. The first night we began training, a week ago, Ford called me Red as he wrapped my hands with white surgical tape. I told him never to call me that again, explaining that someone I hated used to call me Red. So he grinned and switched to Green: "the color of your eyes when you get into the zone. And the color of all your money."

I kind of hate it, but every time he says it, the name makes me push harder. It reminds me of what I'm doing here. Of how I caused Gavin's death, and of how it's my job now to bring the people who killed him to justice.

"That all you got?" Ford bellows, and I spin around to face him. His face is expectant, playful.

"Let's see *you* attack the bag," I say, breathing hard. We've been at it for an hour and a half already, running drills, lifting weights, and now beating up bags and working on technique. This is the eighth night in a row Serge has met me after midnight and driven me to Jimmy's. The eighth night in a row he's waited for me in the car outside, even though I've invited him up every time.

School continues to be awful, with Will making me hang on him at every possible moment and Zahra still only speaking to me when I corner her, and barely even then. Sometimes I catch her looking at me in the halls and at lunch when I'm parading around with Will, her expression sad and confused, as if she can't quite believe her eyes. The sadness in her face gives me a little hope that maybe there's still some part of her that can forgive me, if not understand me. In those moments, I feel like if only I could tell her the whole truth, things between us might be okay again. But then Will catches me looking at her and jiggles his stupid flash drive, and I go right back to hiding behind my wall of lies.

As soon as I get him off my back, I tell myself, I'll tell Z everything.

Besides ballet practice, which is a distraction from everything at school and from the aching pit of grief and guilt inside me, training with Ford has been the only bright spot in my daily slog through life.

"Fine." Ford grins. "Watch and learn."

After Ford does an impressive boxing sequence that ends with a spin-kick, I turn to the mirror and practice my left-hand jab, my weakest punch according to Ford, bobbing and ducking in front of the mirror. My eyes still look haunted, but my body is much stronger than it was a week ago. Hours of sparring, weights, and drills have morphed my scrawny-but-strong limbs into sinewy, toned muscle. My stomach—always flat and toned from ballet—has real definition now. There's an actual six-pack, especially after I've been moving around for a while. And by the end of every workout, my biceps look like they're carved of stone.

"Okay, you again," Ford says, his eyes meeting mine in the mirror as he thrusts his chin toward the bag. A trickle of sweat runs down the side of his jaw. "Take it down this time. That bag killed your boyfriend."

Of course I can't take it down, I think as I take a few big steps back, preparing to come at it with as much force as I can. This is how we end all the sessions—with a final, do-or-die attack where Ford encourages me to go to my "crazy place" and give it all I have. *If you only knew*, I thought the first time he used this phrase. My crazy isn't just a place, it's a whole continent.

I start spinning in circles as I approach, gathering momentum with every turn, then I aim the flat of my foot straight at the chubby center of the bag and make contact. *Hard.* Harder than I've ever kicked before, I realize as I hear a metallic crack. I don't register what I've done until the bag is in midair, flying across the room. It lands with a thud, all two hundred pounds of it draped over a set of barbells forty feet away from where it hung.

"Holy Christ on a cracker!" Ford cries. "Jesus, Green! You snapped the chain!"

My hands on my hips, I look up at where the bag was hanging and see a link of steel with a chunk missing, swinging in the air. "Oops."

Ford looks at me, his mouth hanging open. "Okay, let's assume I'll be able to fix that by morning," he mutters. "No more sparring the bag. You're ready to fight a real person."

"You?" I say, turning in circles as he dances around me and jabs the air with his taped hands.

"You see anyone else here? Come on, Green. Bring it." His smile is wide and confident. I look at my own hands, my pinkie bruised, calluses on my palms covered with the white tape. I asked about gloves the first night I came here. *No gloves*, he'd said. *We do it open-handed in Bedlam. We're out for blood.*

Whatever, I remember thinking as he showed me around Jimmy's Corner. Physical pain, a broken hand, it's nothing compared to how I feel inside. It would feel good, probably.

But now, all I can think about is how much I don't want a punch in the nose, since it would mean an interrogation from my parents and weeks of monitoring, maybe even that anxiety assessment with Principal Bang. More important, I don't want to accidentally kill Ford. I duck down low, protecting my head as Ford and I begin to circle each other.

"Come on," I plead. "Let's not do this."

I feel my heart pumping hard, banging out a *ka-thunk ka-thunk ka-thunk* rhythm in my ears, pushing my blood around my body as I match Ford's shuffle with a step-ball-change dance of my own.

We each take a few swings, but then I land both hands on his shoulders and try to pull him down. "First one to the floor loses." Ford grimaces, his biceps straining and slippery with sweat under my grip. Nervous I'll hurt him, I take it easy. So easy he's able to push me off him, then snakes his leg behind one of mine to take me down. I fall forward, toward him, but catch myself at the last minute, punching my way out of his grip. He's not taking any jabs at my face or body. He's playing nice, too, I realize. Doesn't want to hit a girl. I dance toward him and kick the air in front of him. When he comes close again, I duck low, railroading straight toward his stomach and slamming my right shoulder into his midsection, sending him flying backward so far he's past the edge of the mat. After a moment of shock, he springs up, but I come at him again and slam him to the ground, pinning his windpipe with my forearm, half-sitting, half-lying on him, keeping him pinned according to the rules of the match—rules he taught me.

I look at the mirrored wall for a half-second and see a girl in a black tank top with rippling arms atop a guy twice her size, and it almost feels like a dream, like I'm watching a movie, because it's so hard to believe she's me. Ford's neck is warm and vulnerable under my arm, and I remind myself to hold back.

I ease up a little on his neck and start to count out loud—*one, two, three*—but then I notice Ford is trying to say something, and that he's trying to pull my arm from his throat, and that his face is turning purple. I yank my arm away, scared by my own capacity to hurt, and my obvious inability to control it.

"Sorrysorrysorry," I'm saying over and over, my face redder than his now.

Ford rubs his neck. "It was just my windpipe," he croaks, giving me a funny look. "Who needs a trachea, really?"

My heart kicks when I see the look on his face, the way he tilts his head and studies me, an expression of wonder and something else I can't quite read. "What?" I ask, even though I know what he's thinking—some variation of *Is this for real*?

"Nothing," Ford says, still rubbing his neck as he scoots an inch or two away from me. "I've just never been afraid of a girl before."

My face flushes deeper, like he's caught me without my clothes on. He's the first person aside from Will who sees the dark side of what I can do. "Here's to new experiences."

He laughs, a horsey guffaw that fills the room. "You're going to be a great fighter. You already are."

"I don't know," I mutter, turning away from him to walk to the water fountain, avoiding the mirror, and trying not to pay attention to the fluttery feeling in my stomach. Ford's attention makes me uncomfortable. But it feels good to do something well, to think that maybe I can use what I've learned to take down Rosie and her crew.

Lately, in the few hours of sleep I'm getting after training, my dreams are filled with finding the kidnappers, overpowering them, making them suffer.

All I can do is register what Ford tells me and hope it might be enough to ensure that Rosie is punished, locked away forever in a maximum security wing of Bedlam Prison, a black metal tower on Dead Man's Hill, deep in Exurbia, with narrow slits for windows and a spiked, electrified fence sealing thousands of criminals inside.

I bend over the water fountain, swallowing the lukewarm water that trickles out of it, and picture attacking Rosie, my hands around her neck . . .

Until water shoots up into my eye.

When I let go of the metal spigot, I discover it bent to one side.

I didn't do that . . . did I? I look around quickly, but Ford is busy trying to roll the punching bag back to where it used to hang. If I'm not more careful, I'm going to destroy more than just the boxing studio. A closer look at the water fountain reveals indentations in the metal where I was holding its side.

I swallow hard. Rosie might not make it to Bedlam Prison after all, I realize. Because if I'm as strong as it looks like I am, I might not be able to stop myself from killing her.

CHAPTER 26

When the church bells ring for lunch hour the next day, something like optimism clangs in my chest along with them. Normally lunch is the worst part of my day because I have to spend it with Will and his crowd, playing the part of the loyal if aloof girlfriend. But today I have it to myself because Will has a student council meeting.

I've got my backpack full of books slung over one shoulder as I enter the cafeteria. The smell of marinara sauce and meatballs hangs in the moist air. It's a warmish day for a Bedlam winter, and even though there's a mist of fog in the air, at least fifty students sit outside on the covered patio overlooking the cathedral's courtyard, their coats unbuttoned. The cafeteria is quieter inside as a result, with a hundred juniors and seniors spread out among the round aluminum tables.

I spot Zahra right away, in our usual corner table, against the back wall. She's slumped over her cell phone, her burgundy sweater vest a pilled relic from seventh grade, hugging her curves and looking far less dowdy than it does on me. When she looks up and sees me, I wave my crumpled lunch bag and head toward her. She raises her eyebrows for a second, gives me a neutral look acknowledging my wave, then looks back at her phone. *It's a start*, I think, and keep moving toward her.

I start to pick my way past the cluster of tables in the front, where the junior boys who are into role-playing games tend to congregate, then past two perfume-scented clusters of junior girls Zahra calls Team Ice. Team Ice—the next generation who will inherit Bang's and Fitz's titles as the queen bees of Cathedral when we graduate in the spring—flout the excessive jewelry clause in our uniform handbook, each of them sporting enough diamonds and gems to support a small country for a year. Their leader is Martha Marks, the daughter of Mayor Manny Marks, a tall, gap-toothed brunette who has nurtured a mania for horses since kindergarten. I've known Martha a long time, and she's always been nice to me. For as long as I've been attending charity balls with my parents, she's always been there, one of the small pack of little girls regularly stuffed into a crinoline dress with a red velvet sash. One gala when I was eleven and she was ten, we spent the entire evening hiding under the mayor's table, protected by thick tablecloths, grooming a stable of plastic ponies Martha had brought with her in a pink lunchbox.

She's standing with a few of her friends, whispering about something and eyeing another girl, the only junior in my AP Physics class, Duffy Doolittle. Duffy is five or six tables away, near the windows of the cafeteria, eyeliner smeared under her eyes, her sleek blond hair in a high ponytail on the exact top of her skull. It sprouts from her head like a geyser. She's yelling loudly at someone seated in the group of pillheads who hang out back there. I shouldn't be able to hear—she's too far away—but I pick up something like "I prepaid for a hundred, not fifty!"

I catch sight of Roderick Dodge, a baseball cap pulled low on his head, shrinking away from Duffy. He mumbles something and shrugs.

"Screw you, Roderick!" Duffy says, clearly agitated.

Then Roderick says something else I can't hear, and Duffy goes ballistic. She grabs Roderick by his lapels and yanks him from his seat. She's sweating, like she's been running laps. Now Martha Marks and Team Ice are standing on their chairs, straining to see the fight. I move to one side of them to a spot where I can see a sliver of their faces between onlookers.

Roderick raises his hand to Duffy, then thinks better of it and backs off. "I'm out of here," he mumbles, and starts pushing his way through the crowd toward the exit, but Duffy chases after him, screeching, "There's nowhere to run! I will find you! We had a deal!"

That's when I notice the two uniformed cops watching from the doorway. Suddenly they stride quickly toward Duffy. Her always-pink face is scarlet and pinched with anger.

"This her?" one of the cops asks Principal Bang. Bang nods, and the police begin reciting their ancient script: "Youareunderarrestanythingyousaycanandwillbeheldagainstyou. Nopictureskidsyouknowthelawcameraswillbeconfiscated."

Duffy emits a guttural growl and tries to bolt, but they grab her and tie her wrists with plastic restraints behind her back. She falls to the floor and thrashes in vain to break free. The cops hoist her upright again and say something in her ear, and she hangs her head and walks, handcuffed, flanked by the two cops, her ponytail leading the way like a single antenna.

The room erupts in noisy chatter when she's gone, and I

hear the word *Zenithin* over and over as I walk toward Zahra, who's still surreptitiously videotaping the scene with her phone.

"What's Zenithin?" I say when I reach her. She ends the recording and shoots me a look that says *I'm still mad at you, proceed with caution.*

"You are so out of it." She sighs after a beat. "Zenithin is a stronger, illegal version of Accusolve."

"The study drug?"

"I heard Roderick bought a huge stash of it from some Syndicate dealer. Guess Duffy wanted an edge." Zahra says all this while texting someone on her phone. I get the message. To Zahra, I'm an afterthought at best.

"She's been amazing in physics class," I tell Zahra, feeling awkward about standing and trying to decide if I should pull up a chair. "Practically answers the question before the teacher finishes asking it."

"Zenithin turns you into a machine," Z says, now watching a replay of the arrest video on her phone. "You feel brilliant and unstoppable. But it has a comedown from hell—no sleep, uncontrollable rage. Not my thing," she says with a shrug. "I'm too raged out already." She looks up at me at last and gives a half-smile.

I notice she's wearing eyelash extensions and feel a pang for how it used to be between us. We used to help each other glue them on for special events back during freshman year. Before I wrecked everything and lost her.

"Which reminds me . . . why are you here? Aren't you supposed to be at the power table with his highness Sir Suckwad?"

I look down at my crumpled lunch bag in my hands, suddenly losing my appetite. "I'm sorry, Z. That's what I came over here to tell you. I know this thing with Will doesn't make sense to you, but . . . but I miss you," I say.

She nods tentatively, her lips pressed into a thin line as if to say *I miss you, too.*

It's time, I decide suddenly. I'm telling her the truth about Will, the blackmail, my surgery, everything.

My hands shake as I pull a chair out to sit down with her, the prospect of finally confessing everything so close at hand. But just as I'm about to sit, I hear Will's voice beside me. "*There* you are. Come sit with us, babe."

He puts his hands on my shoulders and squeezes them, hard. It's all I can do not to scream.

"What about the student council?" I shrug his hands off me and turn to face him, even though I'd rather look anywhere else.

"It got postponed. The VP broke her leg skiing or something," Will says.

"That's too bad," I say in monotone. Inside, I'm crestfallen.

"So come on." He's getting impatient, looking over my shoulder to see who's watching us.

"I'm sitting here today." My eyes meet Zahra's. She looks disgusted and a little ill watching me and Will, like she just got a whiff of someone else's fart.

"Anthem, are we back together or not? Because if not, I'll just turn around and walk away. Maybe spend lunch in the computer lab, uploading some old movies . . ." Will chuckles a little, but his threat is anything but funny. Behind him, I see a few people watching us, Olive Ann Bang and Clementine Fitz among them, and the hairs on the back of my neck stand on end.

"Fine," I say icily. "I'm coming."

"Seriously, Anthem?" Zahra calls, shooting me an incredulous look.

"'Seriously, Anthem?'" Will cuts in, mocking Zahra. "You're choosing Will over me?" he continues, his voice high and girlish. His eyes bulge as he turns on Zahra. "Just sit here by yourself and enjoy your irrelevance, okay, Zahra? Nobody cares about your opinion."

"Don't talk to her like that," I say quietly, my face burning as more of Will's admirers turn to watch the fight. "Apologize, Will."

"Or you'll what? Break up with me?" Will laughs. "Sorry, babe, not worth the oxygen."

I stare miserably down at the floor, the black and white tiles smearing into gray. When I look up, Z's eyes meet mine, radiating shock and hurt.

"Wow, Anthem. Thanks for the support," Zahra says in a tight voice. "I'm done here anyway." She pushes her chair away from the table and walks past Will, slamming into his shoulder as she goes, and heads outside to the patio.

"Problem solved!" Will chirps. "Coming, *dear*?"

"I'll be right back," I mutter, then I take off after her.

I catch up with her on the patio and barely touch her shoulder, but she whirls around and shakes me off. "What?" she says tightly.

"Just give me two minutes," I say. "I'm sick about what happened at lunch. That was . . . beyond horrible. I'm so sorry."

"Apology not accepted. How can you be with such a prick?" She's whispering, conscious of kids at nearby tables watching us.

"I realize how it looks," I say in a low voice, grabbing her hand, the hand I first held in kindergarten, when we were paired as buddies on a field trip to the Bedlam Hall of Science. "Just bear with me and soon I'll exp—"

"I think I'm just about done waiting," Zahra snaps, wrenching her hand away like I'm poisonous. Her eyes swimming with hurt tears, she walks backward away from me. "Have fun, okay? I hope he's worth it."

Then she spins around and walks toward the courtyard.

I swallow a howl of frustration as I walk back to Will, my breath coming in short little puffs. Then I almost trip over an empty wrought-iron chair. "Damn it!" I mutter as I shove it out of my way. But I'm out of control and I push too hard. Way too hard, actually. The heavy chair flips and skitters ten feet, clattering off the edge of the patio and onto the half-dead grass that borders it. Everyone turns to stare at me, all lunchtime conversation ceased, all eyes on me.

"What?" I yell. "Haven't you ever seen a chair before?"

I move faster toward the cafeteria doors, my heart ricocheting around my chest like a pinball. Thick black clouds have blotted out the winter sun, and before I get back inside, the dark sky starts to spit fat drops of water. I stand still, fingering the heart pendant at my clavicle as my chest whirs, relieved to be fading back into the background as a dozen kids push past me, pandemonium unleashed as everyone tries to get out of the rain.

Now it's official, I think. *I've lost everything. Even my best friend.*

CHAPTER 27

"From the top," says Madame Petrovsky in her heavy accent, whipping her delicate arms overhead and sending her sheer black scarf floating to the polished wood floor in the process. *"Un, deux, trois, quatre!"* On Madame's count, the twelve of us level sixers take our places for the start of the crucial scene in *Giselle*, the part where Giselle returns to protect her lover, Duke Albrecht.

We dance the routine in silence, as we do most days. Madame believes that we should hear the music inside, take our cues from our body's muscle memory, not from the swells of the violins. All I hear is the *thump-thump* of our toe shoes when we land, the hushed symphony of our collective breath.

A few weeks ago, I was dancing the prima role of Giselle. But after all the rehearsals I've missed, I'm lucky to be in the performance at all. Somehow, I've managed to convince Madame that I can handle dancing in the corps de ballet even after my "sprained ankle" and my "flu," and now it's my job to get every move perfect so she doesn't change her mind. It helps that my new heart allows me to perform better than I ever have.

My first day back in rehearsal, I talked her into giving me a chance to dance the opening act with the other girls, and I managed to nail the routine. Madame gave me a strange look and nodded slowly, then shot me a tentative smile. "I don't know how you did it, Anthem. Beautiful work. You can be in the corps, but Constance will still dance the prima part." The old me would have been devastated to lose the role of Giselle, but all I felt was relief at the chance to return to the normalcy of ballet.

The performance is less than a month away, and rehearsal has left all of us with broken toenails and sore muscles. But my body recovers faster now.

"And pointe. And *pas de jambe*. And *tourne, revele, turne, releve*." Madame recites calmly as we do the group number, all twelve of us leaping and turning in unison, forming a circle that spins out into a line and back again. Blood thrums in my ears, and I feel my heart pumping from the exertion. My limbs are elastic and warm, and even though I returned to ballet only because my parents expected me to, for the past few rehearsal days I've been able to lose myself in the physical release that ballet has always given me. Ballet and my nights training with Ford are the only times I feel like the faintest shadow of my old self is still inside me, buried beneath all the layers of pain.

I grab hands with Nina Chase and Liberty Sewell as we circle up, vaulting ourselves onto our toes for the grande releve, then spinning away from the group in a series of fouettés, feeling airborne when I triple-pirouette into my next mark.

"Anthem, too fast, too high!" Madame looks at me quizzically after I land. "Stay with the group, please. No—what is the word?—pyrotechnics."

I nod and refocus on the mirror, hoping my reflection will help me match the speed and strength of my fellow dancers, reminding myself that just because my heart makes it possible to do things faster and jump higher doesn't mean I can allow myself to do them. At least not right now.

As I dance, hearing only breaths of exertion, gentle thuds of landing after a leap, and the muted tapping of my fellow dancers as we toe-step through the routine, my thoughts move to Zahra, then to Ford. We've sparred every night since I first pinned him to the floor, and each time I beat him easily. Last night, he brought in a cardboard dummy and a switchblade, and taught me how to throw a knife. The flicking motion of the wrist, the arm—it's not so different from ballet, really. I landed the knife in the center of the dummy after a few tries and then sparred with Ford, bringing him to the mat again without much trouble. Each time I beat him, he laughed. *You're a machine, Green!* he said, and high-fived me.

A machine with a machine heart, I think now as I land the final triple-pirouette with my feet within an inch of where I want them on the floor, satisfied that I'm able to mimic the biologically normal dancers in the room.

Just then, across the room, I hear the crunch of bone, followed by a loud scream. Constance Clamm crumples ungracefully to the floor and is clutching her right ankle in pain.

I join the rest of the girls in crowding around her, but Madame shoos us away and runs to her office to get an ice pack from her mini-fridge. "Another ankle," she mutters when she returns. "I cannot believe our misfortune."

"Anthem!" Madame's kohl-lined eyes land on me, and I know without a doubt what she's thinking. *No, no, no,* I want to say, widening my eyes and turning scarlet. *It's not fair. Pick any-one else. Anyone but me.* She motions me closer, then leans over and whispers in my ear.

"You are Giselle again. Take your old role back for now, and we shall see how Constance is doing."

"No!" Constance is crying, having figured out what's going on even as her ankle is swelling to twice its normal size. "I'll be fine tomorrow, I'm sure of it," she whimpers, pressing the ice pack gingerly against her damaged leg.

"Let's wait and see what the doctor says," Madame says consolingly. "For now, Anthem will reprise Giselle."

Constance looks at me miserably, and I can't help but share her misery. There was a time when all I wanted was this role, but that time has passed.

"It's all yours, as soon as you can do it again," I say, trying to be comforting. Constance looks glumly at the ground, nodding, but I can tell she doesn't believe me.

I stay after class to work on the solo, pulling on a pair of tattered sweats over my legs to stay warm now that the rest of the body heat has left the building. The character Giselle is a young girl with a weak heart, ironically. She falls in love with a man who is betrothed to a princess. They have a passionate love affair, and then Giselle dies. But her ghost cannot rest until she knows her lover, Duke Albrecht, is protected against those who want to kill him. *And Giselle protects him,* I say in my head, staring into the mirror. *And then her soul can rest.*

I run through the sequence of the first and second solos a few times each, taking care not to leap too high or spin too fast, modulating my speed to what I used to be able to do. It takes focus not to go too fast.

But my heart revs inside my ribs like an engine thrown into gear, encouraging me to go faster, faster. I stop dancing and look around me. The sun went down over the river long ago, and a starless, foggy night has blanketed the studio in darkness. Madame has gone home. Nobody's here to see me.

I think of the spin kicks I've been practicing with Ford. The punches and hits, the way he's taught me to throw a knife. And then I break out of the routine from *Giselle* and start pirouetting across the room, first doubles, then triples, faster, faster, my heart whirring, until my feet seem to barely touch the floor. I look in the mirror, eyes wide—and see that I'm actually *spinning in the air*. Two, three inches above the floor, hovering in one spot as I spin and spin. A second later, the impossibility of it hits my brain, and I come crashing down, landing ungracefully on my rear end, feet splayed out in front of me.

I shake my head at the mirror.

"No way," I say out loud. "No way is this happening."

"You read my mind," a voice says behind me. In the mirror, I see Ford step out of the shadows at the edge of the room. His sneakers squeak on the polished floor.

"What are you doing here?" I turn around to face him, alarmed. "Is everything okay?"

"Can't a guy sneak into a ballet studio once in a while just because?" Then, more quietly: "I wanted to tell you I can't practice tonight. Jax needs some stuff delivered."

"You could have texted."

"Sometimes I run past here, and when the light was on I figured I'd take a peek. I'm glad I came."

"How long were you watching?"

"Long enough to see how amazing you are." He shakes his head, a half-smile lingering on his face. "Your dancing, I mean," he corrects himself, and I think I see him blush a little.

"Thanks." My face suddenly feels like it's on fire, too, like he's caught me doing something wrong. Which, in a way, he has. It *is* wrong—physically impossible. I walk over to the barre and grab a towel, though there's no sweat on my brow to wipe off. I go through the motions anyway.

"Looks like the transplant gave you a little more than just the ability to run fast and kick my ass in the ring," Ford says gently, joining me near the barre.

"I don't know. Maybe." My eyes meet his in the mirror before I look away. "That's the first time I realized I could . . . do that."

"I think the word for that is *flying*," Ford says, throwing his leg over the bar and mimicking a ballet dancer stretching, awkwardly bending toward his leg and putting his hand over his head and bending until he almost falls over. "It's amazing, Green. Embrace it."

"Whatever," I whisper. "Just one more talent for the freak show."

"You know, they used to say he could fly."

"Who?"

"The Hope." Ford looks at me like I'm an idiot. "Don't tell me you never heard the crazy stories about him."

"Not really," I admit. What is it with South Side boys and the Hope? "But I definitely can't fly. And I'm nothing like the Hope. More like hope*less*."

"You know, you sell yourself short, Green," Ford says, switching legs. "I don't know anything about ballet, but it looks like you're pretty good at that, too."

My eyes prickle with tears for a second. "I used to be really serious about it," I say. "My whole life was kind of geared toward becoming a professional ballet dancer."

"Well, it shows."

"But now . . . it all seems so unimportant." I look down at my feet, at the calluses and bunions and broken toenails from years of ballet. "I mean, I'd trade any talent I have in a second if it meant Gavin was still alive."

"Don't say that." Ford finally takes his leg off the barre and moves closer to me. "Don't give up everything you've worked for. Don't be so willing to trade it away." He pauses, choosing his words carefully. "Take it from me, giving up on something that big isn't . . . it's not a fun road to walk down."

I study his face, unsure if I should push him to tell me more. "You mean you gave up on boxing?"

"Something like that," he says. "But that's a story for another time. Listen, Green. About Gavin . . . Maybe it's time to think about a plan."

"A plan?"

"Finding them." Ford looks at me in the mirror, his eyes serious. "Isn't that why you've been working so hard in the ring? So you can bring them to justice?"

Justice. I blanch at the word. "I don't even know if I believe in justice."

"Well, I didn't believe people could fly until tonight." Ford smiles. "Silly me."

I grimace. "I can't *fly*, Ford."

"Really? It kind of looked like you could." He raises one thick eyebrow. "Want to try again, just to find out? Five bucks says you can stay in the air for thirty seconds."

"Fine," I mutter. I don't want to admit how curious I am to see if I can do it again. "But I want it on record that this is stupid."

"Totally stupid. Making a note of it for the record." Ford pantomimes writing it down on his hand. Then he looks at me expectantly. I make a sound of annoyance in the back of my throat, but he just waits placidly for me to get to it.

"Okay, okay." I square my shoulders and move into fifth position, lifting my arms above my head. Then I begin the sequence.

I repeat the same sequence of steps, the same pirouettes. I use him as a spotter, my eyes landing on his face with every twirl. As I move, I feel my body rising. My toes stop pushing off the floor and instead push off the air.

I'm up. Launched. Spinning in the air. *Flying*.

Ford pushes a button on his phone and looks up at me, pumps his fist in the air, silently mouthing what looks like *wooohooo*.

And just like last time, the minute the fact of what I'm doing fully hits my conscious mind, I get scared and crash to the floor, this time landing flat on my back. "Ow!"

"Oh my God," he says, his eyes shining. "Green! That was twenty-two seconds!" I sit up, leaning over to stretch out my calves, my chest thrumming like a jet engine.

"Think you can do it without spinning?" Ford asks. He circles me, bending down twice to squeeze my arm muscles. I wrap my arms around myself, feeling embarrassed, then mad at myself for being embarrassed. It's just Ford.

"Guess I may as well try," I say. I stand up and move to the corner of the room, the thumping of my heart returning almost back to normal, in that I can only hear it if I really concentrate. When I reach the corner, I turn around, take a big breath in, and start to run. After six or seven strides, I'm in the center of the studio, and I push my arms back hard as I leap upward and out, pushing my right leg out behind me as I jump into the air.

And then I'm airborne, my heart chopping like the blades of a propeller.

I can see in the mirror that I'm much higher up than I should be—closer to the ceiling than the floor—and I stay there longer than I should, moving slowly forward and down. I'm in the air maybe three or four times as long as gravity should allow.

Instead of looking in the mirror at myself, I look at Ford, in front of me in the room. *Don't think about it,* I tell myself. If I think too hard about what I'm doing, I'll fall again.

When I land this time, it's graceful and quiet and clean. I hit the floor gently, bouncing forward once before I'm steady on my toes. My heart is quiet now, humming nicely, like I'm doing exactly what it wants. I put my hand over it, for the first time feeling not just scared of what I can do, but instead sort of . . . proud.

I grin at Ford. "That was pretty cool, right?"

"Mega." Ford shakes his head. "Just . . . yeah. Incredible." He turns away, seeming nervous all of a sudden. Which makes me nervous. Suddenly I'm acutely aware that it's just the two of us, alone together. Standing close. Both of us not sure what to say next.

To my relief, Ford breaks the silence.

"Now tell me, do you think I have a future as a ballet dancer?" He executes a few sloppy twirls, his arms splayed crazily out at his side, the hood of his sweatshirt flying out behind him.

"Anything's possible." I grin, relieved by his silliness. "If you promise to work really hard, I can maybe teach you how to do a plié. Here, grab on to the barre."

"This is gonna come in so handy," Ford jokes, "when dudes

get up in my face in the Lowlands."

"You have no idea." I smile. "Ballet can be very intimidating, if used correctly. Now, straighten up." I put one hand on his lower back and the other on his collarbone, attempting to undo his slouched posture.

"Yes, ma'am."

When I catch a glimpse of my face in the mirror, my eyes are a deeper green again, the same bright emerald shade they turned those first few days after Jax implanted the heart inside me. *Ford is right,* I think. It's time to figure out how to find Rosie.

CHAPTER 28

"You're here!" Jax cries when she finds me and Ford on her doorstep later that night, just after 1:00 A.M. She claps her chapped hands together in front of her like a kid about to open a pile of birthday presents, then engulfs me in a tight hug. "I'm so glad you're all right. I knew you would be. Your speed was *so* impressive the day you ran away. You reminded me of Rat-tat-tat, one of my fastest transplant patients."

"Yeah, sorry about that," I mumble, extracting myself from her embrace and ignoring the comparison she's just made between me and a rat. "I'm pretty fast, I guess."

"And you've been careful to keep moving, to keep eating?"

"I've woken up with blue fingers and lips a couple of times, but yeah, eating seems to keep it at bay."

"Good, good, good," Jax murmurs as she swipes a clipboard from her desk and pulls a pair of bent reading glasses from the pocket of her T-shirt—silkscreened with the periodic table and the words SCIENTISTS DO IT PERIODICALLY—and puts them on. "Patient suffers occasional mechanical slowdown, mitigated by . . . what kind of food?"

"Sugar," I confess. "I never used to eat sweets. But now—"

"You can't get enough of them. A natural side effect. Hummingbirds love nectar, after all," Jax says, trailing off as she finishes her notes on the clipboard, her handwriting a crazy, hieroglyphic scrawl. At last, she shoves her pen into the mass of silver curls piled atop her head. "Anyway, what brings you back to the lab?" She fastens a blood pressure meter onto my arm and pumps the ball until it cuts off my circulation. "Don't mind me, just gathering data. You understand, of course."

"Of course," I say, looking to Ford for help, mouthing *Let's focus* and hoping he can read my lips.

"Speaking of data," Ford says, taking my cue, "I was telling Anthem about the time you hacked into the police datacluster."

"Ah." Jax blushes. "Anthem, I hope you don't think I'm a horrible person. I just like to peek at my file every few weeks, to make sure the trail is still cold."

I shake my head. Hacking into my chest is a thousand times more horrible than a little database exploration, but I keep that thought to myself. "We're looking for someone—"

"Ford's filled me in about the kidnappers, actually," Jax says, undoing the blood pressure cuff and sliding it off my arm. "Sounds like trouble."

"Probably, yeah," I say, staring at the dirty floor. Does this mean she won't help me?

"Don't look so glum, Anthem. Of course I'll help. You're my greatest achievement—how could I say no to you?" Jax grins, then heads toward a wall of file cabinets.

"What is she doing?" I ask Ford. Jax's monkey has begun to screech in his cage, beating his paws against his white tuft of chest hair, baring his sharp little teeth.

"Shut your piehole, Mildred," Ford calls to the monkey, shrugging at my question.

"Mildred?" I snort. "That beast is called Mildred?"

"Named her after my aunt," Jax calls, slamming a file drawer shut and opening two more. The back of her lab coat says BEDLAM GENERAL on it, and I wonder again what she must have done to end up here, with tape on her glasses, leaky pipes, terrible heat, and a rabid monkey. "A real nut job. My aunt, not the monkey, ha-ha." Her nervous laughter echoes in the big room. The monkey howls.

"She's a little paranoid about being traced," Ford whispers. "Gotta be ten different computers and a thousand wires in those drawers."

Soon the three of us are crowded around Jax's laptop, looking at yellow letters on a black screen, full descriptions of perps, in many cases with photographs, either taken by surveillance cameras or mug shots, in the upper right-hand corner of the screen. Jax has hacked into the police database, for what I'm guessing is not the first time this week.

"Okay, let's narrow it to Syndicate," Jax mutters. "Of course, that's nearly everyone these days. . . ."

Indeed: 4,263 results. I sit back on the rolling stool Jax gave me. "This isn't going to help us," I say to Ford.

"Female, Jax. Narrow the search by gender," Ford suggests.

"Aha." Jax's silver curls bob up and down as she bounces on her chair. "Only three hundred fourteen!"

"Can you search by age? She's in her early twenties," I say. "And blond."

Almost instantly, a blurry picture captured by a surveillance camera appears, the date from a year and a half ago in one corner, someone who could be Rosie with shorter, spikier blond hair. A half-smile visible in the blurred pixels that make up her deceptively sweet mouth. Standing next to a taller figure, brunette, face obscured because of the angle of his head. I get chills when I notice what's in the corner of the frame. On the linoleum floor, a kid, lying facedown, hands over his head. My heart breaks when I see he's young enough to have mittens clipped to his jacket. They dangle from his cuffs, shielding his face. A milk carton is on its side next to him in a puddle of milk.

And there she is, *smiling*.

ROSE THORNE: FEMALE, BLOND, 5'4", 120 lbs., tattoo on right shoulder

ALIASES: KATRINA KINICKIE
SHADRA BLACK
GWENDOLYN GOODWIN

CHARGES: Assault, petty theft, grand larceny, grand theft, conspiracy, drug trafficking, accessory to murder. APPREHENDED SPEEDING FROM CRIME SCENE (TEDDY'S ONE STOP SHOPPING, Loc. SOUTHEAST EXURBIA) IN YELLOW LANDPUSHER, LIC. SHOO4512

ARRESTS: 1

CONVICTIONS: 0

PLEA BARGAIN: Plaintiff currently active in the field as Police Informant #5611.

I point to the last section of the screen and elbow Ford. "Does this mean she's working with the police?"

Ford shrugs. "Guess so. Wonder how they'd feel to know their informant killed someone."

I shudder involuntarily, then turn back to the screen. If I deliver an informant to the police, would they just let her go?

ACCOMPLICES AND ASSOCIATES:

Smith Macoumb—WANTED: grand theft, conspiracy, assault

Karl Small—WANTED: assault w/ deadly weapon, drug trafficking

Emmett Cask—WANTED: conspiracy, larceny, assault w/ deadly weapon

Maximillian and Augustus Luz—WANTED: assault, drug trafficking, conspiracy

Jessa Scorpio—WANTED: prostitution, human trafficking, conspiracy, assault

We all fall silent as we read. The only sound in the room is the monkey scraping a metal spoon along the bars of its cage.

Her hair is a lot shorter and more of a golden blond than her current platinum, but the bright red lips, the wide cheekbones, even the way she stands—straight and rigid, commanding much more space than her five-foot-four frame would suggest—are the same. And the name, Rose Thorne, cannot be a coincidence. I flash on the yellow SUV parked outside Dimitri's on the Water.

"It's her," I whisper. "The car and the name match. I'm sure of it."

"This tells us nothing, though," Ford says glumly. "I thought we'd get an address. . . ."

"Well, you've got a good clue right here. All you need to do now," Jax says, "is find the car. How hard could it be?"

"Says the person who hasn't been outside in three years," Ford snorts.

But my heart flutters with adrenaline, picturing Rosie and her goons—her *accomplices and associates*—driving around the city in that gas-guzzling tank of a car, looking for people to rob, kidnap, exploit, and harm. How many more robberies and murders and senseless acts of violence would vanish from the world if only she and her crew were stopped?

I grab Jax's mouse and zoom in on Rosie's face. That smile. The expression of someone who gets away with everything, who thinks it's just so easy to destroy people and walk away.

I need to wipe that smile off her face.

"I'll think of something," I say to nobody in particular. I stand up abruptly and start to pace, racking my brain for the best way to find and track the car.

This isn't just about Gavin anymore. It's about everyone. All the people in this city who are trying to get by, trying to live their lives. Who don't deserve to go out and buy milk and come home with an unshakable case of Bedhead and a lifetime of flinching and cowering and fear.

I grab a notepad from Jax's desk—it says *Vivirax: Because We All Deserve Inner Peace* across the top—and write down the names:

Smith Macoumb
Karl Small
Emmett Cask

Maximillian Luz
Augustus Luz
Jessa Scorpio
Rose Thorne

Then I write down the plate and model of the yellow LandPusher.

CHAPTER 29

The next night is one of the few lately where my parents beat me home. In the dining room, a Bach cantata tinkles out of the built-in speakers, and my parents are seated at the table eating Cornish game hens. An electrical storm has erupted outside the glass walls, and flashes of lightning crackle in the purple night.

"We started," Helene says with a smile when I walk in, a forkful of pale meat paused in midair. "We were famished. It was back-to-back meetings all day, and we have drinks at the police commissioner's later tonight. Hope you don't mind, darling."

"Of course not," I say. "It's nice to see you guys."

"There she is, the prima!" Harris booms. "It's good to lay eyes on you so healthy and strong, kitten. We're like ships in the night lately."

I take my seat at the long rosewood table, where a candelabra with six lit candles casts a pretty glow.

"I know. With ballet and everything, I've just been so busy, and you guys are so swamped with the stadium . . ." I trail off aimlessly as Lily comes in with a plate of Cornish game hen for me, too, a huge cone of wild rice alongside it. She's noticed my new eating habits and has adjusted accordingly by piling on the starches, but the sight of the miniature chicken—legs tied up with cooking string and rosemary sticking out of the cavity where its guts once were—makes me a bit queasy. "Thanks, Lily."

"My pleasure," Lily says, shooting me a smile before she darts back into the kitchen to clean up for the night and head home.

"All caught up on your schoolwork?" Harris asks, plucking the leg bones from the tiny chicken carcass on his plate and sucking the meat off them. I look away, my stomach dropping at the sight.

"Yeah, just one research paper in Propaganda and Politics to go," I say, forcing myself to dig in to the rice. "After that, I'm fully caught up."

"And how are things with Will?" my mother chirps, taking a sip of chardonnay.

"Why does that matter?" I ask quietly. A millisecond later, I regret it. Why can't I just say *Super! Fantastic!* and leave it at that?

"Just making conversation." A flash of emotion—irritation, anger, hurt?—lights up her eyes for a second, and I watch her compose her face back to its neutral mask.

"Your mother is being supportive, is all." Harris shoots me the Look. The one that says *Don't upset your mother, you know how she is.* "We just happen to think Will is a wonderful young man."

A wonderful young sociopath, I think. Looking from my mother to my father, I'm suddenly furious. All they care about is what my relationship with Will means for *them*. A Fleet-Hansen union would lead to the most advantageous business arrangement since aspiring mayor Manny Marks married Belinda Bullett, then the daughter of the chief of police, Branford Bullett Jr.

"Sorry to disappoint you," I say icily, "but I wouldn't count on Will and me being together forever."

"Darling, we just want what's best for you," Helene murmurs, her voice careful. "Nobody is talking about *forever*." She places her manicured hands flat on the rosewood dining table, on either side of her place mat, and stares down at her half-eaten little hen.

"Fine," I say tightly. A bolt of lightning slices through the sky like a knife, and for a half-second we all turn a sickly shade of blue-white. "Sorry."

My father picks up the evening edition of the *Daily Dilemma* from the chair next to where he sits and starts reading.

"Stop me," Harris says through a mouthful of chicken. "I keep reading it over and over. Take it, Leenie."

My mother folds the paper and puts it next to her plate.

CONCERNS OVER FLEET STADIUM PLANS ROCK THE WATERFRONT. I can read the headline upside down.

Helene rolls her eyes. "Oh dear. More protests?"

I grab the paper and open it up to see a picture of a few hundred people with picket signs that say SCHOOLS NOT STADIUMS and RECOVER DON'T RAZE.

"South Siders." He settles back against his chair and tosses a brocade cloth napkin over the bones on his plate. "Never happy with what they're given, these people."

"What exactly have they been given?" I ask, immediately regretting it.

I lock eyes with my father, and something silently passes between us. A challenge.

"Well, Anthem, a new stadium, for one. And jobs." His nostrils flare white.

I nod, staring down at the dining room table, the polished rosewood shiny enough to reflect the red blur of my hair. Then I grab the paper and read the article. "It says here that they don't want their houses razed to make room for it."

"Trust, me, kitten. They'll be a lot better off in the low-income apartment complexes we're building," my father snorts. "All new appliances, no mildew, no graffiti. The best security. Protection from the criminal element. All that, and their beloved KillBall at the stadium! They should be thanking me."

"Looks like they're not in a thankful mood," I murmur, looking more closely at the photo in the paper. Hundreds of people standing with banners waved, arms linked in protest, blocking a line of cranes with wrecking balls dangling from them. On one side of the picture, toward the back, a cluster of five older people are making this funny hand gesture, their fingers crossed and pressed to their chests, level with their hearts.

"What are these people doing with their hands?" I ask, jabbing my finger toward the old people.

"Oh, nothing. That's from before your time." My mother sighs. "Back when the Hope made everyone on the South Side go insane."

The Hope. I think back to Ford in the studio the other night. *They used to say he could fly.* I think of Gavin on our first date, insinuating that the Hope was killed in some sort of planned conspiracy.

"But what does it mean?" I scrutinize the photo. The people with their crossed fingers over their hearts look right at the camera, their expressions calm.

"I suppose it was meant to evoke a victory sign combined with crossing one's fingers for luck," my mother says. "For a while, it was everywhere. That sign, and this chant they were always doing."

"'We will rise,'" Harris says softly, looking up at both of us, his mouth curled into a sad half-smile. Just then there's a crack of thunder. "Regina painted it on her wall, remember, Leenie?"

I open my mouth, then shut it. *Regina?* The perfect blonde in the family photos was a populist? Why would she have cared in the least about the Hope and his movement? I blink. Suddenly I see those exact words inked on the bartender's wrist from the other night.

My mother's gray eyes flash as she pushes her chair away from the table and throws her napkin down on her plate. "Of course I remember."

She gets up and retreats into her bedroom, and just like that, the air in the cupid-ceilinged dining room has gone sour.

My stomach flips as Harris takes a sip from his wineglass and shoots me another version of the Look. This one comes every time one of us mentions Regina. The *Don't pour salt on the wound* look. I raise my eyebrows and shrug, silently reminding him that he's the one who brought up the dead daughter, not me.

Another violent crack of thunder makes us both jump. "I'll take that," he mutters. He grabs the newspaper out of my hands and leaves through the room's other entrance, avoiding my mother. Two minutes later, I hear his office door slam.

I try to imagine my dead sister painting a South Side slogan onto her wall. Was Regina less sheltered from the city than I was? Did my parents humor her when she did it, or was she punished, forced to paint over it immediately? I sit blinking in the empty room, the soft classical music not working to calm my whirling mind. Then I get up and head toward the kitchen to dump my untouched Cornish hen in the trash.

When I reach the kitchen, I'm surprised to see Serge standing at the marble countertop and peeling a tangerine, which looks tiny in his enormous hands.

We trade nervous smiles. I focus my hearing to listen for footsteps coming toward us. Nothing. Lily has gone home for the evening, and my mother is probably popping a couple of Viviraxes in her dressing room to get ready for that police fundraiser they're going to.

"I understand the performance is coming up." Serge is being careful, speaking to me as if we are as we always were—cordial, affectionate, but not intimately involved in each other's daily routine.

I nod. "Just a couple more weeks."

"Are you prepared?"

I shrug. "Getting stronger every day." Which is actually true, I realize. Physically at least, I'm stronger than I've ever been.

Serge puts a hand on top of my head and looks intently into my eyes. What he says next is so quiet it's barely a whisper. "I'd like to help you with your search," he says.

I shoot him a look of surprise. We had discussed what I learned from Jax's database last night in the car, but I thought it was just to make conversation.

"You mean finding . . . those people?" I whisper back.

I stare up at him. His face is calm as he nods almost imperceptibly. I think about his past, working as security for warlords, CEOs, army generals. If anyone is resourceful and knows how to squeeze information out of the city, it's Serge.

"Okay. Thank you." I go to a drawer near the telephone and grab a piece of paper and a pen and write down *Yellow LandPusher. License plate SHOO4512.*

Serge tucks the scrap of paper into his breast pocket. "Consider it done."

I nod, speechless. Amazed that he's in favor of this and that he's willing to help. "Thank you, Serge."

"I'll be in touch." Satisfied, he moves toward the staircase to the lower floor, heading for my father's office.

And then I'm alone in the kitchen with a sink full of dishes. I turn the water in the sink as hot as I can bear it, and stand at the sink methodically sponging the plates, wondering if tonight is the night I get Rosie Thorne off the streets.

CHAPTER 30

Two hours later, my phone buzzes with a text from Serge.

4 Larkspur Lane
(be safe)

This is it. I try not to let my hands shake as I put my phone down and head to my closet. I dress slowly, in a black hooded parka and black jeans, taking care to tuck my hair up into a black beanie. I tell myself not to think too hard about what it will mean to catch up with the LandPusher.

Before I head out, I send a quick text to Ford:

Sorry, 2 tired 2 train 2nite. Gonna go 2 bed early.

I arrange some pillows convincingly in my bed and close my door, then take the service elevator—the only one with no cameras inside it—down to the parking garage and exit through a back door marked MAINTENANCE. As I'm jumping the low back fence that separates Fleet Tower from the building next door, my phone buzzes with a reply.

OK. Nite, Green.

I feel a pang of guilt. The risks I'm about to take are exactly why I don't want to involve Ford. The first time I confronted the kidnappers, Serge was attacked. The second time, Gavin was killed. I couldn't live with myself if something happened to Ford, too. Until he can outrun bullets, I need to do this alone.

I trace the blue dot on the glowing map on my phone to a location in the southeast quadrant of the city, and then I run hard and fast over the Bridge of Forgetting.

My lungs burn, but my feet hardly touch the pavement anymore.

I'm getting faster.

The metalwork of the bridge whizzes by like I'm seeing it from a train window, a blurred black streak. Here and there a car drives past me, but for the most part the streets are quiet in this part of town, and evidence of the Syndicate is less pronounced than elsewhere in the south. Brick row houses and austere apartment buildings line the blocks, their bald hedges neatly trimmed, for the most part. I see a few TVs still on in living rooms, a few people staying up late, but mostly it's quiet, and the air smells like burnt leaves. I stop on a silent street corner and pull out my phone again, then slow to a jog as the map in my phone tells me I'm closing in on the location Serge sent me.

I come to a cul-de-sac, which makes me nervous because there's only one way out. At the end of it sits a wide, squat elementary school. Jackson Jones Elementary. I think back to tenth-grade history and my oral report on Jackson Jones. He was mayor when the Hope was cleaning up the city—until the

Hope vanished and the mayor was killed by a Molotov cocktail thrown through his office window. That was the last time anyone got close to the mayor's office without a full body scan, the last time police were encouraged not to use excessive force. The Jackson Jones laws gave the police a lot more leeway in dealing with crime. When I gave the oral report, I was pretty enthusiastic about the Jackson Jones laws. But now I wonder, *What have they actually done?* The crime ring in Bedlam is larger than ever.

I huff the cold air and walk past a naked flagpole toward the school, where the lights are dimmed but not off. There are no cars in the parking lot in front, so I skirt the edge of the building, ducking low under the bottoms of the windows, and peer around the wide building to the back.

Jackpot. I don't know how he did it, but Serge came through. In front of me is the yellow LandPusher.

I dive into a clump of bushes and wait, keeping my eyes trained on the car. Nobody's inside it. The only movement is a rat scurrying alongside the edge of the building. After a few minutes spent crouched in the bushes, I find the courage to try the double doors of the school, pressing on the door's handle and slowly inching my way inside, biting the sides of my cheeks so that my teeth won't chatter. Inside, it's an ordinary elementary school hallway—dimmed for the evening, kind of run-down, linoleum floors, bulletin boards outside each classroom displaying the work of students. I'm looking at a cluster of sea life collages when I hear glass shattering and a male voice yell, "That's a hundred bucks you just lost us!"

My heart thrums with fear, but I move forward, my head tilted toward the sound. At the end of the hall, bright light spills from an open door. I keep close to the wall, knowing that if the kidnappers choose this moment to step out of the classroom, the shadows will probably not be enough to hide me. My arms are tensed, my body ready to run at any moment.

When I reach the open classroom door, I smell formaldehyde. It reminds me of Hades, of the wall in the coffee shop offering a menu of kidneys and colons. I can hear voices, both male, and I'm certain one of them is Smitty—his dopey slur is unmistakable. It's like he keeps rocks in his mouth. "We taking all of it?" Smitty asks.

"Whatever they got," another guy says. From the volume of their voices, I'm pretty sure they're in the back of the room. I don't dare breathe as I peek inside.

There are several rows of long black lab tables surrounded by stools. A pull-down periodic table flapping in the front of the room. A skeleton standing at attention in one corner. A table against the wall contains metal pans with something gray and slimy in them. Above it hangs a sign—DO NOT DISTURB—DISSECTIONS IN PROGRESS—with a little smiley face beneath the words.

On the front-most table are large beakers, Bunsen burners heaped in a pile, plastic bottles of different-colored solutions, and a few jars filled with powders, one a light blue, the other a light green shade. And a door marked EQUIPMENT, half-open.

I slip inside the room and duck behind one of the lab tables, but before I'm all the way down, one of them has seen me. This one's young, short and stocky with thick black hair, possibly one of the original masked kidnapping crew.

"Freeze," he says, his gun already out. In the hand not holding the gun, he's got a large beaker and a canister of light blue powder tucked under his arm. *Move*, I tell myself. *You're faster than he is.* In a microsecond I've reached the dissection station, where formaldehyde frogs' bulging eyes seem to stare up at me. And as I'd hoped, a few scalpels have been left in their pans.

There's no time to think. He's yelling, but all I hear is a drum-beat of adrenaline. I turn around just as he cocks the gun, the bullet falling into its chamber with a click, loud enough to reach me. I flick my eyes from the short one to Smitty, who has lum-bered out, and then a puff of air escapes my nostrils as I flick my wrist, releasing the scalpel into the air.

Time seems to slow down as the scalpel cartwheels through the room. It makes contact with the short guy's wrist, and his gun fires before he drops it and it clatters to the floor. For a moment I have no idea what's going on except that Smitty is bent over, howling.

I grab a microscope off the dissection table with both hands and charge toward them. The short one clutches his hand, bright red blood pouring from it, smeared all over the linoleum floor, and Smitty, dumb ox that he is, is whimpering and hold-ing his foot. I hesitate for a half-second, then, as if putting a half-dead bird out of its misery, I shut my eyes and slam the heavy base of the microscope down on the short one's head.

He's out cold but breathing. I find Smitty's gun beneath a roll of fat around his belt and pull it free, placing it carefully on the far table. His foot is bleeding all over the place. There's a bullet hole in the tip of his leather boot. Smitty whimpers like a dog as I stand over him. "Don't," he says. "Please don't kill me."

I race to the supply closet and spot a length of rope. Then I remain silent as I tie them both to the radiator. I stand over Smitty.

"Sorry he shot you," I say.

Smitty looks up at me, then away. "Yeah, I bet you are," he mutters.

"Drugs or organs?" I ask, kicking him a little in his ample

thigh when he doesn't answer. His head lolls on his chest, swiveling from right to left as he moans and clutches his foot. "Answer me, Macoumb!"

"We got a guy we sell them to," he manages. "We don't ask any questions."

Small-timers, I realize. Smitty and this other goon are low on the food chain, a minuscule part of the organism that is the Syndicate. I don't know how high up Rosie is, but I intend to find out.

"Is that Karl Small?"

He nods.

"Where is she?" I ask next.

"She moves around." He waves his flabby arm. "She don't tell me when she goes to take a piss or nothing."

A hysterical, onion-scented moan erupts from his huge head. "You gotta move on from this," he says, his eyes meeting mine. "You're gonna get yourself killed. Nobody wants to kill a little girl like you, but you're giving us no choice."

"You killed me already," I say, my voice thick. "This is just my ghost."

"It's not her you want. She's just doing what the Boss told her to."

I stare down at him dumbly. "What boss?"

"The Boss . . ." he trails off, the rest of his sentence unintelligible, his eyes unfocused. I need to call him an ambulance.

I check the restraints, making sure the rope is looped around the radiator enough times and that there's no chance he'll be able to cut or bite through it before the police come. On my way out, I use the hem of my shirt to wipe every surface I think I may have touched, including the scalpel and both of the guns. Then I use a lab apron to put both guns on the table with the chemicals, gently depositing the scalpel inside a thin glass beaker, like a single bloom in a vase.

When I'm outside and breathing the night air again, I force my shaking hands to punch the numbers on my phone, to call the number advertised on every billboard in Bedlam. KEEP BEDLAM LAWFUL: 999-TIPS.

"I'd like to report a robbery in progress at Jackson Jones Elementary," I say, my voice shaking. Just before I hang up, Serge pulls up in the Seraph. I run toward him, my whole body flooded with relief. "Go," I say. "We need to disappear fast."

Serge nods. "Buckle up. I thought you might need assistance." Then the car lurches forward faster than I knew it could.

By the time the wail of sirens pierces the silent net of the black sky, we're already twenty blocks away, approaching the bridge.

I am a phantom who was never there.

CHAPTER 31

The next day, I'm up early enough to grab the *Daily Dilemma* before my father does. Smith Macoumb and Karl Small are front-page news. I read about them with shaking hands, suddenly sure they'll reveal who caught them and tied them up.

> The two are each wanted on several counts of conspiracy, theft, assault, drug trafficking, and larceny.
>
> Police Chief Bullett said in a statement, "Whoever gift-wrapped these two criminals after catching them in the act of stealing from the elementary school, please make yourself known so we can thank you."

I look up from the paper and stare at the fleur-de-lis pattern on the wall opposite me in the hallway. They didn't mention anything about me or what I look like. Maybe they don't want the police to know about me because they hope to retaliate.

I fold up the paper and leave it on the ground in front of the apartment door exactly as I found it, so my father won't notice anything out of the ordinary. I have to be more careful. And I have to go after the others before they come after me.

I head to my room, where I send Serge a text:

I have a few more names. Can you help me track them down?

Then I take out my list from a metal lockbox under my bed and cross off the first two names.

~~Smith Macoumb~~

~~Karl Small~~

At midnight, I take the service elevator down to the parking garage and get into Serge's Motoko.

I sneak a look at him, but his profile is as calm and unflappable as always. "Did you see the paper?"

He nods, a trace of a smile tugging at his mouth.

"What if one of them tells the police who I am? The whole group of them must know I'm the one who turned in Smitty and Karl Small."

"They won't. The Syndicate has a code. They tell the police nothing. And in your case, if they tell the police, you'll implicate them in the murder of the boy. That crime is far worse than what they are wanted for."

I nod, mulling it over as Serge drives the Motoko over the Crime Line on the Bridge of Peace.

We drive for close to an hour through the South Side until we get to the PharmConn plant out on factory row. Factory row is a string of hulking buildings, black with soot, ringing the southern edge of the South Side. Several of them are still operational: the electricity plant, the waste conversion center, the scrap metal yard, the Buzz Beer distillery. Above them looms the nuclear power plant, two round domes with red lights on top. I've been looking at these buildings, their smokestacks belching blue-white steam or yellow smoke, from my bedroom window since I was little.

We pull up alongside the giant PharmConn complex, wrapped in a twelve-foot-high, impenetrable-looking white brick wall. Every few minutes, the deafening *thwunk-thwunk-thwunk* of PharmConn's security helicopter fills the air as it makes its rounds, aiming its searchlight in a circular pattern around the streets. Serge pulls the Motoko up across the street from a door in the white PharmConn security wall. "Every week, Maximillian and Augustus Luz are dispatched here to buy pills from a few of the security guards who steal them during their shifts. They then sell them on the black market."

"How do you know this, Serge?" I duck low in the passenger seat as the PharmConn security searchlight swoops over the car and recedes.

"Contacts," Serge says. "Acquaintances. Friends in low places." He leaves it at that, and I don't push him further. I get out of the Motoko and shut the door as softly as I can, walking back toward the shadows across the street from the gate.

Sure enough, at 1:00 A.M., two people dressed like medics slip out of the side gate carrying duffel bags that say BEDLAM GENERAL. I recognize their slight builds and matching faces as Max and August Luz. I wait until the PharmConn spotlight does another sweep across the block. I know that when the sweep is done, I have about three minutes before it sweeps here again.

I get a running start and scale the wall with two grand jetés, landing lightly on one foot. They don't see me coming.

By the time they're aware of me, one of them is on the ground and I'm tying his hands to his ankles behind his back. The other one—his identical twin, it turns out—charges at me, but thanks to the left hook combination Ford taught me, it takes me less than thirty seconds to land enough blows so that he's flat out on the ground, curled up, grunting, "Enough, enough!"

I tie him to his brother and leave the duffel bag like a gift right next to them, knowing that the sweep is coming again in less than a minute.

"Where is she?" I ask.

"Who?" they ask simultaneously.

"Rose Thorne."

"Why should we tell you?" one says.

"Because if you don't, I'll put your brother in the hospital." To make him think I mean it, I grab his brother by the collar of his coat and lift, raising both of them, tied together as they are, a foot off the ground.

The one I'm holding up whimpers, his eyes saucers full of fear. I've already given him a bloody nose and a fat lip tonight.

"There's a place called Double X. Off Bergamot," he says.

Just then the searchlight starts to travel back toward us. I drop them both to the ground and take off, and in an instant, I'm back in Serge's car, dialing 999-TIPS. I pull my list from my pocket and grab a pen from Serge's dashboard to cross off two more names.

~~Maximillian Luz~~
~~Augustus Luz~~

We get to the Double X in fifteen minutes. It's an almost pitch-black bar filled with Syndicate women. I don't see any men the entire hour and a half I'm there nursing a Sparkle cola.

I keep my eyes trained on the door, but Rosie never makes an appearance.

I'm about to leave when I spot the tall, thin woman with

the long purple hair. Jessa Scorpio. She stands near a curtain in the back of the room, wearing five-inch platform boots, a skirt the size of a napkin, and a black lace tank top with an exaggerated collar. On her head is a velvet top hat. A crowd of women quickly gathers around her, and she passes out small neon-pink glass vials of powder to them all. They each hand her a wad of bills and move away, unscrewing their vials and rubbing the pink powder on their gums.

Then she ducks back behind the curtain.

I slide off my barstool and walk across the barroom, my stomach fizzing with the fight I know is coming.

I lift the curtain to find a dark hallway. At the end of it, I spot her using a key card to get into a back office. She's way down the hall, but I'm there in a heartbeat. Silently, I follow her into the office and close the door behind us.

"Hello, Jessa."

She turns around. When she sees me, she snorts, incredulous. "You've got to be kidding me."

I look around the room, noting several stacks of hundreds stacked up on the shelves above a big safe. Jessa lunges across the messy desk and reaches into a pile of papers, but I get there first.

Beneath the papers, my fingers wrap the handle of a switch-blade.

I unfold it and point it at her chest, and for a moment I imagine what it would feel like to push the blade into her.

I get control of myself and carefully fold it up. "I'm not going to hurt you," I say to her. "Just tell me where Rosie is."

She snorts in response. "I wasn't worried. You're so *pure*."

I take a second to notice the walls. Lined with pictures of girls, women, starting from about age thirteen and going up to around age forty. Then I notice a metal pole off to one side,

232

attached to the ceiling and floor in a corner of the room. "What is this place?"

"Are you that thick?" she says. Then she points to a binder open on the desk. It's full of pictures of girls in sparkly, skimpy clothes. "Those girls out there are all companions," she says.

I look at her blankly.

"The kind you pay by the hour?"

Oh. I swallow, feeling naïve.

"Where is Rosie?" I ask again, shutting the binder as if this can make the fact of what Jessa does for money go away.

"How am I supposed to know? Honey, just forget her. Forget him, too," she says. "You know, you'd make a great companion." Her long fingers wind around a lock of my hair.

I think of all the young girls on the wall forced to sell their bodies for money. Static fills my ears, and I shove her hard in the direction of the metal pole. She hits the wall, and I don't think about it before I slam both hands into the pole and push in her direction. Hoping to . . . I don't know what. Surely I don't think I can actually bend the pole?

But the metal yields immediately, as if it's liquid.

The top of the pole disconnects with the ceiling, and with both my hands, I push the metal pole toward her, pinning her against the wall, the pole curving around her slim torso, tight enough that she can't get out. "What in Bedlam's balls?" She shrieks, terrified. She squirms against it, but she can't move. The metal is too tight against her narrow waist.

She stares at me, speechless now. Visibly trembling. Her top hat fallen to the floor.

I shrug, regaining my composure. "You should reconsider your line of work," I say before I leave. "It'll make you cynical."

I don't like the look on her face as she's figuring out what

I am. It's a mix of fear and pity, and I don't want to be pitied. I leave, shutting the door behind me, and as I walk down the darkened hallway I call the tip line.

Once I'm back in the Motoko with Serge, I pull out the list and cross her off.

~~Jessa Scorpio~~

Now all that's left is Rosie, of course, and one more: Emmett Cask.

I wait a week after Jessa.

The newspaper articles keep coming, and I'm afraid I'll get caught, exposed in front of the whole city. Someone could easily take my picture and sell it to the *Dilemma*. And if that happens, my life as I know it will end. My parents will lock me in the house forever. They'd probably pull me out of school and bring in tutors to finish out my senior year. I'd become a recluse or leave the city altogether. Or worse—my chimeric heart could become the source of study at a lab somewhere.

But then Serge tells me he has a lead on the yellow LandPusher. I decide we should follow it, hoping tonight will be the night I find Rosie.

I find the LandPusher on the bank of the river, just to one side of the Bridge to Nowhere, and climb up into the decorative ironwork beneath the bridge to watch what happens. A black SUV eventually pulls up next to the LandPusher, and a man wearing sunglasses steps out. My stomach drops in anticipation of Rosie, but when the door to the LandPusher opens, it's Emmett Cask, the skinny man with limp blond hair who was my captor just before Gavin was killed.

Emmett hands a suitcase to the man in sunglasses. The man hands him a paper bag in return.

The mural Gavin painted is sixty feet from where I'm hanging in the shadows of the bridge.

The minutes tick by with Emmett talking to his contact. I focus my hearing on what they're saying.

"Tell the Boss we need the same order next week. The club kids love the new strain." Finally, the other guy gets into his SUV and drives away. I'm preparing to confront him when my foot slips and a piece of the old fretwork clangs to the ground.

That's when Emmett looks straight up at the shadow of the bridge, right at me.

"Having fun, princess?" And then he starts to run toward the entrance to the bridge.

I consider my options, my heart galloping. The *slap-slap* of the Midland feels like it's almost surrounding me. I swing out of my hiding spot and climb back onto the bridge itself, which is mostly wooden, made up of rotting boards that look like they might not hold my weight. The freezing kerosene air of the Midland hits my face as I wait for him close to the bridge's end, not far from where it drops off into the river.

He's got his gun out, holding it with both hands. When he's ten feet away from me, I leap toward him, my body moving faster and farther than the laws of gravity allow. He's too surprised to shoot, and when I land, I knock the gun from his hands. But he's strong. He manages to push me away, sending me staggering backward toward the edge of the bridge, where the boards have rotted away and it just stops, cut off in the middle of the water.

He comes at me fast, knocking me down so that half my

body is suspended over the edge of the bridge. The boards cut into my back through my coat, and then I'm almost over the edge, grasping at the air. I scream, my mind careening back to the night on the bridge with Ford.

But before I fall, he grabs me by the arms and drags me back to safety, that same creepy smile on his reptilian lips. "You're not going to get off that easy."

I twist away from him and spot a loose board popping up from the severed bridge. I manage to wrench it most of the way free, pulling with everything I have and scrambling back onto steady footing, squirming out of his grasp.

Everything around him goes white, and the space of seconds ticking by seems to expand. It feels like I have all the time in the world to lift my arms over my head, to turn, to aim, before I smash the board over his skull. The board breaks in half on impact, but he's still standing, and I grab him by his jacket, throwing him hard. He flies into the air and smashes head-on into the railing of the bridge. When I reach him, he is unconscious but breathing.

I pull a length of rope out from the inside of my jacket, and I spend about fifteen minutes wrapping him in it, tying knot after knot until I'm satisfied. Then I wrap the rest of it around a metal girder and send him flying so that he's swinging, suspended from the bridge like an ornament.

After I call the tip line, I climb the scaffolding and hide in the crevasses of the bridge, watching when the police come and search him. They find the paper bag full of drug money he'd stuffed into his jacket pocket. They find his car keys. Then they shove him into a paddy wagon, and he's gone.

When I finally climb down from the scaffolding and begin to jog back to Serge's car, I hear people applauding. I turn to look, thinking there's a fight going on, or a three-card monte game, but all I see are two filth-encrusted teenagers huddled by a fire blazing in a metal drum. They keep clapping, staring right at me. I wave, realizing they must have seen my fight with Emmett Cask. Then one of them crosses her fingers over her heart, standing there solemnly. The sign for the Hope.

Not knowing what to do, I make the sign back at her. *We will rise*, I think. Then I quickly turn around and start to jog away, not wanting them to see Serge's plates. My body aches from the hits Emmett landed, from pulling the board up out of the bridge. My back is still bleeding. But somehow I feel it, too—a funny tingling in my stomach that must be something like hope.

CHAPTER 32

Serge pulls into the Fleet Tower parking garage at 2:10 in the morning. We nod a quick good-bye, and I get out of the car. I wave as he pulls away.

Inside the parking garage, the air is humid and still. I walk over to the elevator bank and press the service elevator button, the slow creep of a smile spreading across my lips. I'm getting closer to Rosie Thorne. The elevator car bounces slightly when it hits the subbasement level, and then the door *ding*s open.

"We've got to stop meeting like this."

My smile dissolves instantly. Will.

I step backward, my eyes locked on his smirking face. His blond curls are wild, frizzing out in all directions, his eyes so bloodshot the whites are solid red, and the skin under his eyes is swollen. He steps out of the elevator, his arms open, about to pull me toward him.

Disgusted, I dart out of his reach. "Don't touch me," I hiss.

"Anthem." He looks at me sideways as if I'm an incorrigible

student who's forgotten my homework. "We both knew there'd come a time when you'd give me what you promised."

"I've done everything I promised," I breathe. "Every stupid thing. Zahra still isn't speaking to me. I guess that makes you happy."

He steps toward me again. I can smell the tang of his sweat, something mineral about it.

"Yes, actually," he muses, reaching out a hand to stroke my cheek, his fingers hot. "It does. She's such a bitch."

"No she isn't. You're deranged," I say, flinching from his touch. I make myself as tall as I can, but I'm still so much smaller than him. "Get out of here. I'll call secu—"

"I don't think you'll call anyone," he says. "Since that would mean waking Mum and Daddy, who might wonder why their dear daughter is in the parking garage at"—he pulls out his antique pocket watch, an affectation given to him by his father the district attorney—"two seventeen in the morning."

I press my lips together, running through my options. He has no chance against me physically, but the last thing I want is for him to get so angry he posts the video.

"Speaking of, Anthem, why are you down here at this hour? I watched you leave through the garage hours ago. Of course, you're too fast to keep up with, so I waited here for you to come back. And now you're back." Will laughs. "And you have blood on your blouse."

I hurriedly button my coat. Emmett Cask put up a good fight. A few drops of blood must have gotten on my shirt when I was tying him to the cement column under the overpass.

"Will," I whisper. "Leave now. If you don't want me to hurt you—"

"You're not going to hurt me, Anthem," Will purrs, stepping

close to me again. "Your new life as a freak is too important to you. Now let's go upstairs and lay down in your bed and do what we should have done months ag—"

Just then, the service entrance door clicks open. Will and I both whirl around, and I'm overjoyed to see Serge's stern face.

"Anthem," Serge says in his deep basso profundo. "You should be in bed. William, I will drive you home."

"Hi, Mr. LaForge," Will says, his voice cracking. "We were just—"

"It is very late," Serge says, his eyes blazing. He puts a protective hand around me, inserting his enormous frame between me and Will. "Too late for you to be here. Anthem needs her rest."

"Right, I just . . . um, okay."

"I will drive you home."

"You don't have to do that."

"I insist." Serge takes Will by his arm and walks him to the Seraph. Over his shoulder, he calls out, "Your parents think you are asleep in your room. I suggest you make your way there quickly."

As Serge pushes Will into the backseat of the car, his hand on his head like a cop escorting a criminal to lockup, my adrenaline starts to ebb and I take a deep, shaky breath. They pull away, and Will's face in the car window is a portrait of fury.

CHAPTER 33

The next morning, my parents and I end up all leaving at the same time. "Catch a ride with us, kitten," Harris says as we get into the elevator, me in my school uniform, my mother in a navy pantsuit with a periwinkle silk shirt, my father in his usual suit and tie, the *Daily Dilemma* tucked under his arm.

"Okay," I say warily.

We pile into the car, which Serge has pulled up to the grand front entrance of Fleet Tower. When I'm seated in the middle seat between my father and mother, Serge nods hello in the front seat, wearing his chauffeur's cap. His eyes meet mine in the rearview, then flick away. A hot blush creeps into my chest and up my neck. What must it be like for him, keeping my secret from my father and mother, his employers, and for so many years, his closest relations?

Next to me in the backseat, my father makes a funny sound in the back of his throat. "Unbelievable," he mutters under his breath.

I turn to look at him, and he's got the front page of the paper in his hands. I freeze when I see the headline, printed in huge letters:

RETURN OF THE HOPE?

Next to it is a picture of Emmett, his face bloodied, squinting in the glare of the flashbulb, tied to the bridge girder.

The article itself is small, and I strain to read it without my father noticing. All I see before we get to school is this:

> For the sixth time in two weeks, a wanted member of the Syndicate has been caught in the act, tied up, and delivered to the Bedlam boys in blue through an anonymous tip. Ariel Siegel, interviewed at the scene, claimed to have seen the whole thing. She said, "What I saw tonight was incredible speed and strength. Beyond what a human being should be able to do. I always knew we'd have a second chance to turn the city around after the Hope disappeared. This is our chance." Ms. Siegel declined to describe this "incredible" person's looks, repeatedly saying "no comment" when pressed for a—

"Anthem." My mother is shaking my arm, and I have to tear my eyes away from the paper. "We're here."

"Sorry." I put my hand against my chest, where my heart is hammering at my rib cage. I hurry out of the car and head toward school, the cathedral tower looming gray and massive in the white morning sky. The headline burned into my retinas, floating in front of me everywhere I turn. I really should start wearing a mask.

"So now you have your father's bodyguard watching out for you?" The sound of Will's voice oozes around the edge of my locker door. I slide my physics and Latin books on top of the teetering pile and have to fight the urge to slam the locker door against his face. Instead, I close my locker and begin to walk away. Fast.

But he's right there alongside me, matching my stride, pushing his way through the pre-homeroom throngs, his blond head held high.

"I don't have time for this right now," I say. All I want to do is go to the computer lab and check all the papers to make sure none of them have a picture or description of me. But I head in the direction of the library instead, because Will and the computer lab don't mix. Not while he's got the footage on his flash drive.

"I don't really care what you have time for," Will hisses. "That was bullshit last night. I'm going to need you to tell your dad's lackey to back off." His eyes bulge out, and he's breathing fast, almost panting, as we head up to the second floor.

I push the library door open, wanting more than anything to head up to the Thesis Tower, alone, away from Will. He's right behind me, though, and when I pause, his hand goes around my waist.

I twist away from him and move to put a study table stacked high with books that need to be reshelved between me and him. "He's not a *lackey*. And he doesn't answer to me."

"Oh, please, Anthem." Will laughs. "That guy would die for you. In fact, I wouldn't be surprised if he's in *love* with you." Will keeps laughing, doubling over, convulsing with it. I've had enough.

"You're even more demented than I thought," I say, my voice rising.

"Oh my God, Anthem, did that hit a little close to home?

Are you, like, having an affair with big man Serge?" Will is breathing shallow breaths, like he can't get enough air.

The edges of my vision blackening with rage, I reach down and grab a thick hardback from the table in front of me and throw it at his head as hard as I can. It grazes his cheek and falls twenty feet behind him.

"Really?" Will yells, his face turning ten shades of pink.

Then a lot of things happen very quickly.

He grabs me by my shoulders, shoving me harder than he should be able to into the side of one of the library stacks. My body slams into the shelves, sending a few dozen books flying off onto the carpeted floor. I push him away, and he staggers, falling over a chair.

"It's your funeral," he says flatly. "Hope you enjoy all the exposure, you stupid little bitch."

Frozen above him, my body shaking with adrenaline, I open my mouth to say *Don't do it, Will,* but I never get the chance.

"From where I stand, there's only one stupid little bitch in the room," a familiar voice growls. Zahra steps out of the stacks on the far wall, the ones that lead to the Thesis Tower. Her CDS cardigan is threaded with hundreds of safety pins; her black hair is dyed an amazing hot orange at the roots. It takes me a second to notice that she's holding a small black canister out in front of her with two hands. "And it's the guy cowering on the floor."

I have never loved anyone as much as I love Zahra right now.

Will backs away, using a chair to pull himself up. "You use that, you'll be expelled," he mutters.

"Do I look like I give a shit about being expelled?" Zahra says, walking closer to him, the pepper spray still held out in front of her. "I think it would be worth it, Willard. Just to hear you cry. You've had a good pepper spraying coming your way for a long, long time."

"Don't do it," I say, my voice hoarse with emotion. "Zahra, I love you, and I can't let you ruin your life for me."

Zahra looks at me, and I see her eyes are glassy. "Who says I'm doing it for you?" She smiles feebly.

In the time it takes for us to have this exchange, Will is on his feet and running for the door. Zahra's clear shot is ruined. "Leave her alone or we'll finish this," she calls just as Will hustles out the door.

"Z," I start, running toward her. "You're amazing. That was like a movie."

"Yeah, it was, wasn't it?" Zahra's face lights up for a second, reliving the triumph, then darkens again. She goes and grabs her book bag from the stacks and puts the pepper spray in a zippered pocket.

"I'm so sorry about everything," I start, moving in to give her a hug. But she steps away from me.

"I know you are. But Ant, things are still seriously messed up between you and me. This gross game Will's playing with you? It needs to stop now." She pauses and gives me a hard look. "We're not remotely okay until it's over with him."

"I just—" I whisper, looking at the floor, desperately wishing I could spell it all out for her. I owe her the truth, now more than ever. "I need a little more time—"

"There is no more time!" Zahra yells, exasperated. "He's a rage-aholic, and it's only going to get worse. I can't watch you do this to yourself anymore."

Just then, the ancient, nearly deaf school librarian, Mr. Deckle, walks in, and the morning bells start to clang. Zahra whirls around, not waiting for an answer.

Zahra moves out the door as quickly as Will did, leaving me in the musty library to explain to Mr. Deckle why there are fifty books on the floor.

I take my bag off my shoulder and start to pick them up while Mr. Deckle goes around opening shades and turning on lights, humming to himself.

Zahra's right. Will *is* a rage-aholic. He's a ticking time bomb, getting crazier, more and more reckless, more erratic.

I gather up piles and piles of books from the floor and line them up on a library cart in the hope that Mr. Deckle won't make me stay and shelve them. My thoughts wander to Duffy Doolittle's arrest a few weeks ago. I picture her sweating, screaming at Roderick, threatening him . . .

I grab the last book off the floor and roll the library cart between the stacks, realizing I finally have something on Will. Something every bit as damaging as what he's got on me.

CHAPTER 34

The Hansens live in a townhouse near the lake, on a street with old-fashioned oil-burning lanterns spaced evenly at the corners of sumptuous lawns. The carved topiary sculptures are thick and green in spite of the cold winter.

It's Wednesday at 7:30. Will is still at Cathedral, heading up a prom budget committee meeting. After ballet, I ran back to school to make sure, peeking into the lit auditorium windows, where Olive Ann was walking the committee through the proposed floor plan. Will stood in the corner of the small group, furiously crunching numbers on his phone. I smiled when I noticed the sheen of sweat on his forehead.

I press a gloved finger to the bell and hold my breath. *Smile,* I remind myself. When the door opens, Will's stepmother is in front of me in a black cocktail dress with a plunging neckline. I blink at her surgically enhanced cleavage, the two tan orbs of her breasts at my eye level, then beam a smile. Her pinched, puzzled face is framed by a swirl of black hair crowned with a diamond tiara.

"Anthem." She air-kisses each of my cheeks, making no physical contact with me, then motions me inside. "Lovely to see you again," she mumbles, approximating a smile as best as her lip injections allow.

"Hi, Lydia," I say, pulling my gloves off and threading my fingers together, blowing into my hands to warm them up. "Sorry to show up like this. I should have called."

"Will's not here . . . he's . . . got a school thing," Lydia says lamely, shrugging her toned shoulders.

"Right." I nod. "Actually, I wanted to talk to you and Rupert."

"Oh." Lydia frowns. "You're lucky you caught us. We're off to the opera."

"It'll just take a minute," I say. She blinks at me, then runs off to get her husband, dashing through the sweeping great room in her bare feet and looking, from the back, like a much younger woman. As Rupert Hansen's third wife, she might be closer to my age than to his.

In a few minutes, District Attorney ("Rupert, please! Ho ho, Anthem, been a few months since I've laid eyes on you, how is it you've grown even more beautiful?") Hansen and Lydia and I are all standing awkwardly together at the entrance of the great room, the fireplace roaring, our shadows flickering on the velvet wallpaper. Rupert Hansen's blond waves are gelled in a deep side part, his temples graying slightly, a small paunch in his belly mostly concealed by a cummerbund, his black bow tie drooping askew around his neck.

Lydia reaches out and straightens her husband's tie. The fire pops and hisses. I clear my throat.

"I'm here because, as you probably know, Will and I are dating again—"

"We couldn't be happier. William needs a girl like you to

keep him grounded," District Attorney Hansen cuts in, flashing a carnivorous smile my way. I have the distinct impression he's ogling me, and I'm glad I'm still wearing my coat. I pull it tighter around my chest and take a breath. *Bombs away.*

"Anyway, I'm worried about him. He's been acting strange lately, and I have reason to believe he's . . ." I've practiced this part, locked inside my bathroom, staring at the mirror. My eyes fill with tears. It's not a hard trick to master, since in my life there are a million good reasons to cry.

"What?" Lydia whispers, grabbing my hand. "Tell us, sweetie. It's okay."

I wipe a few tears away and feign struggling to get my voice under control. "I think Will is addicted to some kind of study drug." I choke out the words as if I'm devastated, then stare down at the carpet, which is a lovely blue and green paisley.

"Will? Are you sure? He's always gotten A's, so I can't see why he'd bother with all that," District Attorney Hansen says.

"I know, that's what's so sad." I sigh. "He doesn't even need them. But I saw him buying a baggie a few days ago, and he's been acting kind of . . . um . . ."

"He's been acting like an ass," Lydia says. We both look at her, and she shrugs. "Come on, Rupert. You know he's never liked me. He's a different person when you're not around. And I agree, Anthem. Lately he's been . . . hyper. Secretive. Angrier than usual."

I nod and try to look sad, but inside I'm ecstatic. I've got an ally in Lydia—someone else who wants Will out of her hair.

"Well." Lydia sighs, but I see her eyes dance with anticipation in the firelight. "Obviously we need to search his room."

"Lydia!" the district attorney says. "This seems rather drastic. Let's at least talk to him first."

"He'd do anything to keep this from you," I say gently. "He might need—"

"An intervention," Lydia interrupts, practically licking her lips at the thought of it. "Rupert, this is not up for discussion. We need to find his . . . what's the word, Anthem?"

I shrug, not wanting to appear too eager. "Stash?"

"Right." She nods. "We need to find his stash."

And then she marches down the hall, District Attorney Hansen trailing reluctantly behind her. I follow at a safe distance, then hover at the threshold of Will's room, watching as Lydia directs her considerable energies to ransacking it. She digs through his possessions like a professional investigator.

I hop nervously from foot to foot, praying I'm right. If I'm wrong, it'll just about ruin me. My breath starts to hitch in my chest when I imagine the scene—Will coming home, his room a mess, his father telling him what I said, demanding to know the truth. Without evidence, he'll weasel out of my accusation, then waste no more time making public the contents of that flash drive.

Lydia moves from the desk to Will's sock drawer. She fishes out a metal box of Bruise-Aids and gives Rupert a meaningful look, her eyebrows raised.

"Just open it, Lydia." Rupert sighs. Will has always said Rupert has a temper, that when he gets mad, he gets very mad, but all I see is a weary man sagging inside his tuxedo, hoping we're wrong. Lydia pops open the metal box and looks inside. Nothing.

I edge my way into the room, looking desperately around me. If I were Will, where would I keep drugs? He was so good at hiding the camera in my room . . . they could be anywhere. Or nowhere. My eyes travel along the wall, wondering about the few framed pictures he has up—a photo of his favorite president, a framed certificate of excellence in student government, a picture of the cast of *That's My Gal*, last year's CDS musical, where he played the lead role of Sammy Stilts, a simple man who is molded into a powerful politician by his scheming wife. . . .

God, Will is such a square. Maybe I'm wrong about him.

But then my gaze lands on a shelf above his bed. There is an old-fashioned gumball machine. A bronzed pair of baby shoes. And four trophies, all lined up. Except for one, which sits at an angle.

That's odd. Will is compulsively neat.

I move closer to the shelf as Lydia rummages around in Will's sweater drawer and D.A. Hansen suggests, "Dear, maybe Anthem was wrong about this."

The trophy is in the shape of a podium, with a small fake gold person leaning on it, speaking into a microphone. It says WILLIAM HANSEN, FIRST PLACE, JUNIOR DEBATE CHAMPIONSHIP.

Lydia comes over and notices the trophy that's askew. When she picks it up, the little gold podium comes off the base, and the thing splits in two in her hands. A small plastic bag filled with fluorescent orange pills falls to the floor.

Lydia's lips purse as she tries to suppress a smile. She might be only slightly less excited about this than I am.

Lydia reaches down and grabs it, wiggling the bag in the air between her two fingers. "Aha!" she exclaims. Then she shoots a look at Rupert. "Sorry, love. But at least now we can get him help."

Rupert dumps a few of the pills into his palm, and we all peer at them. The orange pills are stamped with a black Z on each side. Zenithin. Exactly what Duffy Doolittle was hooked on. "Damn it," Rupert mutters, kicking a loafer Will has left on his bedroom floor. The shoe hits the wall hard. "He could go to jail for possession if I decided to prosecute."

"But you won't," Lydia says, putting a manicured hand on Rupert's arm. He shakes it off.

"I need to make some calls," he says gruffly. "I'm going to kill him." Then he walks out of the room, leaving me and Lydia to stare at the little pile of pills.

An hour later, two gray-uniformed orderlies from Weepee Valley Psychiatric Rehab Unit are standing in the Hansens' kitchen. Lydia is pouring tea for everyone, still in her cocktail dress and bare feet, her tiara askew on top of her head. I've slipped off my boots and perch nervously on the edge of one of the barstools. I've told my parents I'm at Will's, and of course they're overjoyed and said to stay as long as I like. If only they knew why I was really here.

District Attorney Hansen has taken his tuxedo jacket off and paces around the living room in his cummerbund and shirt, the bow tie long since discarded somewhere in his bedroom. He has been on and off the phone with Lyndie Nye for the better part of an hour—apparently she works for the Hansens, too. My extrasensitive hearing has come in handy to piece together the chain of events—Lyndie called Weepee Valley for him, assuring him a dozen times that they would keep Will's sixty-day stint in their rehab facility confidential.

Finally, at 9:20 P.M., we hear the front door open, the bass in Will's headphones blasting a tinny beat into the silent foyer.

A nervous heat rising in my chest, I slip my shoes back on and jump down from the barstool, trailing behind the orderlies and the Hansens. I brace myself for yelling, for Will to lash out, for him to maybe even run. But there's still one more thing I need to do before I leave here tonight . . .

"What's going on?" I hear Will say. I linger in the doorway. "What is this?"

He stares down the orderlies, who stand on either side of him, keeping about a foot of distance, both of them outweighing him by at least fifty pounds. He hasn't put it together yet. I can see it in his eyes—still confident, still prince in his own personal kingdom . . . until he spots me.

"You," Will says, backing away, his eyes narrowed to slits. "What did you do?"

"Anthem came here because she cares about you," Lydia says, tears flowing down her stretched cheeks. "You'll thank her when this is all behind you."

"When what, exactly, is all behind me?" The tenor of his voice rising, Will moves away from the orderlies in the direction of his room, but D.A. Hansen, silent until now, puts a fleshy hand on Will's shoulder.

"No need to run and hide them, William," he says, his voice even and cold.

"Hide what?" Will whirls around and faces us, the whites of his eyes red, his nostrils flared. His forehead glistens under the track lighting.

"Your drugs." His father scowls. "Your drugs that you bought with *my* money. Money I earned trying to keep drugs off the streets. Ironic, isn't it?"

"I don't know what you're talking about."

"Let's skip the denials," D.A. Hansen says, shoving Will toward the orderlies harder than a father should. Will trips on the carpet, his eyes wild and flashing when they meet mine, then he rights himself, looking from me to his father. For a second, I feel a pang of sympathy for Will.

"Go ahead," D.A. Hansen says. "We've scheduled you for sixty days of detox and therapy at Weepee Valley. You'll clean yourself up, and then we will discuss what to do about all this."

"Well, I'm not going," Will squeaks. "Dad, I'm fine. Could not be better."

"Maybe you didn't understand me. We have had you committed. It's not optional," Rupert says.

Will's eyes grow even wider. "Those pills aren't even mine. Tell them, Anthem. Tell them the truth, or should I tell about where you've been going at night?"

The orderlies edge closer to Will now, ready to pack him off in a locked ambulance.

"I already did tell them the truth," I say, stepping closer to him. "You need help, Will. You're paranoid. It's a side effect."

I lean in to kiss his cheek and wrap my hands around his waist. I feel him start to shrug off my embrace, but then he leans into me a little in spite of himself, a part of him wanting to believe I care about him after everything. "It's for your own good, *sweetie*."

He pulls away from me, scowling, still focused on his father. "Dad, I swear, I don't—"

"I don't want to hear it, William. Everything you say to me from now on, I'm going to have to assume is a lie."

Will pulls away from me, his eyes flashing with hatred. "She did this! She framed me, and she planted those pills!"

"I hardly think that's true," Lydia says. "You've been erratic lately. Filled with venom. Staying up till all hours. It's a wonder we didn't suspect it sooner."

I turn around and walk toward D.A. Hansen, my eyes filled

with tears. *Check his pockets,* I mouth.

The district attorney swings into action. "Let's leave your things here, William. You won't need them where you're headed." He nods to the orderlies, who immediately turn his pockets out. A pack of rollies, his wallet, his keys. The key chain fob—the flash drive with my life on it—nestled in the center of the pile like a jewel.

"No!" Will struggles, but the two orderlies are already pulling him out the door. He tries to wrench himself free. "She did this! She's the one!" he screams.

"Don't shoot the messenger, William," his father says.

"Dad! Don't do this! You're making a mistake!" Will is screaming as the orderlies struggle to get him to let go of the door frame.

"Get ahold of yourself," D.A. Hansen hisses, following Will down the front walk. "I will not have my career ruined by my own son. And I will not have a drug addict living under my roof."

"But Dad, it's not even habit-forming!" Will yells, his voice breaking as he thrashes down the walkway, the orderlies gripping each of his arms with both of theirs, barking at him to cooperate.

In all the commotion, nobody notices when I pocket Will's keys.

CHAPTER 35

The day after Will is carted away to Weepee Valley, Ford asks me to meet him somewhere new—a place called Floyd Sherman Field—for one final training session.

I've been using the upcoming *Giselle* performance as an excuse for not meeting him on nights I've been busy tracking and tying up Rosie's goons, but ever since that "return of the Hope" article in the *Dilemma*, I've been spooked. I'm lucky nobody gave me away after the night on the Bridge to Nowhere. Next time, I might not be so lucky.

Why not Jimmy's? I write back.

But all I get is a cryptic *You'll see.*

I have to check the location a few times on my computer before I figure out how to get there—it's about a mile outside the industrial ring that marks the city's borders. Serge is driving my parents to a charity event tonight, so I'll have to travel on foot.

It takes me nearly forty-five minutes to run there, even with my supercharged legs. When I arrive, I find Floyd Sherman Field is an abandoned airport built a hundred years ago, back when Bedlam was a much smaller city. The runways are choked with weeds, the terminals demolished into shattered cement ruins. But a few of the hangars still stand, and one of them glows with a faint light. I move toward it, still puzzled by Ford's choice of venue.

The hangar is a huge A-frame structure, kudzu crawling up the walls, many of its antique windows shattered. Still breathing hard from my run, I duck inside the huge door and press my hands together for warmth. Inside, two working Klieg lights are clipped to the rafters, illuminating Ford's back as he sets up a pyramid of empty beer cans on top of a wide log positioned with the flat part facing up.

"Hey," I say. My voice echoes in the cavernous space.

Ford finishes his pyramid, placing the last Buzz Beer can on top, then waves and walks toward me.

He claps the sides of my arms with his hands and flashes his usual warm smile. "Find the place okay?"

I nod. My stomach hurts. It's time for target practice. "Do we have to do this? I don't think I want to do this."

"Do what? Kill a couple of cans?" Ford shrugs. "It's easy, Green. And you need to be prepared."

"Last time I held a gun at someone, I froze. And Gavin died because of it." I stare down at the cracked cement floor, ancient oil stains reminding me of the inkblot tests they use at school to give the annual anxiety assessments. If Bang had gotten her way last month and made me take another one, I'm sure I would have failed. Luckily, she dropped her crusade after I caught up on all my work.

"That's exactly why we should do this," Ford says gently. "I've taught you all the fighting strategies I know. You're strong,

Anthem. Getting stronger every day, I'm guessing. But if someone holds a gun to your head, you need to know how to handle it."

A shiver passes through me. I hate guns. They're what ruined this city, where anyone at all can get their hands on one if they have enough cash. But I'm already here, and Ford is right. Even if I never bring a gun with me, I should still know what to do if faced with one.

"Fine." I nod, walking to the center of the hangar and turning to face the pyramid. "Let's kill some beer cans."

Ford kneels down on one knee and fishes a gun out of his high-top sneaker. It's grape-juice purple, constructed of the same matte plastic they make toy cars out of. It looks so much like a toy that for a minute I think it is one.

"Looks pretend, right?" he says, reading my mind. "But it's real."

"Purple?" I raise one eyebrow, ribbing him a little. "Interesting choice."

"It's just a loaner," Ford says, blushing as he walks toward me. "It was all my guy was willing to part with."

"Your guy?" Ford has a whole network of people around him that I know nothing about, I realize. I don't even know where he lives. Suddenly, this strikes me as incredibly weird.

"Fred. His name is Fred. Let's concentrate, okay?" And then Ford puts the gun in my hand. I fight the urge to set it on the floor and walk away, instead focusing on the weight of it (heavier than it seems it should be), the texture (smooth on the flank, scored in a diamond pattern on the handle), the size (bigger than Miss Roach's pearl pistol, smaller than the last gun I held, the black one I kicked out of Smitty's hands). My palms are suddenly sweaty, and I wipe first my left and then my right hand on my jeans.

"Okay," Ford says, standing close behind me and slightly to my right. "See this little lever?" He moves his arms around me and touches the small curved safety latch on top of the gun. "Pull that back until you hear a click."

I do it, and hear the bullet fall into the chamber. A sound I've now heard more times than I would like.

"Now stand firm, feet apart, and bring the gun up in front of you with both hands, right index finger on the trigger."

I blow a few strands of hair out of my eyes and assume the position of markswoman. He puts his arms around me until his hands rest lightly on my wrists, raising the gun a little higher.

"Close one eye, and bring the gun level with your open eye so that you see one of the cans just above the muzzle of the gun. After you've got your aim all squared, brace yourself for the impact of the shot. You're pushing the bullet forward with the gun, and the gun is going to push you backward." He speaks softly, precisely. His mouth is just behind my ear, his breath tickling my neck. I stiffen, pulling away a few inches. The closeness suddenly feels too intimate, the silence around us too complete. I squeeze my lips together and tell myself to focus on the task.

"Okay," I say, lining up the top can in the pyramid with the tiny raised part at the end of the gun muzzle. I bend my knees a centimeter more. I brace for impact. "Ready."

"When you press on the trigger, think of it as a squeezing motion. Too hard and fast, and you'll recoil and lose your aim. Just slowly squeeze until it fires. Arms locked. Take a breath in, then let it out slowly as you squeeze." His words unspool in my ear, the precision of his instructions calming me, all my focus now in the path between my right eye and the gun and the can.

I suck air into my nostrils and smell his shampoo. Ford always smells so clean.

I release my breath and squeeze the trigger. The gun fires with a deafening pop, and I feel it through my whole body, the impact knocking me backward off my feet. But then Ford's arms are there, catching me, and I straighten up. I ignore the ringing in my ears—familiar to me from Hades and from the science room—and check the pyramid of cans. It's completely undisturbed. I haven't even grazed my target.

"Good," he says, and somehow I hear him even with the ringing. "Steady your hands and fire again. And this time, hit it."

I repeat all the steps, really focusing on the *U* in BUZZ. When I concentrate, the can almost seems to glow—the background receding behind it and away from it. It's a little bit like my hearing, I guess. When I focus hard on something, I see it extra clearly. I squeeze the trigger, staying put this time and letting my body absorb the impact of the backfire. Instantly, the top beer can goes flying off the pyramid, smacking the brick wall behind it, and falling, crumpled, to the ground.

"Yes!" Ford yells. "Again. All cans must die!"

I line up my shot, this time aiming for the next row of cans atop the pyramid. And again, I nail one. Again and again, the bullets make contact. With every shot, I get better about leaning into the gun so that the recoil doesn't send me flying off my feet. When the gun is empty, Ford shows me how to refill the barrel, and I drop each gold-tipped bullet into its casing, plucking them individually from his callused palm.

We go through five rounds of bullets—the entire box—and I do the last five or six shots standing sideways, running, even, once, just for fun, under one knee. The under-the-knee shot doesn't hit a can, but it gets me a big guffaw and a high five from Ford.

"I think you're officially ready to do battle, with or without a gun," Ford says when all the bullets are gone. He shoots me a funny look, his head cocked to one side. "Not that you waited."

"What do you mean?" I say, feeling my cheeks go hot.

"Come on, Green," he says, kicking a few bullet shells with the tip of his boot. "I read the *Dilemma*. What was the crime blotter headline the other day? Something like . . . VIGILANTE LEAVES CRIMINAL HANGING FROM BRIDGE RAILING?"

"And you assume that was me?" I protest. "That could have been anyone!"

Ford looks at me with raised eyebrows, his arms crossed over his chest. It doesn't take long for both of us to crack up.

"I knew it." Ford grins, pushing me playfully. "Vigilante!"

"Okay, fine," I admit, pushing him back to keep from falling over. "It *may* have been me."

"Guess you've gotten comfortable working alone," Ford says, growing serious. "But next time they might be ready for you. I want to help you, if I can."

I shrug, trying to look noncommittal. I don't want to tell Ford that the reason I work alone is that I can't bear seeing anyone else I care about get hurt. Ford is strong as steel, but if he took a bullet, he would bleed just like anybody else.

"You think about it. For now, let's go look at the bullet holes, vigilante." He pulls me by one arm toward the center of the room, and I scoop up a couple of cans. The bullet holes are almost all directly in the center of each one, a clean hole right through the middle of the *U* in BUZZ.

"Amazing aim," Ford murmurs, squinting through one of the cans out both bullet holes to the other side. "He'd have loved to know you."

"Who?" I say, my eye caught by two sets of initials carved into the smooth top of the log he set the cans up on.

"The Hope."

"How do you know he would have liked me? Maybe he would have hated me."

Ford shakes his head. "When I was six years old, I used to come out here with my older cousin and a few of our rug-rat friends. We'd ride our dirt bikes down the runways, set up little jumps and stuff. There was this guy. Real sad-looking kind of dude, but strong. He could lift a car over his head. I saw it once. He used to train in here. He had a burlap bag of sand he set up, threw a rope over one of the rafters. Nothing fancy, but it was good enough to box with. He let me watch him, even taught me a little bit about throwing a punch. He used to set beer cans up just like this, for target practice. He had a few other guys who came out here sometimes, and later there was even a girl who came, too. They used to have these long meetings where they'd light a fire in a metal drum and talk about all the things they would do to change the city."

I'm listening to Ford, watching the muscles in his face move as he tells his story, his eyes darting around the room but looking inward, at his past. All the while I'm half-conscious of tracing some initials scratched into the log I'm leaning up against. RF + TH, two people in love enough to dig their initials into wood. For a moment, I wish Gavin and I had done the same.

"I was too young to really understand. But later, after he disappeared, I saw his picture on the news, once they finally identified him, and I realized the Hope was the same guy I used to punch a bag of sand with in this place."

"So he was definitely real," I muse, more to myself than to

him. Gavin believed in him, too.

"Of course he was *real*," Ford says sharply. "The city was turning around, Anthem. People believed in each other again, once he got the worst of the crime off the streets. People started talking about a new government, about making things better for everyone, even for the South Side. Don't you remember it?"

"I wasn't born yet," I say.

"I was a little kid, but I remember," Ford says, turning to face me. "And now it's happening again."

I look at him blankly.

"People are talking about what you're doing, Anthem. You're helping break the cycle. It's not that different from what he did," Ford says, his face flushed.

I shake my head, suddenly feeling frustrated. Until now, I thought Ford was the one person who understood what I've been doing, and why. "I'm not the Hope, though. I'm nothing like him. I'm doing this for Gavin, for revenge." I pause and give Ford a sharp look, then pick up a Buzz Beer can and throw it as far as I'm able. It hits the back wall. "I thought you knew that."

"Maybe that's what's driving you now," Ford says. "But I know you see what's going on in this city."

"I guess," I say, not at all certain I see what's going on very clearly at all. When someone close to you has died, it's like wearing a veil. Everything I've seen has been filtered through my grief. I turn away, wishing Ford would stop talking about saving the city. As if I'm all it takes to make this place better. As if I can singlehandedly take down the Boss and the whole Syndicate. As if I'm some kind of savior or hero. Because I'm not. And I don't feel like a motivational speech.

"So the Hope taught you how to box?" I ask, wanting to

change the subject. "And then you became a pro?"

"Something like that," Ford says, looking away. "It isn't worth talking about, trust me."

"Why not?"

"I had to make a lot of compromises." He stops to pick up a few more cans, stacking them back up in a pyramid on the moldy airplane seats. "A few guys high up in the Syndicate were willing to pay me a lot of money to box for them, and I did it, until I couldn't do it anymore."

"Box for them? What does that mean?"

Ford sighs, searching the ceiling as if deciding if he should go on. Then he does. "There are cage fights every month or two in the South Side. Big events. Lots of betting, thousands of bills changing hands depending on who wins. These two Syndicate guys sponsored me. At first, it was fun. I was pretty good." Ford shrugs. I interpret this to mean he was actually *really* good, and that he's just being modest. "I was only sixteen. I was living with my uncle and my cousins, my parents both passed away by this point, both overdosed on droopies. We were so poor, me and my uncle. He works construction and was in a serious dry spell, workwise. And fighting was a way I could make a lot of money. Just one fight a week, and we could all eat. We could pay the rent. Even save a little.

"I got sucked in. At first, I was winning a lot, but . . ." He stops, pressing his lips together as if trying to swallow the rest of the story.

"But?" I put my hand on his forearm for a second, then quickly take it off when he looks at me.

"But six months into it, they realized they could make a lot more money betting against me."

"Betting you'd *lose*?" I ask, mystified. "But they were your sponsors. Isn't that, like, against the rules?"

Ford grimaces as if the memory physically hurts him. "Yeah. Very. They'd bet against me, and since I was the favorite for a while, a ton of money was on me to keep winning. They asked me to throw a fight or two, and they cleaned up."

"So you were losing on purpose?" I ask, trying to keep up.

He nods. "I threw a dozen fights for them. Maybe more. I was drinking a lot, taking Pharms to cope with the humiliation. It wasn't really them asking me so much as threatening me. If I didn't throw fights, they said they would start hurting people close to me. Hurting my family, what little of it I had left. My uncle, my little cousins."

Ford stops to kick a can. We both watch it sail through the air and bounce onto the ground.

"Eventually, I couldn't do it anymore. It felt too dirty, you know? So this one night, I was up against this kid who couldn't have been more than fourteen, who shouldn't have been competing at all he was so young, and I just kept punching, totally raged out on him. I won. I gave the kid a concussion. And my sponsors lost. A lot. Enough so that they threatened to kill me."

"And that's when you dropped out of boxing?"

"Right. Because they would have killed me if I showed my face in there again. So I've been lying low ever since. Just waiting."

"Waiting for what?"

"Dunno." He shrugs, moving closer to me, his voice barely above a whisper. "Maybe for a way to do something real. Something more than keeping Jax in food and formaldehyde. Something bigger. With someone better than me." He stares at me, his brown eyes soft and unfocused, their usual playfulness gone. Then he leans toward me, slowly, slowly.

I feel myself leaning in, too, my eyes closing. I want to feel the heat of his arms through his sweatshirt, wrapped around me. To feel the clean warmth of him . . .

But then my phone buzzes with a text, and the spell is broken. I pull away from Ford, my face on fire as I dig for my phone. It's from Serge.

The LandPusher is out of the impound lot. Heading north on Oleander.

Oleander. Gavin's old street. The scene of their original crime.

"Car's on the move," I mumble, jumping up, my face still warm, my heart racing, guilt flooding my veins. Even though Gavin is dead, it still feels like a betrayal. "I need to find it. To see if Rosie's inside."

Ford nods. "This time I'm coming with you."

I open my mouth to say *No, it's not safe, I can't take that risk,* but there's a hard determination in his jaw that tells me I have to give him this, that if I refuse, he'll find a way to follow me. I let out a defeated puff of air and nod.

I text Serge back, telling him to let me know where the car ends up and that I can be there in half an hour. *Nothing happened,* I tell myself. And nothing will ever happen. My heart is a machine. A biological experiment under my strict control. And I intend to keep it that way.

CHAPTER 36

We leave Floyd Sherman Field with our bulletless gun and an awkward silence between us. Outside, we're all alone for miles, just us and a heavy half-moon hanging low in the sky. The air smells like burnt plastic, like imploded skyscrapers. A waist-high thicket of brown weeds bends in the cold wind.

Searchlights crawl through the clouds miles away, beamed down from a few low-flying helicopters in the far south. A police investigation. Nothing unusual. "It's far," Ford says after we walk a few minutes. "Let's take my car."

Behind a demolished wall of cinder blocks is Ford's car. It's a boxy Halcyon, ten years old at least, the maroon paint job hidden under a layer of sooty dust. The kind of car a grandmother might drive, all ugly lines and wide leather seats.

"This is yours?" I say as we walk toward it, our footsteps crunching under cinder-block shards.

"Sort of." He grins. "Why do you ask?"

"I just . . ." *You can't afford a car.* "You never mentioned having a car."

"Oh, I have tons of cars," Ford says, opening the passenger side door for me. A waft of rose perfume spills out, engulfing us both, and I slide inside. He closes the door behind me, jogs around the front of the car, and hops into the driver's seat. An embroidered picture frame hangs from the rearview, two toddlers beaming in its center. "I just don't have them for very long."

He flips open a section of the dash under the steering column and does something with one hand, hardly looking at it, just feeling with his fingers and humming an aimless tune under his breath. A few blue sparks fly out, and he pulls his hand away. I yelp in surprise as the ancient engine roars to life. Then I roll my eyes at my stupidity. Why *wouldn't* Ford be a car thief?

I lean my head against the ancient, stiffened doily on the seatback and settle in for the drive, pulling up a map of the city on my phone so I can direct Ford which way to go.

Ford shifts into drive and we are on our way, zooming away from Floyd Sherman Field, our headlights the only moving thing in the still landscape, careening down the hill toward the dark sprawl that will connect us to the highway.

We're back on the city grid, in the industrial corridor of the southwest, where Oleander begins. It's a long street, and we're still far from where Gavin lived. I text Serge again, hoping for a quick answer.

A minute later, I get one.

Just parked at a warehouse on Oleander and Nightshade Ave.

I write back right away.

Thanks. I have a ride home. Get some sleep.

We crawl the two blocks with the headlights off. The last thing I want is for them to see us coming.

"Turn right," I say, and he does. A hundred feet in front of us, the yellow LandPusher is parked at a haphazard angle outside a warehouse with the words RID-EX on a faded awning, its back windows covered entirely by orange police impound stickers, big black numbers, and BEDLAM POLICE DEPT. in thick letters.

"Pull up to the curb," I whisper. My fingers begin to pulse with adrenaline, and as Ford struggles to achieve a semblance of parallel parking, I wish we hadn't used up all the ammunition on target practice.

We get out of the car, closing the doors as quietly as possible, and walk slowly through the cold, silent air toward the RID-EX building. Ford bends to move the gun from his boot to the back of his jeans. Then he thinks better of it and offers it to me.

"You keep it," I say. "You can use it to bluff, if nothing else."

He nods, and I see in his eyes that he's nervous. "Anthem." His hand on my wrist. His Adam's apple bobbing as he swallows. "Don't feel like you need to watch out for me, okay? You just worry about you. If anything happens to me, just . . . just make sure you're safe."

I nod, suppressing a flicker of irritation. I shouldn't have let Ford come. "You too," I mutter. "Don't play the hero." But I know he will. If given half a chance, I suddenly realize, Ford will save my life a third time. Or die trying.

We agree, silently, through a few motions of my head, to enter around the back of the warehouse. But both sets of back doors are locked. Ford puts his finger to his lips and pulls out a set of keys, and after wiggling an oddly thick key from his key ring around in the lock for a moment, he succeeds in unlocking the door.

I go first, peering into the dim space to make sure there isn't anyone in back we need to worry about. The place resembles the MegaMart. There are metal shelves every six feet, lined floor-to-ceiling with huge containers. Only instead of cooking oil or drums of tuna fish, all of these containers are marked with a skull and crossbones and the words POISON, DO NOT PUNCTURE, TOXIC.

Following the hum of voices coming from the other side of the room, I motion to Ford, and he follows me down a long drum-lined aisle marked RATS to the front of the warehouse.

When we get closer, I stop to peer between two metal drums, goose bumps rising on my forearms. At a small reception area, an older man counts out money, a lamp casting a concentrated light onto his shabby desk, illuminating two stacks of bills, his hand methodically setting down a third stack.

"Three twenty, three forty, three sixty, three eighty," he drones. And next to him, her back to me, standing between two red drums marked with an outline of a cartoon rat with X's for eyes, I can see the familiar blond hair with the roots growing in. I'm close enough to smell her bubblegum.

It's her, I turn and mouth to Ford. I motion for him to stay hidden. Then I take a gulp of stale air and make my presence known, stepping into the dim circle of light cast by the desk lamp. "Hello, Rosie. Or whatever your name really is."

"Well. Look who it is," she says, turning around and step-ping out of the shadows. Her hair is piled high on top of her head, her leather trench buttoned all the way to her throat, its oversize collar stiff and flared, framing her hard red mouth in its black folds.

"Stavros, take a long walk, wouldya?"

The guard, a stooped man beaten by life, his nose a mass of broken capillaries, looks at me with pity. I motion that it's okay, and he nods, grabbing a bottle of brown alcohol from his desk drawer. "See you next week, then," he says to her.

"Yeah, sure. Go take a nap somewhere. I'll need an hour or so to speak with my . . . friend."

Stavros nods and shuffles out. All the cash he'd been counting remains on the desk, and Rosie goes to scoop it up, stacking it all in a big pile and stuffing it into a black leather handbag. She clicks it closed and smiles at me.

"Aren't you going to introduce your friend?" she says. "Pretty sure I heard two sets of tiptoes scurrying in here."

Ford steps into the circle of light, his face a hard mask of indifference, a boxer's face before the bell. "So this is her?" he says to me, his eyes never leaving Rosie's face.

"It's big, bad me, in the flesh." Miss Roach twirls, her hands fluttering at her sides. She's wearing spectator heels. How very prim.

"It's her," I breathe, suddenly so full of rage that she's alive and Gavin is dead that I feel dizzy, my head exploding with the memory of Gavin looking into my eyes before she shot him, shaking his head, pretending he wasn't scared but his beautiful eyes giving him away as he pleaded with me to go . . . and then her tight smile as she aimed right for his heart. . . .

"Gavin's killer."

She snorts, her hands clasped out in front of her, index fingers out, making the shape of a gun. "You've got a real flair for drama, don't you, sweet pea?" She looks at Ford appreciatively, her heavily lined eyes lingering on him before refocusing on me.

"You murdered him in cold blood, for no reason," I say, my voice shaking. I wonder if I'll be able to restrain myself, to keep myself from hurting her. "And now you need to pay."

"So naïve," she sighs. "I feel sorry for you, almost. Go

home, okay, princess? Focus on this new boy of yours. He looks neglected. Like a lost little puppy."

I launch myself at her, unable to hold back anymore, wanting to rip hunks of her blond hair from her head, to break her bones, to smash in her teeth. In a heartbeat I'm on top of her, knocking her to the floor. I bring my hand up, ready to smash it into her face. When she grins I feel something in my back, a burning sharpness that morphs into a tingling freeze. I've been stunned by a zapper.

I'm immobilized for a second, enough time for her to roll out from under me. Ford is at my side then, checking on me, yelling something that I can't quite hear, his mouth moving as Rosie runs down one of the aisles of chemicals. A few seconds later, I can move and hear again, Ford's hands in my hair. I push him away and jump to my feet again. "I'm going after her."

Ford nods, pulling out his bulletless gun. I motion to him to take the left side of the room, and I take the right.

I run through the warehouse, blinking in the low light, not daring to breathe so that my sensitive ears can better pick up Rosie's footsteps. Halfway down the aisle, shots ring out from the other side of the warehouse.

I sprint through a center aisle that runs horizontally through the maze of poison, careful to keep my footsteps silent in the dark room. Then there's a hissing sound, and I start to panic, my heart thumping with fear. One of the canisters has been punctured and is spraying industrial poison into the air. We need to get out of here. *Now.*

Then there's another gunshot. This time it's closer.

I look up toward the ceiling and notice a hanging metal pallet, dozens of additional barrels of chemicals stacked on top of it. Then I hear breathing. I race toward it, my hands raised like all-too-penetrable shields in front of me.

It's Ford, crouched behind a pile of tubing. He's all right, uninjured. He points silently straight up to the ceiling at the hanging metal pallet filled with heavy drums of poison. He pantomimes it falling.

More gunshots ring out, echoing in the giant warehouse. My ears are ringing, and for a second I can't tell where her voice is coming from.

"Come out, princess," Rosie shouts. "This is what you wanted, isn't it? To die for him? So let's get on with it."

We crouch down and hold our breath as the poison fills the air and Rosie's spectator heels *clack clack clack* on the cement floor, getting closer.

My eyes move to the wall, where there's a red lever connected to a chain wound again and again around a spool. The chain is holding up the pallet dangling above us. I race toward the red lever, taking care to be as silent as I can.

She's only two rows away from us now. I spot the metal of her gun glinting between the skull-stamped drums.

I look back at Ford, who's still crouched on the floor. *Run*, I mouth. *Go now*. I point to the lever and motion to the ceiling where the pallet sways.

He nods curtly, wavers for a moment, then darts toward the front doors.

I see a sliver of Rosie's body through the shelves of poison. She's less than twenty feet away now. I focus on her and realize I can hear her breathing, labored and gasping in the poisoned air. "Come *on* already," she groans. "Let's end this."

Yes, let's, I think, my heart revving in my chest. *You don't deserve to breathe, ever again.*

"Here I am," I say calmly, pressing my body as close to

the wall as I can. As she turns, gun raised, and begins to walk through the aisle toward my voice, I pull the red lever, using all my weight to lean on it until the metal chain starts to unspool. "Good-bye, Rosie."

Above Rosie, the pallet starts to sway. I hold my breath, my mouth filled with the taste of aerosol poison. Just as she steps in front of me, the pallet slams down on the towering shelves. She looks up and realizes what's about to happen, her face frozen in shock. Then in a half-second, the shelves of poison cave inward, sending hundreds of metal canisters raining down on Rosie, burying her underneath.

The avalanche is massive. She doesn't stand a chance.

As the drums and canisters continue to pile on top of her, I push off the wall and sprint around the edge of the room, holding my breath amid the slish and hiss of pinkish rat poison spraying out in all directions.

When I'm nearly out, I hear a pop.

I get outside and just as I'm about to slam the door shut there's the pop of another drum exploding. I turn to see industrial poison blooming into a huge red aerosol cloud. Through the cloud I spot Rosie's high-heeled shoe, her ankle twisted oddly, her body crushed under the weight of the drums of Bug-Off. Bile rises up from my stomach as the bright red cloud engulfs her. I hesitate for a moment before I slam the door.

I run thirty feet away, then lean over and retch, bile coming up, sour on my tongue, and I'm vomiting on asphalt, just a few feet away from the yellow LandPusher, my vision streaked with tears, my whole body shaking.

When my body has expelled everything it can, I let Ford guide me to the car, my throat raw, my eyes burning. He gently puts my arm over his shoulder, not saying a word. He opens the passenger door, and I collapse into the seat.

When he's in the driver's seat, we just sit for a minute, not looking at each other. Outside, eddies of crushed cigarette packs, plastic bags, and the *Daily Dilemma* swirl past. In the distance, neon red and yellow chemicals spray the two front windows of the RID-EX warehouse. My body is violently shaking, watching it. Rosie doused in poison, crushed to death. A gruesome, inhuman death that even she didn't deserve.

"This wasn't what I'd planned," I whisper, tears falling into my mouth. "Not at all."

"I know." Ford grabs my shaking hands in his. "Just breathe. She's gone now. That's all that matters. She's gone, and it's over."

Then I hear the distant wail of a police siren. "Let's go," I say, swallowing hard and shaking my hands free of his. "We can't be here when the police come."

CHAPTER 37

The day before opening night of *Giselle*, I go to Zahra's house on Lakeview Drive, duck my head under the weeping willow in her front yard. I think about all the summers I've spent here, in this yard, the blue stone dappled with sun, building fairy houses out of sticks, Zahra sprinkling them with daisy petals. I wish I could go back to that time, when we were all the other needed or wanted, when we were as alike as twins, when whatever Zahra liked, I liked. Whatever Zahra wore, I wore. Whatever Zahra laughed at, I laughed at. Z's dad used to joke that we shared a brain.

But that's all over now. I bite a ragged cuticle on my thumb and wince at the treatment I've subjected Zahra to lately. The girl who knows me better than anyone, and all I've given her are lies.

I approach her front door slowly, pushing my stocking cap back on my forehead a little. It's late March now, but spring shows no signs of coming. Winter is getting longer every year.

I take a second to check behind me, to scan the block from one side to the other, making sure nobody has followed me. I keep waiting for retaliation, for the Boss or some other Syndicate thug to come after me, or to figure out that Ford was involved and come after him. But nothing happens. Nothing has happened for a week. Just ordinary calm, the regularity of my routine.

I put my hand up to knock but instead, on a hunch, I try the door. It swings open. "Zahra?" I call out, the ticking of the grandfather clock in her tasteful living room the only sound I hear. I breathe in the familiar smell of Z's home: pistachios and furniture polish and bread and flowers from the garden.

A door creaks open upstairs, and Zahra appears on the landing, one hand resting on the banister.

"Hi," she says.

"Hi." I smile as she hesitates on the landing, seemingly deciding if I'm worth coming downstairs for. "I've been looking for you for days."

"Huh." Z shrugs, turning to fuss with her growing-out pixie cut, almost a bob now, the orange ends now pink, studying herself in her grandmother's antique mirror. It's the same one we used to play Bloody Mary in as little girls. "Guess I've been busy."

I take a tentative step toward the stairs, putting one boot tip on the carpeted bottom step. The second step has always squeaked. We both knew to skip it when we snuck upstairs at night after popcorn-fueled movie marathons, or later, when we were older, after coming home late from a school dance or a party. "I miss you," I say simply, my voice breaking. "It's over with Will. I wanted you to know. Not that you should care in the slightest."

"Of course I care," Zahra snaps. "I care about everything. It's you who doesn't have time to care about *me*."

The accusation stings, but she's right. I shake my head. "I've been a terrible friend. I hate what's happened with us. I want to know everything, Z. Everything about what's going on with you. I always did, and I always do."

"Whatever," she says. "You tell me one thing and do another." But I detect the trace of a smile pulling at her lips. "I have to admit, I was impressed when I heard you got Will shipped off to Weepee Valley," she adds slyly.

"Yeah," I say, climbing a few more stairs, careful to skip the squeaky one though nobody's here but us. "I thought you might like that."

"What a psycho." Z shakes her head. "He was always bad news, Anthem. Even before the pills. I couldn't figure out why you didn't see it. It was like he cast a spell on you. . . ."

"I was an idiot."

I breathe a huge involuntary sigh. Things are finally starting to feel okay again. The people who can hurt me are gone. Will is locked away in Weepee Valley for at least another six weeks. I have his flash drive under my bed. Rosie is gone, and though her death makes me a killer, I'm starting to convince myself the world might be better off without her. Only one of us was going to walk out of that warehouse alive. I'm glad it was me.

"You seem good now," Zahra says, studying my face, her head tilted to one side. "Are you good?"

"I think so," I muse. "For the first time in a long time, I'm pretty good. Especially now that I'm here and you haven't thrown a shoe at me."

"I would never throw a shoe at you," Zahra insists. "A magazine, maybe."

"I deserve it."

"Yeah. You kind of do. But I'm tired of hating you. It's giving me zits."

It feels so great to hear her say this that I'm actually dizzy with relief. I grab on to the banister to steady myself, my heart thwacking with joy against my ribs. All this time, I've had a million rationalizations for not telling Z the truth about what I'm doing and what I've become, but being my old self with her feels like such a relief right now that I finally understand my real motivation for hiding what's happened from her:

I need this too badly.

Being the old me—the Anthem who Zahra has always known—means not having to think about the person I've become at night. It's a reprieve from the violence, the pain, the horror of everything that's happened in the South Side. If the girl I am during the day fuses together with the girl I am at night, I won't know who I am anymore.

And for right now, all I want to be is Zahra's friend again.

"You should have seen the look on his face when they carted him away." I fake-sigh, hamming it up as if it's a painful memory. "He was so shocked."

"Details," Z demands, her violet eyes widening, her hands reaching for mine, braceleting my wrists with her fingers. She pulls me into her room, where she'll smoke a rollie out the window and I'll regale her with the debate trophy, Lydia with her tiara, the Weepee orderlies, Will's hissy fit before they took him away. Finally, something I can be totally honest with Zahra about.

It's a start.

CHAPTER 38

My hair is shellacked in a tight bun, metal combs with glittery white feathers firmly affixed to either side of my head. My stage makeup is freshly sealed with a giant puff of powder. I'm wearing an ivory leotard and a stiff tutu the color of cinnamon toast, my toe shoes newly cracked and sewn on to my feet like a second skin.

I am number six in the line of dancers waiting for our first entrance. I roll my shoulders back, raise my arms above my head, take a deep breath, and fold over one final time, my head almost touching my beribboned ankles, as the violins swell with the first notes of the *Giselle* score. I straighten up and lift onto my toes, peeking out at the audience when the heavy red curtains begin to rise. Through the scrim of the wings, I can see a sliver of endless seats that seem to go on forever, all filled. All eyes are trained on the stage, and under violins I can almost hear the collective anticipatory hush of the packed house.

It's opening night at last, and I am pure ballet—my mind

focused, my muscles taut and ready to perform, every step committed to memory, not in my head but in my body. After eight counts, the first dancer flits onto the stage. I am last in the long line of level sixers, just behind Mara Wood. As the line moves forward and I approach the stage, I spot Mayor Marks in the front row next to his pinch-faced wife, her hair styled like a cinnamon bun atop her head. Just behind them are Zahra and her parents, Asher and Melinda Turk. My heart does a cartwheel, and I lift a hand up to wave, forgetting for a second that they can't see me in the wings.

Next to the Turks are my parents. My father is leaning over to whisper something in my mother's ear, and I see her fuchsia lips curl into a hard smile. They've been waiting for this moment a long time. Their daughter, premiering as Giselle. I think of all my years of practice, my dogged, desperate clinging to the routines of a dancer. And I press down on my chest, my scar so faint that all it takes to cover it now is a bit of foundation and some powder.

I turn to the stage, watch the level sixers fan out into a blooming rose of balletic precision. In a few more beats, it's my turn. I rise onto my toes, and the nervous butterflies that filled my stomach backstage are gone now, replaced by muscle memory, by the absence of thought. Through the hot glare of the stage lights, I make out the vague outlines of the full house, the seats packed to the very rear of the rafters at the Bedlam Opera House. The audience is a silent mass, a breathing wall of energy just outside my vision.

And then all I see are my fellow level sixers, whose steps I have made every effort to match—*not too high, not too fast* has been my mantra in rehearsals.

My heart whirring and whirring like an eager dog pulling at a leash, begging me to speed up, I become the dance. Onstage,

I become Giselle, an innocent and sickly maiden who falls pas-
sionately in love. I leap and chasse, I pirouette and fouetté en
pointe, the music moving through me and with me. The energy
from the audience radiates into my limbs, which bend like
rubber bands at my command.

Everything else falls away—Gavin's murder, Ford, the guns,
the fighting, Rosie's gruesome end, the chemical smell of RID-EX
that hangs on me even now, a week after her demise—and I feel
more present in this moment than I've felt in a long time.

Before I know it, the first act is done and I'm pirouetting
offstage. Before the curtain lowers, the lights dim, and for a few
seconds I have a clear view of the audience. Movement in one
of the upper balconies catches my eye, and I crane my neck to
see over Constance's head. Someone is standing, leaning against
the wall behind the six balcony seats that jut out from the wall
above and to the right of the orchestra seats. The only person in
the audience who is standing.

Someone snuck in, I think. Someone who wants me dead. But
then a head moves forward, and I see familiar brown eyes twinkling in the darkness. My stomach tightens, and for a second
it's like my body lifts up and out of itself, flying toward him. He
gives me a thumbs-up and puts two fingers in his mouth and
whistles loudly.

A huge smile stretches my cheeks. I try to shake the sweetness of Ford sneaking into the Bedlam Opera House out of my
head as the curtain falls and intermission begins. Because I
remember this feeling all too well, and where it leads is straight
toward trouble. Toward caring so much about someone that
when you lose them, you lose everything.

The moment I felt this way about Gavin, he was taken away
from me. I can't ever let that happen again. I'm not strong
enough to survive it.

He's just a good friend, I tell myself. And that's all he can ever be.

At the curtain call, I'm breathing hard and revving with adrenaline. We take our final bows, then race offstage, all of us grinning and congratulating one another on getting through it. Everyone's gossiping about seeing scouts in the audience. Sadie Lockwood whispers to me, "You were great. You're getting a spot at the Bedlam Ballet Corps for sure."

"I'm just happy I didn't screw up," I say with a shrug, but part of me hopes she's right. I let myself imagine a future filled with dance, with sore muscles and Epsom salt baths, with aching feet and a constant flow of beautiful music and temperamental choreographers. Everything I always thought I wanted.

I could want it again, maybe. In the ballet corps, I could almost forget about this horrible year, my souvenir heart allowing me to excel as a dancer instead of a killer.

I'm replaying the performance in my head when I open the tiny closet of a dressing room marked ANTHEM FLEET. On the tiny slab of the vanity pushed up against the wall, there's a huge bouquet of bloodred roses wrapped in cellophane. Two dozen at least. It takes up the whole vanity. I pick it up and breathe in the smell, twirling a little. I pluck a tiny black envelope from the blooms.

To our prima.
We love you!
Mom and Dad

I sit down and start unlacing my toe shoes, thoughts of the reception in the lobby with Zahra and both our sets of parents swirling in my mind along with Ford's unexpected appearance in the audience. I hope I can see him before they whisk me away. . . .

But then I look in the mirror.

In the very center of it, someone has taped a card. The invitation is on heavy card stock with fancy engraved lettering.

The Boss invites you to a
SYN new-recruits party!
March 30. Tonight.
2212 Sumac Street
Please dress for success.

An arrow drawn in my dark purple lipstick from act two on the mirror points to the invite. Above it, three words.

We will rise.

I stick my head out the door and check the hallway, but nobody's there except Constance, who is unwinding the ribbons on her toe shoes. I jump back inside and close the door, moving toward the mirror to rip the invitation off and study it, my hands suddenly shaking.

Someone knows who I am and what I've been up to. But who? I stand there blinking. *We will rise.*

My mouth feels like it's full of sand. The Boss. The ringleader. The unseen hand who told Rosie what to do.

I close my eyes and fight a wave of dizziness, the scent of the roses my parents left suddenly cloying as I try to decide what I should do. Sumac Street isn't far from Will's house. It's in the north, in a nice neighborhood. Why would the Syndicate have a party there?

I blink at the mirror, my face covered in white pancake makeup to look like Giselle's ghost, my eyes lined heavily in black that fades to silver. I tilt my head to the right, and Ghost-Anthem tilts hers back at me, green eyes ablaze.

Unless I want to spend my life looking over my shoulder, I need to make sure the Boss is locked away.

Go on, a voice inside me says. *Go on and do it. It would be so easy. You know just where to find him.*

Slowly, I finish untying the ribbons around my toe shoes, then use a pair of nail scissors to cut the stiff fabric off my tired feet. I unclasp my ragged silver-gray ghost-skirt. I shove my feet into a pair of black boots and put on the simple black dress I've brought with me for the reception in the lobby of the Opera House.

By the time my parents come to get me in my dressing room, my ghostly makeup is mostly removed and the invitation is folded into a small square next to my heart, slipped into my bra.

"To the prima!" Harris booms in the lobby of the Opera House, smiling down at me. "And to the entire corps!"

Everyone raises their glass and yells "Hear! Hear!"

There must be a hundred people at the reception, and the room buzzes with conversation. There are tray-passed hors d'oeuvres, miniature crepes, puff pastry filled with duck and quince, mini-toasts with caviar. "Come, Anthem," my mother is saying in my ear. "Let's say hello to Mayor Marks." I let her lead me over to the crowd clustered around the mayor, waving to Martha Marks as my mother pulls me closer.

"Lovely, just lovely," the mayor says, shaking my hand and smiling his huge white smile. He's a short man—maybe half an inch taller than I am—but his head is huge. I stammer out a thank-you as a dozen flashbulbs go off. For a second all I see is pops of blue-white light. When I regain my sight, I turn to my mother, silently asking her permission to move on. I panto-mime eating, and my stomach growls noisily in response.

"Bring me a wine," my mother whispers, and I nod, taking off after a tray of what looks like shrimp satay, carried by a tux-edoed waiter.

Just as I'm reaching out to grab a shrimp skewer, a familiar set of arms embraces me. "Awesome, Green," Ford says in my ear.

"Thanks," I say, pulling two shrimp skewers off the hors d'oeuvres plate before the waiter moves on. "I could have gotten you tickets, you know."

"We like to stand. Don't we?" Ford says, turning his head to the right. I look down and see a little girl who's about five. She's holding on to Ford's pant leg.

"Who's this?" I breathe. She's like a mini-Ford. The olive skin, the flushed cheeks. Only her huge eyes are blue instead of brown, and her curly hair is long and tumbles down her back. She wears a red velvet dress with a thick white sash.

"My youngest cousin, Sam. She's your biggest fan."

I kneel down on one knee and hold out my hand. "Nice to meet you, Sam."

Her hand in mine is impossibly small, lighter than air. Her voice is barely audible, but thanks to my supersonic ears, I hear her perfectly. "Your dancing is the prettiest I've ever seen."

"Thank you." I smile. "I'm sure you're a great dancer, too."

She shakes her head.

"Maybe you could show her a few moves sometime," Ford says, and Sam beams.

"Sounds like a plan," I say, my stomach tickling with a familiar feeling. Then Sam nods and goes back to hiding behind Ford's legs.

"I didn't think I was a ballet kind of guy, but now I totally am," he says as I get to my feet again. "Giselle is kind of a badass."

"She is, isn't she?" I grin. As the party swirls around us, Ford and I just stand there, quiet for a beat too long, blinking at each other. Another second ticks by, and I start to feel uncomfortable about how smiley and floaty he's making me feel.

"I need to get some wine for my mom," I say, feeling warmth move into my cheeks. "Thanks for coming."

"Wait." Ford puts a hand on my arm. "I'm going to take Sam home, but that should only take me half an hour. Want to go out a little later and celebrate what a badass you were tonight?"

I do, I think. That's exactly what I want to do. But I can feel the piece of paper against my chest, the corner of it resting on top of my scar. It feels like unfinished business. If I take care of it, then maybe I can stop walking around in a fog of mourning and fury all the time. Maybe, someday, I can start over.

I shake my head. "I'd love to, but let's do it another night. I'm really beat. I think after this I'm gonna crash."

I pull away from him and wave good-bye to Sam, who smiles shyly. I step backward, because if I don't do it now, I might never be able to. The last thing I see before I turn to get my mother's wine is a funny look clouding Ford's eyes. A mix of hurt and doubt, as if he knows I'm not going home to sleep. He knows me better than that, I realize.

Keep walking, I tell myself, putting one foot in front of the other and pressing through the throngs of people saying *congratulations, prima,* to me, all of them blending into one perfumed mass. Soon this will all be over, and I can hang out with Ford and little Sam and not have to think about the Boss moving around the perimeter of my life, probably killing more innocent people, possibly planning to kill me, too.

CHAPTER 39

The reception devolves into a mass of confusion that I'm able to use to my benefit. Zahra thinks I'm going home with my parents. My parents decide to go out for drinks with the mayor (and Serge is driving them, of course), and I tell them I'm going out with Zahra.

Everyone thinks I'm somewhere else, and I'm able to slip away from the reception alone. I pull my coat around me as I walk down the steps of the Opera House, digging in my bra for the invitation.

And then I'm moving through the clean, well-lit streets of the North Side so fast that I'm practically flying. My lungs burn as they fill with icy air. My black suede boots move through the air, my legs propelling me forward with only occasional contact with the pavement. Pedestrians turn their heads to follow the blur of motion, but nobody chases me. As I run north, I think of my parents, slipping into the Seraph, telling Serge what a great job I did. I think of Zahra and the huge, genuine hug she gave me after the show. I think of Ford walking home with Sam on his shoulders.

Then I stop thinking about what I've left behind and try to focus on what I might find ahead of me. The Boss, whoever he is. The person behind the plot to take Gavin from me. The last domino to fall before I retire from the game of revenge.

Sumac is a long street full of mansions with land around them, each house encircled by a huge security gate and behind that, perfectly trimmed privet hedges that prevent views of anything but beyond the long, winding driveways.

Could this possibly be the location of a Syndicate party?

I skid to a stop in front of 2212 Sumac Street, the last house on the block. Its security fence is older than the others, and the enormous metal gate is open for cars to drive through, festooned with an orange ribbon with a single orange balloon on one end. I hear thumping coming from the house, and opt to skirt the privet hedges instead of walking up the huge gravel driveway, lined on either side by potted rosebushes and traversing a blue-green lawn that should be dead in winter, but isn't. I squint toward the house, sitting at the top of the property, at the top of a sloping hill. It's white limestone with two columns flanking the front door. The house is tall and skinny, built ages ago when mansions were smaller than they are today. Still, it's pretty big. Eight bedrooms at least. I think of what my real estate developer parents would call it—Gothic Revival. Or plantation. Whatever it once was architecturally, it's kind of spoiled by the fact that it has twenty satellite dishes attached to its sides and roof.

At least forty cars are parked in the driveway close to the house, most of them fancy sports cars. Whoever these people are, they have money.

The front doors—gold, enormous, adorned with snarling

lion door knockers—are shut, and I think better of going inside that way. What if there's a security crew manning the door? I move around to the back of the house and easily scale the fence. There, I see a gorgeous S-shaped swimming pool, all lit up with orange and blue lights glowing from the depths of the water. Past the pool is the house, full of modern windows and angles that look nothing like the old-fashioned front. Through all that glass, the scope of the party is clear. There are at least a hundred people dancing inside.

I move toward the back patio next to the house, where a crowd of young Syndicate types dressed up in their finest black leather stand laughing, dancing, and trying to keep warm under a cloud of rollie smoke. I walk up to a girl and boy who look about my age, both of them on the periphery of the crowd.

"Are you guys new recruits?" I ask. The boy is in only a T-shirt in spite of the cold, with orange suspenders attached to his pants. In the orange light coming off the pool, I can see goose bumps on his arms, along with a fresh tattoo on his forearm that looks like it might be getting infected. It says SYNDKID. The girl is small and dark, bundled up in a peacoat. She stumbles onto the lawn from the bottom step, probably drunk. Weirdly, I don't feel afraid of anyone here. Just sad that all these people, most of them not much older than me, are giving their lives to crooks and killers.

"Uh-huh," she says, almost knocking into me. She opens up her coat to show me a gun no bigger than a water pistol. It's hot pink. "Just got this from the Boss. Cute, right?"

I nod and try to smile, though inside I'm recoiling at the sight of yet another gun. There must be hundreds of concealed weapons here. I blow on my hands to keep them warm, and to try to stop them from shaking. "Where is he? I'm supposed to get mine tonight, too."

"Upstairs," she says. "Third floor. Have you ever met him?"

I shake my head.

"He's *so hot*," she whispers. "Like, seriously hot."

I thank her and head inside, pushing my way past the crowd on the steps, into the pounding bass of the party.

The house's interior is gorgeous. My mother would die over the huge, ultramodern kitchen, where every appliance is curved and beautiful, as if imported directly from the future. The walls and countertops are smooth and shiny and white. Touch-screen controls glow on every wall.

People mill around a bar set up on the kitchen island, complete with two female bartenders in white sheath dresses and top hats. All of the party guests wear dark clothes, contrasting with the all-white surroundings. A group of four young guys sits on the counter, looking ecstatic as they sway to the loud music being pumped out of the walls.

I move into the enormous living room, the air hot from all the dancing. A spiderweb of tiny white lights hangs from the soaring ceiling, illuminating a circular black couch. The walls have enormous close-up photographs of the flanks of black horses, their muscles rippling like sand dunes. Everywhere there is hooting and screaming and dancing and sweaty bodies. A beautiful woman dressed in a white toga minidress belted with a gold rope and matching gold heels walks around the perimeter of the room holding a gold tray with tiny paper cups on it.

"Instant Love?" she says to me, shaking the platter a little so that a purple not-quite-solid, not-quite-liquid quivers inside the cups.

"No thanks." I move toward the staircase at the back of the living room. Apparently, Instant Love makes you fall down–wasted. A dozen people are draped along the staircase, laughing hysterically and clutching the banisters for dear life. A few of them have given up trying to stand and are already lying down on the stairs. The music pounds and howls, but I can still hear the whirring of my heart. The closer I get to the third floor, the more terrified I feel. What if this is a trap? What if the Boss invited me here to finish me off?

But I force my feet to keep climbing until I reach the third floor, which is a pitch-black hallway lined with doors. I ball my hands into fists and keep going. At the end of the hallway is a partly open door with a blue light spilling out of it.

I move closer to it, drawn by the sound of laughing women. The hair on the back of my neck stands up when I hear a male voice join them.

It's him. It's got to be.

I peek inside and find a large room covered with TV screens, all of them broadcasting surveillance camera footage from around the city. There must be three hundred of them. They line every inch of the walls except for two large windows. There are even TV screens on the ceiling. The room flickers with an eerie, unsteady light that comes from the movement of people on the surveillance screens.

I push the door open just enough to squeeze inside. In front of me is an enormous desk—the only furniture in the room. Behind it there are four people with their backs to me, watching one of the surveillance screens and laughing—three more toga girls in heels, their skirts barely long enough to cover their behinds, draping themselves around a seated man.

This is him, I think. This is the monster running the Syndicate. The man who took the life of the only boy I've ever loved.

One of the toga girls turns her head and sees me. She elbows another girl, and they move away slightly from the seated guy. I note his black suit jacket. His shaggy brown hair. He gestures with his hand, still talking and watching the surveillance screen. His hand moves through the air, his elegant long fingers as familiar as my own.

It hits me in one sickening rush.

I know it before he even turns around. I stumble backward, suddenly dizzy, and trip over the corner of an Oriental rug, my boot heel landing hard on the floor.

He swings the desk chair around to face me, and the sight of him is so impossible, I forget to breathe.

"You." His eyes flash with surprise that he quickly covers with a smirk. "I wondered if the great avenger would ever show her face. And now you have."

I shake my head. No words come.

"Welcome to my home, Anthem." I'm too sick and horrified to speak. My mind ricochets between the night Gavin was shot—the moldering bookstore, Rosie with her revolver, Gavin's shirt soaked in blood—and what I see in front of me.

Gavin, alive.

I've spent so long replaying it from every angle. My own culpability in Gavin's death, the sadism of Rosie and her goons. There was *so much blood*. Gavin was so pale, so utterly drained of life. I had my arms around him. I saw him die.

And yet. Here he is. In a tux. His black bow tie undone, the ends of it drooping from a starched collar.

In the Boss's house. In the Boss's desk chair. Because the Boss is *Gavin*.

I take another step backward, my whole body shaking.

"Ladies," he says. "We need a minute alone. How about waiting in the bedroom down the hall."

They trip out the door, coltish and giggling, waving good-bye. *Waiting in the bedroom down the hall.* My heart kicks a sharp pain into my chest.

"You look surprised," he says with a smirk. Then he gets to his feet and moves behind me, stopping to pat me on the head like I'm a pet. I jump out of reach and watch, still too shocked to react, as he closes and locks the door.

He moves toward me, and I back up. My eyes are drawn to something gleaming inside his tuxedo jacket. A revolver. His hand drifts slowly, casually toward the gun.

"Gavin?" I whisper, shaking my head, my mind still clutching at the absurd idea that there's been some mistake. Because the truth is just too painful to process. Lies. All of it. A scam. From the night we met, and forever after.

His fingers tighten around the gun handle, and the hot liquid shame coursing through me turns instantly to ice. He pulls the gun from the holster, his finger threaded through the trigger hole.

"So it was all a scam." My voice quavers, but I need to hear him say it. And I need to buy time.

He takes a step closer to me, his hand with the gun in it raised slightly away from his body.

"If you'd just behaved yourself, you would never have had to know," he says. "But no. You're like a boomerang. Toss you away, and you come right back. All you had to do was stay away and go back to your life as a little rich girl. Why was that so *hard* for you?"

His voice is pinched, off-kilter. Not the shy voice I remember, but a deeper, rougher one with a South Side accent.

I shake my head, my mouth open, no idea what to say. Pinpricks of pain are lodged in my chest from the daggers he's throwing. *Little rich girl. Toss you away.*

"Please," I manage, my voice thick. At this close range, he's not going to miss. No matter how fast I am. "Gavin, put away the gun."

My eyes move from the gun to his face. His jaw working, furiously clenching.

"You don't actually think my name is Gavin, do you, *sweet pea*? Just like your name isn't Anthem *Flood*."

"No," I whisper, taking a small step back toward the desk. "I guess I don't."

"Why me?" I ask, stalling him, trying to figure out how to get the gun away from him.

"You don't know how many times I've asked myself that this month." He waves the gun around, breathing fast. "You're all the same, really. Smug. Special snowflakes. Sensitive rare flowers. It's disgusting, what they teach you at the private schools. Though it's been helpful for the rest of us. You've got your heads so far up your own asses, you can't even see when you're being played."

"So there were others." I watch the barrel of the gun circle and swerve in the air as he talks. I've got to keep him talking. If I don't keep him talking, he'll start shooting.

"Come on. You really don't get it? Even now?" His voice goes way up at the end, and he looks incredulous. "It was a *perfect scam*. I perfected it myself. Took me two years. And it worked on twelve girls before you. We never had any problems until you came along, lucky thirteen."

Twelve. I feel bile rising in my throat. I'm backing away, shaking my head.

"And then you couldn't just go home to your ballet slippers and your ponies. And now that it's been in the papers, people are starting to copy you."

"They are?" This is news to me.

"I've lost twenty-six of my guys since you started pulling this vigilante shit. People are calling the cops on us left and right, getting all sanctimonious about cleaning up the city."

A part of me, underneath the shame and humiliation and fear for my life, is a little bit proud.

"You obviously have a death wish." Gavin shrugs. "Why else would you come to a Syndicate recruit party? I was going to leave you be, even after Rosie. But now you know all my secrets. What's a guy to do?" His eyes are cold, a half-smile tugging at one corner of his mouth. A dimple forms below his cut-glass cheekbone.

I open my mouth, but nothing comes out. In the distance, I hear police sirens approaching. Maybe whoever taped the note to my mirror—whoever believes in me, believes that the Syndicate can be stopped—called in a tip. Gavin can't hear the sirens yet. All of the dominoes fallen now. I look around the room. Each TV screen broadcasts a live feed from security cameras all over the city. Behind Gavin on one of the screens, a group of Syndicate guys surround a couple dressed for a night on the town. They grab the woman's purse and frisk the guy until they find his wallet. These are his employees, I realize. The people who pay for this giant house.

"If it makes you feel better, special snowflake"—he cocks the gun—"you were really good in bed."

Hatred bubbling up inside me, I concentrate on the gun. Both his hands encircle it now as he takes aim, one brown eye closed, the eye with the blue smudge in the iris trained on me.

Like a cornered animal, I tense up and get ready to move. My only hope is to come at him, to leap into the air and hope he's too startled to shoot before I land on him. I take a breath, my legs tensed and ready to spring. But then the window behind Gavin shatters and a whole wall of TV screens goes black.

In the remaining light, I make out a figure ducking inside the window dressed all in black, save the white piping down the sides of his workout pants.

Nonononono.

Gavin whirls around just as Ford barrels into him. They struggle and fall onto Gavin's enormous desk, Ford on top, Gavin under him.

Frozen in horror, I watch Gavin's left arm flail behind him as they struggle. And then a shot rings out, muffled by flesh and clothes.

Ford slumps on top of Gavin, both of them sprawled across the giant desk. The figures on the surveillance screens are the only things that move. Ford's body is absolutely still.

CHAPTER 40

The ringing silence after the gunshot is like so many of my nightmares. I run toward them, but my body can't move fast enough. It feels like I'm wading through mud.

Gavin pushes Ford off him onto the floor and stands up, still holding his gun. "Everybody wants to be a hero."

"No," I'm saying over and over. It's like a repeat of when Gavin was shot. A mirror image. Only it's all backward now, because Gavin is alive. And he is the killer. I kneel down next to Ford. He's still conscious, but barely. His hands cover his midsection.

I move his hands aside and peel his sweatshirt up, flinching as he cries out in pain. The pool of blood just below his chest, spreading outward from the hole in his clean white T-shirt. The blood spot the size of a baseball, quickly spreading.

In a second it's a softball. A moment later, a volleyball.

The police sirens I heard before are much louder now. I glance at Gavin and can see that he hears them, too, then focus on Ford, pulling him to me, rocking him back and forth. It's just like before. Only this time, it's not an act. The blood is very real, and very warm. That's the difference, I realize. Gavin's blood was cold. This is hot and sticky, and I can smell the rusty tang of it as it seeps out of him. Ford is so pale, his eyes so black. He's whispering something. I lean in to hear. "Fight."

I turn around. Gavin is aiming the gun at my head, saying something I'm not listening to. The sirens get closer, and the sound mingles with the beating of my blood. I marvel at how blind I was not to notice the sadism in Gavin's eyes. *A stranger,* I think to myself.

And then, like the yellow haze that sits on top of Bedlam on an air-quality alert day, a surreal absence of fear settles over me, and it's as if I've already left my body. I stand up and get ready to kick the gun from his hands, when the sound of the sirens grows from loud to deafening.

Gavin lowers his gun a little, wincing at the noise. "YOU ARE SURROUNDED," a voice booms from a bullhorn in the front of the house. "COME OUT WITH YOUR HANDS UP."

There's the screech of brakes, doors slamming. Riot police shouting over bullhorns, and, from downstairs, the sound of dozens of windows opening all at once, with partiers jumping out them. The wail of sirens fills the blood-scented air of Gavin's office. And then the sound of boots on the stairs. Climbing.

Gavin pushes past me, his eyes completely blank, as if I'm not even here anymore. I'm sure he has a perfect place to hide and hopes to slip out before the cops make it to the third floor.

I watch him run down the hall for a moment before I kneel down again with Ford, listening to him wheeze like a broken accordion.

"Go after him," he manages, each syllable an effort. "He's getting away."

The riot police are thumping up the stairs. It's not long before this whole house fills with feargas or something worse. And Ford has a record of petty theft. They'll think he's Syndicate. He could die before they're done arresting everyone, and they probably wouldn't care.

I shake my head. "Forget him."

Ford's eyes widen, then go kind of blank. He's losing so much blood.

"This is going to hurt," I say, wrapping his arms around my shoulders and pulling him onto my back. He groans, but he holds on as tightly as he can. "Stay with me, Ford," I yell. "You are not allowed to pass out."

"Or you'll kill me," he slurs, his labored breath hot on my ear.

"Good one. Keep the zingers coming, okay?"

I wrap my hand in one of Gavin's luxury curtains and punch out as much broken glass as I can from the window frame, then duck out the window with Ford on my back, moving carefully so as not to cut or scrape him. Below us there's a ledge—I think the kitchen roof. Holding on to Ford, I do the only thing I can think of to get us out. I squeeze his limp arms around my back and jump. Ford howls with pain when we hit the roof and falls from my grasp. I hoist him onto my back again and shimmy down the drainpipe.

Ford's blood has already seeped through his sweatshirt, through my coat. I feel it on my back. Each movement produces a muffled groan.

"We can do this," I say to Ford as we touch down on the blue-green lawn, hoisting him higher onto my shoulders just as the hiss of feargas canisters reaches my ears, loud and sinister even from outside the house. "Just a little longer, okay?" He barely makes a sound even though the jump must have hurt a lot. He's losing consciousness, I realize, my head pounding with raw panic.

I run past the pool and into a thicket of trees, past police cars that are making their way onto the lawn. Luckily, nobody stops us.

There's a gap in the security fence, and I'm just able to squeeze through it with Ford on my shoulders. We run through the yard of another mansion until we reach the street. I turn right, quickening my pace as best I can with Ford's 180-pound body in my arms. I listen desperately, straining my super-charged hearing, the only sound I want to hear Ford's heartbeat in my ears.

CHAPTER 41

Ford's body seems to double in weight as I hurtle through the streets, my throat swelling with a raw ache, my legs pumping faster, faster, even as my arms feel like they can barely hold on to him another second. Every few minutes, I have to stop and change the position I carry him in, moving him from a sort of piggyback to throwing him over one shoulder like a sack of bricks. The entire back of my coat is now saturated with his blood. When I pause to listen for his breathing, it is that of a drowning man, gurgling with what must be blood.

I stop to move Ford's body so it drapes over both my shoulders, and he groans, his liquid breaths coming slower and slower. "Ford!" I scream. "Stay awake! I'm getting you help."

But his eyes are closed. He's probably unconscious. I look around me, turning in a circle, looking for the nearest hospital. The decent hospitals, the ones not overrun by bacteria and death, are all in the direction of what I see now is a line of police cars cordoning off the North Side. The glass trapezoid of Bedlam

University Hospital glitters just up the hill, but holding Ford, how will I ever get past all those police cars? The next closest hospital, about fifteen minutes away, is Saint Savior, a hospital my mother once called a glorified morgue.

Blood seeping from my shoulders down my coat sleeves, I make a snap decision and change course.

"Now we just sew up the wound," Jax says through gritted teeth, a piece of black thread hanging out of her mouth. "And we wait."

I nod miserably. "Okay."

I've stood by and held Ford's hand as Jax cut his blood-soaked shirt off him, searching his closed lids for movement. I've handed her sponges and suction tubes and scalpels when she asks for them. The bullet, gold-tipped, the back of it shredded and now sitting on the table next to me in a clear glass bowl smeared with blood, was lodged in his left lung. Blood had been pooling inside it, nearly drowning him.

Two inches higher, and it would have been his heart. Two inches higher, and he would have died instantly. I shiver in my leotard and tights, the scrubs Jax has loaned me providing no additional warmth.

"Come on," I whisper as Jax threads the needle. Ford's breathing isn't wet and labored anymore. Thanks to the blood dripping into his arm—what kind of blood, or where it came from, I don't dare ask Jax—the monitor attached to his heart emits a steady, regular beep instead of the rapid-fire staccato it was tracking when Jax first put it on him. But his olive skin is still so sallow, and his lung might be damaged for life, the bones around it shattered. *Damaged for life.* "Wake up."

"He's tough," Jax says absently, all her focus on Ford's wound and where best to stitch. "If anyone can handle this, it's Ford."

Just before Jax pushes the needle through his skin, his eyelids flutter open. His brown eyes make contact with mine, and I can see he's still there, still himself. His hand squeezes mine weakly, just for a second, and all the tears I've been holding begin to fall.

"I'm so sorry," I blubber. "You should have let me drown that day. All I do is ruin things and get people hurt—"

I stop, realizing he's trying to speak. His voice is barely a whisper. I lean in, careful not to let my hair dangle across his face. "No sorries," he rasps. "S'okay, Green. . . . My whole life, I've been waiting . . ."

But just as quickly as he woke up, he falls unconscious again.

"Totally normal," Jax says. "He'll be in and out for a while."

I study Jax as she stitches Ford's chest, the needle moving back and forth under his taut, smooth skin. Her tattoo flashes on her arm every other stitch. The little red heart around the word *Noa*.

"Who is Noa?" I ask at last, after Jax ties a knot in the thread and has put a white gauze bandage on top.

Jax purses her lips, not answering for a long time. Finally she looks up at me and takes a breath. "She was my daughter."

Then she corrects herself. "She *is* my daughter. No longer living among us, though."

"I'm sorry," I murmur, my eyes filling up with tears again when I imagine everything Jax has been through. "What happened to her?"

"Congenital defect in the left ventricle of her heart. She was six years old." Jax draws a shaky breath, her blue eyes magnified behind her thick glasses, steady on mine. "She was dying. All the medical interventions had failed. We had the best specialists. I called in every favor I could through the university lab.

And when eight different surgeons told us it was a matter of days before she died, I tried to correct it myself—" She shakes her head and her silver curls bounce. "And . . . I failed. She died on the table. My husband pressed charges. I lost my lab, my license, my family, everything. All at once. And now . . . well, now I'm here." Jax winces, then forces a pained smile.

I study Jax, absorbing this horrible story. A few tears snake again down my cheeks. "How do you do it? How do you go on each day, living with the death of someone you love?"

Jax looks at me and sighs. A sad smile plays at the corners of her lips. "It's things like saving you that give me a little peace. The anomaly isn't being unable to save people—that happens all the time, to all of us, every day. There are people everywhere suffering, people we can't help. It's the few people you *do* help that get you through."

I look at the filthy floor, my throat aching as Jax starts fussing with Ford's breathing tubes.

For the next hour, we both sit silently watching over him, waiting. Ford does not wake up. The only sounds in the lab are his shallow breathing, the heart monitor, and Mildred banging her food dish against the bars of her cage.

My whole life, I've been waiting . . .

I let my fingers travel through his soft black hair.

Wake up, Ford. You're the one, of the two of us, I want to tell him. *The one with no blood on your hands. The one who still has a chance at being happy.* A few salty tears slide into my mouth.

I stare down at him, willing him to wake up and tell me: *What is it you've been waiting for?*

CHAPTER 42

"That's all I know," I say for the twentieth time, making sure to look directly into the eyes of the two police officers seated across from me at a bare metal table bolted to the floor. Liars look away, and I need them to think I have nothing to hide. "I've told you everything."

At least everything I can. Which isn't much.

The police interrogation room is freezing. I shift my weight on the hard metal chair, trying to find a way to get comfortable. But at four in the morning, after everything I've been through tonight, comfort is unlikely to find me ever again.

I know enough to realize I should probably have a lawyer with me, maybe Lyndie Nye, but when I mentioned it, the police said this was just "a little chat about what happened on Sumac Street" and that if I wanted a lawyer, they'd have to alert my parents. Nobody was accusing me of anything, the cops took pains to assure me when they intercepted me outside Fleet Tower a few hours ago. Not yet, anyway.

"It's just, I'm really tired," I say. How long have we been here? Two hours? Three? I've gone over my story a half-dozen times to Officer Rodriguez and Detective Marlowe, but each time they keep demanding more details, finding new ways to ask the same questions. I can't blame them—my story is thin. They know it, I know it, and whoever might be watching me behind the two-way mirror on one side of the room knows it. But I'm not about to tell them about Serge's help, or about the criminals I've left gift wrapped for them. Or about the real reason I ended up at the Boss's house. I could get arrested for a hundred different crimes by now—including manslaughter— even if what I've done has prevented just as many.

And I'm definitely not telling them anything about Ford.

Spread out on the metal table between us are ten black-and-white stills captured by the surveillance cameras connected to the gate of Gavin's house. Turns out he was monitoring everything, even his own place.

One picture is of me, my face turned up toward the camera, my features screwed into a worried grimace. There are several of random partygoers in cars, on motorcycles, and on foot. And one is of Ford, the hood of his sweatshirt obscuring half of his face.

I kept repeating that I didn't know any of these people, but they kept going back to the picture of Ford, asking me if I was sure. I pretended not to know Ford, swallowing the lump of sadness that rose up in me every time my gaze returned to the picture of him. Underneath his hood, he looked panicked. All because of me.

They asked me repeatedly why I was there to begin with, and for a while I just shrugged, opening and closing my mouth like a fish.

Finally I decided I may as well tell them about Gavin. I have no reason to protect him from the police. I told them he was my former boyfriend who'd gotten in touch and said he wanted to meet with me. I played the lovesick little idiot, which was easy since that's what I've been all these weeks.

I recapped what I could, saying that I went to the party and that Gavin was there with a gun. I said I heard people calling him the Boss, and they nodded. Clearly they'd been after him for some time. Over and over, the cops make me relive the humiliation of Gavin's scam. I leave out Ford and the shooting entirely. I would never forgive myself if I implicated Ford in any of this. As long as I remember not to focus my eyes when I look at Ford's picture, I can get through this without crying.

"Okay, Miss Fleet, it has been a very long evening. One final thing I want to clarify: You say the last time you saw alias Gavin Sharp before last night was the night he was allegedly kidnapped?"

"Yes." My voice is small and haggard. I've lied so many times tonight, both actively and through omission. I try to tell them some of the truth, just enough to keep my secrets. But still. "My parents didn't want to negotiate with the kidnappers. They thought it best to call their bluff."

"That must have been hard for you," Rodriguez says. She's tall and broad-shouldered, in her early thirties, buttoned up in a gray suit. She's been acting blasé and bored during the whole interrogation. Bored, or maybe disbelieving. She's played Bad Cop, while Detective Marlowe has been the sympathetic one who brings me a can of Sparkle cola from the vending machine.

I look at the mirrored wall behind them. It's got to be a one-way mirror, just like in cop shows on TV. There could be twenty additional police officers watching. Or nobody. I have no idea.

All I want to do is go home, go to sleep, drop out of the world altogether for as many hours as I can until I sneak out to visit Ford. He's still unconscious in Jax's lab, but I want to go be by his side.

"I already told you, it was *very* hard for me. I was furious at them. But it turns out they were right. I was conned." I say this directly to the mirrored wall, suddenly wishing Harris and Helene were behind it so they could hear me say it.

"And when he called you, you didn't hesitate before going? To a place you'd never been? Didn't think about getting a ride with your parents?" Marlowe's blue-gray eyes meet mine, and I know I shouldn't be reassured by his nicey-nice routine, but I can't help but feel he's my ally here.

"I didn't want to lose time. I was so excited to see him," I say, my voice tight with humiliation all over again. I've already told them all this. "And I knew they wouldn't want to take me to him. Besides, they were going out for the evening."

"And you say when you got there, he told you it was all a con?" Marlowe frowns, shaking his head slightly as if to say *What a scumbag*.

"That's right." My voice is small. It still feels like fifty razor blades cutting into my chest to remember it. Maybe it always will.

"And how did that make you feel?" Rodriguez takes over. "Did it make you angry? I would have wanted to kill a guy who did that to me."

"I wasn't aware this was an anxiety assessment," I say. "But yes, I was upset. I'm not a violent person, though, so killing him didn't enter my mind."

"Just one more clarification, Miss Fleet. The man you knew as Gavin Sharp pulled a gun on you. You were in imminent danger. So I'm puzzled why you didn't stick around when the police arrived. Didn't you want Gavin caught?" Detective Rodriguez raises one eyebrow.

My heart feels like it's being squeezed, and I take a second to think about the best way to handle this question. I'm drawing a blank. I put my hands on the table edge, pressing the pads of my fingers into the cool metal as the seconds tick by. Before I remember not to do it, I'm staring at Ford's picture and my eyes prickle with tears.

"Miss Fleet? Why take off, in that moment? I don't think I quite understood it the first time."

"I was sad. I wanted to be alone." I stare down at the table, my cheeks reddening. "I was . . . embarrassed."

"And the blood we found upstairs? Are you still asking us to believe you have no idea whose it was?"

"I'm not asking you to believe anything," I say. "You can believe anything you want. It probably came from one of the hundreds of people at the party that night. Maybe he shot some people after I left. I didn't see anything, so I really don't know." My voice breaks, and I fall silent, thankful that Jax helped me clean off the blood and loaned me a coat and sweater when I left the lab. Mine were completely saturated with blood.

The three of us stare at one another for what feels like several minutes, nobody speaking. Suddenly I need to get out of here more than ever.

I look at my wrist, wishing there were a watch on it. "Unless you are charging me with a crime, I'm going to have to get home now."

"All right, Miss Fleet," Detective Marlowe says, pushing his chair away from the table and standing up. "We'll have a security detail on you for a few days while we find the where-abouts of the perp."

"I don't need a security detail," I say tightly.

"He could come back and try to hurt you. After all, you've seen his face. He's a very dangerous man."

Let him try, I think, staring at Marlowe petulantly. *Let him dare to try.*

"Fine," I say finally. "But you'll keep your word about this . . . staying between us?"

"Absolutely. And here's my card, in case you lost it the last time." He winks as he hands it to me, which feels simultane-ously creepy and oddly comforting. I pretend I don't notice.

"Great. Thanks." I start to stand up on wobbly, half-asleep legs. "Check the mall, the place they call Hades," I say half-heartedly. Nothing in me believes they have any hope of finding "alias Gavin Sharp," but I may as well give them a fight-ing chance.

"Don't worry. We'll do our job," Officer Rodriguez chimes in, resting a hand lightly on my shoulder and looking me in the eye. "And you do yours, all right? Stay safe out there. Any details you remember after you get some rest will help out tremendously."

Detective Marlowe holds the door open, and I walk through it into the coffee-scented bustle of the police station, where four cops dressed in riot gear are dragging a couple of teenagers down the hall. One of them, a green-haired girl wearing a dirty white faux-fur coat, has a black eye. I swear I see two of the riot cops smile at each other. *We'll do our job,* Officer Rodriguez said. What exactly does that mean in Bedlam, I wonder? Breaking up protests and clubbing people in the face? Gassing people for no reason? Because from what I've seen, it definitely doesn't mean cleaning up the black market, or ending the drug trade, or catching the real criminals who control this town, or making sure good people are safe.

My job, I think bitterly as they usher us down the hall and out to the lobby, *is to forget about all of this. To forget, or die trying.*

I'm too exhausted to run home, so I call a cab. When I get there, it's five in the morning. I eat four of Lily's blueberry muffins, crawl into bed, and fall into a sleep filled with nightmares of Gavin in a police uniform, handcuffing me to the table in the interrogation room, booking me for a thousand different crimes while my parents and Will and Serge look on, their faces blank and impassive, as if I am a stranger to them.

I nap on and off all day, making an appearance for lunch to tell my parents I'm writing a history paper in my room.

Come sundown, I'm wide awake. I need to be near Ford, but there are unmarked cop cars stationed by the front and back doors of Fleet Tower, monitoring everyone who goes in and out. I peer down to the street and realize there's no getting out of here via the ground. I just have to hope the security detail is too busy monitoring the street to spend a second looking at the sky.

I open my window and step out onto my tiny balcony. I turn around and grab on to a gargoyle just above my window, preparing to climb. I should be terrified, but grief and rage have made me sure-footed. Or maybe I just don't care all that much about dying anymore.

It takes less than a minute to lift myself up one story to the roof, my fingers and legs clinging to the few bricks that jut out in a decorative pattern from the façade. I move hand over hand, fighting the wind, and then I pull myself onto the roof to sit on a metal grate in front of the building's tall metal spire.

I sit for a while and stare out at the city that's ruined me. The city we all keep on ruining every day. Before, when I thought Gavin was dead, I was stricken, miserable. But now that I know the truth about how he manipulated me, I'm just . . . empty. And inside the emptiness is a desperate prayer: Let Ford live.

The wind howls in the gray evening, and suddenly I'm thinking about Gavin and how stupid I am for being played like that, and how wrong it is that I'm untouched and Ford is in a coma. My eyes mist with emotion, but I squeeze them shut. I refuse to cry any more tears over Gavin. He doesn't deserve them.

Pathetic, I tell myself. All of it. The stakeouts. The risks. Nearly getting killed at the bookshop, at the bridge, at the school. Training with Ford. Taking out Rosie. All of it for nothing. Everything I've done in the name of saving or avenging Gavin is filthy with his lies.

And yet my heart keeps pointlessly whirring, a turbocharged muscle that doesn't know good from bad or left from right. I am so strong physically—my arms are sculpted, my stomach taut, my ability to run and leap and barely touch the ground is astonishing, even to me—but I've never had less mental clarity than I do right now. I look out over the city, the lake an empty purple disk that killed my sister, the rest of it a heaving mass of suffering and lies.

This city is only fit for dead souls and lost ones.

At last I swallow hard and stand up, bracing for the jump. The building next to Fleet Tower is a corporate hotel called Regal Apartments. Fleet is eighty-seven stories tall, the Regal only sixty or so. It's a long way to their roof.

I swing my arms back and forth, bending and unbending my knees as the icy air whips strands of hair across my face.

I take a few steps back, take a big breath, and without pausing to think, I run. In a moment, I'm leaping off the edge of

Fleet Tower, into the oblivion of the blue-gray sky. My heart revving with adrenaline, I spin through the dusky air, my hood flying up around my head, the flat glass roof of the Regal conservatory racing up to meet my body.

In that moment in the air, my mind veers crazily between total terror and utter confidence. My head beats out a rhythmic *death death death*, but my beating heart assures me I'll live.

I land more lightly than I could have possibly imagined. On two feet, toes pointed outward in first position. But the glass is much more slanted than I realized. I fall forward, pressing my whole body flat against the slippery pane of glass to try to get ahold of it, but the angle is too steep. In a moment I start to slide down it, toward a section of the roof that flattens out.

In the conservatory underneath me, four men in suits and an older woman in a cocktail dress hold champagne flutes and look out at the view. The woman spots me first. I see her pointing, covering her mouth with her hand as I slide down the glass. I press a palm to the window and mouth *Sorry*.

I'll keep jumping from rooftop to rooftop until I'm off my block, out of the range of surveillance. Then I'll run, not slowing down until I get to Ford. And he'll be awake. He has to be.

CHAPTER 43

It's 5:24 A.M. when I arrive. I slow my run to a walk, breathing hard as my feet hit the sidewalk again.

Jax has given me the code to the door, a complicated series of numbers that correlates with her favorite molecular theorem. I pass by the wall of cages, no longer repulsed by the bunnies, the rats, or Mildred, who is passed out in a pile of shredded *Dilemma,* a dried-out carrot in her leathery paw. *I'm one of you,* I think as I run my finger along the cage bars. Experimental. Caged inside invisible bars. I take a deep breath and head down the hall to Ford.

The small room presses in on me as I slide Jax's wheeled stool toward him. Under the now-familiar *bleep*ing of the heart monitor, I listen to Ford's breath. His lungs are clear now, his breathing slow and regular. I put my hand on his soft black hair and examine him. His cheeks are drawn; the bones above the dark hollows alarmingly sharp. His skin has taken on a greenish cast under the fluorescent glare of Jax's tiny back room. I dig a pot of lip balm from my pocket and remove the oxygen mask covering his nose and mouth to dab some of it on his cracked lips.

"You are the kind of boy," I say to him as his lower lip moves under my finger, revealing a few of his teeth, "who would never touch lip balm. I know it."

So wake up and tell me to knock it off, I say silently. His eyes move rapidly under his closed lids, an automatic physical response to dreams, Jax says.

I put the oxygen mask back on, taking care to make sure it's not too tight. His hair is so soft under my palm. I sit in silence, my hand moving through his hair.

"They're still looking for him." I hear the door swing open, the sound of Jax's slippers shuffling in behind me. "Gavin, I mean. I hacked into the police radio and heard them talking about a possible lead."

"They'll never find him," I say, turning to look at Jax. Her glasses are stuck crookedly into her silver pile of hair, and her eyes are bloodshot and puffy with sleep. She wears a Bedlam U sweatshirt and blue scrubs. "Sorry I woke you."

"I like the company, honestly." Jax smiles. "You going to go after him yourself?"

I shake my head and shrug. I don't want any part of it. My nights of chasing bad guys are over. All I feel when I think of Gavin is emptiness, deeper and more complete than guilt or grief ever was. The girl who fell in love with a fictional boyfriend died that night in the river. The girl sitting here with Ford is someone else entirely.

"I'm sure he'll do whatever it takes to keep them off his back. He's smart," I concede. He may be a monster, but it's not everyone who can fake his own kidnapping thirteen times, who can fake his own death.

"You're smart, too," Jax says gently.

"Not smart enough to save him." I sigh, watching Ford's chest rise and fall. "How long do we wait, Jax? I mean, how long until we give up hope?"

"Anthem." Jax gives me a hard look. "You know the answer. We never give up hope."

I nod. Ford's eyelids are still now. His dream, whatever it was, must be changing course.

CHAPTER 44

At 11:30 the next night, I'm bent over my physics homework, the numbers swimming on the page as I drift into what I've come to call the Bad Place—an anxious stew of thoughts where Ford never wakes up, and where Gavin finds me and finishes what he started—when someone pushes my bedroom door open. My whole body clenches in anticipation of one of my parents attempting another of their anxious heart-to-hearts. About graduation, ballet, my future. If only they knew how meaningless it all sounds to me.

It's exhausting pretending to be okay, performing the role of the girl they think they know. But this time, it's not my parents at the door.

"Hello, Anthem. May I have a word?" Serge says.

I nod, blinking away my surprise and straightening up at my desk chair. Even after all we've been through together, he's never sought me out in my room before.

"Of course, come in," I say. I stand up, not sure if I should offer him my chair. Serge is a formal man. Even at this hour, his tie is knotted tightly at his enormous neck, his black suit jacket perfectly smooth across his broad shoulders.

Serge walks in, surprising me by closing the door silently, carefully behind him. "I saw your light on. You're not sleeping much these days," he says, the corners of his mouth turning down.

I shrug. "I don't need as much sleep as I used to."

Serge's thick brows knit together, and he gives me a sharp look as if to say *Let's not pretend we don't know what's really going on here*. I wonder absently if he's been following me, if he knows about my visits to Ford's bedside. Of course, I decide. Serge knows everything.

He walks to my windowed wall and stares out at the city, all searchlights and helicopters at this hour, a few dim fires flickering in the distance. I move to stand next to him, drawn to the man who's been my friend and protector since I can remember. His quiet presence—so different from my parents, with all their questions and demands—is a comfort. I can feel the muscles in my neck and back relax slightly.

"It must be hard for you to imagine," he says, speaking so softly that I have to lean in a bit closer to him to hear, even with my enhanced hearing. "But there was a time when Bedlam was an even darker place than it is today."

I nod. "When the first tube attacks happened, that must have been the worst of it. Because before then, the city must have been so whole. I can't imagine watching the South Side go from a regular place to . . . to this." I wave my hand at the window to include the pitch-black decaying neighborhoods, the city of squatters.

"There were riots. Endless riots in the streets. People were so angry. So many dead each night from the criminal element, so much senseless violence, you cannot imagine it," Serge says. "But then the Hope appeared, and people believed again. People who had given up on Bedlam entirely began to think the city could be rebuilt. That all the scars would one day heal."

"But then he died," I say tightly, resisting the urge to roll my eyes. *Scars don't heal*, I want to say. Maybe on the outside, but inside, they're indelible.

"And yet now, seventeen years later, people are starting to believe again." Serge's eyes light up and bore into mine.

I frown. Seventeen. The same number of years I've been alive.

I open my mouth to reply, but Serge puts a finger to my lips for a second, then turns and walks to the door and puts his hand on the knob. "It would be a shame to fall back into darkness," he says, "before you finish what you've started."

Before I can respond, he's gone. I'm alone in my room again, standing openmouthed, a hundred questions forming, my throat plugged with the weight of what Serge has intimated.

I didn't start any of this, I want to say. Gavin did it all. He took everything from me: my virginity, my love, my mother's necklace, my human heart.

The only thing he hasn't taken from me is my life. Suddenly I feel certain that it's only a matter of time before Gavin surprises me somewhere, that there's a target on my back. And even if he doesn't, how many more girls will he take advantage of in some new city? How many more lives will he wreck? I think of the anonymous soul who snuck backstage to point me toward the Boss. Someone who believed I could topple a major Syndicate player, stop him from destroying what's left of our city.

Then I think of Ford lying in the hospital bed.

Maybe Serge is right. Maybe the only thing to do is to fight.

My stomach churns as I stare at the spot Serge just vacated. It's hard to argue with a man of so few words.

"You're right," I say as I slide into the front seat of the Seraph the next day. Serge is driving me to school, and we're lucky enough not to have my parents with us this morning. I slam the door shut and Serge starts the car, pulling it out of the circular, hedge-lined drive of Fleet Tower without saying a word or even acknowledging my presence. "I want to finish what I started."

Serge nods. "Very well."

"So? What do we do now? How will we find him?"

Serge turns onto Church Row from Foxglove Court, and I spot Olive Ann and Clementine walking to school, their plaid skirts shorter than ever and fluttering as they hoof it down the sidewalk. "I have friends who keep tabs on these things."

I sit back in the seat and shake my head. "Serge, how come you're letting me do all this?"

"Because I know what you are capable of. I know you are ready to do what cannot be done by anyone else."

"What's that?" I joke. "Be a freak of nature?"

"Make the city whole again," Serge says simply.

I nod, staring straight ahead of us at the crosswalk, where a group of ragged protesters are marching with signs that say SOUTH SIDE PRIDE and SCHOOLS NOT STADIUMS. A teenaged girl—my age, or maybe younger—wears a pair of homemade wings on her back and moves silently through the crosswalk, holding a heart-shaped sign that says RISE. A shiver runs through me when I realize they're probably headed to my parents' office, where the police will surely fire water cannons or feargas them until they give up.

"What do you think about the stadium?" I ask Serge.

But then we pull up to the school and Serge reaches over to open my door. "I'll be in touch," he says. "Be careful."

And then he grabs my hand and squeezes, and for a while after that, I feel less alone.

CHAPTER 45

My footsteps crunch on the long gravel driveway leading up to one of the houses in Morass Bluffs, a luxury housing development on the cliffs above the lake that my father's company has been working on forever. The project has been stalled for a while, the houses half-constructed while my father raises more money. He's been complaining about it for two years straight.

The driveway is steep, and I skirt the edge of it, moving alongside a scrim of birch trees. I make sure to put my phone away for fear that the screen might be bright enough to spot from above.

This is where Serge says Gavin is hiding out. This silent hillside hitting up against Lake Morass. It's a great place to hide. Very private. So private, I realize with a shiver, that if Gavin sees me coming, nobody will hear the gunshot.

Don't freeze up, I tell myself as the hill evens out and the trees open up to a circular driveway with a garage on one side and the skeleton of a house—the drywall installed but no windows or doors yet—on the other. The garage is open just a foot, enough for me to spot a familiar motorcycle inside. I grimace when I think of the twelve other girls he charmed with that stupid bike. I used to think I was the kind of girl who didn't fall for clichés, who wanted something more unique than a boy on a motorcycle. Now I know I was exactly like every other girl Gavin fooled—looking for a fantasy, not a real person.

I move away from the garage and head toward the house.

He will have his gun. *You have to be faster than whatever he throws at you*, I tell myself. My body humming with nerves, I move along the outside of the house, keeping my steps as light as possible, terrified to snap a twig or rustle a bush and give him the advantage of knowing I'm here.

I spot a side door with a half-built deck coming off it, the planks uneven and jagged, no railing to protect people from falling straight off the bluff. I peer over the edge of the bluff—spiky black rocks divide the cliffs from the lake.

I inhale hard and jump up onto the deck, then walk through the house's archway into the area that will someday be the kitchen. There's a metal pipe sticking out of the wall where an oven should be, another pipe meant for a sink. The kitchen doesn't have cabinets yet, or counters, but there is a cardboard box in it with several beer bottles and some takeout containers inside.

I move silently through the archway connecting what will someday be the dining room to what will someday be the living room, and then I'm face-to-face with him.

"Hello, Anthem," Gavin says dully, his face twisted into a smile I once longed to see again and now recognize as fake. He's in tuxedo pants and a white V-neck undershirt with his leather jacket on top of it, sitting on a folding chair in the very center of the empty room, a row of beer bottles at his feet. "How nice of you to visit. Beer?"

"Better not," I say, taking a tiny step closer to him, fury swelling in my chest. "It'll slow me down."

And then I launch myself straight at him, pulling him up by the collar of his jacket and sending the folding chair flying out behind him, smashing against the wall. My face is a half-inch away from his, and we're both breathing hard.

"Still in love with me, huh?" he pants. "You're much more aggressive than I remember."

"You're not the only one with a secret identity, *Gavin*," I say just before I knee him in the groin. "That was for the other twelve."

He's moaning on the ground, huddled in a ball. My eyes travel the room in search of something I can use to tie him up. I've come straight from school and have nothing with me.

But he recovers faster than I expect.

Suddenly he's up again, staggering toward the far wall that divides the kitchen from the deck. He puts his hand inside a wide metal pipe in the wall, and just as I reach him he whirls around. In his hands is the same gun he used on Ford.

The static of rage filling my ears, I launch myself into the air, my foot raised. Gavin's mouth drops open, and he is momentarily frozen with shock. A quarter-second later and I'm landing the jump. My foot slams into his chest, sending him crashing through the windowless square cut into the wall. He lands on his back on the planks of the deck, the gun bouncing out of his hand. It slides across the deck and stops a few inches from the edge, which hangs over the cliff, high above the lake.

"You shooting BodMods into your veins or something?" He is breathing hard but undaunted, shifting position so he's a few feet closer to the edge of the deck. "Is that how you killed Rosie, all pumped up on Pharms?"

"Stop moving," I order him, widening my stance as I stand looking down at him. Seeing this new "real" persona—the South Side accent, the sneering way he looks at me—doesn't bother me this time. No part of me still loves him. "She came after me with a gun. Kind of like you just did."

"Well, she learned from the best."

"I just have one question," I say, against my better judgment. "Who painted the mural?"

He smiles pityingly up at me, still half-sprawled on the deck. "She did. All that talent, and still killed by a little girl in a pleated plaid skirt. Tragic."

"You're disgusting," I growl. "All of you." Though the image of Rosie painting—slaving over that mural, copying my face from a photograph they'd secretly taken, working for hours—fills me with remorse. I swallow it down. "Now is when it ends."

"Oh, really?" he asks, still on his back, sprawled out on the deck. "We'll see."

He springs up and forward until he's close enough for me to smell the nicotine and sweat coming off him, his right hand fisted, swinging.

I duck his blows. Avoiding his fists is a lot easier than dodging bullets. I let him take a few more swipes before I land a punch, a right hook to the side of his head. But even though I hit him hard, he manages to grab a fistful of my skirt and take me down with him. We're close to the jagged edge of the deck now, less than three feet away, when he squeezes my arms behind me and rolls me over him so that I'm hanging halfway off the deck, my legs swinging.

Below me, the jagged rocks swirl with whitecaps and litter.

The drop is at least ten stories. A sharp edge of one of the boards bites into my thigh, and I feel blood dripping down my leg.

I manage to wrench my arms free and grab on to the collar of his jacket. As I do, I swing my leg up and kick the gun. It sails off the deck. The drop is so far down that I don't hear it when it falls into the lake.

"How about we both fall off?" he mutters, his teeth gritted.

My face is so close to his that our noses practically touch. "There is no *we*."

He's stronger than I would have expected. With the leverage he has from being on top of me, he shoves me closer to where the deck meets the sky.

In the silence of the struggle, my body beneath his, I look him in the eyes. I make my expression soft, like it was when I loved him. I move my lips forward a centimeter until they brush his, and then my tongue is in his mouth long enough to taste the beer he's been drinking. I feel him stiffen with surprise, but just like Will before, he lets me kiss him. Sex and violence are so intertwined in the minds of men like him. Pathetic.

I bite his lip, hard enough to draw blood. He screams and lets go of my arms to grab his mouth, an instinctive need to touch where the pain is. It's enough time for me to get out from under him.

Furious, his mouth filling with blood, he hurls himself at me again, his arms splayed wide. Just before he reaches me, I spring up, leaping out of his reach at the last second.

Gavin tries to stop. He almost grabs on to the planks of the deck.

But it's too late. He's going too fast.

My breath catches in my throat as he sails—screaming, flailing—over the edge.

I race to the edge of the deck, my whole body shaking at the moment of impact, the instant his bones crack against the rocks far below. He lands flat on his back, his scream silent now, his limbs splayed in unnatural angles. Everything broken, smashed against the black rocks, the blue-black lake lapping at his limbs. His eyes and mouth remain open in a permanent scream.

I feel the bile rising up from my stomach, the taste of Gavin's blood still in my mouth. I turn to retch, the acid taste of my insides bitter and foul. After a few minutes where I can't look, can't move, can't think, I force myself to peek over the deck again.

He's still on the rocks, his eyes unblinking, his arms spread as if in greeting to the sky. His lower half is already covered in water—green scum and white foam move across his legs and torso. I search the lakeshore for beachcombers, homeless people camping out, and any signs of life. It is completely deserted. No boats out on the water.

Soon he will be washed away, eventually found by someone. Maybe buried in the paupers cemetery in a stoneless grave. I'll never learn his real identity. But as I turn away from the lake, I realize I know exactly who he was. He was a liar and a thief and a con artist. He lived off his looks and his charm and his ability to do terrible things and still live with himself. I reach up and grope at my throat. I'm still wearing the necklace he gave me. I yank the heart pendant hard enough to snap the thin gold chain and throw it as far as I can, out toward the lake. I watch as it gets carried by the breeze a moment, twisting in midair before it drops, a tiny glint of gold flashing before it falls out of sight.

CHAPTER 46

Still shaking with adrenaline and shock, I walk past the rows of beer bottles, the folding chair in the living room. I stop and stare at the duffel bag a moment longer, until I can't keep myself from seeing what's inside.

I dump out the bag and dig through the pile with shaking hands. A few pairs of neatly folded designer jeans, two T-shirts, his leather rollie pouch. Three stacks of hundreds, each with paper wrappers around them. All that remains of his life on the run. I sit back on my heels and try to calm my shaky, panicked breathing. That's when I notice the edge of a book sticking out from a pair of folded jeans. I yank it free and study the title: *Collusion: The Secret History of Law Enforcement and the Mob*. The cover features a revolver resting on a pile of money.

I turn it over in my hands and start to flip through it. On the borders of most of the pages there are tiny notes made in pencil.

Numbers, figures. *Names.*

My stomach jumps when I turn to the end.

There's a chart on a blank page toward the back of the book, in tiny, careful print, with lines connecting each name from the top down. At the top, underlined and in darker pencil than the rest: *The Money*.

Farther down the line, I spot Rose T., Smitty M., Jessa S., M. & A. Luz, Karl S., Emmett C., among many other names—at least thirty altogether. My veins turn to ice when I spot a section marked *BPD*. Bedlam Police Department. It's a whole column, with at least forty names. One of which is *Marlowe*. Next to Marlowe is a dash. At the end of the dash is a number. *50,000*.

My head spinning, I carefully refold Gavin's clothes and put everything back in the duffel bag. Everything except the book, which I shove into my back pocket.

My hands are shaking worse than ever when I step out over the threshold of the house. I walk down the driveway and suck air deeply into my lungs, holding my breath as long as I can, hoping it will quiet the scream inside my head.

I'm alone in the alleyway, watching a rat dart in and out of a drainpipe as I pound frantically on Jax's door. I've tried to type in the code, but my hands are still shaking, and I can't seem to keep the numbers in order in my head.

After a few minutes, I finally hear the click of the bolts in the lock. Jax pulls me inside, embracing me, squeezing me so hard I can barely breathe. I sink into her arms, grateful for her warmth against my ice-cold skin.

"Anthem, did you hear me?" She steps away from me and grabs my shoulders, shaking me slightly.

I shake my head, too wrapped up in what I've done to have listened properly.

She's grinning. "He's awake."

"Ford?"

Jax nods, her eyes swimming with tears. "About a half hour ago. Vitals are great. Appears to have no brain injury—"

I race down the hall to the back room and find Ford sitting up, smiling broadly, wearing Jax's Bedlam U sweatshirt and eating a Styrofoam bowl-o-noodles. His lips are still cracked, but his color is restored, his skin no longer the color of an unwatered houseplant.

"Heeeey." He waves, a tangle of noodles dangling from his mouth. He sounds like the slightly drunk host of a party.

"Hi, you." I smile, approaching the gurney slowly, suddenly shy.

He slurps the rest of the noodles into his mouth and puts down the bowl, grinning. "Jax said you carried me here."

I nod.

There's an awkward silence, and I rush to fill it, to tell him how much I missed him, how wrong it was that he was the one to get hurt.

"I'm so sorry about everything, Ford. I should have been able—"

"To stop a bullet from thirty feet away?" he interrupts me.

"But if I hadn't gone to him in the first place . . ." I trail off.

Ford shakes his head, a half-smile lifting his stubbled cheek. "I'm the one who followed you to that party. And I'm pretty sure you're the only reason I'm alive right now. So let's call it even."

I nod miserably, knowing that nothing Ford says will undo what just happened at the lake.

"So did the police find him? Jax told me they were looking."

I stare down at the dirty linoleum floor as my throat fills up with sand.

"Green." Ford reaches out and touches my chin, tries to lift my face again. "What is it?"

"He's dead," I whisper. "First Rosie and now Gavin. I'm a killer now," I finish, shaking, heaving. Ford pulls me toward him, and I collapse against his chest for a minute. "Just like them."

Ford presses me to him and I can hear the slow thump of his heartbeat through the sweatshirt. "No. You're what this city has been waiting for." His voice cracks on the word *waiting,* and he grabs my hand, runs his thumb across my knuckles.

All my life I've been waiting. I feel that same thick warmth spread through my chest again. I think about all the nights I've spent right here, waiting for him to wake up and finish telling me what he was telling me. "You're what *I've* been waiting for."

As he pulls me closer, a tiny section of all the broken pieces inside me fuses back together.

CHAPTER 47

With Ford getting healthier every day and Gavin gone, I have nothing to do except pore over the *Collusion* book, looking for answers to questions that are only half-formed in my mind.

I stare at page four and read a section someone underlined:

The police, in this way, act as enablers of both the corrupt interests of the elite and the corrupt interests of the criminal underclass. And those who do not benefit from this complex exchange of money and power—the ordinary citizens of our vast metropolises—are kept terrified, helpless to change the system.

I look up from my book, my mind on fire. *Photographers will be arrested.* Batons. Feargas. Detective Marlowe. The Money. *Helpless to change the system.* I flip to the back of the book, staring at Gavin's chart until the names begin to swim in front of my eyes.

Lily is singing softly in the kitchen, an old song, something corny about a revolution. I hear the *slish* of her knife as she dices vegetables, preparing canapés for an intimate dinner my parents are hosting here tomorrow night with Mayor Marks and Will's parents. Will is due to be released next month from Weepee Valley. When that happens, I'll have to pay him another visit at home to make sure he keeps quiet.

I don't really sleep much anymore. Now that I've adjusted to my new heart, my body doesn't seem to need more than a couple of hours per night, which makes it easier for me to find time to spend with Ford as he recuperates at home. I've gotten to know his uncle, Abe, and Abe's two daughters, Sam and Sydney, on the rare times I get there during the day. Ford's apartment is a basement one-bedroom not far from the MegaMart. We sparred a few nights ago at Jimmy's Corner, and he lasted longer than I thought he would, and then groused at me for taking it too easy on him.

Every day, I scan the papers for mention of a body washing up on the shores of the lake. I have been rewarded with three others, two young women and an older man. Lake Morass is swimming with corpses.

My father's shoes click down the hall, and I slam *Collusion* shut, careful to shove the book behind a chintz couch cushion before my father gets too close. I jump up, craving I-don't-know-what from him—some combination of reassurance and distraction, maybe—and meet him in the hallway. He's wearing all black. Even his shirt and tie are black.

"Somber," I say lightly, trying to smile. Trying to be the girl I've always been, the hard worker. The future valedictorian. The one he never has to worry about.

"Headed to a funeral, unfortunately," he says, straightening his tie in the mirror before turning to look me over, to scan my eyes for trauma as he has been doing ever since the kidnapping and my three-day disappearance. "No dance class today, kitten?"

"It's Sunday," I remind him. "I'm just sitting around, resting the old muscles. Whose funeral is it?" I smooth my freckled hands over his black suit jacket, plucking a stray thread from his lapel.

"Someone who worked with me," he says. "Young guy, too."

"Was he sick?" Death. Everywhere I turn, there seems to be more death. Do the Fleets attract it, or does it follow everyone?

"Not that I know of. Robbed is my guess. Killed senselessly. They found his body days after the fact," my father sighs. "Tragic, what this city has become. I have half a mind to leave here, to take your mother and you and move to Exurbia or even farther out, to some barricaded hilltop."

His words drop into silence, and my chest blazes with heat. *Killed senselessly.*

"Where did they find the body?"

I study my father's unlined face, his upright posture, the sonic boom of his charisma. "He was checking up on our Morass Bluffs projects, and then, just, *poof.*" He snaps his fingers, pauses for emphasis. "Just like that, he washes up dead in the lake. A terrible thing."

"Oh." The hall goes up at a tilt, and I need to grab the wall for support. I try to focus on the light fixtures, the warm glow of lamplight illuminating the family pictures lining the walls.

The one in front of me was taken before I was born—my mother, my father, and bouncing blond Regina. I've never liked this picture. Regina reaches toward the camera and looks as if she's about to howl. My mother is looking at something off to the right, and my father stares straight ahead, nostrils flared, lips pressed together impatiently.

"Who do you think did it?" I breathe, struggling to push the words out as my father studies me with worried eyes.

"I'm leaving that to the police to figure out," he says. "Some Syndicate thug would be my guess. Don't think about such dark stuff, kitten. I shouldn't have mentioned it."

When I don't answer, he leans down and kisses me on the forehead. "I love you to pieces. You know that, don't you?"

I nod, forcing my lips to curve into a smile for him.

A minute later, I'm waving a feeble good-bye as my father rounds the curve of the hallway and moves out of sight. I press my forehead against the cool wall, black splotches blooming in front of my eyes as words move through my consciousness like water circling the drain.

Recover, don't raze. *They should be thanking me.* Schools not stadiums. *Someone who worked with me.* We will rise. *Some Syndicate thug.* Drinks at the police commissioner's house. *Manny Marks is soft on crime.* Checking up on our Morass Bluffs project. *The Money.*

When the front door clicks shut behind him, I head toward the kitchen, my heart racing, beads of sweat forming on my forehead. I pause in the doorway and watch Lily's knife move through a head of cabbage, slicing it again and again until it's in shreds.

"Hey, Ant," she calls out as I move through the kitchen. "You look like you've just seen a ghost."

I shake my head and smile, though inside I am a ticking bomb.

"Just looking around for something I lost," I murmur.

Then I reach the narrow staircase to my father's office on the lower floor. I don't bother switching on the light. I grab hold of the banister and force my shaking legs to take me downward, into the dark.

ACKNOWLEDGMENTS

My enormous gratitude goes out to everyone who helped shepherd this book into the world:

To the certified genius Sara Shandler, for teaching me how to write for younger readers and giving me a shot at building Bedlam City; to Josh Bank, for trusting me to do it right; to Katie Schwartz, for starting it all; and to the endlessly patient, kind, and hilarious Joelle Hobeika, for always wrapping your razor-sharp notes in the softest velvet as you ushered this book into being. Thanks also to Katie McGee, Aiah Wieder, and Phyllis DeBlanche, for lavishing such careful attention on the manuscript at every stage of the process.

To my editor, Sarah Landis, at HarperTeen, who came back from maternity leave to work her magic on my newly born first draft, for knowing where Anthem's story was going even when I didn't; to the whole team at Harper, for believing in this book and giving it a home; and to my agent, Faye Bender, for your wise counsel and constant reassurance. You are Xanax in human form.

To Michael Cunningham, Josh Henkin, Stacey D'Erasmo, Susan Choi, Mary Morris, Ellen Tremper, Elaine Brooks and everyone at the Brooklyn College MFA program for early encouragement. And to everyone at *One Story*, especially Marie-Helene Bertino, Hannah Tinti, and Maribeth Batcha, for taking this debutante out on the town.

Huge thanks to Lauren Flower, for being my dear friend and fairy godmother for the past twelve years. It's been thrilling to share this journey with you. To the members of my writing group, the Imitative Fallacies: David Ellis, Tom Grattan, Elizabeth Harris, Anne Ray, and Mohan Sikka, your friendship, perspective, and generosity have been invaluable. Special thanks to Helen Phillips for her even-keeled advice about all things publishing, and to the future doctor Adam Brown for teaching me the ins and outs of chimeric heart technology. And to my glamorous neighbor and friend Allison Devers, thank you for the cheerleading and unicorns as I hammered out multiple drafts of this book.

Heaps of appreciation go out to Jessea Hankins, for doing everything first and always letting me follow your lead, and to David Alpher, Mehernaz Hamsayeh, Conor Hankins, Thais Jones, Julia Landau, Jennie Litt, Shasta and Jeremiah Lockwood, Cinque Schatz, and Naomi Schultz for your friendship and support.

Thank you to my parents, Alan and Phyllis Kahaney, for raising me with a love of books and adventure and for always encouraging me to keep writing no matter what; to my sisters, Jeannie Kahaney and Cory Kahaney, who taught me everything I know about tenacity, pluck, and good wine; and to Ariel Segan, the cake maven of New York, for your enthusiasm at every stage of writing this book.

Thank you to Agnes and Ivan Sanders, intrepid in-laws and treasured friends, and to Lizzy and Neil Postrygacz, Ken Misrok, and Rufus Misrok for key plotting advice and inspiration.

To Ezzy, my little love who has been eagerly awaiting the arrival of this book so he can add pictures: Ta-da! Here it is. Let's dance. And to Gabi—my love, my life—thank you doesn't even come close. Ten years ago, you found me on a park bench and stole my heart. It's been yours every day since, still beating like mad, unbroken.